ORIGINS OF
THE WHEEL
OF TIME®

THE LEGENDS AND MYTHOLOGIES
THAT INSPIRED ROBERT JORDAN

ORIGINS OF THE WHEEL OF TIME®

The LEGENDS *and* MYTHOLOGIES
that Inspired ROBERT JORDAN

MICHAEL LIVINGSTON

foreword by Harriet McDougal

Tor Publishing Group **TOR** *New York*

A Tor Book
Published by Tom Doherty Associates / Tor Publishing Group
120 Broadway
New York, NY 10271

www.tor-forge.com

Tor® is a registered trademark of Macmillan Publishing Group, LLC.

The Library of Congress has cataloged the hardcover edition as follows:

Names: Livingston, Michael, 1975– author. | McDougal, Harriet, writer of foreword.
Title: Origins of The wheel of time : the legends and mythologies that inspired Robert
Jordan / Michael Livingston ; foreword by Harriet McDougal.
Description: First edition. | New York : Tor, 2022. | "A Tom Doherty Associates Book." |
Includes bibliographical references and index.
Identifiers: LCCN 2022034285 (print) | LCCN 2022034286 (ebook) |
ISBN 9781250860521 (hardcover) | ISBN 9781250860545 (ebook)
Subjects: LCSH: Jordan, Robert, 1948–2007. Wheel of time. | Jordan, Robert,
1948–2007—Sources. | Jordan, Robert, 1948–2007—Knowledge and learning. |
Jordan, Robert, 1948–2007—Dictionaries. | LCGFT: Literary criticism. | Dictionaries.
Classification: LCC PS3560.O7617 Z77 2022 (print) | LCC PS3560.O7617 (ebook) |
DDC 813/.54—dc23/eng/20220718
LC record available at https://lccn.loc.gov/2022034285
LC ebook record available at https://lccn.loc.gov/2022034286

ISBN 978-1-250-86053-8 (trade paperback)

Our books may be purchased in bulk for promotional, educational, or business use.
Please contact your local bookseller or the Macmillan Corporate and Premium
Sales Department at 1-800-221-7945, extension 5442, or by email at
MacmillanSpecialMarkets@macmillan.com.

First Tor Paperback Edition: 2023

Printed in the United States of America

0 9 8 7 6 5 4 3 2 1

To Robert Jordan

For his Heart,

For his Light,

Forever.

CONTENTS

Northern

the Blight

Aryth

N

S

Morenal
Ocean

Seanchan

Southern

ICE CAP

the Blight

the
Dead Sea

Aiel
Waste

Shara

Sea of Storms

equator

Ocean

the Mad
Lands

0 500 1000 1500 2000
Miles

ICE CAP

Ellisa Mitchell 2022

FOREWORD

I first heard of Michael Livingston in 2008 when he was invited to speak at my late husband's induction into the South Carolina Academy of Authors Literary Hall of Fame. About all I knew about him at that time was that he taught at The Citadel, Jim's alma mater. Michael did such a fine job at that event that I invited him on the spot to speak at another upcoming event, where a permanent display of Jim's memorabilia was being introduced at the Daniel Library at The Citadel. Speaking along with Brandon Sanderson and David Drake, Michael again delivered engaging and insightful remarks.

A couple of years later, Michael was invited to deliver a presentation on The Wheel of Time at a fan event. This was, of course, much more in-depth than his earlier appearances, and it was entirely engrossing. It was quite obvious that he had a great understanding of how Jim had put the series together and the countless sources that he wove into the story. And his rendition of Old English was absolutely wonderful; I wish there were a way to incorporate that into this volume. He delivered the same presentation multiple times, and even when it was scheduled at the earliest slot on the JordanCon schedule, he always had a full room, fully engaged.

Over the years, Michael became a friend, and while we were working on the final three books, Team Jordan consulted with Michael on working out the details of the Last Battle. He was a great help with that, and it was always a joy to discuss the details of The Wheel of Time with him. In thanks for all his assistance, we presented him with the ersatz saber-toothed tiger skull from Jim's office—a saber-toothed tiger that was mentioned in his Wheel of Time presentation.

Last year, Michael asked how we felt about his writing a book regarding the myriad inspirations used by Jim in the series. We thought it sounded like a wonderful idea; he is a marvelous writer and has shown over the years just how much he knows about the subject. So we moved ahead, and by dint of new construction at The Citadel (where we had donated Jim's desk), Michael ended up writing this book at the same desk where Jim had written The Wheel of Time, which we believe is fitting indeed. We hope that you enjoy this glimpse into the story behind the story.

—Harriet McDougal

A LETTER TO READERS
FROM THE AUTHOR

I'm a scholar, an investigator, a historian. I'm a man who weighs facts, examines evidence, and uncovers truth. I'm sensible. I'm responsible.

And I'm here to tell you that magic is real.

Let me prove it to you.

I was fifteen when I pedaled my bike—a black Huffy with dirt tires—across a dusty Albuquerque prairie to reach my local bookshop. I had allowance and birthday money to spend, and a thirst that could only be quenched with a new book. I parked the bike, locked it up, and then perused the shelves for what seemed like hours. The store had these big comfy chairs, I remember—blue and welcoming—and whenever I found a potential new book I'd sit down with it and take the first chapter or two for a quick spin.

I was into fantasy back then—the kind of magic that a fifteen-year-old on a beaten-up bike wanted to believe in as he pedaled his way here and there under the hot sun, ever watchful for scorpions and snakes. The kind of magic that isn't real, of course.

I found such a fantasy on the new release shelves. A big and fat one. *The Eye of the World*, by Robert Jordan. I picked it up. I liked the nifty cover it had on the outside and the cool map it had on the inside. I thought it had the hum of Tolkien.

So I sat down in one of those stuffed blue chairs and started to read.

In pages I was hooked. I spent every dime of the little coin I had and claimed my prize as my own. I tucked it into my backpack and pedaled home faster than I'd ever done before.

Not because of the snakes or the scorpions. Because of the magic.

That magic stayed with me long after I devoured that first book. Every year I saved up to buy the latest volume in The Wheel of Time as soon as I could. I became—I *am*—one of its many millions of fans.

I read the books on the bus to high school. I read them in college and in graduate school, where I earned a Ph.D. and became a specialist on the Middle Ages.

I became—I am—a serious academic. If I should read the chronicler Adam of Usk claiming there was a dragon haunting northern England six hundred years ago, I will find a natural phenomenon to explain it. Because despite my love of fantasy literature—from Homer to *Beowulf* and *Sir Gawain and the Green Knight*, from Tolkien to Jordan and N. K. Jemisin—I know magic isn't real.

And yet . . .

After I graduated, I was asked to interview for a professorship at The Citadel, the Military College of South Carolina. The only thing I really knew about the place came from a single notice on the back of every book of The Wheel of Time in my library: Robert Jordan was a graduate of The Citadel.

I interviewed. I got the job. I moved to Charleston, and every day I walked past the iconic white tower on our campus. Every day, more and more, I wondered if that *meant* something.

A coincidence, of course. Magic isn't real.

And yet . . .

In the fall of 2006, I was talking to The Citadel's *other* Big Name literary alumnus, Pat Conroy, about starting student writing awards to honor him and James O. Rigney, Jr.—the man the world knew as Robert Jordan. Pat suggested he could write Jim to help introduce me. Before I knew it I was exchanging emails with the man who'd given me The Wheel of Time.

I mentioned to Jim I was a fan. I told him at one point that I hoped to publish fiction myself one day, and that I planned to do it with Tor for no other reason than the fact that they'd given people like me his Wheel of Time. He said he looked forward to my success: "You have my best wishes on your rise (soon) to bestsellerdom," he wrote me in early January 2007.

A few months later, he came to the first ceremony to bestow the student award named in his honor. He was already very ill, but he nevertheless cut a dashing figure with his lovely wife and legendary editor, Harriet, by his side. My script had me call out thanks to the English Department for their support. From the first row, Jim grumbled that he'd been an engineering graduate. It was awesome.

We shook hands. I thanked him for helping change my life. He was charming and kind and unforgettable.

The summer passed.

On September 16, I was making photocopies for my class on Norse mythology when I heard that he'd died.

For a moment it felt as if the magic in the world had died, too.

And yet . . .

Not long afterward, the chair of my department called me into his office and told me that Jim had been elected into the South Carolina Academy of Authors. I was asked to give a speech at the ceremony, which would be held at The Citadel.

The event came in March. Harriet was in the front row and I couldn't look at her as I talked. I was too afraid to cry.

But I got through. I sat down. A bit later, Harriet stood up to accept the award for her beloved Jim. She was gracious—by the Light, far more gracious than I could ever be—and then she publicly asked me if I'd come take part in a panel with her and Brandon Sanderson, who'd just been tapped to finish The Wheel of Time.

It might've felt like magic—in that moment I thought I could fly—but magic isn't real.

Later, after that panel, I went to dinner with Harriet and Brandon and Team Jordan. They asked me if I wanted to come and tour Jim's office sometime.

His writing desk was there when I visited: a beautiful old rolltop, where he'd spent countless hours building a world. So was his library and his armory and so much else that he used in the effort. At one point I looked up to see a saber-toothed tiger skull staring down at me and realized I was literally standing in the middle of the Tanchico Museum.

But, I forcibly reminded myself, magic isn't real.

Not long after that I was invited down again. The Estate was going to auction off many of the weapons in his armory to raise money for medical research. They wanted me to pick one first, and they left me alone in his office to decide.

I remember staring at his desk, wanting to sit down but too afraid to do so. I felt a sudden impulse to turn around, and when I did I found my hands reaching past far nicer-looking pieces to pick up an otherwise unremarkable katana leaning against the wall. I don't know why. When I unsheathed it, I saw that it had a dragon etched into its sweeping blade.

I keep the sword in my campus office, and it was there, in later years, that one of my veteran students saw it. Turns out, he'd been deployed in Iraq when his father-in-law, an antiques dealer, had sold that very blade to Jim. He had pictures of the event.

Magic isn't—

I wrote the Shards of Heaven, a trilogy of historical fantasy novels, and achieved that lifelong dream when Tor published them. And though they hardly achieved bestsellerdom, just seeing the books come out was more than I ever thought possible. It felt like a promise fulfilled, like the result of some secret wind pushing at my back.

I continued to give talks on Jim's literary impact over the years. Out of love. Out of a feeling of gratitude. Not long ago, I was invited to a get-together with Team Jordan, and out of the blue Harriet stunned me by gifting me that saber-toothed tiger skull I'd seen in Jim's office on that first visit.

Magic is—

Over this past summer, the administration here at The Citadel wrote me with the news that Harriet had donated Jim's rolltop desk to the school. She'd asked only that it be used and not simply set in a corner.

Days after my eager agreement to have that desk moved into my office—the desk on which he wrote those books, the one I'd been too afraid to sit at before—Tor offered me a contract to write a book about the real world in The Wheel of Time.

Somehow, that kid who pedaled home through the New Mexican dirt with *The Eye of the World* in his backpack would write his own book about The Wheel of Time . . . at Jim's own desk, beneath his dragon-marked sword and his tiger skull, looking out at a white tower amid peaceful trees in a city between two rivers.

Magic—

Is real.

It might've taken a bit for me to get the hint, Jim, but I don't think I can deny it any longer. So thank you. For this. For everything. I promise I'll do everything I can to make *Origins of The Wheel of Time* worthy of the Light of your memory.

The Wheel weaves as the Wheel wills.

I pray it weaves through me.

—Michael Livingston
The Citadel

INTRODUCTION

Many books are liked. Far fewer are beloved. And only the rarest become something even greater: so deeply and passionately beloved that they transcend the pages between their covers and take on life within the lives of their readers. They inspire *dedication*.

James Joyce's *Ulysses* belongs in this category. So do J. R. R. Tolkien's *Lord of the Rings* and J. K. Rowling's Harry Potter books.

And Robert Jordan's Wheel of Time.

As I began writing this book, twins were born to a couple who met each other through their shared love of the Wheel of Time novels. Their children live— their love exists—because James Oliver Rigney, Jr., under the pen name Robert Jordan, wrote one of the bestselling and most beloved fantasy series in history.[1] They're just one of the many, many people I've met over the years who were brought together by the turning of the Wheel.

Ask any two of its millions of fans what they love about The Wheel of Time and you might hear a dozen answers: like our tastes in food, what we appreciate as readers is inevitably and irrevocably personal. But what they all share, in the end, is a love of the intricate world of stories that Jordan created: "Randland," as they often call it.[2]

I can't explain *why* people love The Wheel of Time any more than I can explain why I love cheeseburgers. What I *can* do is explain *how* Jordan created The Wheel of Time. At its core, that's what this book is: a behind-the-scenes story of how Rigney became Jordan both in terms of his biography and his creation—the story of the maker and his making, since you can hardly have one without the other.

Characters within Randland frequently speak of their lives as threads that the Wheel of Time weaves into the Pattern of existence. For most people, this process is passively reactive: when their actions make unexpected changes, these are incorporated into a new design within the ever-evolving Pattern. Most people have, to use the terms of our world today, free will.

But not everyone. For if *everyone* had free will, there would be no Pattern at all. The world would devolve into chaos. So for a rare few people, the Wheel must bend their lives—and most importantly the lives of those around them—in order to create the Pattern. In Randland, these people are called *ta'veren.*

In this sense, we can think of the Wheel of Time like the most masterful conductor. Among our many discordant tunes, her ear detects harmony, induces a rhythm, and from chaos makes ordered music. But managing that direction, creating that beat that holds it all together, means that someone—a strong drum in the back, perhaps—must move to the nodding of her baton.

If this is all sounding a bit like the Moirai—Greek mythology's thread-cutting Fates—it's for good reason. The Pattern, the threads, the Wheel . . . Jordan absolutely expected us to recognize real-world mythological parallels behind these ideas. He was actively using them. They were the roots of his story.

The *roots,* mind you. Not the restraints. The fantasy that bloomed atop them, so carefully tended by Jordan, went far beyond the myths and the legends that gave it rise. As we will learn, one of the keys to how Jordan did what he did—and perhaps a key to why it has appealed to so many people—is that he enmeshed our collective reality with his own personal faith, experience, and imagination. Between fate and free will, between chaos and order, he sought a balance of all. A wheel out of balance, after all, would be a wheel that spins awry.

That Jordan accomplished what he did—and his Wheel of Time has had the impact that it has—no doubt marks him as *ta'veren* in our own reality, but it's important to say up front that he didn't turn the Wheel alone.

There was, at the center of everything, his editor-turned-wife, Harriet McDougal. There were his friends and family. There were his key assistants, Maria Simons and Alan Romanczuk. There was his publisher, Tom Doherty. There was Brandon Sanderson, the man who took up the pen when Jordan could not. And there were, alongside so many others, Jordan's millions of fans.

All of them play roles in what follows.

This book has two parts.

The first part provides a look at who Jordan was, how he worked, and why he holds such an important place in modern literature. The central argument here is that Jordan is what I call an "American Tolkien": that the best way to understand what he was doing in The Wheel of Time—and how he was doing it—is to understand what Tolkien had done in *The Lord of the Rings*. Tolkien threw down a gauntlet with that work, challenging other writers with what and how they could create. Many wrote fantasies after Tolkien. Many of them sold extremely well. None, I think, picked up that gauntlet quite the way Jordan did. There is nothing simple, nothing small, in his work. The Wheel of Time is the height of seriousness, a vision that cuts to the heart of our cultural, political, and religious worldviews in the way only a fantasy can: it is not in the mirror, after all, that we see the truth of ourselves; it is in the eyes of strangers in unfamiliar lands.

The second part of this book is a glossary that reveals the "real world" in The Wheel of Time. In some sense we've already started this process with recognizing the real-world mythology of the Moirai that's partially behind Jordan's concept of the Pattern. But we'll see that this is only scratching the surface. The most central truth of Jordan's fantasy is that it's built out of a great many of our own myths and legends.

King Arthur is in The Wheel of Time. Merlin, too. But so are Alexander the Great and the Apollo space program. The Norse gods and Napoleon's greatest victory.

It's astonishing how much is in these books once you see what he was doing.

New readers continue to discover The Wheel of Time. You may be one of them. So it's important I say this up front:

SPOILER ALERT

This book is **Full Spoilers**, folks. It would be impossible to discuss the materials from which Jordan crafted this series without addressing the full scope of the characters and events in The Wheel of Time (and even parts of Jordan's other works, too). So I'm holding nothing back. If you go to the entry on the Last Battle, you'll see that I spoil *everything*. Look up Rand al'Thor, and I give the whole game away.

In other words, if you haven't finished the series yet and don't want spoilers, you may want to wait to read this book until you've turned the last pages and closed the final volume, *A Memory of Light*. Yes, I know that means a few million words might stand between you and what I've got to say, but it'll be worth it, I promise.

If you're done or just don't mind a few spoilers, though, read on and enjoy!

So that's what this book is.

Here's what it's not:

It is not, in any way, a replacement or even a rival for the two remarkable books already put out by Robert Jordan and the Rigney Estate: *The Wheel of Time Companion* (2015) and its predecessor, cowritten by Robert Jordan and Teresa Patterson, *The World of Robert Jordan's The Wheel of Time* (1997). Those works are exclusively Randland focused. They provide "in-world" backstory to The Wheel of Time: the histories of characters and nations and so much else. This book is instead "out-world" focused: a guide to the real world within this fantasy creation.

To put it another way: If you want to know Graendel's role in the death of another character, then the best place for answers is *The Wheel of Time Companion.* If, on the other hand, you want to know how Jordan built the murderous Graendel out of the monstrous Grendel in *Beowulf,* then this is the book for you.

NAMES AND NOTES IN THIS BOOK

Robert Jordan's fans are extraordinary. Since 2009 they have been running an annual convention—JordanCon—devoted to his works and the love of fantasy literature. There are multiple websites devoted to the intricate parsing of the details of his world or the friendly interconnection of those who love it: Dragonmount, Theoryland, and the Thirteenth Depository are just a few of these sites that you'll see cited within these pages. All are incredible resources, each of them paving a unique path to a more complete understanding of Randland long before I came along. I owe them all my thanks.

One result of this longtime, vibrant connection between the author and his fans is the feeling that they were, in some measure, family. This relationship came into sharp relief when Jordan became ill and passed away. In hope and prayer, in grief and mourning, the community was bound ever more tightly together. Jordan's widow wasn't "Mrs. Jordan" or "Mrs. Rigney." She was, quite beautifully, "Harriet." Jordan's assistants were likewise known by their first names. So, too, was Brandon Sanderson when he became bound with the Jordan legacy.

Wonderful and heartwarming as this is, it has presented a slight problem for me. Traditional formatting would have me referring to Jordan's incomparable assistant Maria Simons as "Simons," but this isn't at all how the core of fandom knows her. To them, she is simply "Maria." And though it risks informality, I have followed the practice of the fans in these familiar naming traditions.

There is also the matter of how to refer to the author himself. Robert Jordan was one of several pseudonyms used by James Oliver Rigney, Jr., who was known to his friends and family as Jim. His fans, meanwhile, often referred to him as "Mr. Jordan" or "the Creator." I have, as a matter of standard practice, opted to refer to him simply as "Jordan" throughout this book—even when referencing times before he himself took that name in print. While this wasn't the name he'd have answered to for much of his life, it's the name by which he was most famously known.

After Jordan's death, Harriet gave most of his personal papers to the College of Charleston, which today keeps close watch over the materials within the special collections at Addlestone Library: the James Oliver Rigney, Jr., Papers (MSS 0197). I have made extensive use of this valuable archive, which I will refer to throughout simply as "the Rigney Papers." I'm grateful to its custodians for making this trove available to my research, and I'm grateful to the Rigney Estate for their permission to quote so liberally from it.

One last thing: People often use the word *myth* to signal that a story is false . . . but this is itself a false notion. There is no value judgment in the word. Academically speaking, a mythology is simply a group of stories, collectively endorsed by an institution, that narrates an ideology for that institution. We tend to think of such stories as being cosmological (teaching how the universe works), and many certainly are. But they can also serve any number of other functions for an institution, from sociological (teaching how society works) to pedagogical (teaching valuable lessons) or even metaphysical (teaching a sense of wonder). Regardless of their function, the question of whether these stories are true or false is an entirely separate issue from the acknowledgment that they exist for a group of people and can be valued as such. There is little question that Jordan was devout in his personal faith, just as ancient Egyptians were devout in theirs, and just as you might be in yours. Each of these religions—Jordan's and the Egyptians' and yours if you have one—will in this book be referred to as mythologies. This shouldn't be seen as an attempt to diminish or denigrate any of them.

Okay, *this* is really the last thing: Spoilers abound. Seriously. It's so important I'm saying it twice. If you don't want spoilers, turn back now.

You've been warned.

THE WHEELWRIGHT: THE LIFE OF ROBERT JORDAN

James Oliver Rigney, Jr.—the man who would become Robert Jordan—was born on October 17, 1948, in Charleston, South Carolina. It was, as he'd later point out, the Chinese Year of the Rat.[1] He was the second of the three sons of James Oliver and Eva May Rigney (née Grooms) who regularly attended a downtown Baptist church. He was nevertheless born under the care of Catholics at an infirmary: "My mother believed the nuns gave better care than anyone else," he recalled.[2]

His father had been in the Pacific in World War II, earning a Bronze Star for valor and a recommendation for a Silver Star, while working ground reconnaissance behind Japanese lines in places whose names would become synonymous with horror. Guadalcanal. Bougainville. Luzon. His son recalled the elder Rigney's trauma with vivid awareness: "For years afterward he would sometimes wake up in the night, sweating, afraid that in his sleep, in his remembered dreams, he might have hurt the wife he loved."[3] Family was the center of his world. He was a police officer, but money was tight:

Police officers were very poorly paid in those days, and he was an honest man. He would not even accept the Christmas turkeys that everyone else thought were perfectly all right. Instead, to take care of his family, he worked another full-time job as a carpenter, and took house-painting jobs whenever and wherever he could find them. Later, when he worked for the South Carolina State Ports Authority, he would take every bit of overtime he could find, even if it meant that sometimes he came home with just enough time to bathe and eat and go right back to work. Whatever burden he had to carry, he carried; if the weight of it made his knees buckle, he never complained—he just got back up and carried it on, carried it as long as it was his to carry.[4]

Harriet later described her husband's childhood circumstances as having been "*real* poor,"[5] but Jordan himself seemed hesitant to paint such a bleak picture of his youth, perhaps due to his keen awareness that there were others who'd had to make do with far less than he'd had.[6] Instead, he recalled his childhood, and especially his father, with clear love and respect:

As for my idol, that is my father, now deceased. He was a wonderful man, with a rich life. I'll try to paint a small picture. He got his first car, a Model A, at the age of thirteen because he had the habit of hitching rides with bootleggers in the Tennessee mountains, and after he was in a wreck where the driver ran off and my father told the police who had been chasing them that he had been driving, his father decided to put an end to the hitching. He was a noted middleweight boxer in the 1930s, rising in the rankings, but stopped after he badly injured another man in the ring. He was a veteran of WWII who spent a lot of time behind the Japanese lines, a quiet, gentle man who taught me to rebuild automobile engines, to hunt and fish. He told stories over the campfire when we were out hunting or fishing, thus starting me on the road to storytelling myself. He never said a word about me stealing shotgun shells from his stock so a known bootlegger and poacher would take me into the woods with him. Well, I didn't know about the poaching until later. But Junior knew more about the woods than anybody else I've ever met. My father was a poker shark with a photographic memory who allowed me to sit in for three hands whenever the weekly game was at our house, even when I was young enough to need to sit on three encyclopedias to be able to get my arms on the table. He staked me, he ate the losses, and we split any winnings I had. I did win one of those hands while sitting on stacked up Encyclopedia Americanas. He told my brothers and me that he had few requirements of us. Be honest. Keep your word always. Try to do better with your life than he had done with his. And whatever you decided to be, whether it was a college professor or an auto mechanic, be the best at it that you could manage to be. Yes, he was, and is, my idol.[7]

His mother, Jordan said, "was very beautiful. She looked like Ava Gardner's sister—the prettier one. She was a housewife. The only job she ever had was in World War II when everyone was employed—she did something then in defense."[8]

When he was four years old, Jordan taught himself to read with the incidental aid of his brother Ted, who was twelve years older and was often put in charge of "babysitting the brat."

He wanted to keep my hands out of his goldfish bowl and his terrarium, and keep my hands off his balsa wood planes. And he found that if he read to me and moved his finger along the line, I would sit beside him and stare at the page.

Now he was not about to read children's books: he was reading me fairly adult novels. I don't know when I made the connection between the words he was saying and the symbols on the page. But one night my parents came home; he stuck the book back on the shelf, and I wanted more. So I pulled the book down and struggled through to the end. *White Fang*: that was the first book I ever read, if you want to call it reading. I did get a sense of the story.

When my brother found out that I could do this, he started to supply me with books because that would keep me quiet. When he got guilty about letting me take books off my parents' shelves, he would bring me a book for a 10- or 12-year-old. My great-uncles also supplied me with books, so I had a great clutch of pre–World War I boys' books.

I did think about writing when I was very little. But writers didn't seem to make a living in the United States as writers. All sorts of fellows wrote books but they all had something else they did for the money. That's the way it seemed. And those who did, lived in Cuba or the South of France or Italy. I might have been precocious but I wasn't so sure about moving to Italy. . . . [9]

By the time he was five, Jordan was tackling Mark Twain and Jules Verne on his own and had developed a love of books. Reading "was galvanizing," he later said, "better than a movie. I could visualize all of it in my head."[10] He remained an avid reader for the rest of his life—his library held over fourteen thousand books when he died.

He attended a public elementary school starting at age six, and found himself quickly butting up against the restrictions on what was expected of his reading level and his own far more advanced position. His solution was to go to the public library, but he was forced to "sneak out of the children's section to a reading room on the second floor," where the books he actually wanted to read were to be found.[11] Whenever he was denied his desired reading material, he would take to reading the encyclopedias in the reference section. By the time he was eight years old, biographer David Aiken explains, Jordan's high intelligence and voracious appetite for information were beginning to cause him problems: "He had the knowledge of an eight-year-old, but the outlook and perception of someone in his twenties." Teachers at school weren't prepared to handle his questions as a result. Neither were the teachers in church: "I was one of the few kids I know of who was sometimes told to sit outside the Sunday School classroom."[12]

Around this time, Jordan had to switch schools to one in a different part of town. And then, in the middle of it all, the household was further shaken when his mother suddenly took ill.

The added strain began when my mother had her first nervous break-down, when I was eight. Those continued at regular intervals, neces-sitating her being hospitalized. I think that these two things—the fact that I was a precocious little monster in some ways, and that my mother had nervous breakdowns—in my case that was enough child-hood stress to improve my chances as a writer, looking back at it rather coldly.[13]

Through it all, he had two constants in his life: books and sports. "I made it through Machiavelli's *The Prince* by age twelve," he said, "which may have begun to cure me of romantic illusions."[14] As for athletics, he played anything he could. As he got older, he particularly excelled in football: he was ultimately over six feet tall—every bit the part of the linebacker he played on the field.

When he was in high school his family moved to Johns Island, out-side of Charleston. His new high school didn't have a football team, or many of the other sports he enjoyed. But he did what he could:

By and large I found school boring. Most of the time I could do a solid B, B+, perhaps an A, without studying. And since I was an athlete, that was considered sterling! . . .

As for writing, I thought again about doing that, at 10 and 16 and 20. I said, "It would be a useless exercise. What am I supposed to write about? I haven't seen enough of life, so anything I write is going to be empty."[15]

After graduating from St. John's High School in 1966, Jordan was recruited to play football at Clemson University and received a schol-arship. He elected to major in electrical engineering, but the experi-ence did not go well. The long-ahead-of-the-curve young man suddenly found himself unprepared for the moment:

I went to university and discovered that trying to carry a very heavy load in academic subjects and play football, I needed to know how to study. And that was something I had never learned how to do, so I floundered quite badly. At the end of a year at university I went into the army and went to Vietnam.[16]

VIETNAM

Rudderless, Jordan had volunteered for enlistment in the U.S. Army. And after basic training at Fort Jackson, he was off to war in May 1968 (see photo insert, page 1). He would spend two tours in Vietnam. Or, as he counted them, the next "two years, two months, and twenty-two days" of his life.[17]

Originally assigned to a clerical role, Jordan managed to get himself posted as a helicopter door gunner so he could be closer to where the action was, then advanced to crew chief: he served with the Sixty-Eighth Assault Helicopter Company, a.k.a. the Top Tigers, of the 145th Combat Aviation Battalion, Twelfth Aviation Group, First Aviation Brigade.

> I've always been a military history buff. But when I was in Vietnam I wasn't thinking history or strategy: I was thinking staying alive, and occasionally taking an R&R to Australia where I'd go to the beach and drink a lot of beer and try to meet a schoolteacher on vacation.
>
> I sort of knew in a way what to expect because military service has always been a family tradition. All my brothers, my father and my uncles, my grandfather and my great-uncles went into the military— some enlisted, most as officers, some made careers, some did not. But you did your basic service and if there was any shooting going on, you went where the guns were.[18]

Just how much his war experience had affected his later makeup as a writer came up often in interviews, and Jordan was hesitant to admit to an intentional correlation between his writings and his experiences. His response to such questions most often fell along lines such as this, from an interview just two years before his death:

I've certainly used some things from Vietnam. I know what it is like to
have someone trying to kill me. Me in particular. Not some random
guy. Me. I know what it is like to kill someone. I know how the first
time feels, and how that is different from the fifth, or the tenth. These
things certainly went into the characters I've written. That wasn't deliberate. Who you are is constructed in large part from what you have
experienced and how you reacted to those experiences. Whatever you
write is filtered through who you are. So the influence has to be there.[19]

Only once did he admit to an actual one-to-one correlation between
his experience at war and his books. In the sixth novel of The Wheel
of Time, the protagonist, Rand, memorizes the face of a young woman
who'd died to protect him:

A Maiden was straightening Desora's body; she had raised Desora's
veil. She reached to stop him when he touched that piece of black
algode, then hesitated, looking at his face, and settled back on her
haunches.
   Lifting the veil, he memorized Desora's face. She looked as if she
were sleeping now. Desora, of the Musara sept of the Reyn Aiel. So
many names. Liah, of the Cosaida Chareen, and Dailen, of the Nine
Valleys Taardad, and Lamelle, of the Smoke Water Miagoma, and . . .
So many. Sometimes he ran down that list name by name.[20]

It's only a few sentences. A minute, perhaps two, in Rand's life. But
to readers familiar with trauma the passage was searing. Asked in 1994
whether the scene owed anything to his military experience, Jordan replied that it did:

I suppose, actually, that particular thing came from the only time I
was really shaken in combat in shooting at somebody, or shooting *at*
somebody. I had to, uh, I was shooting back at some people on a sam-
pan and a woman came out and pulled up an AK-47, and I didn't

hesitate about shooting her. But that stuck with me. I was raised in a very old-fashioned sort of way. You don't hurt women—you don't *do* that. That's the one thing that stuck with me for a long, long time.[21]

War is filled with such horrific events, no matter the side or the cause. This was one of many reasons that Jordan was particularly uncomfortable with the idea that he'd done anything heroic during his time in Vietnam, though he was ultimately decorated with a Distinguished Flying Cross with Oak Leaf Cluster, a Bronze Star with "V," and two Vietnamese Crosses of Gallantry with Palm. Asked about how he'd earned these military honors, he was intrinsically self-effacing:

Everyone knows about one way of winning a medal. That is, to see something which needs to be done and to consciously do it at the risk of your life. I never did this. Relatively few people do, which is why we mark out those who do as heroes.

But at other times, you can realize that you are going to die in a very few minutes, except that if you do something incredibly stupid, you might just have a small chance of living. And against all reason, it works. Or you take a step without thinking, and then it's too late to turn back, maybe because turning back is just as dangerous as going on, or even more dangerous, or maybe because you know that you will have to look in the shaving mirror, and that every time you do, you will remember that you turned back. So you keep going. Or perhaps it's because you are with your friends, and you have to back their play, even if it's crazy, because they're your friends, because they've backed your play, even when it was crazy.

I was with a group of men who had a certain air about them, and if you didn't have it when you joined them, you soon absorbed it. A plaque in our day room read: Anybody can dance with the Devil's daughter, but we tell her old man to his face. At a time like that, in a place like that, you're all young and crazy, and if you've been there long enough, you know you're going to die. Not from old age; next month, next week, tomorrow. Now, maybe. It's going to happen, so what does it matter? In the end, for most of us, the medals boiled down to managing not to die. If you're alive when the higher-ups think you should be dead, it discombobulates their brains, so they hang a bit of something on you to balance things in their own heads. That's how it happened for me. That is why I am not I repeat, not! a hero. I just managed to stay alive. And I even managed to get sane again. Reasonably sane, anyway.[22]

There were nevertheless hints of actions done. In 2002, commenting on mortality, Jordan said:

I was 19 when I realized I was going to die for sure. On my first tour in Vietnam, the helicopter I was in blew up and threw me into the jungle. I got up and ran back through the lines of an NVA ambush—I didn't know it was there—I just knew the other chopper was in that direction.

This knowledge changes your view of the world. I think it gives you a certain maturity. Perhaps maturity is the knowledge that everything is going to change, that neither you nor anything you see is going to go on forever.[23]

Only toward the end of his years did more detailed stories about his service get out. While Jordan was fighting the illness that would eventually take his life, his close cousin, Wilson Grooms, took over the writing of Jordan's blog, providing updates on the beloved author's condition. In one exchange, he referenced a family story about Jordan shooting down a rocket-propelled grenade (RPG) in flight.[24] This prompted Jordan to tell the tale himself a few weeks later:

I think I need to put a few things straight about this whole shooting down an rpg in flight thing. First off, it definitely comes under do not try this at home even if you ARE an expert. Expert is defined as anyone who has tried it once and is still breathing. You see, there aren't many reasons to try such a thing. But when looking right shows certain death coming hotfoot, and looking left shows a crack in the wall that you couldn't scrape through [sic] one time in a million . . . one in ten million . . . you instinctively make a dive for the crack. Now I was very lucky. Very lucky. I just happened to be laying down suppression not very far from Mr. NVA when he took his shot, so I only has [sic] a small arc to cover. Just a quick shift of the wrist. Still, a lot of luck involved. When the pilot asked what happened, I just said an rpg went off prematurely. I figured he wouldn't believe what happened. Even some guys who saw it all from other choppers didn't believe. I heard a lot of "You know, it almost looked like you shot that thing out of the air" and "You were really lucky that thing went off prematurely. I never heard of that happening before."

Now there's the matter of actually seeing the rpg in flight. That came from being in the Zone. An RPG is a rocket propelled grenade, and it is fast, fast, fast. I've heard a lot of athletes and sportscasters talk about being in the Zone, but I think most of them simply mean they played their A-game. But they weren't in the Zone, because in the Zone, you don't make mistakes. None. I discovered this playing baseball and basketball and later football. You can't always get there, certainly not at will, but when you do. . . . What happens is that while you are moving at normal speed, everybody else, everything else, is moving in slow motion. Passes float like they were drifting through honey. You have all the time in the world to position yourself. And your vision improves, sharpens. The quarterback has carried out a perfect bootleg. Everybody thinks that fullback coming up the middle has the ball. But even if you didn't catch the motion when the QB tucked the ball behind his leg, you spot that tiny sliver of ball that just barely shows, and you're right there to meet him when he reaches the line. Maybe you drop him for a loss before he can get his pass off. In the Zone. That's the only reason I could make this play.

On another note, I was riding an M-60 on a pintle mount, not a .50 cal. We only had a limited number of Ma-deuces, and we had to be careful not to let any IG inspectors see them because we weren't authorized to have any at all. Don't know whether I could have done it with a .50, frankly. A matter of just that much more weight to swing, that much more inertia to overcome. It was damned close even with a 60.[25]

Jordan's time in the war was deeply traumatizing. He left changed. He referenced this himself in the same post, when he told a further story about the two nicknames he had in Vietnam:

First up was Ganesha, after the Hindu god called the Remover of Obstacles. He's the one with the elephant head. That one stuck with me, but I gained another that I didn't like so much. The Iceman. One day, we had what the Aussies called a bit of a brass-up. Just our ship alone, but we caught an NVA battalion crossing a river, and wonder of wonders, we got permission to fire before they finished. The gunner had a round explode in the chamber, jamming his 60, and the fool had left his barrel bag, with spares, back in the revetment. So while he was frantically rummaging under my seat for my barrel bag, it was over to me, young and crazy, standing on the skid, singing something by the Stones at the [top] of my lungs with the mike keyed so the others could listen in, and Lord, Lord, I rode that 60. 3000 rounds, an empty ammo box, and a smoking barrel that I had burned out because I didn't want to take the time to change. We got ordered out right after I went dry, so the artillery could open up, and of course, the arty took credit for every body recovered, but we could count how many bodies were floating in the river when we pulled out. The next day in the orderly room an officer with a literary bent announced my entrance with "Behold, the Iceman cometh." For those of you unfamiliar with Eugene O'Neil [sic], the Iceman was Death. I hated that name, but I couldn't shake it. And, to tell you the truth, by that time maybe it fit. I have, or used to have, a photo of a young man sitting on a log eating C-rations with a pair of chopsticks. There are three dead NVA laid out in a line just beside him. He didn't kill them. He didn't choose to sit there because of the bodies. It was just the most convenient place to sit. The bodies don't bother him. He doesn't care. They're just part of the landscape. The young man is glancing at the camera, and you know in one look that you aren't going to take this guy home to meet your parents. Back in the world, you wouldn't want him in your neighborhood, because he is cold, cold, cold. I strangled that SOB, drove a stake through his heart, and buried him face down under a crossroad outside Saigon before coming home, because I knew that guy wasn't made to survive in a civilian environment. I think he's gone. All of him. I hope so. I much prefer being remembered as Ganesha, the Remover of Obstacles.[26]

Jordan long had the intention to write a book looking back on his experiences. It was for this reason that he insisted on writing fiction under a pseudonym: only the story about his own life would appear under his own name. It would be a difficult undertaking, he admitted in a 1991 interview: "But the difficulty of approaching a book on Vietnam may prevent me from doing it. There are an awful lot of people who haven't come to grips with the war, what it did to them, how it changed them."[27] By 1998, he was even less sure he'd be able to do it:

I don't try to write about Vietnam; I thought I would, once, but now, I don't believe I could make myself. But I know the confusion, uncertainty and outright ignorance of anything you can't see that exists once the fighting starts; I don't think war will ever become sufficiently high-tech to completely dispel "the fog of war." So I can put these sensations into my writing.[28]

HOME AGAIN

Returning home to Charleston, Jordan was convinced to enroll as a veteran student at The Citadel, the Military College of South Carolina. Eschewing many campus activities, he mostly kept to himself: now that he was out of the army he grew out dashing waves of hair and a mustache. Though he was not at the top of his class, it's clear he was no slouch in his chosen field of physics: "I had everything lined up," he later said, "to go to graduate school for a doctorate in quantum optics."

I was very interested in theoretical physics. But I was tired of school, and I wanted to get on with my life. The government at this point was recruiting engineers, physicists and others, who they then sent to a school to study nuclear engineering. So I became an engineer, and for a long time I designed procedures to test and overhaul reactors on United States naval vessels.[29]

His job took him to the Charleston Naval Shipyard, not far from where his father had worked. It was there, in early 1977, on his way back to his office from the dry dock, that his "foot slipped on a railroad junction box."[30] When he fell, he shredded the ligaments in his knee. Surgeons did what they could to reconstruct the joint, but for the rest of his life Jordan would sometimes need a cane to walk. Nor was the tragedy finished: while he was recovering, postsurgical blood clots broke free and entered his lungs. If he hadn't already been in the hospital, he almost assuredly would have died.

Thirty years old and already having faced death in war and in peace, Jordan determined that "life was too short" not to do something he loved.[31] Finding the books he was reading to pass the months of recovery time unsatisfactory, he decided to write his own:

I remember picking up a book by an author I knew I liked, reading a few paragraphs and tossing it across the room and saying, "Oh God, I could do better than that." Then I thought, "All right son, it's time to put up or shut up."[32]

By his own account, it took him three and a half months to complete his first book, "writing longhand on legal yellow pads. When I went back to work I typed it up in the evenings and made the changes, and sent it off to a publisher." The book turned out to be a fantasy novel, *Warrior of the Altaii*. The publisher was DAW Books. Though it was his first attempt at something few could manage, the talent and potential were recognizable. In August of 1977 DAW made an offer on the book. But a month later, after Jordan asked for changes to the contract's subsidiary rights terms, the offer was withdrawn.

HARRIET, ALWAYS

Meanwhile, one of the greatest editors of science fiction and fantasy was moving back home to Charleston herself. Harriet McDougal (née Popham) was born on August 4, 1939, into a very different part of the city than the poor, hardscrabble one in which Jordan had grown up. Her father was a career navy man who would retire as an admiral. While he was at sea during World War II, her mother took out a mortgage in her own name to buy out her three siblings' shares of the home on Tradd Street that they'd inherited from their mother: a house built around 1797 whose fence, of all things, was praised by the writer H. P. Lovecraft in his published walking tour of the city.

After the war was over, Harriet's father was acting commandant of the naval shipyard in Charleston (where Jordan, by happenstance, would later be injured). This took the family to quarters on base. But when that tour of duty ended he retired and they moved downtown.

Afforded an excellent education growing up, Harriet graduated from Harvard-Radcliffe in 1960 with a degree in English. A chance contact landed her a job in publishing. She moved to New York City, became an editor at John Wiley & Sons, and before long married her first husband, Ed McDougal. By 1970, they'd divorced, and she was raising their son, Will McDougal, alone. All the while, her star continued to rise as an editor. Working at Grosset & Dunlap, she met publisher Tom Doherty. When he became publisher for Ace Books in 1975, she took the position of his editorial director and oversaw a period of "tremendous growth," as Doherty later recalled.[33] By 1977, he'd named her vice-president at Ace, but the death of her parents convinced her to resign the position and move back to Charleston. Two generations of women had owned the home on Tradd Street. She would be the third.

To help pay the bills, Harriet contracted with attorney and former counsel to Dell Books, Richard Gallen, on a profit-sharing agreement to start her own imprint, Popham Press. While shopping at a local book-store on King Street called The Book Bag, Harriet was told by the man-ager that there was a local man who came in from time to time and had said he was writing a book. Having no business cards, Harriet hand-wrote her name and number on a three-by-five-inch index card in case the man came in again.

The man, of course, was Jordan (see photo insert, page 2).

At the time, Harriet was looking for "a writer who could write bod-ice rippers, sexy historicals aimed at a female audience."[34] When Jordan finally called her, she told him as much. He insisted he was writing just that. He was thinking, he later recalled, of an old lesson in acting:

> If someone comes to you and says, "There is this audition you ought to go to. I know you're just right for the part. You'll get it. You *will* get it. No doubt. You can ride a horse, can't you?" You say, "Oh, yes! Yes! I was born in the saddle. Oh yes. I was." And then you go out and learn to ride a horse.[35]

Invited to her home for a talk, he "made up a bodice ripper synopsis on the drive."[36] Harriet recognized potential problems with the outline, which she recounted as an "awful" idea: "All I remember was that the obligatory sex scene involved a duck." Still, she knew DAW had offered him an initial book contract for *Warrior of the Altaii,* so she suggested he give the bodice ripper a try.

That book contract was also on Jordan's mind. "It didn't matter" that the second letter from DAW had withdrawn the offer, he later recalled, "because I decided I would ignore the second letter":

> The first letter [from DAW] said I could write. There were things happening at work that I found very irritating. So I cleared my desk and I completed every project in the pipeline, and I laid down my resignation.
>
> "You can't go!"
>
> I said, "Read the resignation. I'm going."

I was told, "If you do this, you'll never work for the United States government again."

I said, "Could I have that in writing?"[37]

Jordan moved back home with his parents, who did everything they could to support his new direction: "My father always said you have to do what you want to do. It's your life. Nobody can live it for you and you can't live it for anybody else."[38]

The book he was working on, as Harriet had suspected it would be, was not good. Three hundred pages into the project, he set it aside.

Harriet, in "a slow patch" eight months after their initial meeting, called to see how he was progressing. He told her the bodice ripper had failed. She pushed him to let her look at the still-unpublished *Warrior of the Altaii*, which he was reluctant to do: he knew "barbarian fantasy" wasn't what her Popham Press was after and didn't want her to think that was all he could do. Harriet convinced him to let her take a look anyway. He dropped off the manuscript at her home.

When he showed up early to a subsequent meeting to discuss the pages, Jordan overheard Harriet complaining to another author that no one would write a historical set in South Carolina that wasn't about the Civil War. So when it was his turn to go in, he was ready. She told him that he was right that *Warrior of the Altaii* wasn't what she wanted, but it had absolutely convinced her that he could write a good book. With a smile, he responded that he'd actually been thinking of writing a historical novel set in South Carolina. He promised her an outline of just such a book the following day. Unlike the bodice ripper, this book worked. Soon enough, he had a contract for what would become his first published novel: a story of the American Revolution that would tell some of what he felt were the "forgotten" aspects of the history of the South at the time.[39] Largely set in Charleston, the book was called *The Fallon Blood* and was edited by Mc-Dougal. In 1980, it was published by her Popham Press—distributed by Ace Books—under Jordan's first pseudonym, Reagan O'Neal.

Meanwhile, Harriet had suggested he send *Warrior of the Altaii* to Doherty, who passed it along to Jim Baen at Ace in April 1980. Revisions would be requested, but requests were not immediately forthcoming. Around the same time, Doherty left Ace Books and started his own publishing company: Tom Doherty Associates. One of his first calls was to Harriet in Charleston: "I'm not asking you to move back," he told her, "I'm just asking you to edit."[40] She agreed to come on board as the vice-president and editorial director of the newly founded Tor Books, on the agreement that she could telecommute from Charleston. She would ultimately edit many important science fiction and fantasy books of the era.

Jordan and Harriet began dating soon after he finished a book tour in support of *The Fallon Blood,* and the two were married on March 28, 1981. Before long, he converted to her religion—"The males in my family have always taken the religion of the women they marry"—and the couple began attending an Episcopal church.[41] Around the same time, his second novel, *The Fallon Pride,* was published by Tor. A third installment of the Revolution trilogy, *The Fallon Legacy,* followed in 1982. That same year he published the novel *Cheyenne Raiders*—this time under the name Jackson O'Reilly—which he'd sold to a different editor to avoid the feeling that he'd been published due to his wife alone. From that point forward, however, Harriet continued to serve as his editor, as she would for the rest of his career.

It was in this period, with four novels under his belt—and a fifth, *Warrior of the Altaii,* still in editorial limbo—that Jordan became Jordan.

Doherty had just acquired the rights to publish a new novel featuring Robert E. Howard's Conan the Barbarian character, and with a new Conan movie starring Arnold Schwarzenegger due in 1982, he asked Harriet to find someone who could write a barbarian fantasy in short order. She offered up her new husband. Jordan at first declined, as he "was dubious about the prospect of writing in someone else's universe."[42] Convinced by a persistent Harriet, however, he "was surprised to find it a kick," and he ultimately produced seven successful Conan novels in the next two years: *Conan the Barbarian: Conan the Invincible* (1982), *Conan the Defender* (1982), *Conan the Unconquered* (1983), *Conan the*

Triumphant (1983), *Conan the Magnificent* (1984), *Conan the Destroyer* (1984), and *Conan the Victorious* (1984). All of them were written under a new pseudonym: Robert Jordan.

Amid this flurry of productivity, the rights to *Warrior of the Altaii* were reverted to Jordan in 1983, but he didn't re-attempt to publish the book. His mind was elsewhere. He'd started several other stories over the years—in his unpublished papers are early drafts of a thriller novel, *April the 15th;* a science fiction novel, *Jon One-Eye;* and a Western, *Morgan,* among other writings[43]—but a new fantasy series had been percolating in his mind.

The Wheel of Time was about to be born.

Already a popular author, Jordan began the journey toward international bestselling phenomenon when Tor published *The Eye of the World* in 1990. It was the first of a planned six books in The Wheel of Time— all to be edited by Harriet, of course. The second book in the series, *The Great Hunt,* was already nearly complete when the first was released, so it was published later that same year.

Explanation of how the project developed is detailed below. For now, it's enough to know that subsequent volumes in the series (and works related to it) appeared with regularity over the next fifteen years, considerably outstripping the original six-book vision as the scope of the project grew: *The Dragon Reborn* (1991), *The Shadow Rising* (1992), *The Fires of Heaven* (1993), *Lord of Chaos* (1994, a Locus Award Nominee), *A Crown of Swords* (1996), *The World of Robert Jordan's The Wheel of Time* (1997, with Teresa Patterson), *The Path of Daggers* (1998), *New Spring* (1998, a novella), *Winter's Heart* (2000), *Crossroads of Twilight* (2003), *New Spring: The Novel* (2004), and *Knife of Dreams* (2005). Beginning with *The Path of Daggers,* each release of the main sequence of books reached number one on the *New York Times* Best Seller list.[44] For his accumulated publication successes and his lifetime of service, he was awarded an honorary doctorate in literature from his alma mater, The Citadel, in 1999.

Randland was ultimately one of the most extraordinary feats of world-building in fantasy, and that meant work. Each volume of The

Wheel of Time was a massive undertaking, ranging between 226,000 words (*The Path of Daggers*) and nearly 400,000 words (*The Shadow Rising*), with intricate plotting across multiple story lines and viewpoints.

Jordan's offices reflected this scale. They were located in the former carriage house on the Tradd Street property—where Harriet had first lived in 1944 and 1945 while her mother was still renting out the big house. Though he started on the second floor, Jordan's office eventually encompassed the first floor, amid a visual cacophony. There were enough weapons of all stripes—from the ancient world to the modern—to fill a small armory. There were piles of papers. Treasured bits and pieces of artwork and collectibles. Gifts from fans. A skeleton wearing a horned helmet. A dartboard. Smoking pipes. Racks of hats. Hundreds of CDs of every genre (though in his early years he liked to write to classical music in particular). Telescopes. And thousands upon thousands of books on shelves that groaned from the weight: history, mythology, philosophy, and an array of fiction from old mysteries and Westerns to new science fiction and fantasy novels. Upstairs was still more. Each and every piece of it, directly or indirectly, was a spoke that turned the massive and evolving work that was The Wheel of Time.

For all this, his writing space itself was relatively small. To get to it, one had to pass through this labyrinth of the mind to a small office in the corner. There, close beside a window, sat an antique rolltop desk that they'd bought from a store on King Street. It was heavy oak, a little worn where his right elbow long lay upon it. It was here—amid still more papers and books, in air that had the tinge of idling pipe smoke—that he wrote the words that would be devoured by millions.[45]

For years, two assistants shared space with Jordan in the carriage house. Both played pivotal roles in The Wheel of Time. The first was Maria Livingston Simons.[46] She'd begun working for Jordan in 1996. Initially tasked with overseeing fan mail and some light administrative work on a part-time basis, she was his full-time assistant within a year. Among her initial jobs was to take on the enormous task of organizing Jordan's notes on The Wheel of Time, which were already running to thousands of pages of material. From there, she became his continuity editor and general research assistant. She was, he often said, his "right arm," and her constant checking and rechecking of textual questions made her the foremost authority on Randland outside of Jordan and Harriet themselves. Jordan often politely answered fans' questions with the expression "RAFO," meaning "Read and Find Out"; an eventual corollary was "MAFO," meaning "Ask Maria and Find Out."

Year by year, Maria saw her duties expand, to the point that it was difficult for her to serve effectively as Jordan's research assistant while also efficiently managing the growing number of jobs that an internationally bestselling book series demanded. More help was needed. So in 2001, on Maria's advice, Jordan interviewed and then hired Alan Romanczuk to be his new research assistant. In addition to its many general responsibilities, the job entailed the coordination of timelines and characters. This became Alan's specialty. Jordan also frequently leaned on him for help managing the gritty action sequences in the books.

Jordan's workday changed little over the years. He was a daily writer, who in his advice to new writers recommended establishing a set output to be achieved every day.[47] His personal routine was to make his way to the carriage house after breakfast, often entering with a smile and a song. He was particularly fond of sea shanties, among other things, and carried a fine tune. He attended first to phone messages and letters that were organized and prioritized by Maria. He'd then attend to necessary emails, getting the business of the day done as quickly as possible.

Administrative tasks complete, Jordan shifted into writing mode. Once focused, he would neglect to notice the passing of time and the ways of the world—lunch, storms, and much else slipped by—before darkness and the fear of missing out on dinner with Harriet would send him back into the house. Six-to-eight-hour workdays for five days a week were common at the start of a book project, he said in 1994: "After a while, this gets to be: drink a quart or two of strong coffee, write for twelve to fourteen hours a day, and do this seven days a week. Eventually the book is finished or I am dead."[48] Helping to keep him sane despite the grueling routine was Harriet, of course:

Sometimes my wife will say to me, you're working too hard, go fishing, and sometimes I will. And sometimes she will say to me, I want you to see something on the porch, and when I go downstairs, there's a fishing guide waiting, and she tells me to go away and fish. That's about it except for the occasional stops to fish when I'm traveling, there's too much to write and not enough years. She's a wonderful person, the empress of the known universe![49]

Jordan had a systematic mind. He made task lists—often typed out—to make the most efficient use of his time, ranging from a daily to-do list to what tools ought to be carried in a car.[50] This same level of organizational thinking applied in his fiction writing. He took copious notes to deepen and enrich his work: lists of where real-world crops were grown and what time of year they were planted and harvested, for example, as well as lists of trees that included notice about when and where they would grow but also how their bark felt to the touch and the shape of their limbs.[51]

Given the intricate plotting and detailed specificity of The Wheel of Time, it's surely not surprising that Jordan ultimately had tens of thousands of pages of closely guarded notes and background materials. Nor is it a shock to learn that he continuously drafted and redrafted his chapters before he deemed them ready for other eyes. Harriet, in the role of editor, said she often didn't get to see the work until he was on his twelfth draft. A surviving typescript for The Great Hunt, as an example, begins with the twenty-fifth version of the prologue, the twenty-ninth version of chapter 1, the thirty-second version of chapter 2 . . . and it still doesn't match the final printed text.[52]

Though most writers tend to write their stories in a generally linear fashion—that is, working on them in the order they'd appear in the book or even in their own timeline—Jordan sometimes wrote nonlinearly, moving from scene to scene as it inspired him. Despite the sprawling plots of his books, he was nevertheless able to keep the whole of his advancing narrative in his mind.

Jordan's author's biography, with some minor changes, was consistently some variation of what appeared on the dust jacket of the first books: "Robert Jordan is a graduate of The Citadel and lives in Charleston, S.C." The simplicity of this snapshot became famous in its own right—its sparseness even providing a source of some mystery for readers—but it's not what Jordan originally considered. Instead, his notes reveal drafts of a far larger biographical sketch to accompany the first novel. Of the two versions that remain, this is the more complete:

Robert Jordan was born on 17 October 1948, the Chinese Year of the Rat, in Charleston, South Carolina, where he now lives in a two-hundred year old house. He served two tours in Vietnam, and his decorations include the Distinguished Flying Cross, the Bronze Star with 'V' and two Vietnamese Crosses of Gallantry. A graduate of The Citadel (The Military College of South Carolina), he has a degree in Physics, and before resigning to write full-time he was a nuclear engineer for the United States government. In addition to fantasy, he has written historical novels, westerns and international intrigue, and he is also an editorial consultant for Tor Books. His hobbies include hunting, fishing, poker, chess, go and shogi, as well as collecting Oriental and African art. He is a devoted pipe-smoker, and both a Ricardian and a Sherlockian. He is an advocate of Solar Power Satellites, the Strategic Defense Initiative, the industrialization of space, the colonization of the Moon, Mars and beyond, and O'Neill colonies. Politically he considers himself a Libertarian Monarchist. He has just finished the sequel to THE EYE OF THE WORLD, and is working on the third book of THE WHEEL OF TIME.[53]

Because it was ghost-written for another author, the book of "international intrigue" he references doesn't appear on his own bibliography: to date, this thriller has not been identified.

Jordan took roughly fifteen months to complete each of the first six books in The Wheel of Time. He'd had a head start in the early years—

the first two books were completed before anyone could read them—but the plan to put out a new volume every year soon became difficult, especially with ever larger publicity tours eating up ever more of his time and energy. Whereas most fiction books were turned in to the publisher close to a year in advance of publication, *Lord of Chaos* was turned in to Tor in August of 1994, just two months before it appeared on shelves. And there was no rest for the weary: Jordan was immediately sent on a grueling promotional tour of nineteen cities in twenty-three days. Knowing that there'd be no chance of getting the seventh book, *A Crown of Swords,* delivered in time, Tor pushed back the deadline by a year. It was still barely enough: Jordan took twenty-two months to write the volume, and it was printed mere weeks after he was done.

Something had to give. When Jordan hand-delivered the completed book to Doherty in New York City, his friend and publisher was stunned at his appearance: "I could see how tired he was. I felt kind of guilty because we'd all been pushing so hard to get it finished," Tom recalled. "I said to him, 'Much as I hate to tell you this, you've got to slow down, you've got to take care of yourself.'"[54]

It was a wake-up call that helped Jordan adapt to a more forgiving delivery schedule that would better ensure his long-term productivity:

> Publishers don't say that. What publishers say is, "You don't have to worry about the deadline. You could meet the deadline if you didn't sleep so much. You know, it's a proven fact that sleep causes cancer. Nobody who doesn't sleep has ever come down with cancer."[55]

His rate of publication slowed, but it hardly stopped. The Wheel of Time was still turning, with a new book appearing every couple of years. Fans numbered in the millions. The internet enabled them to gather in world-spanning forums, discussing and dissecting his work. Though rooted in a stark vision of good and evil, his stories grew in complexity and depth. Asked what they were ultimately about, though, Jordan gave a simple response: "Life changes. Deal."[56]

It was about to.

AMYLOIDOSIS

On March 23, 2006, Jordan announced in a letter to *Locus* that he had been diagnosed with amyloidosis, a rare disease in which abnormal proteins, called amyloids, build up in the body. If these build up in the organs, they can cause organ failure and death. In Jordan's case, the amyloid proteins were depositing in his heart, a condition that had an untreated median life expectancy of one year. His treatment plan, he reported, had a median life expectancy of four years postdiagnosis. At the time, he optimistically pronounced his intention to beat such a record.

> Everybody knows or has heard of someone who was told they had five years to live, only that was twenty years ago and here they [*sic*] guy is, still around and kicking. I mean to beat him. I sat down and figured out how long it would take me to write all of the books I currently have in mind, without adding anything new and without trying [to] rush anything. The figure I came up with was thirty years. Now, I'm fifty-seven, so anyone my age hoping for another thirty years is asking for a fair bit, but I don't care. That is my minimum goal. I am going to finish those books, all of them, and that is that.[57]

The most pressing concern for everyone, of course, was Jordan's immediate health. But there was, alongside it, the question of what would happen with the still-unfinished Wheel of Time, which had fans around the world awaiting its conclusion.

Knife of Dreams, the eleventh book in the series, had been published the previous October, and Jordan was confident that he needed only a single twelfth volume—to be entitled *A Memory of Light*—to complete The Wheel of Time. He admitted, though, that it might run to thousands of pages and "you might need a forklift to get it out the door."[58] He reassured his fans that he himself would finish the book, but by December he conceded that he was making plans just in case: "I'm getting out notes, so if the worst actually happens, someone could finish *A Memory of Light* and have it end the way I want it to end," he said in an interview. "But I hope to be around to actually finish it myself."[59]

As Jordan underwent a sequence of standard and soon experimental drug treatments under the care of the Mayo Clinic, his fans clung to whatever news about his condition that they could get. When he was well enough, he posted to a blog on Dragonmount, a fan website dedicated to The Wheel of Time. When he wasn't up to it, his cousin Wilson Grooms—who'd been so close to Jordan growing up that he was considered a fourth brother—posted updates on his behalf.

Jordan was fighting for his life, and fighting hard, but as the months went by the prognosis didn't seem to improve. The question of how The Wheel of Time could be finished with his condition was increasingly on his mind. To help him produce as much working material as he could, his computer was moved to his bedside, and Jordan called upon the two assistants who'd done so much to help him over the years: Maria and Alan. Together with Harriet, they would soon become known to the fanbase as "Team Jordan." They collectively attended to both his personal struggle with amyloidosis and his professional directive that they aid him in putting together the vision for the final volume of The Wheel of Time.

Initially, the goal was to gather this information so that he'd be able to complete the work himself when his strength returned. This was the plan, and certainly no one at the house on Tradd Street dared suggest otherwise.

Though there were days when a quiet shadow lay about the house and gardens, there were just as equally days of light and laughter. Jordan faced his illness with grace. Harriet refused to be anything but his pillar of strength. Wilson and his wife were frequent visitors, doing their best to keep spirits up. Even when the author was no longer able to make it into his office, Team Jordan gathered with him in the house on Fridays. Jordan, Alan recalled, "who always became a gleeman whenever a group gathered around him, seemed to take pleasure telling stories, some tales taller than others." For all the difficulties, it was "a warm memory . . .

a time of special bonding for us, a time when we truly became Team Jordan."[60]

Month by month, though, the possibility that he would not recover became more and more present. Though in earlier years he'd spoken of how his notes should be destroyed at his death—"I've arranged for all of my hard drives to be reformatted six times, every bit of paper which mentions anything about the books will be burned!" he said in a 1998 interview[61]—it was clear now that those notes would be vital for anyone trying to finish what he could not. Jordan had no hesitations now. He was determined that another writer should indeed be chosen to complete his great work. As for who that would be, he said, it would be up to Harriet.

Forever Harriet.

On Saturday evening, September 1, Jordan had a burst of strength and lucidity. Harriet was there, and Wilson as well. Also there was Lese Corrigan, an artist and friend of the family who'd painted a portrait of Jordan. She put a pen to paper to preserve what came next. Harriet took notes, too. Over the next two and a half hours, Jordan told them the story of the end of The Wheel of Time: "he became the Gleeman," Wilson reported, "and told the bones of it ALL."[62] Partway through, Jordan needed to take a break. Wilson took the opportunity to rush to Walmart, where he bought a tape recorder. On his return, Jordan dictated still further prose for the last book.

The end, Jordan had long said, was in his mind from the start. He could've written it out at any time. The only thing that might have changed would have been the final word.

Team Jordan had it now. The final chapter. The final word.

That Sunday evening, Maria came and sat with Jordan. She was given all the notes that Lese and Harriet had taken. She and Alan had by now built a long list of questions about the series that needed to be answered. Jordan tried to answer every question he could. Team Jordan recorded every word his failing heart gave him time to relay. He remained in good spirits. In an interview published in a local newspaper on September

13, he said that while he was for the moment bound to a wheelchair, he nevertheless still aimed to "keep marching for the horizon." He was fighting and wouldn't give up. "I've got promises to keep."[63]

On September 10, rumors of the author's deteriorating condition had grown loud enough that the family released a statement that Jordan, while seriously ill, was by no means receiving Last Rites: "I just got off the telephone with him," Wilson reported, "and he's surrounded by laughing friends and relatives and is about to enjoy a shrimp-based bowl of gumbo. He got a chuckle out of news of his impending departure."[64]

His body, though, was indeed failing him.

Maria, who knew The Wheel of Time better than anyone, was working through a list of still-unanswered questions that the team had written down. She spent time with him on Friday, September 14, taking notes as he chose the winner of a calendar art contest for Tor.[65] She wanted to ask him about some of the remaining questions on her list, but he was clearly tired and needed rest. She marked her place on her page of queries. She'd get the answers when she came back on Monday.

That chance never came.

James Oliver Rigney, Jr., quietly slipped away at 2:45 P.M. on Sunday, September 16, 2007. His last words were a whisper of love to his wife.

Wilson Grooms announced his cousin's death on Jordan's personal blog, setting off a wave of mourning around the world. "He never wavered in his faith," Wilson said in making the announcement, "nor questioned our God's timing."[66] Harriet, in the days to come, privately penned a testament to her heartbreak:

Always he started with a wind:

"The English wind blew the dust of the road in Michael Fallon's face."

"The wind scorched across Tripoli harbor."

". . . the wind blew east, out across the Sand Hills. . . ."

And all the others.

Breathing life into the ink and paper.

On September 16 I sat with him as his breath slowed and slowed, and then was gone.

And he was gone.

He had a bad disease and I had learned the hard thing—that some things I could not remedy or even improve. The hardest thing: I could not breathe for him.

Last spring I had a dream—a hospital, where they said he had to go downstairs, so they could take some blood—I said, oh, take mine, no need to disturb him—mine is the same, will tell you what you need to know about him.

But it's not true.

Breath is only ours no matter what the love.

I've come pretty close to my own death lately, with two minor heart surgeries since August 10. Since those events I cannot tell which heart is breaking, except that I still breathe.

He came like the wind, like the wind touched everything, and like the wind is gone.

The breeze today feels very good.[67]

Publicly, hearkening back to that final interview that he'd given just days before his passing, she assured those in mourning that he'd marched just as he'd promised them all he would: "He marched toward that horizon until he crossed it, where we cannot follow yet. The word now, the only possible word, is Onward."[68]

Onward. Not away from Jordan, but in advance of his legacy. He'd made her promise the book would be finished, and even through her tears she was determined to see it done.

Jordan's earthly remains were cremated, and his funeral was held in Charleston's St. Stephen's Episcopal Church on September 19. Among the friends and family in attendance were his publisher and friend of three and a half decades, Tom Doherty, as well as a handful of representatives of the enormous fandom that had been built around his work. The burial that afternoon took place in a small, private ceremony on the grounds of St. James Goose Creek. The stone is simple (see photo insert, page 3):

FATHER STORYTELLER
SOLDIER SINGER

COMPLETING THE WHEEL

Among the many who mourned Jordan around the world was a young, up-and-coming writer named Brandon Sanderson, whose own books were being published by Tor. On his personal blog, he posted a eulogy for Jordan on the day of the funeral, explaining how important The Wheel of Time had been to him in his development.

> I still think *Eye* is one of the greatest fantasy books ever written. It signifies an era, the culmination of the epic quest genre which had been brewing since Tolkien initiated it in the 60's. The Wheel of Time dominated my reading during the 90's, influencing heavily my first few attempts at my own fantasy novels. I think it did that to pretty much all of us; even many of the most literarily snobbish of fantasy readers were youths when I was, and read *Eye of the World* when I did.[69]

Sanderson went on to trace the arc of his career by his evolving feelings toward The Wheel of Time. He acknowledged that there were many authors who would "see this as an opportunity, not a tragedy." They were no doubt already circling for the chance to step into Jordan's shoes and complete the bestselling series. He did not volunteer himself for the task.

> Personally, I simply feel indebted to you. You showed me what it was to have vision and scope in a fantasy series—you showed me what could be done. I still believe that without your success, many younger authors like myself would never have had a chance at publishing their dreams.
>   You go quietly, but leave us trembling.[70]

It was this post that a friend of Harriet's, Elise Matthesen, came upon while looking for tributes to Jordan. On a gut feeling, she printed it out and gave it to her friend to read. Harriet, moved by Brandon's words and noting that he was a Tor author, subsequently called Doherty and asked him to send one of Brandon's novels for her to read. He sent Brandon's novel *Mistborn,* which had been published the previous year. The day it arrived in the mail, she read the first fifty pages of the book and fell asleep—not out of boredom, but out of the sheer relief that she'd found a writer who could do justice to her husband's vision.

On September 26, Harriet called Brandon at home. Asleep, he missed the call, and she left him a simple message: "Hello, Brandon Sanderson. This is Harriet McDougal Rigney. I am Robert Jordan's widow. I would like you to call me. There's something I want to talk to you about."[71] Returning her call after he awoke, he didn't get through. Wondering what was happening—telling himself that she'd only called to thank him for his kind words—he dialed up his then editor at Tor, Moshe Feder. Once more, the call wasn't picked up. At this point, Brandon tried calling his agent, Joshua Bilmes, but again he received no answer. Finally, he reached another editor at Tor, Patrick Nielsen Hayden, who replied only that it was what Brandon probably thought it was. For Brandon, this was his first inkling that he was being considered for the honor of finishing The Wheel of Time.

Later in the day, Harriet returned his call and told him that his name was on the list of potential authors and asked if he'd be willing to do it. Unknown to him, the list was extremely short—there was only one name on it. Though initially struck speechless at the offer, he managed to tell her that he'd need time to think about it.

He knew that it was a once-in-a-lifetime possibility. For someone who'd grown up with the books, it was in some measure a dream come true. It was also, by any measure, a significant business opportunity: if previous books in the series were any indication, he was being given the chance to coauthor what would presumably become an immediate bestseller.

It was nevertheless a hard choice. His gut feeling was that if Robert Jordan couldn't finish the series then perhaps no one should. At the same time, it was apparent that Jordan had tasked Harriet with finding someone to do it. So it was going to happen, with or without him.

In the end, he felt that there couldn't be that many people who were both capable fantasy writers *and* fans of The Wheel of Time who'd be willing to take on the task: if he said no, there was a chance that someone would be chosen who had only one of those qualifications, and the series would inevitably suffer for it. So he wrote Harriet, expressing his gratitude and his enthusiastic interest. By the end of October, she'd invited him to Charleston for an initial meeting in December 2007.

As he'd later recount, she picked him up at the airport and brought him to the house on Tradd Street in the evening. She offered him some soup, since he'd not had dinner. Instead, he asked if he could see the ending. Harriet laughed and gave him what would become the epilogue of the series: what Jordan had divulged on that magical gleeman's night. Without knowing it, Brandon sat down to read it in Jordan's own chair.

All told, there were roughly two hundred manuscript pages of book-specific notes left behind. Some of the pages were outlines for complete scenes—bits and pieces of what became the published prologues for the final three books, for instance, as well as the all-important epilogue of *A Memory of Light*—but others were only hints of plots and solutions. And then there were the thousands upon thousands of pages of series-related notes, glossaries, lists, and other working materials Jordan had left behind in his personal files.

It was all they had, and it left so very much undone.

There wasn't a full outline. There wasn't a sequenced plot. Most of the puzzles had only pieces of the solution. One of the questions that Maria never got to ask Jordan—the next one on her list on that Friday before he passed—was about the final moment in the series: "How did Rand light his pipe?" The answer to this, and everything else, now fell to Brandon and Team Jordan.

Taking with him that initial bundle of materials and Harriet's blessing to get to work, Brandon returned to Utah and set himself the task of rereading the entirety of The Wheel of Time. While he put together his own ideas through this process—no small feat in and of itself—Team Jordan continued to mine and organize what Jordan had left behind, collating everything they thought would be useful to the man tasked with completing the vision.

The task was monumental, akin to designing and then building a skyscraper from the foundation up, knowing only the final form of the front door, a room here and there, and perhaps the staircase to the roof. Those *had* to be there, and they had to stand up straight and be of a seamless whole with everything else in the building and the surrounding city blocks. Along the way, there was also a keen awareness that Jordan had made and then cast aside many plans throughout the writing of the series. Did they need to use *all* the hints in the years and years of notes? Surely not, since at times those notes didn't even agree with each other. Jordan had a habit of stockpiling old files, after all: a boon for the later researcher, but a nightmare for the present writer. It was daunting.

In the spring of 2008, they all gathered in Charleston. As Brandon recalled:

I asked for big sheets of butcher paper, and upon this I started writing down characters, plots, goals, and sequences as headings. Then, we brainstormed answers to holes. I often presented my (somewhat daring) plans for sequences Robert Jordan had not outlined. I think a lot of the things I suggested were surprising to Team Jordan—and made them worried.

My argument was this, however: Robert Jordan would not have kept the last book stale. He wouldn't have done everything as expected. He wouldn't have flatlined the character arcs, he wouldn't have stopped the world-building. If we played this book safe, we'd end up with a bland climax to the series. Harriet agreed, and told me to proceed with some of these plans—but with the warning that as editor, she would read and see if I pulled off the sequences. If I did, they'd go in the books. If I didn't, we'd remove them.

This ended up working really well. It allowed me to exercise artistic freedom, driving the books in directions I felt they needed to go without limitations. Granted, I had a personal rule—I didn't contradict Robert Jordan's previous books, and if he had finished a scene in the notes, we were going to use it.[72]

For the next months, Brandon worked feverishly to build out what they'd come up with. Notes, queries, and ideas flew back and forth between his home in Utah and the house on Tradd Street. Everyone was determined to develop a coherent vision for the book that would be as true to Jordan's plans as possible. "My goal," Brandon later said, "was not to *fix* The Wheel of Time. My goal was to give the best ending possible to the fans." That said, he still found places to try to update the image of Randland in ways that he suspected Jordan might have done had he lived long enough. Though The Wheel of Time had already depicted some limited same sex relationships between women, for instance, most especially in the prequel novel *New Spring*, "there were no gay men. But there are gay men in the real world, so I added them in." Similarly, Brandon felt that Jordan's "idea of female privilege" as the typical experience of life in Randland—a reversal of the male privilege that characterized Jordan's generation—was quite "progressive for [Jordan's] time, but I thought in reality there should be less belligerence" in how it manifested itself. As a result, he tried to make subtle shifts in the ways men and women interacted with each other as the Last Battle approached.[73]

The further into this work Brandon got, the bigger it got. As Jordan had promised, the final volume was going to be a logistical nightmare for the publisher. Accordingly, by the new year, Tor was worried and began suggesting that the final book be split into multiple volumes. Brandon initially advocated for a single volume—because it's what Jordan had said he wanted—but he admitted he knew they were running up against the physical realities of how a book could even be bound and sold:

When Harriet asked me about splitting the book, she wondered if there was a natural breaking point. I told her breaking it once wouldn't work—but breaking it twice might. I didn't feel *A Memory of Light* would work as two volumes. Looking at my outline and what I needed to accomplish, two books would either mean one very long book and one normal-sized one, or two books split equally. Both would have been awkward. The former because doing a double-sized Wheel of Time book would have the same problems as just printing the original 2000-page novel. 1400 pages isn't much better in publishing terms. 1000, like some of the Wheel of Time books, already pushes against those limits.

The second option—two 1000-page books—was even more of a problem. If we cut it in the middle like that, we'd get the first half of all four plot sequences I mentioned above—but none of their climaxes. This (writing one book as a setup book, with the payoffs mostly happening in another book) was an experiment that Robert Jordan had already attempted, and he had spoken of the problems it created. He was a better writer than I am, and if he couldn't accomplish such a split, I didn't want to attempt it.

Instead, I felt that splitting the book as three books would allow us to have complete arcs in each one. Two, actually, for each of *The Gathering Storm* and *Towers of Midnight*—followed by the climactic book, *A Memory of Light*. So I set out to divide the plots and decide what would go where.[74]

It was settled. What Jordan had hoped would be a single final volume would be three coauthored books: *The Gathering Storm* (2009), *Towers of Midnight* (2010), and *A Memory of Light* (2013). Some fans grumbled that this was stretching out the story for financial reasons—hinting that Jordan himself would not have approved—but nothing could have been further from the truth. Brandon and Team Jordan were only doing the best they could to deliver well-crafted stories that would wrap up the myriad loose ends and satisfy the voracious appetites of that vast readership. As for the question of whether Jordan would have done the same . . . The Wheel of Time was supposed to be six books long before it became nine before he'd written eleven and hoped to finish it in twelve. Had Jordan lived to complete the work himself, it's unlikely he would've managed to fit all that needed to be done within the single book he'd promised. Light knows, it might well have grown even beyond the fourteen volumes that Brandon and Team Jordan ultimately delivered. In truth, it doesn't matter. The Pattern was woven. The Wheel turned.

In the years that followed the completion of The Wheel of Time, Team Jordan also compiled *The Wheel of Time Companion*. This important work pulled together Jordan's vast array of notes on his world to produce an extraordinary encyclopedia of Randland—even solving a few lingering mysteries along the way. If there was any doubt about the monumental nature of what Jordan had done, the *Companion* dispelled them at once. It was the perfect coda to a song sung across decades.

Jordan's life was far more than his words. It was far, far more than this chapter has shown. He was, as Harriet had memorialized, like the wind that had touched everything before it was gone. The passing of that wind was not an ending. There are, as he himself wrote, neither beginnings nor endings to the turning of the Wheel of Time. Even all these years later, with every turning page, the leaves still sway with his memory.

His untimely passing affected his millions of readers very deeply, but there's no question that his stories and his dreams live on. Sanderson may have finished its final books, but The Wheel of Time, Jordan's lasting legacy, will never be complete. It cannot be. After all, our futures, and even the fullness of our pasts, remain for us forever incomplete. In memory, as in hope and dream, there's always another chapter to be written.

THE AXLE AND THE WHEEL: TOLKIEN AND JORDAN

J ordan had experienced a great deal of success writing his Conan novels, but along the way there had been limitations on what he could do. He was writing within the bounds of another author's world. What Robert E. Howard had built was wonderful, and the challenge of those constraints was unexpectedly exciting, but Jordan was anxious to work on his own. The Wheel of Time was, for him, a chance to break out of that shell, a chance to create something wholly his own. This was one reason he was drawn to fantasy. Another reason, as he would later report, is that fantasy lay at the very heart of what he wanted to say:

> One of my themes is (and it's one reason I wrote the books as fantasies) there is good, there is evil, there is right, there is wrong—it does exist. If you do that in a mainstream novel you are accused of being judgmental unless you've chosen the right political viewpoint.[1]

Fantasy has evolved enormously over the years, in part due to the influence of writers like Jordan. So what *is* a fantasy?

Gene Wolfe—like Jordan, a luminary of the fantasy genre—is said to have quipped that "all novels are fantasies. Some are more honest about it."

There's enormous truth in this. Whether our stories are built on everyday reality or not, we paint the details of our tales large and small with the constructions of our imagination. Even our memories can be fantasies of who we want to believe we were or are or might be.

Most people use a far more narrow view of what makes a book "fantasy." Some call it speculative fiction that cannot occur in the real world. Others say it has to have magic. Or dragons. Or maybe both. How the genre is defined, in the end, depends a great deal on who is defining it.

Unfortunately, one of the ways that many people define the genre is by separating "serious writing" from "mere fantasy." The implication could not be more clear. The one is to be valued, studied, and discussed. The other is not.

This is nonsense.

Fantasy lives and breathes at the very core of our culture. It is arguably the very oldest mode of writing we have, dating back to the imaginative stories our most distant ancestors told each other to explain the passing of the seasons and the stars, to cope with life and death. "What other forms of fiction," Doherty has asked, "what other kinds of writing have spoken down through the years, between the ages, to so many different people?"[2]

To call something "mere fantasy" is to disregard it, perhaps even discard it, but every time I hear the phrase I'm instead reminded of a most extraordinary fantasy of the mere: *Beowulf,* one of the greatest epics in English. That magnificent poem, after all, is a fantasy by any definition possible. The mere-creatures Grendel and his mother aren't real. Neither is the dragon that Beowulf must defeat. Beowulf picking up his sword in his old age is surely its own kind of fantasy, too.

Our literary history is filled with fantasy, in fact. We just don't always call it that.

When the monstrous Green Knight stoops to retrieve his own head from the stone floor of King Arthur's court, when he holds it out before the terrified, astonished, and brutally ignorant knights and ladies, and when it *speaks*, we know *Sir Gawain and the Green Knight* for the fantasy that it is.

The tale of Geoffrey Chaucer's delightful Wife of Bath is nothing if not a fantasy. So, too, is the tale of his Nun's Priest.

To the realms of fantasy belong the fairies both noble and nefarious in Shakespeare's *Midsummer Night's Dream*, the spirits of his *Tempest*, the witching sisters of his mighty *Macbeth*.

Virgil's Aeneas under the onslaught of vindictive gods; Spenser's Redcrosse Knight and the serpent Error; Dante's descent through the terrors of the Inferno; Tennyson's *Idylls of the King*; Homer's heroes at the gates of distant Troy: all of them, fantasies.

From the *Epic of Gilgamesh* to the *Nibelungenlied*, it would be difficult, if not impossible, to find a genre that has done more to shape the very thinking of the human species than fantasy has. "Fantasy literature as a genre," John Timmerman has said, "has the capacity to move a reader powerfully. And the motions and emotions involved are not simply visceral as is the case with much modern literature—but spiritual. It affects one's beliefs, one's way of viewing life, one's hopes and dreams and faith."[3] J. R. R. Tolkien, writing in defense of the genre he had chosen for commenting on our own, all-too-real, perilous world, states that "fantasy remains a human right: we make it in our measure and in our derivative mode, because we are made: and not only made, but made in the image and likeness of a Maker."[4]

Despite all this, that sense of being "mere fantasy" still trails the genre in our modern world like a most unwelcome shadow. Among the handful of fantasy writers to escape that shadow, none looms larger than Tolkien. Not only did he do more than anyone else to shape modern fantasy, but he has also inspired reams of literary criticism in multiple regular, peer-reviewed journals.

TOLKIEN AND JORDAN

As it happens, Jordan was compared to Tolkien almost from the beginning. When the first volume of The Wheel of Time, *The Eye of the*

World, was published in 1990, multiple reviews recognized a connection between them. As the series grew in popularity, so, too, did the comparisons. *Publishers Weekly* said, "This intricate allegorical fantasy recalls the works of Tolkien because of its intensity and warmth." *The New York Times* suggested that "Robert Jordan has come to dominate the world Tolkien began to reveal."

Later reviewers would go even further. By the publication of the eighth book, *The Path of Daggers,* Jordan was widely praised as the American heir of the British master. Yet recognition that he was going *beyond* where Tolkien did was also growing. As Edward Rothstein noted in a glowing column in *The New York Times* (1998):

> The genre's founding masterworks by Tolkien, who fought in World War I, were begun on the eve of Britain's entry into World War II and are fraught with nostalgia. Mr. Jordan, the Vietnam vet, is creating an American, late-20th-century counterpart. But something different is also happening in Mr. Jordan's series, where nostalgia is replaced by somberness.[5]

There is much in this observation that still rings true, even now that the series is completed. The Wheel of Time is assuredly Tolkien-like in many of its features, most obviously in its beginning in *The Eye of the World.* There are the broad strokes of good and evil, of course, but the parallels can also be found in the details. Jordan's Two Rivers is very much a stand-in for Tolkien's Shire. His Emond's Field is, minus the hobbit-holes, a mirror of the earlier Hobbiton: it's a happy small town where the tavern inn is the center of society and the lack of big problems makes small matters seem a grave concern. The initial chase of Rand al'Thor by Trollocs and Myrddraal is not at all dissimilar to Frodo's flight from Orcs and Nazgûl. Black riders hint at Tolkien's Black Riders. Jordan's mysterious swordsman of the north, Lan, has more than a few characteristics in common with Tolkien's Aragorn. Even the slow plotting at the start of *The Eye of the World* is an even match for the slow plotting at the start of Tolkien's *Fellowship of the Ring.* The echoes, once you begin looking for them, are everywhere at the start. They're quite impossible to miss.

This wasn't a mistake, and it certainly wasn't a secret.

The most obvious reason for this is that Jordan counted on the comfort that this would bring to his readers. If you know and love *The Lord of the Rings,* he seems to say, then you'll love The Wheel of Time. As he himself put it in 2002:

> In the first chapters of *The Eye of the World,* I tried for a Tolkienesque feel without trying to copy Tolkien's style, but that was by way of saying to the reader, okay, this is familiar, this is something you recognize, now let's go where you haven't been before. I like taking a familiar theme, something people think they know and know where it must be heading, then standing it on its ear or giving it a twist that subverts what you thought you knew. I must admit that I occasionally drop in a reference—for example, there's an inn called The Nine Rings, and Loial is seen reading a book entitled *To Sail Beyond the Sunset*—but it isn't a regular thing by any means.[6]

Jordan unquestionably loved Tolkien's work: "My favorite fantasy novel is *The Lord of the Rings,* hands down," he said in 2005. Even so, he had no intention of simply rewriting Tolkien's masterpiece: "The largest effect that it had on my writing was a desire to be the flip side of the coin, to take the comfortable old tropes and put a different spin on them."[7] To take one early deviation from those books, Jordan's decision to make his "Gandalf" a woman thankfully doesn't feel as bold today as it did in 1990, but in some measure this is because of the ways in which Jordan's own popularity so thoroughly recast the genre.

Having engaged the reader's goodwill through his use of a Tolkien-like setup, Jordan aimed to build out his own world in the genre, deviating from the accepted model to construct the story he longed to tell. It's clear that this was part of the plan from the beginning. Asked about the comparison between his work and *The Lord of the Rings* in 1991, just after the first two books had been released, Jordan said:

On the one hand, I'm flattered. On the other, I would have to say it's overplayed. On the third hand, Tolkien encompassed so much in The Lord of the Rings and other books that he did for fantasy what Beethoven did for music.

For a long time, it was believed that no one did anything that did not build on Beethoven. For his part, Tolkien did provide a foundation while himself building on an existing tradition. Although it's difficult now to forge a singular place in this foundation, people like Stephen R. Donaldson are doing it. I hope I am as well.[8]

Jordan's reference to the fact that The Lord of the Rings was also built on an older foundation is important to note. As it turns out, Jordan had a deep understanding of how Tolkien's Middle-earth had been made, and that process would absolutely inform his own world-building.

HOW TOLKIEN DID IT

In the year 2000, Tom Shippey, the scholar who has done more than anyone else to solidify the legitimacy of Tolkien studies in academia, released perhaps his finest book on J. R. R. Tolkien. The work was sub-titled "Author of the Century," and it immediately caused a storm surge of critical concerns. It was one thing, it seems, for poll after poll to reveal The Lord of the Rings to be, at least in the public's eyes, the most influential and well-loved book of the twentieth century. A wide-ranging 1999 poll from Amazon.com had in fact awarded it the title of the greatest book of the millennium, which was no small taters no matter which way you cut them. Still, those polls could be dismissed by the critical elite. Popularity has nothing to do with quality, they said. Shippey's defense of Tolkien, however, was rather difficult to dismiss. It was an academic line drawn in the sand that drew critics out of the woodwork, most of whom cried foul that Shippey dared, with the title of his book, to call Tolkien the author of the twentieth century.

"What about Hemingway?" they exclaimed with increasing ire. "My god, what about Joyce?"

Shippey, for his part, found these questions odd, since it meant that so many of the offended critics had missed a crucial detail that they ought to have noticed right away. They were, after all, professional readers: his subtitle was simply "Author of the Century." Not "*The* Author of the Century." His thesis was not that Tolkien should stand alone, but that he should stand alongside: he was an author of the twentieth century, his work embodying its hopes and its horrors just as surely and strongly as anything by Hemingway, Orwell, Huxley, or Vonnegut. In his influences, in his obvious impact, Tolkien thereby ought to be considered, Shippey argued, as perhaps one of the great authors of the century. His was an argument for placement in the canon, not canonization.

As we'll see, Jordan created a work of literature that is best understood through the lens of Tolkien's own creative project. What Tolkien began with *The Lord of the Rings,* Jordan completed in The Wheel of Time, even if that series—like Tolkien's own legends of the *Silmarillion*—remained technically unfinished with his untimely passing. We come closest to understanding the impact of The Wheel of Time, therefore, by building on the work of academics like Shippey, by throwing more stones upon the foundations laid in Tolkien studies, knowing that the tower we build thereby might give us the chance, in the end, to see the sea.

So let's begin with the deceptively simple matter of what it was that Tolkien was up to in his creation of Middle-earth. And for that we need to understand, at a root level, what Tolkien did for a living.

Tolkien was a philologist by both trade and mind-set. Like me, he was a professional academic who taught medieval literature at the university and wrote in his spare time between grading student papers. Tolkien's first published book of Middle-earth, *The Hobbit,* was supposedly begun when he was grading exams in his office one hot summer day, exhausted and no doubt exasperated. He turned the page of one of the exams to find that the student had left the next page, as he put it, "blessedly blank." On that blank page, Tolkien wrote, for reasons he could never explain, the following: "In a hole in the ground there lived a hobbit."

Tolkien stopped grading, and he then spent quite a long time staring at the words he'd mindlessly written. And because he was a philologist, he stared in particular at that last word—*hobbit*—trying to figure out what it meant. He couldn't recall having ever seen it before.[9] That search for meaning ultimately dovetailed with a history of elves and men that he'd been pondering in the trenches of the First World War, and from their creative combination Middle-earth was born. To understand Tolkien at all—and, as we'll see, the same ought to be said of Jordan—you must understand that he was a philologist at heart, the kind of person who would, in the end, construct a world out of a word.

Philology literally means "love of learning," which is something that one hopes has been around as long as humans have had the ability to think. Yet when we say that Tolkien was a philologist we have something more specific in mind, something that could be said to begin in 1786 in Calcutta, then the capital of British India.

Sir William Jones had founded the Asiatic Society two years earlier to promote the academic study of India and the East, and on this occasion he gave a lecture to the society about some correspondences he'd been noticing between the languages of Latin, Greek, Sanskrit, and Persian. The languages were similar enough at times that he suggested they must be "sprung from some common source which, perhaps, no longer exists."

Numerous scholars poured their minds into the exploration of such linguistic connections, and by the middle of the nineteenth century they had determined many of the laws that govern language change— the reasons, for example, that we don't pronounce English the same way we did in the year 1000.

As a case in point, here are the first lines of *Beowulf,* which was copied down in Old English over a thousand years ago:

> Hwæt! We Gardena in geardagum,
> þeodcyninga, þrym gefrunon,
> hu ða æþelingas ellen fremedon.
> Oft Scyld Scefing sceaþena þreatum,
> monegum mægþum, meodosetla ofteah,
> egsode eorlas. Syððan ærest wearð

feasceaft funden, he þæs frofre gebad,
weox under wolcnum, weorðmyndum þah,
oðþæt him æghwylc þara ymbsittendra
ofer hronrade hyran scolde,
gomban gyldan. þæt wæs god cyning!

[Hey! Of the Spear-Danes in days past,
of those clan-kings, of their fame we've heard:
how their princes performed intrepid deeds.
How Shield, Sheaf's son, from enemy threats,
from many peoples, often seized mead-benches
and menaced the fearsome Heruli. This was after he was
found helpless and flat-broke. But he knew how to overcome,
and he grew under the clouds, gathering glory,
until each of their neighboring nations
beyond the whale-road had to bow to him,
and give tribute. *That* was a good king!][10]

And here, as a more recent example, is a bit of Chaucer's London-dialect Middle English, the opening of *The Canterbury Tales,* which is a mere six hundred years old:

Whan that Aprille with his shoures soote,
The droghte of March hath perced to the roote,
And bathed every veyne in swich licóur
Of which vertú engendred is the flour;
Whan Zephirus eek with his swete breeth
Inspired hath in every holt and heeth
The tendre croppes, and the yonge sonne
Hath in the Ram his halfe cours y-ronne,
And smale foweles maken melodye,
That slepen al the nyght with open ye,
So priketh hem Natúre in hir corages,
Thanne longen folk to goon on pilgrimages,

And palmeres for to seken straunge strondes,
To ferne halwes, kowthe in sondry londes;
And specially, from every shires ende
Of Engelond, to Caunterbury they wende,
The hooly blisful martir for to seke,
That hem hath holpen whan that they were seeke.

[When April, with its sweet showers,
has pierced the drought of March to the root,
and bathed every vine in that liquid
whose essence engenders the flowers;
when the west wind with his sweet breath
has inspired in every farm and field
the tender crops, and the young sun
has half-run its course through Ares,
and small birds make melody,
and sleep all night with an open eye—
their courage pricked to it by Nature—
then people long to go on pilgrimages,
and pilgrims to seek foreign shores,
to distant shrines, rumored in sundry lands;
And especially, from every shire's end
of England, to Canterbury they went,
to seek the holy blissful martyr,
who had helped them when they were sick.]

As scholars figured out the laws that took us from *Beowulf* to Chaucer to the words you're reading now, they were able to run those laws "backward" from the oldest records—works like *Beowulf*—working further and further back in time until what once had been different languages started to coalesce into one.

The correspondences Jones had seen in 1786 were, it turned out, right on target: behind Latin, Greek, Sanskrit, and Persian—among many other languages—is a single language that no longer survives but almost undoubtedly existed. We call it Proto-Indo-European, and we mark its words with asterisks, because they no longer exist in their original form; they're known only by the evolved remnants that they've left behind. Here, for example, we can see the similarities between the word for "eye" in several different languages, along with the theoretically constructed Proto-Indo-European originator behind them all:

Greek	Latin	Sanskrit	German	P.I.E.
osse	oculus	áksi	auge	*hokws

What's interesting about Tolkien's personal brand of philology, though, is that for him the history of words was a means to profound cultural insight.

As one example, Modern Hindustani *dudh*, which has the same root as we have in our Modern English word *daughter*, doesn't mean "daughter," but "milk."[11] So *duhitar*, the Hindustani cognate to English *daughter*, means not "daughter" but "little milker." From this linguistic connection, we suspect that a family's daughter, in that distant Indo-European culture that gave rise to both Hindustani and English, must have traditionally done the milking of the livestock. They were the little milkers. For philologists, the modern remnants of dead languages, like overgrown ruins in an ancient landscape, provide a window into the past that would otherwise be closed to us forever. The words quite literally tell stories.

Let me give just one more example of this, brought up by Tolkien himself after his son Christopher sent him a copy of one of his school papers, which he'd written on the history of Northern Europe. Tolkien praised the paper, but wrote to his son: "All the same, I suddenly realized that I am a *pure* philologist. I like history, and am moved by it, but its finest moments for me are those in which it throws light on words and names! Several people (and I agree) spoke to me of the art with which you made the beady-eyed Attila on his couch almost vividly present. Yet oddly, I find the thing that thrills my nerves is the one you mentioned casually: *atta, attila*. Without those syllables the whole great drama both of history and legend loses savour for me."[12]

What was Tolkien talking about? Well, Attila is a Hun, a mortal enemy of the Goths, yet his name, *Attila,* is the diminutive form of the Gothic word for "father" (*atta*). *Attila,* in other words, means "little father" in Gothic. This raises the tantalizing possibility that there were Goths in Attila's army, a fact that would rewrite known history. Such is the power of philology to reveal that which is otherwise hidden.

I've gone on about this at some length because it's the same thing that Tolkien was doing in his fiction. Tolkien was always careful to term his mythology as one that is ultimately meant to be associated with our world, fantastic though it might seem at times: "This is a story of long ago," he writes in the foreword to *The Hobbit*—not, we should note, "a story of long ago in a galaxy far, far away" or the like. Thus Middle-earth's legends are connected to *our* legends, its languages to our languages, and its people to our people—if all at a distance deep in the fictional mists before recorded history. Middle-earth, in other words, is the result of the application of philological principles (finding words behind words, stories behind stories) to mythology. Shippey has elsewhere termed the resulting mythology-behind-mythologies that Tolkien constructed an "asterisk-reality," thus underscoring its philological basis since, as noted earlier, words whose prior existences are rooted out by linguistic laws are typically preceded by asterisks to mark their "invention" as missing links in the evolutionary chain of language.[13]

This is not to say that Tolkien thought that the Battle for Helm's Deep truly occurred somewhere in, say, Eastern Europe, but that something like Helm's Deep *could* have occurred there, and perhaps that something like it *should* have occurred there.

This scientifically creative process is precisely the mantle that Jordan inherited from Tolkien, albeit on a different scale and by a different procedure. Whereas Tolkien built from the nitty-gritty of words and languages both real and invented, Jordan built from the larger scope of our cultural inheritance. Where Tolkien is said to have aimed to create a "mythology for England," Jordan aimed for something even more daring and profound: a "mythology for humanity."

But before we get too far into the literary details of this process, we need also to understand the deeply personal aspect of Tolkien's fiction. Here, too, we will see commonalities with Jordan.

Tolkien's *Lord of the Rings*, though published widely only in the 1950s, was a work rooted in his experiences of the First World War. Tolkien was twenty-three when he left Oxford and his new wife, Edith, on March 22, 1916, to go to France to serve as a signal officer with the Lancashire Fusiliers. His destination: the Battle of the Somme. He lost all but one of his friends at the "meatgrinder," as he termed it, and he might himself have died in those killing fields if he'd not developed trench fever and been shipped back to England to recuperate.

Though he'd toyed with invented languages and stories before the war, it was only in the wake of that horror that he began to construct a formal mythology of Middle-earth, and indeed we can see the marks of the Somme and its aftermath across his work.

As but one more example, I've written elsewhere about how Frodo is almost certainly suffering from post-traumatic stress disorder, more commonly termed "shell shock," a condition first diagnosed among the hollowed faces of men at the Battle of the Somme. In fact, I suspect writing Frodo was a way for Tolkien to cope with his own psychological difficulties as a result of what he had seen and done in the war.[14] Even so, Frodo is not simply a personal foil for his creator. He also has mythological ties to the Hebrew prophets Enoch and Elijah, to Norse religion, and to the Christian Everyman.

The major result of these many creative strands, *The Lord of the Rings*, was, as we all know, a really big hit, so it's no surprise that a great many writers had to react to his work in one way or another, like Roger Zelazny, with his *Nine Princes in Amber*, which debuted in the early 1970s, or Terry Brooks with *The Sword of Shannara* and Stephen R. Donaldson with *Lord Foul's Bane*, both of which debuted in 1977. Popular though these works were in their time, they responded to *what* Tolkien had made, not *how* he had made it.

It wasn't until the release of Jordan's *The Eye of the World* in 1990 that we see someone taking up Tolkien's flag with authority. The Wheel of Time series that it began is a true successor, a true heir, to the kind of mythically philological trail of creation that Tolkien had blazed some fifty years earlier. Like Tolkien's Middle-earth, Jordan's Randland is a myth behind myths. The wondrous Age of Legends, the "far past" of Jordan's plotlines in The Wheel of Time, is our mythically Atlantean past just as surely as is Tolkien's story of the fall of Númenor from *The Silmarillion*. Again and again in Jordan's work we see this same kind of mythological revision that is the hallmark of Tolkien.

Just to give you a feel for it:

Jordan's Artur Paendrag is our King Arthur, son of Uther Pendragon. The *sa'angreal* in his books have clear roots in the stories of the Holy Grail. The Dark One Shai'tan is related to Satan. Sammael is based in part on the Talmudic angel of death. The final battle of Tarmon Gai'don owes more than just its name to biblical Armageddon. Lews Therin echoes the "Light-bearer," Lucifer. The list could go on and on.

The list—well, a partial one—is this book.

And not just in this mythological foundation is Jordan akin to Tolkien. As we've seen, from 1968 to 1970 Jordan served his country for two tours in Vietnam, in the midst of heavy conflict as an army helicopter gunner. He was, like Tolkien, someone who had experienced the horror of modern warfare firsthand and was undoubtedly shaped by it.

HOW JORDAN DID IT

For all these similarities, however, Jordan is not simply a Tolkien imitator. I have elsewhere called him "an American Tolkien," and that adjective signifies more than just nationality in this case. It points to a significant difference in his creative approach. America is, famously, a melting pot of culture, and Jordan subsumed this same quality in The Wheel of Time. Tolkien wanted to construct a myth for England and so confined himself often to what he considered a Western cultural heritage, but Jordan aimed at much bigger things. Everything was fair game for his creation, from Eastern myths to Native American cosmology. There are connections seemingly everywhere.

In fact, Jordan's grand project involved not just story and myth, but even material culture.

The primary weapon for the medieval samurai, the katana is a rightfully famed symbol of both Japanese craftsmanship and the codes of honor by which the samurai lived (see photo insert, page 4a). This particular example of a katana comes from Robert Jordan's personal armory. It is, according to the label of the antiques dealer who sold it to him, a "Turn of the Century Samurai Sword" with a "Handforged blade signed by [the] owner and swordsmith." Interestingly, it has a dragon-marked blade. Whenever he could, Jordan had objects like this literally at hand when he was writing his books. And it shows.

Jordan also authorized "heron-marked" blades imagined from the series, produced to his specifications (see photo insert, page 4b). A weapon associated with a true artist's mastery of the bladed fight, the heron-marked sword bears not just a little resemblance to Jordan's katana. Easy to note is the slightly backswept, single-edged blade, which adds velocity to what is primarily a slashing weapon.

Both weapons are delicate enough to be handled with one hand, but they have hilts long enough for two, much like a medieval European hand-and-a-half sword.

Where the katana whispers "grace and flow," the fourteenth-century blade of England's Black Prince (see photo insert, page 4c) gutturally screams "strength and crushing blows." You can see how differently this weapon is designed from its contemporary Japanese counterpart.

Look again, then, at Jordan's creation: the heron-marked blade. An Eastern edge, but a Western sword's weight. An Eastern point, but a Western guard. And a hilt that seems to be both at once.

In other words, Jordan has applied philological principles to material culture, something Tolkien never dared in quite the same way. Jordan created a sword that unites the finest of both East and West. Physical artifacts like his katana were a driving force to his vision no less than the myths that they represent and re-create.

Even setting this aside, though, we can be certain that objects like this spurred Jordan's creative energy. There's no doubt that he physically held such weapons in his hands now and again in order to make his vivid writing more real; we also cannot doubt that he held them in his *mind*, too, using such material evidence to widen the scope of The Wheel of Time as far and as deep into human culture as he could manage.

But even *this* isn't the full story of Jordan's methods. You might well note that when I earlier listed examples of the real-world myths behind Randland stories I was careful not to present them as equivalences. The Battle of Malden is spelled rather like the Battle of Maldon, but its ground and tactics are far closer to what Jordan thought had happened at the Battle of Crécy. And to say that Lews Therin "equals" Lucifer in all his manifestations is to tread on somewhat shaky ground.

We also have to temper our urge to see connections everywhere— and what those connections mean when we find them.

The White Tower of Tar Valon, for instance, appears to have been visibly modeled on Padgett-Thomas Barracks (see photo insert, page 5), the most recognizable building on the campus of The Citadel, where Robert Jordan earned his college degree. There's no doubt he had it in mind. But if the college's isolated campus is compared to the island-city of Tar Valon in the books, we see that the parallel is tinged with irony: Citadel cadets were exclusively male when Jordan attended the school; the Aes Sedai are exclusively female.

Or take the symbol that must be followed through testing to become an Aes Sedai: a hexagram, or six-pointed star. This important Aes Sedai symbol, in our world, is the Star of David, the marker of Judaism and of God's Chosen People, the Jews, whose cultural identity is passed through matrilineal lines, an interesting connection to the White Tower's own focus on the feminine. It's a fascinating association, but it isn't an equation. The Aes Sedai are not a cipher for real-world Jewish peoples.

Tolkien once railed against the idea that *The Lord of the Rings* was an allegory, because, in his opinion, proper allegory implies that a reader can swap elements from one story out for another in a one-to-one relationship. As he wrote: "I cordially dislike allegory in all its manifestations, and always have done so since I grew old and wary enough to detect its presence." It was his distrust of allegory that prevented him from fully enjoying almost every work by his friend C. S. Lewis, and much has been made of the possibility that their different reactions to the form are the result of their individual religious beliefs.

Jordan's opinion on allegories was far closer to that of Tolkien than, say, Lewis: in The Wheel of Time, pure equivalence is a rare thing.

To take one instance, we'll see that his character Mat is an amalgamation of the Norse gods Odin, Loki, and Heimdall, along with Native American Coyote, Egyptian Anubis, and Celtic Math, as well as real-world figures, such as the American Revolution's Swamp Fox, Francis Marion. The whole history of humanity was grist for Jordan's creative mill, and it left pieces of these men and gods scattered here and there throughout this character and that arc throughout The Wheel of Time. But just because something happened to Odin doesn't mean it must happen to Mat. Rather, it means that the interference of legend and history, of history and legend, was a grounding principle of Jordan's vision: time is cyclical—a wheel—and, in its repetitious spin, history repeats itself again and again.

In this understanding of the nature of time, too, we see separation between this "American Tolkien" and his British forebear. Tolkien, a devout Catholic, followed the example of Saint Augustine in viewing the world as subject to a dynamic, unidirectional scheme of time. In chronological philosophy, this is called the "A-theory" of time, where time passes like an arrow, advancing undeviatingly from some beginning to some ending point. In A-theory, only the present time is truly real, as the past is finished and the future is indeterminate and unfixed—except, perhaps, from the point of view of God.[15]

A-theory is the most familiar philosophy of time in human experience, reflected even at such a base level as our language, with its system of tenses past, present, and future. Yet this is not the philosophy that governs Randland. Quite to the contrary, Jordan is right in line with some current theories of quantum physics, which function within what we call the "B-theory" of time, where past, present, and future are all equally real. According to B-theorists, the future is just as fixed and determined as the past, we just happen to know less about it: our distinctions of time are a product of our limited minds. Jordan's work echoes this: time is caught in an endless, cyclical wheel. The future is past, the past is future, now is then, and then is now. If you stand on a wheel, after all, it doesn't matter which way you walk, you'll get back to the same place. Indeed, a simultaneity of time is about the only way to make sense of the magic of balefire in Jordan's novels.

This basic temporal fact, often missed by readers, sheds light on a number of apparent anomalies in this fantasy.

In *The Shadow Rising,* for example, one of the characters enters the Tanchico Museum of the Panarch's Palace. She sees, first, the skeleton of what's undoubtedly a saber-toothed tiger (Jordan kept the skull of one in his office, and it's looking down upon me as I write this). Gazing around in further wonder, she finds

A silvery thing in another cabinet, like a three-pointed star inside a circle . . . made of no substance she knew; it was softer than metal, scratched and gouged, yet even older than any of the ancient bones. From ten paces she could sense pride and vanity.[16]

Why is a Mercedes-Benz hood ornament in the Panarch's Palace? How on Earth is this supposed to make any sense?

Well, to begin with, we must admit that, like Tolkien's Middle-earth, Jordan's world *is* Earth. *Our* Earth. But unlike Tolkien's A-theory sub-creation, which was meant to be our past, Jordan's B-theory subcreation is our past, our present, *and* our future. The cyclical nature of Jordan's time means the Age of Legends is Atlantean myth and Golden Age history—but also science fictional vision. His heron-marked blade is both the asterisk-sword behind both Eastern and Western weapons and the idealized sword-to-come that has been grown from the foundation of such legendary blades.

For once, the fateful decision of bookstores and publishers to collapse Fantasy and Science Fiction into the same rows of shelves is perfectly fitting. The Wheel of Time is both.

The gleeman Thom Merrilin actually tells us as much when he first appears in The Wheel of Time. After introducing himself as a storyteller—he is, we'll see, a character rooted in both Merlin the magician and one of the greatest bards of myth—what he goes on to say is this:

> I have *all* stories, mind you now, of Ages that were and will be. Ages when men ruled the heavens and the stars, and Ages when man roamed as brother to the animals. Ages of wonder, and Ages of horror. Ages ended by fire raining from the skies, and Ages doomed by snow and ice covering land and sea. I have all stories, and I will tell all stories.[17]

Thom speaks not only for himself, but for the greater work of literature of which he is a part. This is The Wheel of Time at its heart: *All stories.*

THE WHEEL TURNS: JORDAN AT WORK

W hat The Wheel of Time became is not how The Wheel of Time began.

The basic idea for the books began percolating in Jordan's mind sometime in the mid-1970s with a simple question:

> The first idea that came to me, the first thought, was what is it really like to be the savior of mankind? What's it really like to be tapped on the shoulder and told you are the savior of mankind, and oh by the way, we expect you to go mad and die in order to fulfill prophecy and save everybody. That was the genesis.[1]

The idea simmered in Jordan's mind for years, so he was hardly starting from scratch when, in 1983, Tom Doherty began wondering if Jordan could build upon the success of his Conan novels with a fantasy book or a series that was all his own: "I knew he could do more," Doherty later recalled.[2]

Jordan's initial conception was that The Wheel of Time would be one single, big book, but after some discussion with Doherty, he thought it *might* turn out to be a trilogy. Doherty felt certain it would go even longer: "I just didn't believe it would get done in three books, because by then I knew how Jim liked to tell a story."[3] So although Jordan "didn't have much beyond ideas," Doherty offered him a six-book contract for an entirely unwritten book series: The Wheel of Time.

In retrospect, the idea for the story at that point owed a great deal to Jordan's own life experience of having left Charleston for Vietnam:

> When I first started thinking of what would turn into The Wheel of Time, Rand and his foster father were one character. Not a 50-ish man and his teenage foster son. But a man in his 30s who had run away from a quiet country village seeking adventure, had become a soldier, and now after 20 years of that, world weary and tired, who has come home to his pastoral village seeking peace and quiet, only to find that the world and prophecy are hard on his heels. You can see that that's a much different character than what I ended up with when I started writing. I may actually use *him* someday.[4]

The degree to which Jordan was filtering his own life experiences through his work has largely been unnoticed, though it should not come as a surprise. Tolkien had done the same thing before him, as had many another writer dealing with trauma. Team Jordan member Alan Romanczuk, himself a Vietnam veteran, recognized exactly this reflection within The Wheel of Time—along with the ways in which it connected to Jordan's inclusivity:

> [Jordan] was in many ways a good ole' boy to the end, having spent most of his life in the South Carolina Lowcountry. He had his rough edges. We all do. But he never showed bias against anyone because of the way they looked or because of their lifestyle, not if they weren't hurting other people. And I don't think his tolerance came altogether from his parents or his time sitting in church pews. I think a lot came from his time in Vietnam.

In a war zone you learn pretty quickly who your friends are and who are not. You go through a lot of tough situations, and you need to share your fears, your disgust, your depression with others. Guys don't usually do that in so many words; a beer or a card game will do. So the barrier that separates you from those who are different gets a crack in it, as you come to know that some of your most reliable companions might be that Black guy with a pair of jacks across the table from you, or the Latino sitting on his bunk reading a letter from his sweetheart back home, or the Filipino who tells jokes you don't understand—and not necessarily the ones you would have hung out with back home. You guys are in this together, fighting a common enemy, and you pick your allies carefully.

And then maybe the situation gets more serious—you kill your first Charlie. Maybe you can see the dead kid, no older than you, with a slightly different skin tone from you and eyes of a different shape, but . . . someone trying to do his job just like you are. That's when the barrier is shattered. A switch flips; dead boy isn't a g, or a f devil, or the enemy. Not what they told you. He's just, except for a few superficial differences, a human like you.

You're torn up inside, if you're sane and there's a shred of decency in your heart, but you have a lot of time left in this war. So to cope you lock the soft vulnerable part of yourself away until your tour of duty is up. There's time for compassion later, if there is a later.

Then you get home and your biggest struggle becomes how do you become normal again, how do you cleanse the taint that fills you? There are all kinds of ways to cope, including falling to pieces. One man's way, [Jordan]'s way, was to write a series of books about a bunch [of] kids from Emond's Field.[5]

There was, of course, far more to The Wheel of Time than simply the psychological repercussions of Vietnam upon Jordan's life. It was also a hero's journey, a fight between good and evil, a meditation on free will, and a good deal more. We can uncover much of this scope, and how he constructed it, by examining Jordan's working notes, drafts, and correspondence, which are today held in the special collections of the College of Charleston.

THE FIRST PIECES OF THE PUZZLE

Most of these papers are open to the public, though a few parts of the collection will remain sealed until 2037. What's there is, by any measure, a wealth of material. Though these notes are generally undated beyond loose ranges—those of the early period are catalogued as being composed between 1984 and 1989—a close examination of their contents allows for the creation of a tentative chronology. This, in turn, enables an unprecedented look into Jordan's working processes as he developed his basic book concept into something that would fulfill the contract he'd signed with Doherty.

Jordan's library ran to many thousands of books. He was a voracious consumer of the written word. But the preserved notes make clear that three works absolutely dominated his early decisions regarding the scope and course of The Wheel of Time. One, as we've seen, was *The Lord of the Rings*. Jordan was roughly following Tolkien's process of creation; he was also trying to catch the same "feel" in his opening chapters and in his landscape: one of his earliest notes has him even constructing a list of "Examples of Kinds of Names as Used in Tolkien."[6]

The second dominant book was *Le Morte d'Arthur*, composed by the "knyght presoner Thomas Malleorre," as the author identifies himself in the book—that is, by the imprisoned Thomas Malory. Though other candidates exist, this Malory was almost assuredly that Thomas Malory who was born in 1416, inherited his father's estates in 1434, and was first imprisoned in 1451 after attempting the murder of the Duke of Buckingham, being accused of raping two women, and robbing Coombe Abbey. Though an escape artist, he could never stay out of trouble too long. During his final imprisonment, beginning in 1468, he likely wrote the book that he called *The Hoole Book of Kyng Arthur and of His Noble Knyghtes of the Rounde Table*. In 1485, it was printed by William Caxton, who gave it the title by which it is now known. It quickly became very popular, and the rapid reproduction of copies of *Le Morte d'Arthur*—thanks to the invention of the printing press—meant it attained a foothold on the culture far larger than Arthurian stories that had been around for far longer but had spent that time being copied out slowly by hand, letter by individual letter. Another reason for Malory's popularity is that he didn't tell a single story of Arthur; instead, he tried to tell all of them. Or, perhaps better said, he tried to create a new single story out of a great many stories that were then in existence. Whether, as a result, he should be credited as a writer or simply a compiler remains a point of scholarly debate. But the undeniable fact is that Malory's *Morte d'Arthur* became the most famous accounting of the legends of King Arthur. Its stories percolated through culture not just by its written word, but also by innumerable retellings in song, art, and film. Not surprisingly, the majority of the earliest files related to The Wheel of Time are likewise notes taken from Malory's work: Jordan, at the start of his thinking, was summarizing Arthurian plots and name lists. He was circling, it seems, around the idea of writing a new fantasy in the Arthurian mode. One of those early notes, in fact, is a related study of "The Arthur Legend as Portrayed in *Excalibur* (As Example of Adaptation)"—this being John Boorman's famous 1981 film based on Malory's work. "A comparisom [*sic*] of this with the basic Arthur legend and with Malory gives a good idea of just how flexible the entire concept is," Jordan wrote at the top of the page.[7]

THE WHITE GODDESS

The third book that dominates Jordan's early notes—and thus the making of The Wheel of Time—is Robert Graves' *The White Goddess: A Historical Grammar of Poetic Myth,* which was first printed in 1948, though repeatedly reprinted and enlarged through 1961. Harriet had suggested the book to Jordan, and he dove into it wholeheartedly. Graves, perhaps best known for his novel *I, Claudius,* was also a renowned poet—one fascinated with the idea of mythology and the past. *The White Goddess* grows out of this fascination.

It should be said that few academics think *The White Goddess* reflects reality. Graves greatly misunderstood many of the cultural artifacts he was studying, and his readiness to assume connections between the names of gods in highly separate times and places simply because their names had some vague superficial similarity led him to make numerous claims that are, by any scholarly measure, indefensible. By the dictates of his similar-letters-means-same-origin logic, for instance, we would need to equate Satan and Santa—which is (I hope) ludicrous. The sheer enthusiasm Graves had for his project, though, was unmistakable and, for many readers, unshakable. More than that, the story he told could be appealing. It was, at its core, a kind of conspiracy theory. Those sell.

The basic conspiracy story Graves told was that the original, prehistoric culture of Europe—Graves assumes that this modern political construct can map to our distant past—was matriarchal and centered on the worship of a supreme moon goddess. This goddess was typically associated with the color white, and she appeared in one or all of three forms (or phases): maiden, mother, or crone. Depending on the context, these forms represented birth, procreation, and death; spring, summer, and winter; or the new moon, full moon, and waning moon. This moon goddess often had a son, who became her consort, lover, and sacrificial victim as she birthed another son to replace him. Male gods came and went. Only she endured. But then this triple goddess, as Graves termed his invention, was wrongly and at times violently deposed by the worship of the male deities, which are associated with the sun. Matriarchy itself was lost. Patriarchy reigned. Like a figure seen through trees, this triple goddess could be perceived—so Graves thought—by reading between the lines of ancient and medieval poetry and myth from Egypt and the Holy Land to the British Isles. Though largely forgotten, this goddess was and is the one truth, Graves suggests, and thus the one muse to whom poets should look for inspiration.

Tolkien had paved the way for building a myth behind myths into fantasy, but in *The White Goddess* Jordan found another inspirational muse. He could now build Tolkien's concept on a bigger scale, weaving a pattern from the threads of "poets and gleemen"[8] that Graves had compiled and the Arthurian stories that Malory had compiled—as well as anything else he could find in history and myth. "The Wheel of Time is in effect a re-creation of the source of legends," he later said.

> I gathered together a lot of legends, fairy tales, and folk tales from around the world and stripped away the cultural references, so that just the bare story was left. Then I reverse-engineered them.
>
> You might recall a game: I've heard it called "Whispers," I've heard it called "Telephone"—a child's game. If you remember, the last child in the row stood up and said aloud, and what actually happened is what's on the piece of paper. So I've reverse-engineered to try and get back to something like what the piece of paper says. King Arthur is there, but most people don't recognize him right off. And there are a lot of other myths and legends too, although King Arthur is the most easily recognizable. As a matter of fact, I was shocked that some people didn't realize that Arthur was in the books until they read the third volume.[9]

In the early stages of this process, Jordan mined *The White Goddess* early and often, clearly fascinated by the breaks it made from the traditional mythic world championed by Tolkien and other authors. *The Lord of the Rings,* somewhat famously, had a handful of female characters at best, and it was hardly unique: patriarchal traditions were the norm across much literature and story. Graves insisted this was no natural condition. To the contrary, he argued that his triple goddess was not just an older and more pure deity, but that she represented a more proper world in which women rightfully held positions of power. So many of the ills of our world, he suggested, arise because we have forgotten this fundamental truth and have instead promoted a male-dominant view. Graves, like Tolkien, had fought at the Battle of the Somme in World War I. It's easy to see how he'd come to his view that the unchecked powers of men would lead to horrors untold.

Jordan had lived through two tours in Vietnam. Before the war, he'd played football at Clemson. And after the war, he'd taken his degree at the then all-male Citadel, which at that time remained defiantly proud of its patriarchal traditions. He, too, knew the potential madness of a world dominated by men.

Jordan could see that things were beginning to change, at least. In 1981, Sandra Day O'Connor was appointed to the Supreme Court. In 1983, Sally Ride went to space. It was a start, but things were hardly in balance.

Balance.

It was in Vietnam that Jordan was first exposed to the Eastern philosophies in which balance was taught as an ideal. The yin and yang of ancient Chinese philosophies like Confucianism and Taoism gave visual symbolism to the harmonic concept: two interlocked "teardrops"—one black, one white—inscribed in a circle.

There was a difference, though. A proper yin-yang symbol has a small circle of the oppositional color in each of the two sides: the black teardrop contains a white circle; the white teardrop contains a black circle. These smaller shapes are fundamental to the philosophy, marking the two halves as absences rather than opposites. There is darkness in the light, light in the darkness. Life exists in the dynamic of the push and pull between them, for a static existence is no life at all. Thus the ideal end goal within such a philosophy isn't to remove one side or the other, but to keep them in balance. This was the duality of existence. The light that couldn't exist without darkness. Good and evil. Order and disorder. The visible and invisible. Only together could such concepts have meaning, and only in the point of balance between them—the middle way, as Confucius taught—could there be stability. But Jordan's symbol in The Wheel of Time lacks the smaller circles within the teardrops. As early as his background notes around 1987 he was already describing a more simplified "yin-and-yang" symbol:

NOTE: it has been so long since men and women worked together that the original symbol for an Aes Sedai, a circle, half black and half white (i.e. the yin-and-yang symbol), has been forgotten by all but scholars of history among the Aes Sedai. The symbol has now been split, the upward pointing white portion (called the White Flame, or the Falme [sic] of Tar Valon) now being used as the sign of the female Aes Sedai, while the downward pointing black portion is called the Dragon's Fang. The Dragon's Fang is a symbol of evil, and is painted on someone's door if they are being accused of evil, or as a hex.[10]

The original Aes Sedai symbol, in other words, is twice-broken—at least if we are to judge it against the true yin-yang symbol. Not only has the unified circle been split into two distinct halves, but those two halves are wrongly presented as "purified" and independent forms rather than interdependent, dynamic concepts.

This might seem like a mere oversight, but few things in The Wheel of Time are genuine mistakes, as far as I can tell, especially when it comes to such core tenets of the mythologies and principles Jordan was using to construct his world. He could have gotten the yin-yang symbol correct. He chose not to do so. Instead of the dynamic truth, he made the original symbol of the Aes Sedai exclusively binary.

BINARIES IN THE WHEEL

Categorizing the world by binaries is a common human behavior—life and death, predator and prey, us and them—but it nevertheless raises questions that need to be addressed.

In particular, many readers today may find the binary nature of gender in The Wheel of Time to be deeply problematic. It's not just that

Jordan's characters are identified as male or female in binary terms, but the fact that this binary is integrated into the very fabric of the universe symbolized by the original Aes Sedai symbol: men can strictly access the "male" half of the One Power, called *saidin,* which has been tainted by the Dark One; women can strictly access the "female" half of the One Power, called *saidar,* which remains untainted. What makes a person "male" or "female" seems simple enough at the beginning of the story: the determinant appears to be biology. As the story unfolds, however, this is undercut by at least one character who finds themselves moved from one biological sex to another without their "gendered" power changing. These abilities are thus tied to an individual's internal gender identity rather than their external biological identity, though the rarity of such characters strongly implies that in The Wheel of Time it is typical for gender identity to match biological identity.

Though Jordan ultimately intends for this binary concept to point toward an erasure of the patriarchy and a unification of men and women, some readers today might instead see this concept as exclusionary: it provides no clear representation for those who don't fit these binary terms. It's important to acknowledge this.

I've little doubt that if Jordan were writing today he would work to create a world that felt more inclusive for nonbinary readers. He would also, I think, do even more to negotiate what is now more widely known about the complex and constructed relationships between biological sex, gender identity, and sexual identity. He would do this, I suspect, because The Wheel of Time was, in its origination, absolutely intended to be corrective of the harms faced by those who suffered from the social and cultural antagonisms of the patriarchal, binary world in which he'd grown up.

> I was thinking about what the world would be like if there had never been any need for a struggle for women's rights, or if that struggle had taken place so long ago that it just wasn't relevant any longer. No one thinks it's odd to see women as high-ranking politicians, or working

on the docks. No one ever thinks that something is or isn't a suitable job for a woman.[11]

Whether he *succeeded* in his aim to create a broadly feminist fantasy is a separate issue from the fact that this was clearly what he was aiming to do. In this regard, it's also important to recall the background of the literary landscape in which his work existed, as well as the restrictions he had admittedly placed upon himself by building his story from existing myths. The "savior" of The Wheel of Time in this age was a man, for instance, but is this because Jordan thought men superior to women? There's no indication of this from his notes or from interviews with those who knew him. Instead, his savior was a man because it more closely tied to the myths that his story was built from and needed to grow into as the Wheel turned—a story about broken masculinity in need of correction.

Beyond all this, though, we must also remember that Jordan was limited by the characters and their world. For instance, the male half of the One Power is described in the books as a powerfully wild force that must be wrestled into submission before it can be channeled, whereas the female half is described as a gentler power to which channelers must surrender. Some have taken this to imply that Jordan himself believed in a stereotype of powerful men and weak women. But, more likely, this kind of description is exactly what it appears to be: the limited understanding of the characters within his story, who can only comprehend their experiences against the background of their own lives in their own world. The original Aes Sedai symbol, in which the two halves unite together in harmony, is a fuller truth than the more ignorant world in which our characters begin—that world in which a Dragon's Fang can be a hex—but it is still very much not the *full* truth. We know this, because we have the real yin-yang. But it's also baked into the series itself, because if there's one thing that the final moments of the series make clear, it is that even our most enlightened characters are still limited in what they're capable of knowing. Their understanding of the world is demonstrably incomplete, and so is ours. Ages turn. The world changes.

Rand lit the pipe.

THE FIRST ATTEMPT

That end, of course, was decades away from the beginning.

In Jordan's early notes, we see the author working to build on the concept of binaries and the need for balance. This basic notion of The Wheel of Time is clear within his first attempt at an outline, at a point when his hero had shifted from an older man to a still unnamed "Young man (age unspecified, but 18–25) in small village":

> The powers weilded [sic] by men and those weilded by women come from different sources, some thought from the female and male principles that represented the balance of nature. The two sources of power were compliments [sic], yin and yang, like yet unlike, touching yet not blending, and each was unreachable by a member of the wrong sex. Each had some abilities not available to the other, each did many thing [sic] that the other did, but in a different way, but neither could be said to be superior to the other.[12]

Balance wasn't the only cosmological difference that the young man from South Carolina found in the landscapes of Vietnam. Growing up, his Christian worldview had been determinedly directional. History had a beginning point, a Creator and a moment of Creation. It had been made, so the Bible taught, ex nihilo—out of nothing. So, too, would it have an ending point: in the last battle at the end of time the world would be unmade at Armageddon. Many people of faith that Jordan encountered in Southeast Asia believed nothing like this. For them, time wasn't an arrow from beginning to ending. It was instead an ever-revolving wheel with neither beginning nor end. Nor did it come from nothing. It cycled upon itself, reissuing in its dualities from the central force of the universe.

Putting together his thoughts for The Wheel of Time, Jordan was clearly attempting to reconcile these ideas. Christianity had an echo of dualism in the struggle between good and evil, between God and Satan. The world he was building would have this, too: a struggle between the harmonic balance crafted by the Creator and the discordant destruction of a powerful figure from another world that he initially named "Sa'khan"—a name he'd apparently derived in an attempt to find a middle ground between the demonic Satan of Christianity and the powerful khans that had historically invaded Europe from Central Asia during the Middle Ages:

Those weilders [sic] of Power discovered the existance [sic] of other worlds, other universes. In order to exchange knowledge they attempted contact with those worlds, but for years all such failed. Then they succeeded beyond their wildest dreams and darkest nightmares. They not [only] made contact, and shared knowledge, but much of the knowledge they received seemed obscure and impossible to use. They were told of a land of peace and plenty, like their own, but too late they discovered the truth. That other world was dying, blighted by the evil uses to which power had been put, corrupted to the point where even powers could sustain life only in the bleakest terms. Worse, the knowledge they had given enabled the lords of that other world to break into the world of our story. (SHOULD THESE HAVE SOURCE MORE EVIL THAN MERELY LORDS????)

The greatest and most vicious of those lords was Sa'khan. The armies that followed him came to be known as the Forsaken, men, half-men and not-men twisted and without souls. (GET A GOOD NAME FOR SA'KANH'S*LIEUTENANTS.)* A war of powers ensued, blasting the earth. A man named* _____,*and called the Dragon, was the leader of humankind in the war, and it was largely his skill as a weilder [sic] of power and his rediscovery of the arts of war that enabled any resistance to Sa'kahn at all.[13]

Jordan was still working out a great many aspects of this vision—as evidenced by his all-caps notes to himself and his blank space for the name of humankind's leader—but readers of the Wheel of Time will already recognize the seeds of what would eventually grow. Sa'khan would become Shai'tan: not just an invading lord from another planet or universe but the ultimate will of evil within a dualistic cosmology. The Forsaken would morph from the general armies of this malevolent force to the "good name" Jordan wanted for this being's lieutenants. Even the eventual naming of the Blight within Randland is foreshadowed here, in the "blighted" nature of the other world.

And already there is the Dragon.

The Dragon as the title given to a man who at the cost of cataclysmic tumults and widespread deaths defeated this Dark One's forces long ago—and who is now remembered through the haze of time as both a savior and a devil—is yet another instance of Vietnam working its way into Jordan's expanding mythology. For someone growing up in America, there had been numerous stories of dragons. The Lernaean Hydra from Greek mythology. The dragon that kills Beowulf. Smaug in *The Hobbit*. The monstrous beasts that had to be killed by Saint George and Saint Michael. All were pictured as creatures of destruction and ill intent. Very different were the dragons from the cultures he encountered in Vietnam, where the mythical creatures were connected with the life-giving rain, as well as the prosperity and power of the country itself. These were beings to be honored, not monsters to be feared. What a dragon was—what Jordan's Dragon would be—depended on who was observing it.

And there were still more dragons of story. A dragon-like serpent eating its own tail appears in iconography across the ancient world. Called the ouroboros (from the Greek for "tail-eating"), it was typically a symbol of the never-ending cycle of life and death—a symbol, Jordan recognized, not unlike a mythological wheel of time. The same imagery appears in Norse mythology with the great world-serpent Jörmungandr, which encircled the earth. But here the image wasn't meant to perpetuate itself forever: at some point Jörmungandr would let go of its tail and awaken. The thrashing of the seas at that moment would be a signal that the age-ending cataclysm of Ragnarok had begun. And while Thor would defeat the mighty serpent in that great battle, a bite from Jörmungandr's fangs would leave the god dying: only nine steps would he take after victory, nine steps and then death.

There was a dragon at the end of Christian mythology, too. The book of Revelation—the last book in the Bible—tells the story of the Apocalypse. The text is full of cryptic allusions that have over the centuries busied many a scholar and believer seeking signs that the end of times was upon them. Jordan, too, was fascinated by it: among his early Wheel of Time notes are handwritten pages outlining its steps, taken from the King James Version.[14]

According to its writer—traditionally Saint John—"the Lion of the tribe of Judah, the Root of David" (Revelation 5:5) would open a scroll with seven seals upon it, thus beginning the Apocalypse. Jordan, reading these passages, copied out the scriptural descriptions of the seven seals (Revelation 6–8), noting the tumult that would accompany these steps toward the end of time. He then subsumed much of this into his growing vision: there would be seven seals that closed off the "Bore" that had been made between the world of his story and the world of the Dark One, and these seals would need to be broken if a final confrontation with evil was to be achieved. What's more, the idea of the cataclysmic ending of an age would become integral to his Wheel of Time. The Hindu cycle of time had many hundreds of ages, but his would spin far tighter: just seven ages, with the transitions between them marked by the same kinds of destruction that accompanied the opening of the seven seals in Revelation—times so horrific that to those living through them they would seem to be the end of everything.[15] But it would never *be* the end. Not truly. The Wheel would keep turning, and it would have its fitting symbol: "The Great Serpent that eats its own tail, and is the symbol of time, and of eternity," he later wrote.[16] Here, too, he made a synergy of myth. Norse Ragnarok, set in motion by the dragon-like Jörmungandr, would mean the death of Thor, Odin, and the rest of the gods, but it wouldn't truly be the end of creation. The world would continue, renewed with new people and new gods.

As we've seen, Jordan's first attempt at an outline from all of this was clearly a work in progress. Again and again he leaves queries for himself, prompts to fill in the gaps in what he was putting together. Among those queries were checks to ensure that he wasn't encroaching too much on the work of other writers. Thinking about how the Dragon had wrought enormous destruction upon the world, he wonders if this is "Too close to Kevin Landwaster?"—referring to a similar figure within the mythology of Stephen R. Donaldson's Chronicles of Thomas Covenant.[17] More globally, Jordan was also still feeling out—rather amusingly—where his work would fall within the genre:

> HOW MANY TRADITIONAL FANTASY ELELMENTS [sic] DO WE HAVE? IF SO, UNDER WHAT CONDITIONS, AND IN WHAT MAN-IFESTATIONS? GIANTS? ELVES? DWARVES? TROLLS? OGRES? (No fucking unicorns, that's for damned sure!) DRAGONS? BEASTS OF MYSTERY AND MAGIC? SENTIENT ANIMALS? SENTIENT PLANTS? SPIRITS? GODS?
>
> THERE MUST BE SOME CREATURES THAT ARE°OF°THE POWERS IN SOME FASHION. OF THESE, THOSE THAT ARE°OF°THE MALE SOURCE POWER WILL OF COURSE BE CORRUPTED IN ONE DEGREE OR ANOTHER.[18]

RHYS AL'THOR

It's hard to tell how quickly The Wheel of Time developed in Jordan's mind. The notes we have are largely undated, so the best we can manage is a rough sense of their order, which tells us little about the amount of time that elapsed between them. It was around this same time in the mid-1980s, though, that Jordan began working to develop a cast for this Arthur-influenced story. That meant, first and foremost, that he needed a name for the "young man" hero that he'd been imagining. He needed his King Arthur.[19]

We don't know exactly when Jordan noticed the similarity between the names Arthur and Thor, but it must have seemed a thunderous stroke when he did: Arthur was connected with myths of dragons through his father, Uther Pendragon; Thor would defeat the dragon-like world-serpent at Ragnarok. If Jordan was going to write a story that was built from our myths—or from which our myths could be built—then this similarity was too good an opportunity to pass up. His hero, he decided, would be named "Al'thur."[20]

It didn't last long. Not much later, he decided that the spelling "al'Thor" was better, as it more clearly referenced the Norse god and echoed both the Welsh patronymic naming convention where *ab* means "son of" and the Arabic prefix *al-*, which is a definite article meaning "the." His *al'Thor* was thus the "son of Thor," "*the* Thor," and "Arthur," depending on how you looked at it.

So what would be the hero's *first* name?

At the head of an early compilation of his notes from *The White Goddess* and other sources, Jordan gave an initial answer: "Rhys al'Thor: the hero of the Wheel of Time. The Dragon Reborn. The Hammer."[21] Strangely, the only Rhys named in the text of *The White Goddess* that he was also mining at the time is a little-known, lesser Welsh prince, Rhys Gryg (Graves calls him "Rhys Ieuanc"), who is mentioned only because he was the patron of a bard who wrote a poem complaining about other bards. A man with a rather unremarkable career—he's a far cry from someone liable to have the nickname "the Hammer"—Rhys Gryg seems a terribly unlikely candidate for the namesake of Jordan's Dragon Reborn. Where, then, did the name Rhys come from?

It may be that Jordan simply liked the look or sound of the name. Not everything need be loaded with meaning. That said, it should be noted that Jordan was a dedicated Ricardian: he was fascinated with the story of King Richard III, who was killed at the Battle of Bosworth Field in 1485. As it happens, the man long credited with killing the king in that bloody fight was a Welsh nobleman named Rhys ap Thomas—and in many tellings he did so with a war hammer. What's more, Jordan might well have known that the name *Rhys* comes from the Old Welsh, meaning "fiery warrior," which could fit well with the notion that the Dragon Reborn would bring such destruction on the world. That association with "fire" might also help to explain why Jordan decided early on that his hero would have red hair.

In these and other notes from *The White Goddess* are more bits and pieces that were simmering toward a plot. His story would have, he decided,

> Wardens: (alt. 'Warders') men who watch the borders of human lands against the prophecied [*sic*] return of evil. They are warriors. Each has some abilities that are gifted from the Power, but they themselves have no use of the Power. Each has bonded himself to a female weilder [*sic*] of Power. She cannot compel him to obey her, but if she commands in a certain way and he disobeys, the bonding is broken and the gifts lost. These gifts include a 'sense' for the presence of evil, a marvelous amount of self-healing ability, and a retarding of aging.[22]

As for those female wielders of the "Power," he found a name for them, too: the Aes Sedai. In Irish mythology, the *aos sí* are faerie from the Otherworld: fierce, frightening, and strange. Graves gave their name using the alternative spelling "Aes Sidhe," which Jordan initially adopted. Later, he transliterated this using a modern English pronunciation rather than an Irish one, creating his own name for the magical, otherworldly women in his story. Searching for a structure to organize their society, he pulled in the kind of institutional governance that was found in the pre-modern convents of the Catholic Church.

And more and more names were swirling in his mind, ready to be fixed into a plot. Handwritten on the back of these same notes is a list that includes Lewin, Thom, Emon, Jaim, Elaida, and Mina, among other possibilities—none of them yet characters, but all of them inspired by his reading and his imagination.[23]

Not surprisingly, Jordan further delved into Malory's *Morte d'Arthur* for more background on Rhys and his world. We have today a set of notes, taken down in Jordan's own hand on lined yellow paper, regarding characters from this Arthurian legend. It's arguably the closest thing we have to the moment of the making of one of the bestselling fantasies in history. In hastily scribbled notes (see photo insert, page 6), Jordan records how Merlin was imprisoned in a cave: "by Nyneve?" He notes how Sir Tristram, one of Arthur's knights, fights a green giant in *Le Morte d'Arthur*. Then, on the following page, he provides a list of connections between Arthur's cast and the one he was inventing:

Merlin : Amyrlen
Duke of Tintagel : [blank]
Igraine : Tigraine
Uther : [blank]
Arthur : Rhys al'Thor
Gwynevere : Gwyn al'Veer
Morgan le Fay : Emorgaine
King Lot : (?) Lor
Margawse : Morgase
Gawain : Gwayne
Gareth : Garth[24]

Lines connect "Amyrlen" and "Emorgaine," an indication that he was apparently thinking of combining these figures into a single character. A similar matching runs between "Morgan le Fay" and "Morgawse." Subsequent pages draw out the relationships between Jordan's Arthurian characters and their Arthurian legends. Inspired by *The White Goddess*, Jordan's Merlin figure, the "Amyrlen," would be a woman: "Emorgaine, leader of Aes Sedai." His Arthur would be "Rhys al'Thor." Though not yet named, his King Uther Pendragon would naturally be "Rhys's father," and Queen Igraine would be "Rhys's mother." Gwynevere would be a "village girl." He would combine Morgan le Fay with Queen Morgawse, who would be an Aes Sedai and "Rhys's aunt, though he doesn't know it." Her husband would be Jordan's still-unnamed echo of King Lot, and her son would be his Sir Gawain and would support Rhys. Sir Gareth would be rolled up into "one of [the] village lads." Sir Mordred, who in the Arthurian legends causes Arthur's death, would be "Morgawse's son (potential power weilder)." Jordan's Sir Lancelot would be "Lan, the Warder," who would be connected with the Aes Sedai. Sir Galahad would be Lan's son, who "does not know his father."

Step by step, his mythology advanced. "Emorgaine" became "Moiraine," with its additional echo of the Moirai of Greek myth, thereby speaking to the way people might think of her as a puppet master of sorts. Amyrlin would become the title given to the leader of the Aes Sedai, rather than an individual name.

Sometime before 1987, Jordan again tried to pull his thoughts together into an outline for the first book of The Wheel of Time, which he was now planning to call *The Eye of the World*. The main character was still Rhys, and Jordan still had a great many questions about the shape of what would happen, but the story was far more complete. The outline begins:

Rhys al'Thor is, he belives [*sic*], the son of a widowed farmer and sheepherder living outside a small village. The village is preparing for one of the yearly festivals (?which one?). There are rumors of strange sightings, but because the source is thought to be a man of the village who is always sour and predicting disaster few take them seriously.

In the night the farm is attacked by strange men, seemingly half-beast, who kill even the farm animals they come on. Rhys and his father defend themselves, managing to kill the attacking beast men, but Rhys' 'father' is badly injured, and the wounds appear to be getting infected even as they look. With their horse dead (?or did they have one??poorer??simpler?) Rhys, though in a state of near shock (Who were the attackers, he wonders, and why did they come? They are like nothing he has ever seen before, nor like anything he remembers hearing of.) must construct a platform he will drag behind him to carry his father to the village, where ther [*sic*] is an old woman who knows much about healing.

On the way Rhys' 'father' begins to talk deliriously. He talks of being a soldier twenty years past when savage tribesmen, horse-mounted clans, invaded the land. He had been a soldier for some time, but was ready to buy a farm and stop when the invasion came. [SEE REASON FOR INVASION, BELOW. REVEAL NOW, OR LATER? OR PART NOW?] He fought in a great battle before Dragonmount, where the invasion was supposedly turned back. [WAS IT IN TRUTH, OR DID THEY TURN BACK FOR SOME OTHER REASON, PERHAPS BE-CAUSE THEIR PURPOSE HAD BEEN CARRIED OUT?] As the battle was ending he found a woman, a warrior of the enemy, on the slopes of Dragonmount, dying of her wounds. She was pregnant, and though it was obviously not time for the baby to be born, her wounds had brought on labor. He helped the woman birth her child, and buried her when she died. He and his wife had had several children, but none survived, so he took the child to his wife, and she took it as her own. They named it Rhys.[25]

Though he wasn't sure how he'd get to that point, Jordan thought the story would ultimately become a quest to find the "Green-God" who could help Rhys defeat the dark forces of Sa'khan. In the end, this being would be revealed to be not a god at all but a construct of the Power who watches over a magical pool. Aiding the hero in his quest, this construct would be destroyed and a temporary victory achieved.

1987: RAND AL'THOR

Only one of the notes Jordan left behind in this period is clearly dated: the second version of a "namelist" for *The Eye of the World*, which was printed from his computer on "1 JUNE 1987."[26] It's a list of names for characters, things, and places for the book—some already in use, some there in case the author needed a name for something while he was writing. Jordan was clearly fond of such lists. His notes are full of them, and they grew increasingly large as the series advanced. This early one is already thirty-three pages long, with Jordan's handwritten notes making numerous further adjustments.

Several changes to Jordan's story had by now taken place. The Dark One was no longer Sa'khan. He'd been renamed Sha'tan—more recognizably connected to Satan—and was thus on his way to becoming the Shai'tan of the actual published books. The Ogyr, as the Ogier were then called, had previously been described as being short and somewhat akin to

Tolkien's dwarves. That basic indebtedness was still there, but they were now of greater than human height, more akin to the traditional depictions of the ogres that they were intended to recall most directly:

> Ogyr: a mountain people. Very tall and very stockily built, men and women alike. Men wear full beards and hair very long. Very flat of face. Considered ugly by most who know of them. Excellent stoneworkers. Major occupations are stoneworking and forresting [sic]. Goats tended by children. Men speak of forests and trees as if they were a flock of animals.[27]

The name of Jordan's protagonist had also changed by this point. He was no longer Rhys. He was now—and would be from here on out—Rand al'Thor.[28]

As with the original name of Rhys, Jordan left no notes directly explaining why he'd picked the name Rand. There's no obvious example to draw from in Graves' *White Goddess* or Malory's *Morte d'Arthur*, though it should be noted that the main character of Jordan's unpublished Western, *Morgan*, was named Randall (Ran) Morgan.

If he had a source beyond simple affection for the name, Rand likely came from Tolkien's *Lord of the Rings*, where an alternative name for the wizard Gandalf was Mithrandir, meaning "grey wanderer" in the Sindarin language of the Elves. This was an imaginary language, but Tolkien hadn't invented it out of whole cloth. His Sindarin verb *randir* was almost assuredly indebted to the same verb in Old French, meaning "to run." Atop this, the name Rand in English derives from Old English *Randulf*—meaning "shield-wolf," a metaphor for a good protector. This, too, would be a match for Jordan's hero: a magic-wielding protector hurrying to save the world, who would ultimately be left a wanderer within it:

> Having finally conquered and bound Sha'tan, Rand thinks to disappear, faking his own death. Moiraine, Arinel [an early name for Elayne], Equene [Egwene], and others of his closest friends are among those who are not fooled and will not let him go alone.[29]

Rand's adopted father also had a name now: Tam, which Jordan had first put in his lists of potential names as being short for "Tamtrim."[30] His source for the name was Mesopotamian mythology: Tammuz (more properly Dumuzid) was a god of shepherds and, more generally, the life-giving growth of plants—or, as Jordan had it in his notes from *The White Goddess,* a "corn god."[31] Dumuzid was also in some stories a heroic warrior-king, whose death and rebirth symbolized the seasons. This was a fitting match for the man who'd left war behind to become a farmer and a father to a young shepherd, a veteran of battles who would very nearly die when their village was attacked.

As the Tamtrim in his word lists became simply Tam, that missing second syllable made its way to a related name: Matrim, with its shortened form of Mat, who was at this point marked for inclusion in the book—though exactly who he'd be wasn't yet defined.[32]

Also now appearing was Thom Merilyn, the name that would become the gleeman Thom Merrilin.[33] In origin it was an obvious derivation of Merlin—as Amyrlin had been—tied to a shortened form of Thomas. That first name, perhaps, was a wink to his friend and publisher, Tom Doherty—a master of stories if ever there was one!

Other names that would become familiar to readers of the series were also showing up on the author's word lists, though mostly without any sense of who they'd become. Jaem is there (an equivalent, Jordan noted, for "Jim"). So are Haral ("Harold") Luhhan, Samel ("Samuel") Crawe, Ewin, Tigraine ("mother of Rand"), Elayna ("Elaine"), Min ("short for Minalea; Minoralie"), Marin, the *sa'angreal* and *angreal* ("Sangreal, the Grail"), Caemlyn ("capital of Andor"), Steddings, Cenn, Elffin ("A slender, small man.????"), Kadsuane, Logain, Seanchan, Bran ("a god betrayed by his kin and slain"), Baalzamon ("in the Trolloc tongue means 'Heart of the Dark'"), Aginor, Congar, Finngar, Elyas, Lanfear, the Kai Shan ("diademed battle lords"), Messana, Oliva, Fail(e) ("accent grave over the a"), and many other names or parts of names.[34]

The next sequence in the notes built upon this, and one gets the impression of a rapid expansion in the plot, the characters, and the world in 1987–1988. Aside from names, Jordan was also compiling other lists:

of vegetation, of jobs, of songs, of idioms and sayings. Laboriously, he was building a living, breathing world.

In large measure, this was a time of addition, though a few changes stand out in these notes. He dropped plans that would have introduced a complicated set of religions operating in the Westlands—shifting these instead into the cultural mentalities of groups like the Children of the Light, the Red Ajah, and the Tuatha'an. He also toyed with changes to the *sa'angreal.* That word was, as his notes just mentioned make clear, an echo of the Sangreal, the name given to the Holy Grail in Malory and other works of Arthurian literature. In The Wheel of Time, it would refer to various objects that were imbued with the One Power or could focus the wielding of it. For a time, though, Jordan decided that these would instead be called *cris.*[35] This notion was built from the Javanese kris, an asymmetrical, finely crafted dagger believed to have magical properties. After more consideration, he returned to using the word *sa'angreal* generally, but maintained that those of them that were weapons—in particular, a set of power-imbued swords in what would become the Stone of Tear—would be called *cris.*[36] The distinction didn't last, though, and his notes soon reverted to *sa'angreal* even for these.

Another change from this period is that the figure of the peddler who would visit Emond's Field at the start of the books at last received a name: Eward White, "though he is somewhat reluctant to give his surname," Jordan noted to himself.[37] The presence of this man had been included from some of the earliest attempts at an outline, with him growing more mysterious in seemingly every revision Jordan made. At first he was torn to shreds in the subsequent attack made on the village, but soon enough Jordan was slipping ambiguity into his fate, before deciding to make him appear in a big city later on—much as he does in the published *Eye of the World.* The peddler was hardly the complex character of Padan Fain, but he was clearly well on his way.

Also getting a name at this point—a *full* name, that is—was Nyneve, as she was then spelled. The Wisdom of Emond's Field had actually been one of the first members of Jordan's cast: she echoed Nimue, from the Arthurian legend, one of several figures that Graves identified as a glimpse of his elusive "white goddess."[38] Jordan's earliest notes from *Le Morte d'Arthur* are a mere half page long, but half of that is given over to part of her story:

> Merlin's pursuit of Nyneve, and his teaching of her. Finally wearying of his attempts on her maidenhead, she manages to trick him into an enchanted cavern, sealing him up alive for all time.
>
> Nyneve fell in love with Sir Pelleas, after cruelly exposing the cold woman whom he had futilely loved for some years.[39]

Jordan, like Graves, was clearly fascinated by this woman, and in some of his early thoughts about The Wheel of Time he followed suit in giving her a darker role that's far more grim than that which was in the final books. She would, he first thought, cause Lan to oppose Rand "at some time," and she herself would be

> raped by one of the Forsaken in *The Eye of the World*. Later, this makes her vulnerable to the Dark One's forces. She is killed, then later reappears, brought back from the dead. She claims she was not killed, or at least that some special abilities of a distant Power weilder [sic] saved her. In fact she has been brought back by the Dark One and is serving him.
>
> Moiraine will ascend to the Amyrlin Seat.
>
> Nyneve will at some point after Moiraine takes the Amyrlin Seat seemingly slay Moiraine, or cause Moiraine's death. This should involve something about a cave. In fact, Moiraine will be trapped halfway between life and death. She will eventually be able to return to the world of men, or be brought back. Whether this is an actual rebirth, or whether she returns in some fashion other than as a living, breathing human is yet to be decided.[40]

Much of this was tied to Malory, with Moiraine as a figuration of Merlin, and Jordan fortunately pulled away from this kind of strict reimagining as he continued to plot the books. Thus while Moiraine is indeed similarly imprisoned and trapped—within the Tower of Ghenjei instead of a cave—it wasn't by Nynaeve's hand. The Wisdom of Emond's Field had evolved, by then, into a character fully for the good.

At any rate, while Jordan's final version of the character had the name Nynaeve al'Meara, his first attempt at a last name for her was Nyneve Bayal.[41] This family name derived from Belili, which Graves believed to be the Sumerian White Goddess—the sister or lover of the "corn god" Tammuz—whose name had been warped into the wicked god Belial of the Bible, as well as "the Slavonic word *beli* meaning 'white' and the Latin *bellus* meaning 'beautiful'."[42] Though little of this is technically true, Graves' theories here were nevertheless a perfect fit for Jordan's efforts to unite mythologies. This was also, by a rather twisting road, probably how the author ended up with the name of Bela for Rand's stout, shaggy mare.

It wasn't just the plot of Nynaeve that became less dark over time. Seemingly everything was more grim in its original conception. The process of cutting a man off from the One Power wasn't called gentling at first, though we have record of Jordan rambling his way to the term while describing a process that was far, far worse than what it would become:

The only way to avoid this fate [of a man going mad] is to be gelded, and to accept a form of lobotomy performed with the power that makes the victim very passive, incapable of violence, and receptive to being commanded. Some men wish to follow the paths of knowledge and power, and so accept the price. Some men (and some women) have such an ingrained afinity [*sic*] for the powers that they would be weilders [*sic*] whether they trained or not. To find these males, so they will not become dangers to the land, there are testings at a certain age, and those found are taken into training. The males must, of course, be gelded and have the rest performed as well. (ANOTHER NAME MUST BE USED FOR THIS. THE VERY PRACTICE IS NOT WELL KNOWN. MOST PEOPLE THINK THE EFFECTS OF MEN OF USING POWER

CAUSE THE SOFTENED FEATURES AND HIGH VOICES, ETC.)
The girls are simply trained.

Sane men manage to escape the testing, or find their affinity only later [in] life, though these are very few. Many of these refuse to accept the fate that must be theirs for the safety of the land. They wreek [*sic*] much harm until they are found and captured. Teams of woman weilders [*sic*] of power search out these men, and "gentle" them. Once the power has taken a good hold, the "gentling" process has a more profound affect [*sic*], so that thye [*sic*] become little more than vegetables. Those who escape find not only increasing madness, but physical afflictions (MUST HAVE ATTRIBUTES OF A PLAGUE, IF THIS IS TO BE USED.) so that male victims of some diseases are actually slain out of fear in some villages and towns.[43]

THE TEST MANUSCRIPT

At long last, after years of planning, Jordan felt confident enough in the world he'd built to try his hand at writing the first book of The Wheel of Time. The result of these labors is the "Test Manuscript" for *The Eye of the World,* which exists today in a printout that's been heavily edited by both Jordan and Harriet (see photo insert, page 7).[44]

The basic story, for the most part, is close to what would become the final plot. The most striking differences are in the names of characters. The peddler Eward White was now Mikal Fain, for example, which brought him one step closer to the Padan Fain that he would become. Jordan was in this case strongly playing off what he'd found in *The White Goddess:* Graves believed that the male archangel Michael comes from a female goddess Michal who had made the first man, Adam. Jordan's peddler, having the name "Mikal Fain," was "feigning" being what he was not: unlike the benevolent goddess Michal, he was a man with ill intent.

More interesting are Rand's friends, whose names in the Test Manuscript are Matrim Piket, Dannil Aybara, and Perrin Dael. These are quite different names from the final versions of Matrim Cauthon and

Perrin Aybara that appeared in *The Eye of the World*—and a Dannil who didn't appear at all.

In the text, that is. Dannil Lewin, as his name became, lasted long enough in Jordan's drafts that he was still part of the copy sent to cover artist Darrell K. Sweet. A close inspection of his depiction of the original party on horseback reveals that there's one boy too many in the group: Dannil was still there. He was, Jordan later said, excised from the book when Harriet noted how little he contributed to the plot. Jordan replied that he'd have something important to do "around book 5." Harriet responded, "Well, this series may never get to book 5."[45]

So Dannil was written out of *The Eye of the World*.[46] And the story, as a result, was tightened up. Here, for instance, is the meeting of Rand with several of his friends, compared between the Test Manuscript and the published version of *The Eye of the World*:

Test Manuscript

Rand and Mat edged into the crowd, trying to get as close to the wagon as they could. Ewin, with the license of his youth, wriggled and dodged all the way to the front, but Rand stopped when the villagers pressed about him so that he could go no further without pushing. He was enough taller than anyone else near him to see everything from there, and close enough to hear whatever the peddler had to say. Mat halted beside him, though not without an envious look after Ewin. Dannil Aybara and Perrin Dael sidled through the press to them.

"I had been thinking you were going to stay out on the farm through the whole Festival," Perrin shouted at Rand over the clamor. The curly-haired blacksmith's apprentice was so stocky as to seem a man and a half wide, with arms and shoulders thick enough to rival those of Master Luhhan himself.

Dannil, a farmer's son whose slight build contrasted sharply with Perrin, shouted, "My father and I met the wagon as we were coming into the village." Normally he was sober and thoughtful, but now his dark eyes shone with excitement. "Imagine it! Spring Festival and a peddler, both at the same time."

"You don't know a quarter of it," Mat laughed at them.[47]

The Eye of the World

Rand and Mat edged into the crowd, trying to get as close to the wagon as they could. Rand would have stopped halfway, but Mat wiggled through the press, pulling Rand behind him, until they were right behind the Council.

"I had been thinking you were going to stay out on the farm through the whole Festival," Perrin Aybara shouted at Rand over the clamor. Half a head shorter than Rand, the curly-haired blacksmith's apprentice was so stocky as to seem a man and a half wide, with arms and shoulders thick enough to rival those of Master Luhhan himself. He could easily have pushed through the throng, but that was not his way. He picked his path carefully, offering apologies anyway, and tried not to jostle anyone as he worked through the crowd to Rand and Mat. "Imagine it," he said when he finally reached them. "Bel Tine and a peddler, both together. I'll bet there really are fireworks."

"You don't know a quarter of it." Mat laughed.[48]

Though he was removed, Dannil's initial existence in the book further illuminates Jordan's continuing mythological work: the character was intended to recall the hero of the biblical book of Daniel, who was considered a prophet in later Christian tradition. Aybara, his last name when he first appeared, likely reflects the Welsh *ab Aaron,* "the son of Aaron"—the biblical brother of Moses from whom the high priests of the Israelites claimed descent. Later, that last name was transferred to Perrin, whose name came from Perun, a Slavic god of war and sky whose weapon of choice was an axe. Making that switch, Jordan gave Dannil a new last name: Lewin, which he got from Lleu Llaw Gyffes—a heroic figure in Welsh mythology who made frequent appearances in Graves' *White Goddess* in conjunction with the source of Matrim's name: Math fab Mathonwy. A king of Gwynedd, Math would reportedly die unless he was at war or resting his feet in the lap of a virgin. For many years his maiden footholder was Goewin, but Math's nephew Gilfaethwy became obsessed with her. With the help of his brother Gwydion, Gilfaethwy managed to trick Math into going to war on a neighboring kingdom. While the king was away fighting, Gilfaethwy raped Goewin. When Math returned and discovered what had happened, he punished his nephews by turning them into wild animals for three years; he took Goewin for his wife. When this punishment was over, Math needed a new virgin on which to rest his feet, and Gwydion (human once again) suggested his sister Arianrhod (who incidentally gave her name to *Tel'aran'rhiod* in Jordan's mythology). During the testing of her virginity, Arianrhod prematurely gave birth to two children: one who would become a sea creature and the other who would become the mythological hero Lleu Llaw Gyffes, meaning "Fair-Haired Boy with a Skillful Hand." The continuation of Math's story revealed him to be a symbol for goodness and good luck—both fitting for the supernatural luck of Jordan's Mat.

Mat's initial last name, Piket, was likewise fitting given his character's draw to gambling. Piquet is a thirty-two-card trick-taking game for two players that dates back to the sixteenth century. It's one of the oldest card games still played today. Whether because he didn't like it aesthetically or perhaps thought it too redundant with the roots of Mat's first name, Jordan later abandoned this in favor of something to reflect another aspect of the young man's nature: his fear of the Aes Sedai. This emotional response from people within Randland, Jordan thought, was not unlike the early modern fears of witchcraft in our own world. As it happens, one of the key figures in the famous Salem witch trials of 1692—and an enthusiastic supporter of the executions that followed—was the Puritan minister Cotton Mather (1663–1728). It was a name that was too delightful an echo to pass up, especially given that the womanizing Mat was hardly a Puritan. Matrim Cauthon he would be.

REVISION 23

The Test Manuscript gave Jordan confidence that he had a working fantasy novel, and Harriet's guidance helped him further refine it into something that was ready to be shared with Tor. Jordan made the changes, resulting in the next version of *The Eye of the World* that survives in his papers: the "Revision 23 Manuscript."[49]

Each iteration was bringing the text closer to what fans would recognize. The Ogier who joined Rand on his quest had previously been named Jak Vladad.[50] He became Loial, a word of obvious but important origins in reflecting his loyalty. The Dragon had been Jaren Telamon,[51] but as Jordan composed a prologue that would be focused on him, the name became Lews Therin Telamon.[52]

This latter name change is especially interesting for the way it reverberates through Jordan's thinking at the time. Telamon, in Greek mythology, is the father of Greater Ajax, one of the Greek heroes in Homer's *Iliad*. Likely due to a story of him hastily constructing an altar of stone to prevent his death at the hands of Hercules, Telamon's name was subsequently given to the architectural feature of stone columns in the shape of men. In The Wheel of Time, the Dragon had made of himself a different kind of colossal stone altar: Dragonmount.

Telamon's *first* first name, Jaren (and later Jaran), was less direct but arguably more impactful. Jordan had early on made notes from Graves' *White Goddess* about "Ja(h): as a man's name."[53] It's clear enough to see why. In that text, Graves had identified Jah as the name for the Hebrew God in the Bible.[54] Looking it up in his own King James Bible, Jordan would've found this passage in the Psalms:

> Let God arise, let his enemies be scattered: let them also that hate him flee before him. As smoke is driven away, so drive them away: as wax melteth before the fire, so let the wicked perish at the presence of God. But let the righteous be glad; let them rejoice before God: yea, let them exceedingly rejoice. Sing unto God, sing praises to his name: extol him that rideth upon the heavens by his name Jah, and rejoice before him. (Psalm 68:1–4)

The Dragon held a role similar to Jah in The Wheel of Time—unparalleled power and a personal struggle with the evil forces—yet Jordan had no intention of implying an equation between his fictional

Dragon and his own personal Deity. So the author wanted a name that could still echo Jah while also moving perceptively away from it. His solution was to add a second syllable, and he once again got it from Graves, who believed that the mythical creature of Geryon was a darker, male counterpart to his ideal White Goddess.[55] The resulting Jaran was an excellent fit for his Dragon: an extremely powerful man who was responsible for bringing a taint upon the male half of the One Power.

Despite the fact that this was a fitting match for his character, Jordan continued to fiddle with the Dragon's name. And, in the end, he decided to make the switch to Lews Therin Telamon. It may be that echoing Jah, even so stealthily, was still too close to his personal faith. One clue that this is so is in the fact that the new first name echoed something quite the opposite: *lucifer*, meaning "light-bearer," was considered an alternative name for the Devil in Christian mythology. But, as Jordan well knew, this wasn't the original way the name was used. It started, in fact, as a simple reference to the "morning star"—that is, the planet Venus, which often appears just before the dawn. Isaiah 14:12 condemns a Babylonian king by referring to him as a morning star that falls to earth, and Christian writers later connected that passage from the Old Testament with an unrelated passage from the New Testament: Luke 10:18, in which Satan (i.e., the Devil) is described as falling from Heaven. Remarkably, the planet Venus meanwhile became a symbol associated with John the Baptist. Just as Venus is a forerunner for the light of the Sun, John the Baptist was a forerunner for the "light" of the Christian Messiah (i.e., the Son). Jordan realized that the duality of these two readings of the morning star—one the great evil and the other bringing about the great good—were an ideal fit for the Dragon's role in The Wheel of Time, with none of the theological baggage that Jaran had. And so, as he was putting the final touches on the first draft of *The Eye of the World,* he renamed the Dragon.

After reading the first third of the book, Harriet called Tom Doherty at Tor and said he needed to look at it. When he asked why, she replied, "Because either I've fallen into the wife trap or this thing is wonderful!"[56]

Doherty asked for it at once. A typescript was produced and sent to New York, along with a description of what Jordan was thinking would happen in the subsequent books that would collectively be The Wheel of Time. Jordan made no secret of the mythologies and messages that were undergirding the entire project:

> The story will take in parts not only of the most obvious myths (Arthur and Thor) but others, as well. Parts of the Arthurian legend will be blended with Norse myth, Greek myth and others. These will not be taken whole, however. What will be done is to show occurences [*sic*] which could, over thousands of years, be distorted into the sources of these myths. Additionally, some of the things that will become major myths will not involve Rand directly, but rather people around him, including others of the young men from his village. Also, as should be evident from the list of events above, the story will in no way be limited to happenings out of mythology.
>
> There will be stories and legends in the world of the story that have their roots in our time. [Examples: Len, who flew to the moon in the belly of a fiery eagle, and his daughter, Salia who learned to walk among the stars. Also, Anla and Lisbet, two sisters, one of whom was a great ruler and the other a great counselor.]
>
> The main thrust of the story will not be how fact becomes legend, however. Rather it will explore the nature of good and evil, of free will and the duty owed by the individual to humanity as a whole, of why and how mankind makes the choice to oppose evil, and the harm that can be done in the name of good.
>
> People who do not champion and support good are acquiescing in the press of evil.
>
> Some people who believe they are championing good actually fight [for] the cause of evil, for they would bind the free will given by the Creator.[57]

Doherty read the book as soon as it came in, and he immediately loved it: "Harriet said it was great," he recalled, "and I *did* think it was great!"[58]

Jordan, relieved, set to work polishing up the first book while also diving deeper into the second, *The Great Hunt*, which was already far along in the drafting stage. He also set about trying to coalesce his notes and sources into a more concrete synopsis and outline for the series.

The full arc of The Wheel of Time, and the lessons it would teach, were already clear in his mind:

Rand will flee his fate at first, but flight will only bring him into further conflict with Sha'tan and the Forsaken. Reluctantly convinced that he is indeed the Dragon, he will attempt to act the part, only to discover that many (including the Aes Sedai) believe he is another false Dragon, and that some humans, both knowingly and unknowingly, are serving Sha'tan. Nevertheless he will attempt to unite the people to oppose Sha'tan's minions, to unite them by force if necessary.

Wielding power far beyond that any human has ever handled before he attempts to destroy Sha'tan, and fails disastrously. Once again he is driven into flight. And Sha'tan has at last been freed totally from his prison, bringing greater misery and strife to the world than ever before. Hopeless now, Rand sets out to fight Sha'tan and the Forsaken as best he can alone, yet now he finds that allies come to him unbidden, almost by accident, it seems. It is now that he realizes why he failed to unite humanity. By attempting to force humankind to oppose evil he was attempting to circumvent the free will that the Creator had made a central part of all humans.

In a final confrontation Rand binds Sha'tan away from the world once more. Some of those who support him want him to destroy Sha'tan, but he knows now that to attempt to do so would be disastrous even if he succeeded, which he does not believe he can. Evil—which Sha'tan is, just as the Creator is good—cannot be destroyed any more than can Good. Evil must be opposed by people who chose [sic] to champion Good, but without Evil as a counter-balance to Good, free will is no more. The removal of Evil, or the possibility of Evil, from the world would destroy humanity as surely as the removal of Good, or the possibility of Good, for free will is an integral part of humankind.

Humanity, to be human, must have something to oppose and something to support, and the free choice of which will be which. People of
future Ages, and the people of his own Age, will always have to make
their own choice between Good and Evil.[59]

Balance.

And the freedom to choose a place for or against that balance, come
what may.

That was all it was. And all it would be was everything.

The Wheel of Time had begun.

Doherty was right, of course: Jordan wrote longer than he initially
thought he would. The planned six books became nine, which became
twelve, which became fourteen and a prequel and the promise unful-
filled of further prequels and "outrigger" novels, as the author described
them, that would follow some of the main characters forward beyond
the main plot of The Wheel of Time.

Jordan was often accused of having deliberately stretched the story
out for financial gain. It's an accusation that's no doubt born of a fan's
frustration that the end hadn't come despite the hundreds of thousands
of words that were piling up. It's understandable. But there's no evidence
that this was so.

What *was* happening was that The Wheel of Time had become something far more than Jordan had originally conceived. He was, at heart,
a writer who discovered his plots and his characters. He knew where he
was going, and he began in a direction to get there, but if the unfolding
narrative twisted and turned along the way it would be because it was
meant to do so. As long as he got to the end he intended, it was fine.

Along the way, it was becoming, in so many ways, more serious. In
the original Test Manuscript, for instance, after Nynaeve appeared at
the Stag and Lion Inn, Rand had an exchange with "Eguene" in which
she talked about now having "a chance to be something more than a
sheepfarmer's wife,"[60] after which he was accosted by Min, who dragged

him into a straw-filled storage shed in the stableyard. There, abruptly, she seduced him:

He turned to leave, and for the first time in what seemed like forever a crack appeared in the calm he had come to accept as normal. Min was pulling her baggy shirt off over her head.

"W-w-what are you doing?" he demanded.

She clutched the shirt to her chest in both hands, and this time he did not wonder at the red in her cheeks. It seemed the least that was called for. "What I must," she said, then amended it. "What I want to. The Creator alone knows why, but even if it is fate, I don't regret it."

She let the shirt fall.

He still knew he could move a [*sic*] smoothly as a hawk on the wing, and he was as ready as a horse at the start of a race, but whatever it was he was ready for, this was not it. All he could do was stare as she put a hand against his chest and backheeled him onto the piled straw.

He was old enough not to be totally innocent, not completely, but this was beyond his experience. Shock made him splutter incoherently—he could imagine what he would have said if he had been able to manage speech—while Min stripped away all of his calm readiness as swiftly as she stripped away his clothing. One clear thought did surface: she was a broomstraw, and he was a whirlwind? Had she ever gotten that backwards!

Later, while he lay, still gasping for breath, on straw that crackled when he moved, the sound of someone humming made him lift his head. It was Min making the little tune, like the quiet songs of contentment he had heard women sing while at their spinning, but different, too. She settled her bulky shirt with a twitch of her shoulders—she was already completely dressed—and began coming [*sic*] her hair into place with her fingers, picking out bits of straw.

"I . . . I'm sorry," he said, and flinched as her song cut off in mid-note and she rounded on him with narrowed eyes and a voice like silk-wrapped steel.

"What did you say?"

"I . . . I shouldn't have. . . ."

His face flamed, and he swallowed hard and took a deep breath. The odd calm that had shrouded him was only a memory, but he fervently wished he had it back.

"I can't take you with me, and I can't stay. Either would be too dangerous, you must believe me. You could wait for me, though. Back in Emond's Field, the Wisdom performs marriages. There must be someone here—. What am I thinking? Nynaeve is here. But what am I going to tell Eguene? We've been promised since—. What are you laughing at?"

Min had sagged against the front wall, quivering and stuffing her fist in her mouth in an attempt to stifle her mirth. Even when she finally got it under control enough to speak she was apt to break into giggles at odd moments. "Oh, my fine downcountry sheepherder. Do you really think you have to. . . . Do downcountry girls never take downcountry boys for a romp in the hayloft?"

"I won't say no one ever steals a march on the marriage ceremony, but this is different. The Light help me, but I've pickled myself for good this time."

She came over to squat on her haunches beside him, with her arms crossed on her knees and an expression that seemed equal parts amusment [*sic*], exasperation and fondness. "The first thing, you wooly lamb you, is that you did not trip me, I tripped you. The second thing is that I have no intention of marrying you, or anyone else. Not yet, at least. Maybe not ever. I don't see why I should have all the troubles of marriage when I can have the fun without it."

Rand snorted. "You're trying to sound like one of those women in the stories, the ones who . . . who have dozens of lovers, but I heard you cry out when I . . . when. . . ." His face reddened, but not as red as hers.

He avoided looking at her directly, and she seemed to find her knees fascinating, but there was a touch of defiance in her voice. "Some things are meant to be. It doesn't mean they will happen, just that it's right that they should. This was meant to be, and I don't regret a bit of it. Do you?"

A Two Rivers' upbringing would not let him call it right, and his feelings for Eguene muddled matters even more, but honesty, and a hint of warning of her question, made him say, "No, I don't regret it."

The smile that blossomed on Min's face at his answer was enough to have warmed him on a cold winter night. She leaned forward to kiss him, a light brush across the lips even warmer than her smile, then sprang to her feet with a laugh. "I won't wait for you, and I won't follow after you, but this is not the last . . . meeting between us. It was my choice. I could have walked away, but I chose to tangle my future with yours, and, the Light help me, I won't regret it no matter what comes." And, so quickly she almost seemed to vanish, she was out of the door and had shut it behind her.

With her going Rand suddenly realized that he was cold. And the straw itched. Scrambling to his feet, he began searching out his clothes, and tried not to think of how they had gotten so scattered and buried in the straw. Persistent wisps of hay clung to every garment, and he had to make sure every last bit was gone before anyone saw him. Right, Min had called it, but he only knew that he now had still another secret to keep. And his headache was back, too.[61]

The scene was cut entirely from the published version of *The Eye of the World.* Instead of a sudden sexual fling, the relationship between Min and Rand was instead allowed the room to grow in a far richer, far more rewarding way. In fact, it isn't until the seventh book of the series, *A Crown of Swords,* that they sleep together, and the sequence as we finally received it is far more emotionally mature and meaningful—an indication of not just how the story had changed, but also how Jordan had grown as a writer:

His arms went around her slowly, gently. "Oh, Min, you have more pain than pleasure from your gift. If I could take your pain, I would, Min. I would."

Slowly it penetrated that he was trembling, too. Light, he tried so hard to be iron, to be what he thought the Dragon Reborn must, but it cut him when somebody died because of him, Colavaere probably no less than Fel. He bled for everyone harmed, and tried to pretend he did not.

"Kiss me," she mumbled. When he did not move, she looked up. He blinked at her uncertainly, eyes now blue, now gray, a morning sky. "I'm not teasing." How often had she teased him, sitting on his lap, kissing him, calling him sheepherder because she dared not say his name for fear he might hear the caress? He put up with it because he thought she *was* teasing and would stop if she believed it did not affect him. Hah! Aunt Jan and Aunt Rana said you should not kiss a man unless you intended to marry him, but Aunt Mirren seemed to know a little more of the world. She said you should not kiss a man too casually because men fell in love so easily. "I'm cold inside, sheepherder. Colavaere, and Master Fel. . . . I need to feel warm flesh. I need. . . . Please?"

His head lowered so slowly. It was a brother's kiss, at first, mild as milk-water, soothing, comforting. Then it became something else. Not at all soothing. Jerking upright, he tried to pull away. "Min, I can't. I have no right—"

Seizing two handfuls of his hair, she pulled his mouth back down, and after a little while, he stopped fighting. She was not certain whether her hands began tearing at the laces of his shirt first or his at hers, but of one thing she was absolutely sure. If he even tried to stop now, she was going to fetch one of Riallin's spears, all of them, and stab him.[62]

How much more confident and complex Jordan's vision became is also evident in a comparison between the early outlines and the finished product. In one of his first outlines for "Books Two Through Six" quoted above, Jordan includes an incomplete "List of Incidents" that will happen along the way.[63] Some, like Rand faking his own death at the end, survived more or less intact. Others shifted a great deal.

For example, Jordan thought that Rand would be "shipwrecked on the coast of a Blight" and find himself in a land broken into city-states, each ruled by Aes Sedai. "Given to a woman who is a daughter of one of the rulers and a general in her own right despite her youth," Rand would fall in love with her, and she with him. Eventually, he would be forced to use his power to fight off the Dark One in this place. To avoid being gentled by the Aes Sedai, he would leave, and the young woman would go with him, bringing with her an army that would help him take the Stone of Stair (i.e., the Stone of Tear).

In its final form in the books, the land in question became Seanchan, and what Jordan had imagined as a single plotline centered on Rand was broken up significantly: the patchwork of city-states ruled by Aes Sedai is what Luthair Paendrag Mondwin found when he arrived in the lands during the Hawkwing era—though by sail rather than shipwreck. In fact, Luthair's success in overtaking and unifying Seanchan gave him the nickname "the Hammer," which Jordan had brought over from his early thoughts on Rand. Other parts of the plot do connect to Rand himself, though differences abound. Rand doesn't go to Seanchan; instead, they invade the Westlands and arrive at his doorstep. And it's not the Seanchan who help Rand enter the Stone of Tear, it's the Aiel. Most importantly, it isn't Rand who falls in love with the young general who is also a ruler, it's *Mat*.

The evolution of this Seanchan plotline neatly illustrates another of the vital changes that the series underwent as Jordan wrote. Rather than focusing solely on the character of Rand, he had his secondary characters begin taking primary positions within books. As they did so, a single plotline grew into many, which was more realistic and more exciting. Jordan was also—paradoxical though it might seem—trying to *tighten* his narrative. Sending Rand to Seanchan by ship for a series of adventures and battles would have added an enormous amount of world-building. Realizing this, he decided to bring these encounters to the Westlands so that the story would move along faster and more efficiently. It would also introduce more chances to dive into the complicated politics of a land invaded—something he'd seen firsthand in Vietnam.

Simultaneously, Jordan was also letting go of many of the Arthurian plotlines that he'd originally envisioned. In the original concept, for instance, Rand's first ally after he accepted his status as the Dragon Reborn was to be "Morgase, who becomes his lover for a time. This makes Galad his bitter opponent, and sends Galad over to Sha'tan." Morgase, meanwhile, would "do a great deal of harm to people in the name of good." In the Arthurian legends, Morgause was Arthur's aunt. For a time she became Arthur's lover, thereby giving birth to the child who would ultimately kill him: Mordred. The Arthurian Galahad, meanwhile, was the son of Lancelot and the grail-bearer, Elaine of Corbenic. Jordan built off this foundation, but what he built was both simpler and more complicated. His final Galad was, in keeping with his Arthurian forebear, a good man; the idea of his going over to the Dark One was entirely abandoned. But, rather than being the child of Lan and Elayne (the Lancelot and Elaine analogues), he was the child of Rand's mother and her first husband, Taringail Damodred. After her death, Taringail married Morgase, making her something of an aunt-in-law. The child of this union was Elayne Trakand, and it was she—not her mother—with whom Rand fell in love. Instead, Morgase's initial lover was Thom Merrilin. Jordan *did* anticipate that Rand would also fall in love with Elayne, though, in an early glimpse into the triple-bonded relationship that his hero would ultimately fall into:

> Rand is taken prisoner by the Queen of the land where he was raised, Elyn's mother. The queen wants to kill him, but Elyn manages to get the sentence commuted. As a price for this, though, Elyn is forced to pronounce the alternate sentence. Rand is blinded by hot irons and turned loose to wander as a beggar. This is the lowest point for him, when he feels that everyone, even Elyn, has abandoned him. [NOTE: he will regain his sight later.][64]

In the final scope, of course, Elayne's mother would be Morgase, and no such imprisonment happened. Morgase truly did do much misguided harm in The Wheel of Time, but it was largely driven by the machinations of other evil forces. And while Rand *did* ultimately go blind in the books, it wasn't the result of a physical punishment. As for the idea that he would be a beggar for a time, one might imagine that

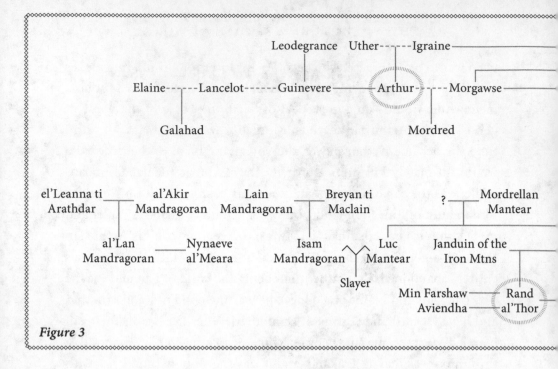

Figure 3

this is a reflection of his final moments at the end of the series, when he's wandering off alone—except that readers will know he had quite a few coins in his purse at that point, and that he was anticipating Elayne and the others joining him soon. By these kinds of changes Jordan tightened his narrative scope in terms of the kingdoms and personnel involved while, once again, entering into political spaces that fascinated him personally. How far in total he had shifted away from a mere rewriting of the Arthurian legends—while still relying upon them—can be seen by comparing the final version of the "family trees" surrounding Jordan's Rand al'Thor and Malory's King Arthur (see above).

As the mythic and legendary bracing diminished over time—particularly so with the secondary plotlines and characters—Jordan brought in more and more ideas of his own invention, along with a number of Easter eggs for watchful readers. Three Aes Sedai who play a key role in Mat's story line, for instance, are Teslyn, Edesina, and Joline. These names reflect the inventors and scientists Nikola Tesla (1856–1943), Thomas Alva Edison (1847–1931), and James Prescott Joule (1818–89), but the parallels have no apparent impact or purpose within the text beyond being something that, if noticed, might make the reader

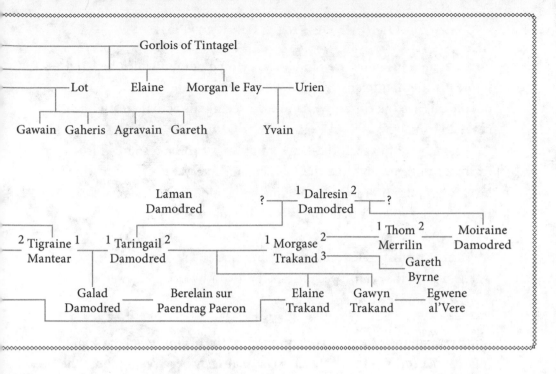

smile.[65] There are also, both in the later books by Jordan and in those cowritten with Sanderson, a high number of tuckerizations: names derived from fans, friends, or fellow authors.[66]

RAMBLING THROUGH TAIMANDRED

The full richness of The Wheel of Time, as we're seeing, resulted from the ways in which Jordan's characters were allowed to grow beyond their original models. Rand isn't *just* a King Arthur or any other source. He's himself, Rand al'Thor, and the central way in which Jordan shaped his character and his life events was unscripted: he never wrote from a strict outline. Instead, he wrote through a state of constant dialogue with his developing story. In this process, his preferred mode of creativity was brainstorming in what he called "ramblings": opening a fresh document, he would begin writing what he then knew about a character, sequence, or scene. Along the way, he would ask questions of himself, even raise objections against himself, all within a written stream of consciousness. Sometimes these ramblings would evolve into the solutions to problems. Other times they would serve only to solidify what the problems really were. Among his notes are ramblings, printed out, on which he hand-wrote his attempts to answer his own still-unanswered questions. These documents are the closest we can get to seeing his actual creative process laid bare.

As one might expect, these raw ramblings can be a source for unexpected information, like the moment in a very early one in which he changed, in mid-ramble, the name he would give to the region surrounding the village where The Wheel of Time would start:

> There is regular traffic among the four villages, but few people leave the district they call 'Tween Rivers (or Two Rivers?), and fewer still of those who leave come back again.[67]

This rambling process served him well at the beginning of the books. It lies at the core of much of what we have already been seeing about the development of The Wheel of Time. It's important to recognize, however, that this active creative process didn't remotely cease when the writing of the series began in earnest. Jordan's ramblings remained an integral part of his work until the end. And they sometimes made him change his mind or his plans.

To imagine that an author never changes their mind about their plots or characters—especially in a work as massively complex as The Wheel of Time—would be foolish. We've already seen an enormous amount of evidence for the ways in which Jordan was shifting his story over time, improving and refining. Another example of this—interesting both for its ramifications within the narrative and its importance to the fans—is the shifting identity of the character Demandred. It's a perfect microcosm of not just Jordan's ceaseless creative process, but also the kinds of problems it left Brandon and Team Jordan in the wake of his passing.

Demandred is one of the Forsaken. These thirteen figures were enormously powerful Aes Sedai from the Age of Legends who'd gone over into the service of the Dark One in return for promises of power and immortality. Their rebirth into Randland at the time of the story, hidden within the guises of other people, allowed them to work toward effecting the Dark One's victory over the Dragon Reborn—as well as their individual victories over each other as they endlessly vied to be the most beloved of their Great Lord. There's no question that the Forsaken played roles in the books that were every bit as important as those of the main characters.

And yet, even after completing *The Great Hunt* and preparing to work on the third book in the series, *The Dragon Reborn,* Jordan clearly hadn't settled on the names of the Forsaken. As he then had them, the list was this:

(1) Ishamael (who is called Ba'alzamon)

(2) Lanfear (who sometimes calls herself Selene, among other names.)

(3) Aginor: dead

(4) Balthamel: dead

(5) De'ath

(6) Moloc (one of the most vicious)

(7) Be'aldrid

(8) Maladour

(9) Malifecin

(10) Sha'rein

(11) Savintar

(12) Sammael

(13) Rahvin[68]

This is not, as readers know, a match to the names of the thirteen as they appear in the final books: Ishamael, Lanfear, Aginor, Balthamel, Demandred, Asmodean, Be'lal, Graendal, Moghedien, Semirhage, Mesaana, Sammael, and Rahvin.

Our first surprise, then, is that Demandred wasn't always Demandred. My guess is that he was originally the "De'ath" Forsaken. This change, though, wasn't one that had any effect on the readers, since it happened behind the scenes. "De'ath" doesn't make an appearance in the series.

More noticeable, though, is how Jordan's discovery method of writing meant that Demandred developed even *after* he appeared on the pages of his books.

That appearance happened in *Lord of Chaos,* the sixth book in The Wheel of Time, which was published in 1994. In the prologue of that book, the Forsaken Demandred goes to Shayol Ghul to answer the summons of the Dark One. There, the Dark One asks of him, "WOULD YOU UNLEASH THE BALEFIRE IN MY SERVICE, DEMANDRED?" When Demandred agrees that he'll follow orders, the Dark One tells him he will "HEAR WHO WILL DIE AND WHO LIVE"—news that prompts "tears of joy" to run down the Forsaken's face.[69] Then, at the end of the book, after the climactic Battle of Dumai's Wells, Demandred once again speaks with the Dark One:

> Demandred knelt in the Pit of Doom, and for once he did not care that Shaidar Haran watched his trembling with that eyeless, impassive gaze. "Have I not done well, Great Lord?"
>
> The Great Lord's laughter filled Demandred's head.[70]

One implication of this framing in *Lord of Chaos* was that the Battle of Dumai's Wells—in which the *saidin* power of the Black Tower was released in a devastating strike against the Shaido Aiel attacking Rand—was ultimately part of the Dark One's plan, orchestrated by Demandred. It was a victory for the Shadow, not the Light. More than that, it suggested to many readers that Mazrim Taim, the male channeler who led that devastating display of power, was none other than the disguised Forsaken himself. Popularly, this became known as the Taimandred Theory.

While appearing at DragonCon in 2005, a decade after the publication of *Lord of Chaos,* Jordan was asked if he was surprised by the Taimandred Theory, or if the clues leading to it were "a deliberate ruse to lead your readers astray?" He answered, "I was surprised . . . but I wasn't going to disabuse you of it for a while, I like to watch you squirm."[71] He was stating, quite clearly, something he'd expressed in other settings: Taimandred wasn't true.

If we rewind back to Jordan's own notes, however, we can see that at least at the time Jordan was writing *Lord of Chaos,* Taimandred *was* absolutely true.

It just didn't stay that way.

Such an enormous change is difficult for some readers to accept. Understandably, they are seeking consistency. But there's a fundamental disconnection between the truth of the series as a final, finished product and the truth of the author's ongoing creative process as they were written. This is especially so when that process, as Jordan's did, relies upon and responds to changing ideas and research.

So when Jordan was starting to write *Lord of Chaos,* he indeed *thought* Mazrim Taim was the Forsaken Demandred in disguise. He recorded as much in his private notes, in which he twice noted that "Taim/Demandred showed up" at Dumai's Wells.[72] He even underscored and put it in bold font when he was summing up the works of the Forsaken so far:

Demandred: Hated/feared/despised Lews Therin. Like Lanfear, he plays for larger stakes than most of the others, who are trying to stake out worldly kingdoms. HE WILL SHOW UP CLAIMING TO BE **MAZRIM TAIM**, TAKING ADVANTAGE OF RAND'S AMNESTY.[73]

More than this, Jordan is also clear that at this point in time he intended for Demandred to have been the one who'd killed his fellow Forsaken Asmodean in a surprising twist at the end of the previous book, *Fires of Heaven.* The mystery of that murder was a particular favorite of many readers, with "Who killed Asmodean?" being a rally cry for countless fan debates. As he was working on *Lord of Chaos,* he wrote of Nynaeve:

She does not know that Aginor (Osan'gar) and Balthamel (Aran'gar) were resurrected, the latter as a woman who is now masquerading as Halima, Delana's secretary/companion.

She knows that Moghedien was prisoner, of course. Until she is/ was informed by Egwene, Siuan or Leane, she thinks Moghedien is still a prisoner.

She does <u>not</u> know that Asmodean was a prisoner of Rand, nor, of course, that he was killed by Demandred.[74]

In both regards, Jordan changed his mind. Mazrim Taim, he ultimately decided, was a high-powered male channeler who'd been captured by Aes Sedai but freed by Demandred, who recruited him as a Darkfriend. And it was the Forsaken Graendal, not Demandred, who killed Asmodean.[75]

Precisely *when* he changed these things and *why* he did so is unclear. It may be that he felt fans had picked up on the Taim-Demandred connection too easily, and he altered it in an effort to keep them guessing. This would certainly be a flattering thing to think as a fan, though in truth it could just as well have been due to an entirely different reason of story, the result of some other rambling that wasn't handed down to us.

Sadly, we'll never know. Jordan shared a great deal with Harriet and the other members of Team Jordan, but he hardly told them everything. And all that was left in the notes that survived was this: as Jordan turned his eye toward book 12, he was pondering explanations of what balefire horror Demandred had committed at the order of the Dark One in *Lord of Chaos*.

Is balefire being used, perhaps in secret by Demandred at the DO's order, per LoC (?), thus causing the reality waves and ripples? It is a possibility, a partial posssibility [*sic*], but it would be hard to do in secret and still on a scale to cause those ripples. Unless done in Shara, say, or in Seanchan. Even if a city is balefired and vanishes, even after the actions of its inhabitants are canceled out and even effects caused by its existence during the time that has now been wiped out, people remember that it was there once even if they can't find any proof of it.[76]

The explanation for that *had* apparently been connected to Dumai's Wells somehow, but with Demandred and Taim separated that no longer worked. Jordan might have tried to wriggle out of the bind by suggesting that because Taim was following Demandred's orders, it could be said that they'd both "showed up" at the battle—even if only *one* had done so in person—but it doesn't seem he was interested in doing this. Instead, he was planning to ramble through it, to find another explanation.

So it fell to Brandon. Team Jordan had pulled aside this note that Jordan had made to himself, and it was Brandon who recognized in it the potential to solve two problems at a single stroke. Though Seanchan had already been a major part of the books and would have a significant role in the Last Battle, Shara had done nothing of the sort. But if Demandred had been doing the Dark One's bidding there since as far back as *Lord of Chaos*, the references in that book would once more make sense. At the same time, Demandred—now under the guise of a new character called Bao the Wyld, named for Jordan reader Bao Pham—would also be able to bring a Sharan army to the Last Battle. It was such an elegant solution that Brandon strongly suspects it's very much what Jordan would've done had he lived long enough to do so.[77]

SEQUELS AND PREQUELS

If it hasn't already been made clear, the amount of world-building that Jordan achieved—in his novels, of course, but also within the tens of thousands of pages of his notes—is breathtaking. The authorized *Wheel of Time Companion* made the contents of a wide swath of these background materials available to the fans, but despite its size it only scratched the surface of what Jordan had in his mind and intended one day to produce.

Jordan said publicly that he planned to write a trilogy of "outrigger" novels after completing the main sequence of The Wheel of Time. These would have been set five to ten years after the conclusion of The Wheel of Time and focused on Mat, Tuon, and the changes faced by Seanchan as a result of the events of the Last Battle. Unfortunately, Jordan's untimely death meant that little writing related to this story was ever produced. There was no complete outline. All that survives, in fact, are two tantalizing sentences. One depicts Mat lying in a cold gutter, the dice having failed him. The other sees Perrin on a boat, sailing to Seanchan to kill an old friend. Given such sparse information, any attempt to create a plot from such few details would owe more to another author's imagination than to Jordan's vision.

Jordan had also hoped to write another couple of prequels to stand alongside his successful *New Spring* novel. Here, the copious backstory materials that he had already composed make it far easier to reconstruct the story lines that he likely intended to write. One book would have focused on Tam. In many respects this would have been the story that Jordan had set out to write in the first place, so many years ago. It would have recounted the years before and during the Aiel War, in which Tam was thrust into the nightmare of a horrific conflict that culminated in a singular moment of grace: Tam finding Rand's dying mother on the slopes of Dragonmount during the Battle of Shining Walls and deciding to save her child—and thus the world. Another prequel novel he had planned to write would have revealed how Moiraine and Lan arrived in the Two Rivers just in time to rescue Rand and his friends from the assault of the Dark One. Between them, these books might also have weaved through the details of much that is only hinted at in the course of the published novels, but for which more information exists in the notes: from Gitara Moroso's prophecy to the creation of Slayer. As with the outrigger novels, however, Jordan's archived papers contain no complete sequences or outlines to know for certain.

That we never received Jordan's vision for these further stories is a loss—especially as it seems clear that he *had* a vision. Though he might ramble through points in the process of writing, Jordan nevertheless had an enormous continuity of story in his mind and in his notes. Countless details wouldn't appear in the course of The Wheel of Time, but he nevertheless knew them. He had worked them out. From his earliest scribbling of notes on King Arthur, he had built a dynamic world whose history stretched out for millennia.

In fact, one could argue that the background work for The Wheel of Time might well extend back to his very earliest writings as an author. His first novel, *Warrior of the Altaii*, was at last published in 2019. Readers examining it found a great many parallels between this first

Robert Jordan in Saigon, 1968. This picture, among others, is on permanent display in the Daniel Library of Jordan's alma mater, The Citadel. *Courtesy of the Rigney Estate*

Robert Jordan, photographed by Harriet during a trip to Wales in the late 1990s.
Courtesy of Harriet McDougal

"Father Storyteller Soldier Singer": Robert Jordan's grave as it appears today, in front of an Anglican church completed in 1719, outside Charleston, South Carolina.
Courtesy of Michael Livingston

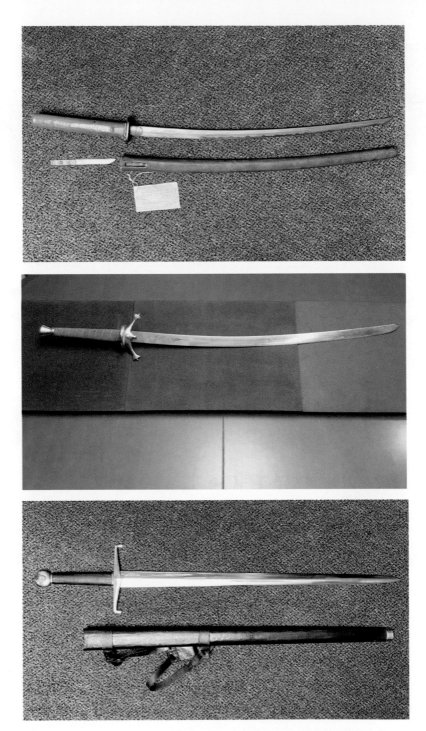

Top: Jordan's dragon-marked katana; middle: the heron-marked blade from Jordan's personal collection; bottom: a replica of the sword of the Black Prince. *Top: Courtesy of Michael Livingston; middle: Courtesy of the College of Charleston Special Collections; bottom: Courtesy of Michael Livingston*

Completed in 2004, Padgett-Thomas Barracks at The Citadel is a nearly exact external copy of the barracks that had stood there since 1922: Jordan's original White Tower and a well-recognized symbol for his alma mater. *Courtesy of Michael Livingston*

FORESTOR

CHARYOT : Morgan le Fay's stronghold

merlin : Amyrlen ←

Duke of Sintagail :

Igraine : Tigraine

Uther :

Arthur : Rhys al'Shor

Gwynevere : Gawin d'Veer

× Morgan le Fay → Emorgaine ←

(?) King Lot : (?) Lot

Margawse : Morgase

Gawain (?) Gwayne

Gareth : (?) Garth

J ordan's early handwritten notes connecting King Arthur to The Wheel of Time.
Courtesy of the College of Charleston Special Collections

Chapter I

The Dark Rider

The west wind flailed out of the Mountains of Mist, ~~a wind-born among~~
~~searing crags whose snow-capped peaks were ever-hidden by the clouds that named~~
~~them.~~ Across the Sand Hills ~~the wind sped~~ and into the ancient, tangled forest
of the Westwood. Along with grit from the hills it bore an icy chill as if it
would rather carry snow, for all that spring should have come to the Two Rivers
a good month since.

Gusts plastered Rand al'Thor's earth-colored cloak to his back, then
whipped it about his long shanks. He wished his coat were heavier, or that he
had worn two shirts underneath. He wished he could pull his thick, wool cloak
closer, too, but he had to keep his arms free for the bow he carried with an
arrow nocked and ready. The quiver of arrows slung on his shoulder did nothing
to help either. His gray eyes searched the all but leafless wood without pause
as he walked warily down the rock-strewn track called the Quarry Road. No one
knew why it was named so, ~~but many places in the Two Rivers had names so old~~
~~that no one remembered from where they came. Stories were sometimes told at~~
~~night in front of fireplaces~~ ~~with them,~~ ~~but there were ten stories~~
~~for every name, and it was seldom two of them agreed on much beyond the name.~~
~~itself.~~

Occasionally Rand glanced at his father over the back of the shaggy brown

The first page of the "Test Manuscript" for *The Eye of the World*. The edits are in Jordan's hand. *Courtesy of the College of Charleston Special Collections*

Perhaps five hundred years old, the Angel Oak on Johns Island, South Carolina, is over sixty-six feet in height, with 17,200 square feet of shade beneath its long limbs. Little wonder it inspired Jordan's *Avendesora*! *Courtesy of Michael Livingston*

Jordan fantasy and the eventual Wheel of Time. Geographically, for instance, the earlier world of *Altaii* is in many respects a mirror image of the later Westlands, from the placement of rivers to the great mountain range along one edge. In *Altaii,* those mountains are the Backbone of the World; in The Wheel of Time, they are the Spine of the World. The earlier barren and dry land of the Plain at the feet of those mountains, with its nomadic warrior people called the Altaii, becomes in The Wheel of Time a similar land on the other side of the Spine, where the Aiel live in the Aiel Waste. Crossing that land is a great gash in the landscape: in *Altaii,* it's the Great Ravine; in The Wheel of Time, it's the Great Rift. Farther into the continent depicted in *Altaii,* rising high above a diagonal range of hills, is a great mountain called the Heights of Tybal; in the Westlands, this is Dragonmount.

Wulfgar is unquestionably a precursor to Lan in terms of his stoic warrior mentality, but he's likewise a precursor to Rand in the ways he begins to bring men into the circle of typically female magic within the world. Being of the Altaii, he is akin to an Aiel commander—perhaps like Rand's biological father, Janduin, had we met him in Jordan's planned prequel novels—though the Altaii, unlike the Aiel, are a remarkable cavalry force. Mayra is a precursor to Nynaeve. The Sisters of Wisdom are a precursor to the Aes Sedai and the Wise Ones. Their oath-binding objects are a precursor to the Oath Rod. The slave-based culture of the Lantans is a precursor to the slave-based culture of the Seanchan. Wulfgar interacts with a queen named Elana in *Altaii,* and one of Rand's three loves is the eventual queen Elayne. In fact, in the original typescripts of *Altaii,* Wulfgar is likewise with multiple women at the end of his story, though under highly different circumstances.[78]

It's clear that, as he worked on The Wheel of Time, Jordan was in some sense reworking themes and ideas that he'd first sketched out in *Warrior of the Altaii.* Perhaps the most fascinating question in this regard is what drew him to these specific themes and images. Why was he captivated by the image of a great gash cutting through a barren landscape, for instance? Was it a fascination with the Grand Canyon? Was it something he'd seen from the helicopter door in Vietnam? For much of it, we simply don't know.

We can guess, though, at why Wulfgar was for a time connected to multiple women, and Rand very certainly was in the final product. Graves' *White Goddess* had meshed perfectly with Jordan's idea of cyclical time, myth, and legend. More than that, it had neatly fit with how he wanted to show that the madness of men could only be made sane through the balance of women. The end result of his protagonists' heroic journeys would be the formal establishment of that balance, the establishment of a more properly ordered society. Rand's three loves— Aviendha, Elayne, and Min—are nothing less than the triple goddess combined with Arthurian myth and made incarnate in The Wheel of Time. As Jordan wrote in his early notes: "THE THREE WOMEN OF THE STORY WILL BE PERCEIVED NOT ONLY AS THE THREE WHO TOOK ARTHUR TO AVALON, BUT ALSO AS THE ORIGIN OF THE TRIPLE-GODDESS PERSONIFIED AS MAIDEN, NYMPH AND HAG."[79] As ever, Jordan was here looking forward and back: using myths and legends while also creating the very substance from which those myths and legends could be built.

The Wheel of Time is a generational work. Some three decades separate its first pages from its last pages. It took two authors to complete, with the help of an extraordinary team of assistants. It was, in the end, far more than what it was intended to be. But even as it stretched out and grew more intricate than its creator had foreseen, The Wheel of Time never lost sight of Jordan's central vision. David Aiken, in a 1999 biography of the man, summed it up well:

In complex plots, Jordan creates characters who must make one difficult decision after another. They have to ask what is the right thing to do in situations where the consequences are unforeseeable. What seems good may cause great harm. What is perceived as helpful may actually be destructive. Time and again Jordan's characters must learn to deal with the ambiguities of life by doing their best in situations with imponderable outcomes: "If you have done good and the result is that tens of thousands of people starve to death, did you really do good? If you did what was right and the result is that hundreds of thousands of people must flee from their homes with nothing but what they have on their backs, was what you did really right?"[80]

THE REAL WORLD
IN THE
WHEEL OF TIME

What follows is a glossary to some of the people, places, and things that influenced elements of Jordan's Wheel of Time. Entries are listed here by Randland terminology, and boldface is used to indicate additional terms that have entries in the glossary. So if you want to know the myths from which **Rand al'Thor** was built, look him up under that name. But if you want to know all the *other* places (partial spoiler alert!) where Jordan used the myths of King Arthur, you will need to look Arthur up in the general index at the end of the book.

As I said at the outset, this book isn't the place to explain the in-world workings and histories of The Wheel of Time. All that and so much more can be found in the wonderful *Wheel of Time Companion*. The purpose here is only to identify some of the known sources that Jordan used in creating it. At times this process of identification will nevertheless require reference to **Randland** histories; please know once again that this text is therefore **Full Spoilers** to all the published materials of The Wheel of Time. I make no effort here to hide the twists and turns of characters and events. This is everything exposed, from **Lews Therin** to the **Last Battle** and back again.

JORDAN'S METHODS

Jordan followed a number of procedures for the creation of story and name ideas. He was, as we have seen, fond of brainstorming through ideas, and so he kept many lists of potential threads and characters. Some were simply a name he'd seen on a map or a word he'd come across in one language or another and had grabbed for no more identifiable reason than that he was apparently fond of how it looked and sounded. Most of these instances have not been recorded here since they do not add substantially to any insight into the books. Many others, however, were picked up through his voracious reading across a wide variety of literary genres and nonfiction subjects. These could slip their way into his Wheel of Time either directly or indirectly as they percolated through his imagination.

When Jordan consciously chose to incorporate references to history and myth, he very often did so by taking names as they're known today and "breaking" them by spelling them wrong, or otherwise veiling them in accordance with the fact that languages change in time, and memories fade even faster. The idea was that these echoes could be at least theoretically defended on historical linguistic terms. Jordan wasn't trying to hide his sources, in other words. His obfuscations weren't meant to throw readers off the scent. To the contrary, they were simply the result of his dedication to the central concept of time and the passing of ages within his fictional world.

In the last chapter we saw the work of this "reverse engineering" that he was engaged in, going all the way back to his earliest handwritten notes on Malory's *Morte d'Arthur*. This process was ongoing. At an early point, for instance, he was taking stock of Chiron, the centaur who taught many of the heroes of Greek mythology. In the middle of this, he made a parenthetical note to himself on how he might incorporate this figure into The Wheel of Time: "Chei as a title, combined with a name beginning with Ron."[1] Though this particular instance did not work its way into the final books, it's an excellent hint of what follows in the guide below. Again and again we will see Jordan following this kind of methodology.[2] Indeed, reverse engineering his reverse engineering, as it were, has been one of the foremost means of unlocking this level of his text.

To make this possible, I have spent years trying to get as close to Jordan's mind as I can. I've read his books (those published and those not), measured the contents of his library, combed the thousands of pages of notes he left behind. I've talked to his friends. I've tested the patience of Team Jordan—the indefatigable Harriet, Maria, Alan, and Brandon—to be sure that what I say here is as confirmed as it can be.

But I'm not Jordan. I've delved deep enough into his mind and his methods to know that in the end a guide like this cannot be exhaustive. Nearly every entry here should be understood to carry the disclaimer "and more": few things in The Wheel of Time are "just" a rewriting of something from myth or history. Besides this, any attempt to note every parallel Jordan used in composing just the single character of Rand and everything he ever said or did would be a book unto itself. To do such work for the whole of the series would create a book, as Jordan once suggested he'd write, that would need a wheelbarrow. For reasons of space, therefore, I have constrained the entries below to the information most likely to be interesting to the reader trying to understand the origins of The Wheel of Time. And, because this is an authorized book, I have also constrained my write-ups to those matters in which we have the highest degree of confidence.

So this book isn't the end of this work. It's a foundation upon which astute readers can build, working to find more in The Wheel of Time— much more—than I've put in these pages.

I hope you'll be one of them.

A

Abdel Omerna. Abdel (more frequently Abdul) means "servant" in Arabic, and his surname seems to derive from *omertà,* the Mafia code of silence (itself derived from the word for "humility"). The name fits **Pedron Niall**'s decoy spymaster well: he was obedient to what he believed to be his duty to the **Whitecloak** "family," even to the point of murdering Niall.

Abell Cauthon. The father of Matrim Cauthon, Abell is a farmer and horse trader. His name derives not from the biblical story of Cain and Abel (where Cain was the farmer who murdered his brother Abel the shepherd) but from Sir Ebel, a knight in Malory who plays a role in the story of Sir Palamides. On his surname, see **Matrim Cauthon**.

a'dam. This word for the *ter'angreal* that was used among the **Seanchan** to control a channeler— originally made up of a silver bracelet on the controller (*sul'dam*) and a collar on the one controlled (*damane*)—appears to be derived not from the  name Adam, but from the phrase "a domme," which refers to a dominant woman within certain BDSM relationships. Similarly, the word *sul'dam* is meant to echo both the phrase "sole domme" (that is, a single dominant) and the word *sultan* (meaning "rulership"). The *damane,* by extension, comes from the word *domain,* as those who are controlled in this way are considered to be owned. A key difference between the slavery systems of the Seanchan and the real-world BDSM relationships whose terminology Jordan echoes here is that the latter are based entirely on the willing and informed consent of individuals. Seanchan enslavement, on the other hand, depends on forced or socially coerced brainwashing that erases the individual, a disturbing practice that is intended to recall the very real horrors of chattel slavery in America. Most particularly, it reflects upon the role of human enslavement in the history of Charleston, South Carolina, whose old slave markets were a mere twenty-minute walk from Jordan's home.

Adan. A direct ancestor of **Rand al'Thor**, Adan suffered numerous family tragedies and was witness to the splintering off of the **Tuatha'an** from the **Aiel**. In his continued devotion to protect the relics of the **Aes Sedai** despite suffering assault and attack, Adan derives from Saint Aidan (ca. 590–651), who founded Lindisfarne Priory and was instrumental in converting much of Northumbria to Christianity.

Aelfinn. See **Eelfinn**.

Aemon al Caar al Thorin. Aemon gives his name to **Emond's Field**. His first name, Aemon, ultimately derives from Old English *Eadmund*, meaning "wealth-protector," which is a fitting name for the famed last king of the vanished realm of **Manetheren**. His grandfather's name, Thorin, is a nod to Tolkien's Thorin Oakenshield, a name that was itself taken from the Dvergatal ("Catalogue of Dwarves") in the Old Norse Eddic poem *Völuspá*. Interestingly, in Jordan's original notes, his name was Morgalen.[1]

Aes Sedai. The *aos sí* of Irish mythology are faerie from the Otherworld: fierce, frightening, and strange. Among the times when the *aos sí* were thought likely to appear and cause mischief in communities was Beltane (see **Beltine**). One of the many alternative spellings for these mysterious beings in Old Irish is *aes sídhe*,  which is similarly pronounced; the naming of Jordan's Aes Sedai is the result of mispronouncing this older form using traditional English letter sounds. His Aes Sedai bring the magical otherworldliness of the Irish *aos sí* together within a structure that he likened to the medieval convents of the Catholic Church (see **Amyrlin Seat**).

Age of Legends. Another name for the Second Age to the current turning of the Wheel of Time. The Age of Legends began as a seemingly utopian period in human history in which men and women worked the **One Power** in harmony and for the common good. It has roots in both Golden Age myths of an idyllic past and science fiction stories of a technologically superior future. Tracked against Hesiod's Five Ages of Man, the Second Age would have been the Silver Age of Demigods, with the present age of the story the Bronze Age of humanity.

Agelmar Jagad. The name of Agelmar, the Lord of Fal Dara, comes from a character in Robert Holdstock's *Mythago Wood*, a 1984 novel (World Fantasy Award for Best Novel in 1985) that, like The Wheel of Time, depicts figures from myth recurring in various forms. As for Agelmar's surname in The Wheel of Time, Jagad derives from the word *jagged*, fitting for a man described as having a hard face.

Aginor. Originally named **Ishar Morrad Chuain**, he became the **Forsaken** Aginor and created the **Trollocs** and many other creatures of the Dark One. Jordan took his Forsaken name from the Greek mythological figure of Agenor, the king of Tyre. In Graves' *White Goddess* (231–32), Jordan would have found the theory that Agenor, also known as Chnas, represented invasions into the Mediterranean basin that pushed aside the older form of goddess worship and took centuries to repel;[2] the Forsaken's destructive Shadowspawn echo just this. After his destruction at the **Eye of the World**, Aginor was reincarnated by the Dark One as **Osan'gar**.

Agni Neres. Agni's name is shared by the Hindu god of fire (Graves' *White Goddess*, 294) and Nereus, the Old Man of the Sea in Greek mythology: a suitable match for the irritable captain of the riverboat *Riverserpent*—and a smuggler on the side.

Ahf'frait. The name of this band of **Trollocs** echoes the word *ifrit*, a demon in Islamic mythology. See **Trolloc Bands**.

Aiel. The idea of people living in a harsh desert landscape beside a great chain of mountains is one that came to Jordan early: *Altaii* has a similar concept, and the Aiel are present in some of the earliest Wheel of Time notes: "They are infantry, in many ways like a cross between the Apache and the Zulu, with touches of Cheyenne. Physically, most are tall, with blonde or reddish hair and blue or blue-gray eyes most common."[3] To this he added elements of the culture of the Bedouins and the Irish—the latter, he said, at least initially intended as a joking comment against the tendency of novelists to all have the same kind of desert people (see **Tuatha'an**). Indeed, it's nevertheless been commented upon that Jordan's Aiel are strikingly similar to the Fremen from Frank Herbert's *Dune* (1965). That similarity, however, is almost entirely the result of Herbert and Jordan using the same source materials of the real world: in particular, the ancient Israelites who wandered in the desert while awaiting their entry into what they believed was their Promised Land. In this respect, **Rand al'Thor** plays a role akin to both Moses and, at least within Christian mythology, Jesus (as the Messiah who both splits and saves the Jews). Other notable Jewish parallels include the **Aiel Tribes** and, somewhat obviously, their name: Aiel derives from *Israel*. Their connections to Native Americans (particularly Plains Indians) should not be forgotten, however: from their rituals to their clan names, Jordan made frequent recourse to them. On their weapons, which come from the Zulu, see *darei*.

Aiel Tribes. There are twelve clans of the Aiel: Black Eyes (Seia Doon), Brothers of the Eagle (Far Aldazar Din), Dawn Runners (Rahien Sorei), Knife Hands (Sovin Nai), Maidens of the Spear (Far Dareis Mai), Mountain Dancers (Hama N'dore), Night Spears (Cor Darei), Red Shields (Aethan Dor), Stone Dogs (Shae'en M'taal), Thunder Walkers (Sha'mad Conde), True Bloods (Tain Shari), and Water Seekers (Duadhe Mahdi'in). These parallel the twelve tribes of the ancient Israelites after the tribe of Joseph split into the tribes of Manasseh and Ephraim. At that point, twelve of the now thirteen tribes were given part of the Holy Land; the one omitted was the tribe of Levi, whose duty it was to administer the Temple in Jerusalem. The Tribe of Levi thus has its parallel in the extinct clan of the Jenn Aiel, whose duty was to administer the city of **Rhuidean**. *Their* name, as it happens, derived from the Jenn-Air stove in Jordan's kitchen.

Ailil Riatin. Though she's a noblewoman, Ailil echoes a king, Ailill, whose name Jordan found in Graves' *White Goddess* (214). The Irish myth of the *Táin* tells the story of a destructive war against Ulster led by Queen Medb and King Ailill of Connacht. That war, like the competition between noble houses in which Riatin takes part, has tragically petty origins. As for her surname, it echoes the senseless destruction of *rioting*.

Ailron Rovere Lukan. Jordan's early notes contain copious discussions of trees and their symbolisms, gleaned from Graves' *White Goddess* and other sources. One of these trees was the alder, which grows "by riversides";[4] the Old English form of *alder* is the source of the name *Ailron*. As for the rest of the king's name, his inability to rule his own land (**Pedron Niall** ruled **Amadicia** in all but name) left him metaphorically *roving,* and the crushing defeat he suffered against the **Seanchan** had a parallel in the historical Battle of Pharsalus in 48 BC, where Caesar crushed Pompey the Great and ended the civil war. The most famous account of that event, the *Pharsalia,* was written by the Roman poet Lucan (AD 39–65), who ran afoul of Nero and was forced to commit suicide.

Ajah. The idea of the Ajah is rooted in the religious orders of the medieval Church that undergird much of the **Aes Sedai**: these are internal, self-organized groups built around a specific set of principles within the larger hierarchy under the direction of the Pope (or the **Amyrlin Seat**). Historically, these religious orders were identifiable by the colors of their robes: Franciscan monks wore brown, Dominicans wore white, Benedictines wore black, and so forth. Unlike religious orders whose hierarchies are clear to outsiders, however, the authority of Aes Sedai within their Ajah were only internally known. Jordan compared this to his own experiences with the practices of Freemasonry, "where the town banker or mayor might hold an insignificant office or none at all, while a mechanic or the banker's chauffeur might be grand master."[5]

Alanna Mosvani. Her name deriving from both the Irish word for "child" and the Gaelic word for "beauty," Alanna is both beautiful and naive. Her surname may have been lifted from the word *Movanic,* an alternative name for the third, spiritual plane of existence in theosophy.

Al'ghol. The name of this band of **Trollocs** echoes the word *ghoul*. See **Trolloc Bands**.

Alise Tenjile. Her surname appears to be derived from the Arabic word for "sending down"—i.e., as revelation is sent down from God.

Alivia. Olive trees take a prominent place in the mythologies of the Mediterranean: in Greek and Roman mythology, the olive branch was a symbol of both peace and victory. Christian writers read this same symbolism into Genesis 8:11, where a dove returning an olive branch to Noah's Ark signified that the chaos of the Great Flood was over. The olive branch thereby came to represent the peace brought by the Holy Spirit through baptism as a Christian. Her most essential role in The Wheel of Time was to bring peace to **Rand al'Thor** by helping him pass through the "baptism" of his death and his rebirth as a man with a clean slate on his life.

Alliandre Maritha Kigarin. A queen of **Ghealdan**. Her first two names derive from *Alexander* and the Aramaic word for "lady" or "mistress." Kigarin appears to have been adopted from the Welsh community of Cilgerran, whose prominent castle is believed by some to be the one from which Owain of Powys brought destruction on his family by abducting Nest in 1109—an event often likened to Paris' taking of Helen that precipitated the Trojan War.

Almen Bunt. An older farmer caught up in the events of The Wheel of Time—including the need to lay down his tools to participate in the Last Battle—Almen represents "all men," a figure like the eponymous protagonist of the famous fifteenth-century play *Everyman*.

Almurat Mor. The name of Almurat, a determined **Seanchan** Seeker for Truth, derives from Arabic *murad*, meaning "will," while his surname derives from the word *Moor*, used by medieval Europeans to refer to the Muslims of the Iberian Peninsula and northern Africa.

Alric. Like many men in his role, **Siuan Sanche**'s Warder has a name associated with military history. In this case, it comes from Alaric the Visigoth, who famously sacked Rome in 410.

Alsalam Saeed Almadar. The king of **Arad Doman**; his name derives from the Arabic words for "peace" and "happiness," while his surname (and home) comes from the Arabic word for "circuit." More than this, he echoes biblical Absalom (2 Samuel), who rebelled against the rule of his father King David and sent his kingdom into a chaos of civil war. Alsalam's disappearance from his kingdom likewise brought chaos to Arad Doman.

Alsbet Luhhan. Her first name is no doubt a nod to the memory of **Elsbet** in **Randland**. As for her surname, see her husband, **Haral Luhhan**.

Altara. A kingdom of weak bonds between highly autonomous city-states, populated by olive-skinned lovers of cheese and seafood, Altara reflects Italy, with its capital city of Ebou Dar combining aspects of Venice (its canals, festivals, and reputation for lacework) and Rome (a city built on the ruins of another). Its name appears to derive from the small town of Altare, Italy, which is near Genoa, another one of the centers of power in the history of the region.

Aludra Nendenhald. As an **Illuminator** who could make fireworks in the night sky, Aludra fittingly shares the Arabic name (meaning "the maiden") long given to a double star in the constellation Canis Major. Her surname alludes to Thomas Mendenhall, an ensign aboard the brig *Nancy* in June 1776, who on the orders of his captain created an American flag that was raised up her mast in place of the British one while in port at St. Thomas: the first flying of the American flag in a foreign port. Just weeks later, hauling gunpowder and chased by British warships, the *Nancy* was run aground at Turtle Gut Inlet, near the mouth of Delaware Bay. The Americans resourcefully removed 265 of the 286 kegs of precious explosive in her hold, then improvised a long fuse to the rest, using the ship's sail. When the last sailor off the ship lowered the American flag before he fled, British forces declared victory and hastily boarded. They were killed when the remaining kegs ignited in an explosion felt for miles.

Alviarin Freidhen. Her name derives from Latin *alvearium*, meaning a "beehive"; chosen by **Ishamael** to be head of the Black Ajah, she was indeed the center of a buzzing nest of dangerous bees. Her surname derives from the German *Frieden*, meaning "peace," which appeared frequently in German propaganda as the end goal of Hitler's Nazi regime.

Alys. A favorite alias of **Moiraine Damodred**. Jordan found this name in *The White Goddess* (247), where Graves argues that this goddess name has connections to apples and, in turn, to Avalon—the mythical island with connections to **Tar Valon** and **Rand al'Thor** (i.e., King Arthur).

Amadicia. With its laws against channeling, its unofficial rule by the quasi-theocratic **Whitecloaks**, and its fashions, Amadicia reflects the early communities of America—including those of the Puritans and their descendants—but Jordan no doubt had an eye toward the Crusader States of the Middle Ages, as well. As for its name, it probably derives from *Amadís de Gaula,* a popular chivalric romance from late-medieval Spain. The story represents an ideal knight of the time and was extremely influential among conquistadores—the sort of thing that would likely appeal to Whitecloaks.

Amaresu. The female champion of the Light—a counterpart to the Dragon—she wields the Sword of the Sun as one of the **Heroes of the Horn**. Jordan based her on Amaterasu-Omikami, the goddess of the sun in Japanese mythology.

Amayar. Hindu belief suggests that this world is not as it appears to be, that what we see is *Maya* (often translated to mean "illusion"). In The Wheel of Time, the Amayar similarly believe that the world in which they live is "Illusion." When Rand destroyed the **Choedan Kal** on their island of **Tremalking**, the Amayar understood this as an indication that the "end of the Illusion" had come and so committed mass suicide. Though there are many religiously motivated suicides in history, Jordan was most probably thinking of the Peoples Temple in Jonestown, Guyana, where more than 900 followers of Jim Jones killed themselves and their children.

Amyrlin Seat. The **Aes Sedai** first came into being under the direction of **Tamyrlin**, the first person to learn how to channel the **One Power**. As they organized themselves, their leader took Tamyrlin's name as a title. The identification of this authority with a seat parallels the practice of the Catholic Church: the seat of a bishopric is so named because the bishop has a chair (Latin: *cathedra*) within its cathedral. Above this, the Pope oversees the whole of the Catholic Church from the Chair of St. Peter. A similar practice exists for Jordan's own Anglican faith, but it was the connection to Catholic practice that he highlighted in his early notes: "People speak of the Amyrlin Seat as the Catholic Church might speak of donning the Shoes of the Fisherman or ascending to the Holy See of Rome."[6] The split in the Tower during the series, which results in competing Amyrlins, parallels the Western Schism (1378–1415), during which time rival Popes ruled from Rome and Avignon, both claiming supremacy over the Church. As for the name Amyrlin, Jordan derived it from Merlin, with an original spelling of *Amyrlen*. The idea, it seems, was to use Merlin as a title: the leader of the Aes Sedai was "a Merlin," Amyrlin.

Anath Dorje. An alias of **Semirhage**, her first name recalls the Semitic war goddess Anat (often spelled *Anath*), whom Graves associated with Athena in *The White Goddess* (362). Her surname refers to a ritual weapon (more commonly called a *vajra*) that represents both a diamond and a thunderbolt—an indestructible object and an irresistible force, respectively.

Andor. This is the original name of Númenor, according to Tolkien's *Silmarillion,* where it may derive from biblical Endor. Jordan might also have condensed it from the name of the small country of Andorra in the Pyrenees. In any case, Andor in The Wheel of Time undoubtedly represents England. In particular, especially within the initial books, it represents a thinly veiled echo of the realm of King Arthur, with its capital at Camelot (Andor's **Caemlyn**), updated to the Elizabethan era.

angreal. See *sa'angreal*.

Anla. *Chicago Sun-Times* columnist Ruth Crowley created the pen name "Ann Landers" for an advice column beginning in 1943. From 1955 to 2002 the increasingly popular "Ask Ann Landers" column continued under the authorship of Esther Lederer, and the pseudonym became synonymous with wise counsel. See **Elsbet**.

Annoura Larisen. In Malory, Annowre is a wicked enchantress who attempts to seduce King Arthur by magical means. When this fails, she attempts to kill him in the Perilous Forest but is foiled by Nimue and Tristram. King Arthur beheads her as she tries to flee. Annoura is hardly so perilous in The Wheel of Time.

Aptarigine Cycle. This cycle of stories involving the generations of a family calls to mind Jordan's own *Fallon Blood* series of books.

Arad Doman. The country of Arad Doman, with its capital of Bandar Eban, is highly influenced by the culture of Arab domains, such as Iran, in which the city of Bandar Ebbas is found. The name quite literally comes from the English *arid domain*. Bandar Eban's Terhana Library, for instance, echoes Iran's capital, Tehran, and a great many Domani names are derived from Arabic. That said, it should be noted that Arad Doman is a false representation: as one example, its reputation for seductive women in diaphanous clothing owes far more to European male fantasies of the harem than the reality experienced by women in these lands.

Arafel. One of the Borderland nations, Arafel gets its name from Amrafel, the king of Shinar in Genesis 14:1. In culture, it has some echoes of the Steppe, but its capital of **Shol Arbela** almost certainly gets its name from the Persian city of Arbela. (See also **Shienar**.)

Aram. There are several people with the name Aram in myth and legend. In several medieval Arthurian texts (but not Malory), Aram is one of Arthur's most diplomatic knights. In the Bible, Aram is the son of Shem taken to be the ancestor of the Aramean people of Mesopotamia. When it comes to Jordan's source, more probable than any of these is Padan Aram, a land repeatedly mentioned in Genesis. According to the fourth-century Jewish midrashic interpretation of Rabbi Isaac, the region was populated with deceitful wicked-doers. Unfortunately, this fits with the arc of the once-gentle **Tuatha'an** all too well. (See also **Padan Fain**.)

Aran'gar. After **Balthamel** and **Aginor** were killed at the **Eye of the World**, the Dark One resurrected them both. The soul of **Balthamel** was put into a woman's body and he was given the name Aran'gar. This appears at first glance to echo *anger*, and many readers have thereby assumed that the change of Balthamel's physical gender—while leaving intact his psychological identity and even his connection to the male half of the **One Power**—reflects the Dark One's anger at his failure to defeat the **Dragon Reborn**. The idea that a character forced to live a transgender life would be serving a punishment has upset many readers, though it should be noted that the real difficulty for the **Forsaken** in this instance derives from the fact that he knew and lived a completely cisgendered existence before the change.

In any event, it seems unlikely that the Dark One intended this as a punishment. No similar act is taken against Aginor after his identical failure, after all: he is resurrected as a man named **Osan'gar**. The Dark One changed Balthamel's physical gender not to torture him but because that change could be made useful: Aran'gar was able to infiltrate many places as a woman that he could not have accessed as a man.

Put simply, Aran'gar doesn't come from *anger*. It seems instead that the previously womanizing Balthamel—originally a historian named **Eval Ramman**, who specialized in lost, distant cultures—gets his new name from *Ananga Ranga*, the title of a book written in India in the fifteenth or sixteenth century. A sex manual in the mode of the more famous *Kama Sutra*, this book focuses on the need for people to attend to the sexual pleasures of their partners in order to achieve harmony in their relationships. Though the text is aimed at monogamous, heterosexual relationships, Balthamel adapts to his own situation by learning about sexual pleasure from both sides across a wide variety of partners.

Beyond this, as was often the case, Jordan chose a spelling that would capture still more meaning. Aran'gar and Osan'gar are said to be the names of twin daggers in the Old Tongue: the word *gār* means "spear" in Old English.

Artur Hawkwing. King Arthur is such an iconic figure in myth and legend—not to mention in fantasy literature—that Jordan opted to split him into several characters (see, e.g., **Rand al'Thor**). In the most popular stories of King Arthur, he was the son of the High King, Uther Pendragon, and he and his knights were engaged in various quests, including the one to find the Holy Grail (Old French *Sang-real;* see **sa'angreal**). Connections to this identity are already made clear in Hawkwing's full name of Artur Paendrag Tanreall. Jordan's change from Pendragon to Paendrag allows him to also parallel the character to the patron saint of Ireland, Patrick (Irish *Pádraig*). Other sources for this character include both Alexander the Great and Charlemagne. See **Heroes of the Horn**.

Artur Paendrag Tanreall. See **Artur Hawkwing**.

Aryth Ocean. In one of his early brainstorming name lists, Jordan left an unanswered query to himself: "Aryth is OT? NT?"[7] The categorizing of words as being Old Tongue or New Tongue does not yet appear to have been in place—and, in any case, the word *aryth* doesn't appear in his later glossary of the Old Tongue—so it seems more likely that Jordan was here using the standard abbreviations for the Old Testament and New Testament of the Bible. More specifically, he was likely remembering the fact that in the Old Testament story of the Exodus, the Israelites cross what is called in Hebrew the "Sea of Reeds." The Greek Septuagint translated this as "ἐρυθρά θάλασσα," Erythrà Thálassa, meaning "Red Sea," which was subsequently followed (and popularized in English) by the King James Version of the Bible. At least in his original vision, therefore, it appears that Jordan's concept of **Rand al'Thor** needing to cross the Aryth to **Seanchan** and back was seen as an echo of the Israelites' time in Egypt and their exodus from it under the leadership of Moses.

Asha'man. This is one of the more remarkably layered word constructions Jordan achieved. At its core, the word splices *Asha* and *man*—the former a fundamental concept in Zoroastrian theology, roughly translated as "natural truth." Combined, however, Asha'man echoes Ahriman, the *destructive* spiritual force of evil in Zoroastrianism. At the same time, the word also called to mind ash trees, which appear frequently in Graves' *White Goddess,* with Jordan noting that "the Three Norns of Sandinavian [*sic*] legend, the Triple Goddess, dispensced [*sic*] justice under an ash."[8] The Asha'man, then, were meant to dispense the justice of a natural truth—but were perverted to do evil.

Ashandarei. The name that **Birgitte Silverbow** gave to **Matrim Cauthon**'s magical, glaive-like weapon appears to combine the Spanish *ascenderé*, meaning "I will ascend," with *assegai*, the name given to the light spears utilized by the Zulu before they adopted the use of gunpowder weapons. See *darei*.

Asmodean. This **Forsaken** was named for the demonic figure of Asmodeus, who appears in the deuterocanonical book of Tobit and came to represent a threatening figure of unbridled lust. His original name was **Joar Addam Nessosin**.

Atha'an Miere. Like the land-roving **Tuatha'an**, the sea-roving Atha'an Miere were derived from the Tuatha Dé Danann of Irish mythology. In *The White Goddess*, Graves speculates that these beings of the Otherworld were originally immigrants driven out of Greece. Furthermore, he suggests that they were exiled in two waves: one by land and a later one by sea.[9] The Old English word for the sea is *mere*. See also **Sea Folk**.

Avar Hachami. A Warder; his surname comes from Hachiman, the Shinto god of archery and war. His given name echoes the Avars, a people of the Caucasus.

Avendesora. The last known **chora tree**, it grows in **Rhuidean**. The story of **Ghoetam** associates the tree with Buddha and the Bodhi Tree, while its attribution as the "Tree of Life" associates it with Yggdrasil in Norse mythology and the Edenic Tree of Life in Judeo-Christian mythologies. Jordan based it on the Angel Oak on Johns Island (see photo insert, page 8), just outside his hometown of Charleston—a mile and a half from where he graduated high school. Its name appears to derive from Low German *avend* ("evening") and Japanese *sora* ("sky"): even at full noon, the Angel Oak is so massive it creates a kind of perpetual evening beneath its branches.

Avendoraldera. The act of **Laman Damodred** cutting down this tree, grown from a sapling of *Avendesora* and given to **Cairhien** by the **Aiel**, caused the Aiel Wars: its name might have derived from "*Avendesora* of the old era."

Aviendha. In Welsh mythology, an *awenydd* is a poet or soothsayer (from Awen, the muse-like personification of poetic inspiration).

Jordan likely first came across the term in Graves' *White Goddess*.[10] Among Aviendha's many hallmarks are the visions she has had of her relationship with **Rand al'Thor** and her ability to recognize the true intent of weaves she's never seen before.

B

Ba'alzamon. This name, by which **Ishamael** began to refer to himself, refers to the ancient Middle Eastern deity Ba'alshamin. One of the related forms of the god's name, Beelzebub, is often mistaken to be an alternate name for Satan—just as many people mistake Ishamael for **Shai'tan** himself.

Baerlon. The first major town visited by the main characters from **Emond's Field**, Baerlon was originally named "Marilyn" in Jordan's notes.[11] Its eventual name was derived from Caerleon, site of a Roman fortress in Wales (its name means "fortress of the legion" in Welsh). Caerleon was frequently associated with the Arthurian legends; Malory has Arthur crowned there.

Baldhere. His name derives from the Old English, meaning "bold army," which indeed he led. It's tempting to see in his name an echo also of the Norse god Baldr, but there's little commonality between that doomed deity and the actions or fate of heroic Baldhere in The Wheel of Time.

balefire. In medieval England, a bale-fire was a ritual bonfire, often associated with a funeral pyre or a sacrificial burning. The word combines the Old Norse (*bál*) and Old English (*fyr*) words for fire, thus literally translating as "fire-fire"—a fitting name to give a magical fire in Jordan's Wheel of Time: a fire so fierce it can burn away a person's existence entirely!

Balthamel. One of the **Forsaken**. Balthamel's name derives from Balthazar, an alternative form of Belshazzar. The idiom "seeing the writing on the wall" comes from the biblical story of Belshazzar's Feast, when as one of the chief administrators of Babylon during the time of the Babylonian Exile, he used the looted riches of Jerusalem to throw elaborate feasts and so earned the enmity of God (Daniel 5). Belshazzar's focus on his own bodily desires over what was right has a match in Balthamel's own love of bodily excesses. His original name was **Eval Ramman**, and after he was killed by the **Green Man** at the **Eye of the World** he was reincarnated as **Aran'gar**.

Ban al'Seen. Though he shares a name with Malory's King Ban, the father of Lancelot in the Arthurian myth, that role more closely ties to Akir Mandragoran in The Wheel of Time, who is the father of the Lancelot analogue, **Lan Mandragoran**. Jordan instead based his Ban on a different character from Malory: Sir Balan, destined to be killed by his brother Sir Balin. Graves believed these were vestiges of the older gods Bran and Beli.[12]

Band of the Red Hand. The symbol of the Red Hand was adopted by the Uí Néill of Ulster and is thus often called "the Red Hand of Ulster," but it has deep roots across Gaelic culture, with many different clans claiming it as a symbol—with different stories about its origin. In The Wheel of Time, **Matrim Cauthon** organizes an independent military order under the name, which is taken from a legendary group of heroes whose name in the Old Tongue was *Shen an Calhar* (that is, Shannon, County Clare, Ireland).

Barid Bel Medar. Despite similarities with the names of a number of historical figures—from a ninth-century king of Dublin (Bárid mac Ímair) to several rulers of the Barid Sultanate (among them Ali Barid Shah I)—the original name of **Demandred** is likely a construct built out of the English words *barren* and *murder*, which Jordan had as name roots in his notes. To these, he added Bel, the name of a Babylonian deity.

Basene. An alias of the sensual **Graendal**, who took it when pretending to be an aging lady in Arad Doman. The name comes from the Arabic word *basama*, meaning "delight."

Bayle Domon. Captain of the ship *Spray*, he would well know of the need to *bail* water, from which is name derives. As for his surname, Bayle was a strong man whose bulk might have been mistaken for fat: that is, he appeared to be a *dough-man*.

Bela. This shaggy brown mare's name echoes the French word *belle*, meaning "beautiful" . . . and she damn well is!

Be'lal. The **Forsaken** originally named **Duram Laddel Cham**, Be'lal takes his name from biblical *Belial*, a Hebrew word meaning "worthless" that came to be used as a name for a leader of evil forces on Earth.

Belinde. White-haired, thin, and ceaselessly plotting, Belinde owes her name to *Betlinde*, which means "bright serpent" in Old High German.

Bel Tine. Beltane is a Gaelic May Day festival: a celebration of the beginning of summer marked by the lighting of bonfires. Many Beltane traditions were meant to appease the *aos sí*, who were particularly active in the world at Beltane and at Samhain, its oppositional moment of the year as the start of winter. During these periods the borders between worlds thinned. See **Aes Sedai**.

Berelain sur Paendrag Paeron. Her name *Paendrag* associates her with Arthurian myth (see **Artur Hawkwing**). Accordingly, it's reasonable to suspect that her first name likely derives from Elaine of Corbenic, who tricked Lancelot into sleeping with her (thinking she was Guinevere) and thus became pregnant with Lancelot's son, Galahad. In The Wheel of Time, Berelain tries to seduce **Perrin Aybara** and, having failed, deceives people into thinking that she has indeed slept with him. Ultimately, however, she falls in love with **Galad Damodred** (a parallel to Galahad). During the Last Battle she takes Galad's *ter'angreal* to **Lan Mandragoran**—just as Elaine of Corbenic heals Lancelot with the Grail in the Arthurian legend. Her surname appears to derive from María Eva Duarte de Perón (i.e., Evita), the popular First Lady of Argentina from 1946–52.

Berisha Terakuni. Berisha and one of her antagonists, **Meidani Eschede**, appear to be tied to the politics of modern Albania.[13] Sali Ram Berisha was the second president of the country (1992–97); the collapse of his government resulted in the election of a socialist successor, Rexhep Qemal Meidani, whose own government would crumble, too.

Bhan'sheen. The name of this band of **Trollocs** echoes the word *ban-shee*, a supernatural creature in Celtic mythology and folklore. See **Trolloc Bands**.

Birgitte Silverbow. Named for Brigid, whom Graves had noted as a Celtic triple goddess—"the Brigit of Poetry, the Brigit of Healing and the Brigit of Smithcraft"—who derived from an Aegean moon goddess.[14] This speculation of a lunar connection recalled to Jordan's mind the Greek moon goddess, Artemis, who was also goddess of the hunt: her icon is a silver bow (akin to a crescent moon). She is one of the **Heroes of the Horn**.

Black Fever. An epidemic during the time of **Artur Paendrag Tanreall**. The Black Fever's death toll of one-tenth of the population is a literal decimation (killing one of ten). In its name, however, it echoes the historical Black Death, which killed a far greater percentage of the population of Europe in the fourteenth century.

Blaes of Matuchin. A **Hero of the Horn** whose name derives from the phrase "blades of *matachín*"—the latter a Spanish dance involving swords that was imported to the Americas by at least the seventeenth century. The highly symbolic dance is meant to reveal the hard-fought victory of good over evil.

Blind Pig, The. An inn in Chachin; its name derives from a pub called The Blind Tiger, a ten-minute walk from Jordan's home.

Bors. See **Jaichim Carridin**.

Bowl of the Winds. In Welsh mythology, the enchantress Ceridwen has a cauldron that contains poetic inspiration. That inspiration, in turn, is often given physical form in the wind. See, for instance, Percy Bysshe Shelley's "Ode to the West Wind," in which he calls on the "wild West Wind" to rise up, a weather-quaking "clarion o'er the dreaming earth"—to bring him the inspiration to compose new things.

Brandelwyn al'Vere. In Malory and many other Arthurian myths, Guinevere's father is King Leodegrance of Cameliard, but some Welsh stories alternatively name him as a giant named Ogyrvan (see **Ogier**). Jordan found this in Graves' *White Goddess*, which lists him as Ogyr Vran and claims him as a form of Welsh mythology's Brân the Blessed.[15] Further, making the name *Bran* a shortened form of a longer *Brandelwyn* allowed Jordan to once more nod toward Tolkien's *Lord of the Rings*: the Brandywine is the name of the river that the hobbits must cross at Bucklebury Ferry in order to escape the Black Riders hunting them in the Shire.

Branlet Gilyard. The word *bran* means "raven" in Welsh, and the suffix *-let* is a diminutive in English that derives from Old French. Branlet's name thus means "little raven." As for his surname, the similarly pronounced Gaillard Center, just over a mile from Jordan's home, is the main theater for large concerts, shows, and other performance arts events in downtown Charleston.

Brend. An alias of **Sammael**, referring to the Bren light machine gun, used by British forces through much of the twentieth century.

Buad of Albhain. One of the **Heroes of the Horn**, she is Boudica, the queen of the Iceni tribe of Britain (often called Albion) who led an enormous revolt against Roman rule in 60 or 61. Boudica's name means "victory"—in Classical Irish, *buadh*.

C

Caemlyn. Jordan's kingdom of **Andor** is full of parallels to Arthurian mythology, so it's little surprise that the name of its capital is also Arthurian. In this case, it is a combination of two Arthurian locations: King Arthur's traditional capital at Camelot, as well as Camlann, the location of his final battle, where he was mortally wounded. In the original notes for The Wheel of Time, the **Last Battle** was to take place outside the ruins of Caemlyn.[16] (See also **Canluum**.)

cadin'sor. The name for the daily garb of the **Aiel** may derive from the Italian verb *cadenzare*, meaning to regulate the pace of an action, like walking. This would make some sense: the Aiel, of course, never get to where they're going by riding.

Cadsuane Melaidhrin. The name appears in Jordan's notes as early as 1987, before the writing of *The Eye of the World*. It appears that he derived it from *coxswain,* the title given to the individual officer in charge of steering and navigation on a boat. In The Wheel of Time, Cadsuane likewise does everything she can to steer **Rand al'Thor**. Though it is close to Spanish *malandrín,* meaning "scoundrel," her surname appears to be made up by Jordan.

Cairhien. From its fashions and its architecture to its devotion to the political machinations of the Game of Houses, the country of Cairhien and its Sun Throne strongly reflect the kingdom of France during the rule of the so-called Sun King, Louis  XIV (1638–1715). The name might have been taken from Querrien, a small commune in Brittany, but more likely it's Jordan's attempt to create a word that would have a French feel while also fitting the feel of the other materials he was using to construct The Wheel of Time (a *caer* in Welsh means a fortification).

Calian the Chooser. One of the **Heroes of the Horn** along with her brother, **Shivan the Hunter**, Calian echoes Kali, a Hindu goddess of both creation and destruction.

Callandor. A powerful weapon in the Stone of Tear that could only be retrieved by the Dragon Reborn, *Callandor* is an obvious parallel to the Arthurian Sword in the Stone, Excalibur. The name of that legendary weapon had derived from Welsh *Caledfwlch,* which became Latin *Caliburn* before reaching its final, familiar form in English. Jordan's *Callandor* is a distant echo of this Latin name while also providing a wink at the reader: "Call **Andor**."

Canluum. The name of this small town in **Kandor**, in which the climactic events of Jordan's Wheel of Time prequel *New Spring* take place, appears to be based on Camlann, a traditional location for King Arthur's final battle, where he was mortally wounded. Though Jordan had originally intended for the **Last Battle** to happen outside **Caemlyn**, by the time he was writing *New Spring* he may have changed it to this region in order to frame the final moments of The Wheel of Time with the prequel novel. In any event, the eventual location was the **Field of Merrilor**.

Car'a'carn. Meaning "chief of chiefs" in the Old Tongue of The Wheel of Time, *Car'a'carn* reflects the phrasing "king of kings" or "lord of lords," which is three times used to refer to Jesus in the Bible (1 Timothy 6:15, Revelation 17:14, 19:16). Jordan's word *car,* reflecting Polish and other Slavic languages, derives from Latin *Caesar.* It's also possible, though uncertain, that he may also have been nodding toward the deity Car, which Graves had speculated was a Latinization of another name for an Old Testament deity, spelled *Q're* and cognate to the Keres (singular, Ker), figures of Greek mythology who descend upon the battle-slain akin to the Valkyries of Norse mythology (Graves, *White Goddess,* 330).

Caralain Grass. These extraordinary grasslands, crossed by few aside from the **Tuatha'an**, are reminiscent of the Great Plains of the United States. Their name and appearance, however, derive from the long-bladed sweetgrass that grows in the Lowcountry of South Carolina. The weaving of sweetgrass baskets began with techniques brought to America through the slave trade, and today these traditions are maintained by the Gullah artists who often sell their remarkable work on the sidewalks of downtown Charleston, near Jordan's home.

Carleon. One of the High Lords of Tear, he objected to many of the new policies that **Rand al'Thor** tried to implement after he seized the Stone of Tear. He subsequently died in a "hunting accident." In this, he parallels Carloman II (866–884), king of West Francia, who also died while hunting.

Children of the Light. See **Whitecloaks**.

Choedan Kal. Welsh *coeden* means "tree" in the singular form, and Hebrew *qahal* means an "assembly" or "congregation." Jordan's combination of them is therefore something of a paradox: an assembly of a single tree. In The Wheel of Time, however, this makes some sense. The Choedan Kal are two enormous *sa'angreal*, each representing one branch of the **One Power**.

chora tree. Jordan derived the name from the so-called coral trees (genus *Erythrina*) that grow in tropical regions.

Colavaere Saighan. The fact that Colavaere's surname echoes Saigon, the capital of South Vietnam, may be an indicator of Jordan's intentions for her character. If her first name derives from Latin—as seems likely—then her whole name translates to something like "we had protected Saigon," which would be a statement of important meaning for a veteran of the war like Jordan.

Companions. The elite fighting force of **Illian**, the Companions are based on the *Hetairoi* ("Companions"), a powerful cavalry that made up the most prestigious, elite fighting force of the Macedonian army in the age of Philip II and Alexander the Great. The *Hetairoi* were limited in number and centered on the person of the king, who personally commanded the largest of their squadrons.

Congars. Often twinned as local busybodies, the families of the Congars and Coplins are an echo of the hobbit family names Bolgers and Boffins in Tolkien's *Lord of the Rings*. Jordan likely derived the name Congar from the Congaree River and National Park, which is close to Charleston, South Carolina.

Coplins. See **Congars**.

Corlan Dashiva. The name given to the reincarnated **Aginor**, it derives from the Welsh *córlann*, which refers to the architectural feature of a choir or chancel in a Christian church: the place from which songs of praise ring out. In Aginor's case, these songs praise not the Creator, but something similar to Shiva, the Hindu goddess of destruction. It is from this that his surname derives.

Couladin. Leader of the **Shaido** and a false *Car'a'carn*. Couladin's name derives from the historical Battle of Culloden, in which Bonnie Prince Charlie's attempt to defend his claim to be the rightful king of England was defeated. See also **Cuallin Dhen, Battle of**.

Cuallin Dhen, Battle of. A fight in which the queen of **Andor** rallied her routed forces to turn and fight—and thus win the victory—Cuallin Dhen gets its name from the historical Battle of Culloden, which was fought on April 16, 1746. Culloden pitted British forces against the Jacobites led by Charles Edward Stuart, known popularly as Bonnie Prince Charlie. The outcome of the battles are hardly the same: unlike the queen of Andor, Stuart absolutely failed to stop his routed forces from being driven from the field. Culloden thus marked the collapse of the Jacobite cause rather than its glorious triumph.

Culain. A great general of the past who opposed Artur Hawkwing Tanreall—one whose memories Mat can now access—Culain is derived from the Irish mythological hero Cú Chulainn. In the epic *Táin Bó Cúailnge*, it is Cú Chulainn alone who defends Ulster against the invasion of Queen Medb of Connacht.

Culain's Hound. An inn in **Caemlyn**. Its name recalls the Irish mythological hero Cú Chulainn, whose name means "Culann's Hound." According to the stories, the future Cú Chulainn was just a boy when he visited Culann the Smith, whose home was guarded by a massive and ferocious dog. It attacked the young man, and in self-defense he killed it. When he saw Culann's sorrow, he offered to serve as a guard himself while a new watchdog was reared, thus earning his name. See **Culain**.

Cyndane. This appearance of **Lanfear** combines Cynthia, an alternative name for Artemis (Greek goddess of the moon and the hunt), with the word *Dane*, which in the Middle Ages was a generic term for the Vikings, who raided across the North Sea in their search for silver among other resources. Jordan's Cyndane has silver-blond hair and blue eyes.

D

da'covale. The **Seanchan** term for an enslaved person. Jordan may have derived it from the term *covalence*, which refers to a bond of shared electrons between two atoms. No matter how the Seanchan try to think otherwise, however, enslavement is, to the contrary, an entirely one-sided relationship.

Dael al'Taron. The name *Dael* entered into Jordan's mind early: it was the original surname of **Perrin Aybara**. Jordan likely found it in the Ulster Cycle of Irish mythology, where the hero Celtchar has a loyal but monstrous dog named Dóelchú—often Anglicized as Dael—that he must kill in order to bring peace to Ulster. (There is also a Georgian goddess of the hunt named Dael, but there's little indication Jordan knew of her.) Dael's surname echoes Taran, the protagonist of Lloyd Alexander's Prydain Chronicles (see also **Taran Ferry**).

Dain Bornhald. A **Whitecloak** who is strongly adversarial to Perrin Aybara, he shares his name with Dáinn (meaning "dead"), one of the dwarves in Norse mythology (and thus with a dwarf in Tolkien's writings). The origin of his surname is unknown, though it appears early in Jordan's notes.[18] See **Geofram Bornhald**.

damane. See *a'dam*.

Dannil Lewin. Dannil originally appeared in the name Dannil Aybara, before that character was combined with Perrin Dael to create **Perrin Aybara** (see also **Dael al'Taron**). Jordan got the name from the hero of the biblical book of Daniel, who was considered a prophet in later Christian tradition. Dannil's surname was derived from Lleu Llaw Gyffes, a heroic figure in Welsh mythology who makes frequent appearances in Graves' *White Goddess*—very often in conjunction with Math fab Mathonwy, who gave his name to **Matrim Cauthon**.

darei. The light spears utilized by the **Aiel** parallel a shortened *assagai*, called an *iklwa*—supposedly because of the sound made when it was pulled out of a victim's body—that became  the standard weapon of Zulu warriors after the reforms of King Shaka (1787–1828). See also *ashandarei*.

Darith, King. It's possible that the interrupted reference to a **Randland** story about "King Darith and the Fall of the House of—" is a loose remembrance of King Darius of Persia, whose family was defeated by Alexander the Great. Given the surrounding symbolisms of The Wheel of Time, however, another likely candidate is Roderick, the main character in Edgar Allan Poe's 1839 short story "The Fall of the House of Usher." In a madness driven by his isolation, Roderick entombs his twin sister, Madeline, alive. Upon escaping, she frightens Roderick to death before dying herself. Their great ancestral mansion then splits in two, the moon shining through the gap, before it sinks into a lake. Poe spent a year of his life in Jordan's hometown of Charleston, and local legend has it that the poet's beloved Annabel Lee is buried in the graveyard of the Unitarian Church just two blocks from Jordan's home.

Darkfriends. In his early notes for The Wheel of Time, Jordan described a related group of "humans who trade with the Trolloc, without being actively agents of the Dark One," with an additional handwritten note to himself that they were "not particularly nice folk, just the same."[19]

Darlin Sisnera. His surname derives from Francisco Jiménez de Cisneros (1436–1517)—in Spain called simply Cisneros—an enormously influential cardinal and statesman during his lifetime who is widely regarded as a key figure in creating the Spanish Golden Age.

Da'shain Aiel. The name given to the pacifist people who followed "the Way of the Leaf" and gave rise to the modern **Aiel**, Da'shain derives from a Japanese word referring to a member of a company.

Davram t'Ghaline Bashere. One of the five great captains of the Westlands and highly loyal to the **Dragon Reborn**; his name derives from *Avram,* the original name of the Patriarch Abraham in the Old Testament. On his surname, see **Faile Bashere**.

Deain. The **Aes Sedai** who invented the *a'dam*, only to be leashed by it, has a parallel in the Greek mythological story of Deïanira, the wife of Hercules. When the centaur Nessus attempted to rape her, Hercules shot him with an arrow. Dying, the centaur told her that his blood, mixed with oil, would create a love potion that would ensure her husband's faithfulness. She collected some of the blood and later put it on Hercules' shirt. In truth, it was a poison that burned away her husband's skin, and he threw himself onto a funeral pyre. After his death, a distraught Deïanira committed suicide.

Demandred. Born **Barid Bel Medar**. His name as one of the **Forsaken** is a combination of the words *demon* and *dread,* while also reflecting both the verb *demand* and the name of Mordred, who kills King Arthur in Malory.

Demetre Marcolin. Though his name bears a close similarity to that of the Greek goddess of the earth's fertility, Demeter, it's more likely indebted to Demetrius, the name of several kings and military leaders in the Classical world.

Dhai'mon. The name of this band of **Trollocs** echoes the word *demon*. See **Trolloc Bands**.

Dha'vol. The name of this band of **Trollocs** echoes the word *devil*. See **Trolloc Bands**.

Dhjin'nen. The name of this band of **Trollocs** echoes the word *djinn,* a supernatural being in Arabic mythology. See **Trolloc Bands**.

Dhurran. A breed of large, strong horse in The Wheel of Time, known for its *endurance*—from which the name is derived.

Donel do Morny a'Lordeine. His first name derives from Gaelic *Dòmhnall,* meaning "world-ruler." His surname is an archaic form of *lordling,* meaning a "little lord."

Draghkar. These bat-like humanoid creatures that suck the soul of their victims were inspired by crossing the titular character of Bram Stoker's *Dracula* with the undead *draugr* of Norse mythology.

Dragon Banner. A white banner deco-rated with a serpent of scarlet and gold, the Dragon Banner combines two historical standards of Wales. The first is the badge traditionally attributed to Cadwaladr ap Cadwallon, a seventh-century king of Gwynedd: this was a red dragon on a white background. In subsequent centuries, Cadwaladr was seen as a kind of savior figure who could rise again to lead the Welsh to a prophesied victory over their enemies. Among those Welsh leaders who were seen to fulfill this role was Owain Glyndŵr, who led a rebellion against the English beginning in 1400. His personal banner was a quartered red-and-gold standard of four lions rampant, themselves alternating in red and gold, but as the self-proclaimed Prince of Wales he began flying another banner beginning in 1401: a golden dragon on a white background.

Dragonmount. There are a great number of lonely mountains in the world, but fewer loom larger in fantasy literature than Tolkien's Lonely Mountain and Mount Doom. Jordan has combined these

models into a single, lonely volcano in the form of Dragonmount—
and then paired it with a second volcanic mountain at **Shayol Ghul**.
The pairing—one associated with hope and one with doom—is a
physical manifestation of balance in the world of The Wheel of Time.

Dragon Reborn. The dragon was the traditional symbol of both Wales
and King Arthur (see **Dragon Banner**). Of the king, popular legend
says that he is sleeping—usually at Avalon (see **Tar Valon**)—until
he's needed once again. When the time comes, he'll reawaken and
lead his people to victory.

dragons. An invention of **Aludra Nendenhald**, these weapons launch
a firework rocket mounted to a bundle of explosive gunpowder (a
"dragon egg"). They are, in essence, the primitive equivalent to
rocket-propelled grenade launchers—weapons Jordan had seen far
too closely in Vietnam.

Duhara Basaheen. The word *dohara* means "double" in Hindi, which
is a hint at her duplicitous nature. More direct is her surname, which
derives from a form common to many martial arts: *Passai* or *Bassai*
(Korean *Ba Sa Hee*). This technique, which translates as "to Penetrate
a Fortress," is ample indication that Duhara, a Darkfriend, is infil-
trating the fortress of **Tar Valon**.

Dumai's Wells, Battle of. An oasis of three stone wells between **Cairhien**
and **Tar Valon**, Dumai's Wells was the location of an enormous battle
in which a party of **Aes Sedai** holding an imprisoned **Rand al'Thor**
was attacked by a much larger army of **Shaido Aiel**—only to see that
army attacked in turn by a force led by **Perrin Aybara** that was intent
on rescuing Rand. In the climactic moments, **Asha'man** appeared
and released the cataclysmic force of the **One Power** upon the Shaido.

Jordan based the engagement on a few historical battles, the first
of which is the Battle of Badr, fought on March 13, 624. The prophet
of Islam, Muhammad, had migrated with his followers from Mecca
to Medina in 622, an event called the Hegira. This set off a series
of small-scale conflicts between the two cities as they jockeyed for
power and the protection of trading routes. In 624, Muhammad set
out from Medina to capture an approaching Meccan caravan. An

army set out from Mecca to protect it. The forces met at Badr, a valley between large sand dunes where several trading roads met beside an oasis of wells. Muhammad had just over three hundred Muslims at his command. The men of Mecca had at least three times as many. After a series of duels at the well controlled by the Muslims, the Meccans launched a shower of arrows at the Muslims. Then they charged. Muhammad, in prayer, waited until the last moment to order his outnumbered men forward. When they did, the counterattack not only repulsed the Meccan charge but sent it into rout. According to the Qur'an, the Muslim success had a divine component: Allah had sent down a host of a thousand angels to join them in the charge (8:9–12).

The other relevant engagement was the Battle of Rorke's Drift, fought on the night of January 22, 1879, during the Anglo-Zulu War. In this engagement, a group of around 150 British and colonial troops at the small mission station of Rorke's Drift were completely surrounded by several thousand Zulu warriors. With a loosely fortified position and the use of gunpowder weapons, the beleaguered British held, losing only seventeen men in the face of the onslaught.

Duram Laddel Cham. The original name of **Be'lal**. His surname reflects Cham (more often spelled Ham), the youngest of the three sons of Noah and father of Canaan. In Genesis 9:20–27, Cham sees his father naked—a transgression that results in Noah cursing his descendants, beginning with Canaan.

E

Eamon Valda. The successor to **Pedron Niall** as commander of the **Whitecloaks**, Eamon very likely recalls Éamon de Valera, an Irish statesman. De Valera first came to prominence during the 1916 Easter Rising, for which he was imprisoned and nearly executed. He ultimately rose to become the third president of Ireland.

Easar Togita. The king of **Shienar**; his name likely derives from Elasar, a kingdom listed alongside the kingdom of Shinar in Genesis 14:1. His surname reflects his qualities as a superior military commander, as it echoes the Japanese word for the square in which troops gathered to receive orders.

Ebou Dar. The capital city of **Altara**, it is split in two halves by the large bay of the River Eldar. A port city of canals built upon the ruins of an older city, it combines the historical cities of Rome and Venice, Italy, with hints of the cultures of Byzantium. Its name, however, seems to derive from Abu Dhabi.

Eelfinn. This name appears early in Jordan's notes for The Wheel of Time, where it is recorded as "a man's name. A slender, small man."[20] He'd found it in Graves' *White Goddess,* which recounted the legend of how the relatively weak Elffin ap Gwyddno, a prince of Gwynedd, had gone fishing and instead  pulled from the waters a miraculous child named Gwion, who grew up to become a bard and take the name Taliesin. Disentangling this myth, and the ways in which it pointed toward a pan-European, pre-Christian mythology worshipping the triple goddess of maiden-mother-crone, is the most central feature of Graves' work. Reading this book, Jordan also noted numerous references to the Queen of Elfin (i.e., Elfland, Álfheimr in Norse mythology), the fairyland remnant of that forgotten goddess, who is as treacherous as she is seductive. From these roots, Jordan fashioned the Aelfinn and the Eelfinn, two separate but related species of humanoids existing in a world paradoxically connected and disconnected from our world—just as is the land of the faerie, with its Seelie and Unseelie Courts—who could offer three answers or three wishes for a price. In this latter respect, they are combined with popular conceptions of the genie, with its roots in the Islamic mythological notion of the djinn (see **Tower of Ghenjei**). See **Snakes and Foxes**.

Egeanin Sarna. A **Seanchan** ship captain who became the Warder of **Egwene al'Vere**. The origins of Egeanin's name are in the Mediterranean Sea: from the island of Sardegna in its center to the Aegean Sea at its eastern end.

Egwene al'Vere. King Arthur's wife, Guinevere, has diverse roles in literature. In one medieval story, "The Rise of Gawain, Nephew of

Arthur," Guinevere has magical abilities, but in most texts she is depicted as a queen who caused the downfall of the kingdom through her infidelity. Early stories tie her affair to Mordred, but by the time of Malory it was most commonly tied to Lancelot. After her husband fell at the Battle of Camlann, most stories depict her retiring to a life as a nun (see **Aes Sedai**). In The Wheel of Time, Egwene seems initially destined to marry **Rand al'Thor** (a cognate to Arthur), but as the story grows her role is increasingly independent. Using Portal Stones, in fact, Rand sees alternative lives in which he did marry Egwene, with the result of the Dark One achieving victory—just as Arthur's marriage to Guinevere would ultimately unmake his kingdom. Instead, Rand falls in love with three other women, paralleling both a Welsh folktale of Arthur marrying not one but *three* women named Guinevere (*Trioedd Ynys Prydein,* no. 56) and Graves' triple-goddess figure in *The White Goddess.*

Einor Saren. A **Whitecloak** commander; his name associates him with warfare. His first name come from Old Norse *Einarr,* meaning "a warrior." His surname derives from Surena, the commander of the forces of the Parthian Empire who decisively defeated the Roman legions of Crassus at the Battle of Carrhae in 53 BC.

Elaida do Avriny a'Roihan. One of the overkingdoms of medieval Ireland was Ulaid (in Latin, *Ulidia*): it encompassed much of modern Ulster, with some stories fixing its southern border at the River Boyne—in Irish, the *Abhainn na Bóinne*. Elaida's name seems to derive from this Irish mix (as might her Red Ajah itself). Perhaps the most famous story of the Ulaid people is the early Irish epic *Táin Bó Cúailnge,* in which Connacht makes war on Ulster in order to steal a prized bull. Due to a curse on Ulster, only the teenaged Cú Chulainn can defend the people. The bull is nevertheless taken. Jordan makes direct reference to the episode, though switching Elaida to the side of Connacht: when **Rand al'Thor** was captured by her **Aes Sedai**, she was sent a message that "the ring has been placed in the bull's nose."[21]

Elan Morin Tedronai. A nihilist philosopher who became **Ishamael** in The Wheel of Time; his first name appears to derive from Elam, son of Shem son of Noah (Genesis 10:22). Several biblical prophecies reference the region named for Elam, including Jeremiah 49:34–39, which states that God will scatter its people and make it captive. Elan's surname also appears to be biblical, relating to "Chedorlaomer king of Elam and Tidal king of nations" (Genesis 14:1).

Elayne Trakand. There are several women in Arthurian myth named Elaine. Among them are Elaine of Astolat (sometimes called the Lady of Shalott), whose unrequited love for Lancelot causes her death; Elaine of Benwick, who is the mother of Lancelot; Elaine of Corbenic, the Grail Maiden who conceives of Lancelot's son, Galahad; Elaine of Garlot, who is a sister to Morgan le Fay and Morgause (and thus half-sister to King Arthur). Jordan's Elayne seems most indebted to Elaine of Garlot, but rather than a sister of Morgause she is the daughter of Queen **Morgase**, and rather than a half-sister to Arthur she is one of the three loves of **Rand al'Thor**. In this, Jordan reflects more contemporary Arthurian stories that often portray three queens taking the dying king to Avalon for healing and, in legend, an eventual return.

Eldrith Jhondar. An archaic word in English, *eldritch* was popularized in literature by H. P. Lovecraft, who used it to refer to unnatural, often horrific dangers—a suitable name for a member of the Black Ajah. In depicting her murderous hatred of cats, Jordan nods to one of Lovecraft's most famous short stories, "The Cats of Ulthar."

Elfraed Guitama. A leader who tried to seize the empire of **Artur Hawkwing** after his death; his name likely combines the names of the historical figures Alfred the Great and Gautama.

Elsbet. That the fabled "Queen of All" refers to a Queen Elizabeth is without doubt: the only question is which one? Queen Elizabeth II (b. 1926) ruled England throughout the Cold War; a reference to her ruling everything would refer not to her place in geopolitics but to her place in Jordan's faith as an Episcopalian: as monarch she is the supreme governor of the Church of England, from which the Episcopal Church split during the American Revolution. On balance, however, Jordan more likely had in mind Queen Elizabeth I (1533–1603), around whom there was such a significant devotion that, as Graves noted in *The White Goddess,* "she was popularly regarded as a sort of deity."[22] Elizabeth's mother was Anne Boleyn, and a later successor was Queen Anne (1665–1714), which would be enough to connect her to a "sister" named Anne as legend turned to myth with the turning of the Wheel. That Anne, of course, became further muddled into **Anla**.

Else Grinwell. Not every name Jordan created was based on some grand connection. Some are so direct as to be amusing. Such is the case with the flirtatious Else Grinwell: *Elsa grins well.*

Elyas Machera. Elias is a name shared by several excellent knights and warriors in Arthurian legend, including, in Malory, the leader of a Saxon army who nearly bested Tristram in one-on-one combat. Elyas is indeed a great warrior, but he's also a **wolfbrother**. In his ability to shift between worlds, he could also be a nod to the biblical prophet Elijah, who is frequently referenced in *The White Goddess* by the Greek spelling of his name, *Elias*. According to 2 Kings 2:3–9, Elijah never died: he was taken up into heaven by a whirlwind.

Emond's Field. Though canonically derived from the name of **Aemon al Caar al Thorin** within The Wheel of Time, the name of the village where **Rand al'Thor** and the other main characters grew up might well owe something to the Harmon Field recreational area in Charleston, which the athletic Jordan would have known well in his youth.

Emond's glory. This purple flower, found in the royal gardens of **Cairhien**, might well be a purple morning glory: better known as the blue dawn flower. They grow in front of Jordan's home in Charleston.

Erinin, River. Jordan took the name of the river that runs by **Tar Valon** and the seat of "a Merlin," the **Amyrlin Seat**, from "the Land of Erin"—a romantic formulation meaning Ireland (from *Éirinn*, the dative case of the Irish word for Ireland, *Éire*). He found it in Graves' *White Goddess*, where Erin is discussed in conjunction with Merlin.[23]

Ethenielle Kirukon Materasu. She is the queen of **Kandor**, and her name comes from *Ethanael,* meaning "God-given strength." Her surname ties her to Amaterasu-Omikami, the goddess of the sun in Japanese mythology (see **Amaresu**).

Eval Ramman. The original name of **Balthamel**, it has biblical origins. Eval is taken not from the word *evil,* but from Ebal, a mountain cursed by God in the Bible (Deuteronomy 11:29). His surname is taken from Rimmon, either as an alternate form of the Syrian deity Baal or a temple for his worship (2 Kings 5:18).

Evanellein Lorn. A member of the Black Ajah. Her name combines that of Eve, the first woman created in the Bible (Genesis 2–3), with the English word *forlorn.*

Ewin Finngar. His surname likely associates him with Fionn mac Cumhaill, better known in English as Finn MacCool.

Eye of the World. Building as it does toward the apocalyptic notion of a **Last Battle** between darkness and the Light, The Wheel of Time has many origin points in the Christian book of Revelation. In that text, the end-times are said to begin with the breaking of the seven seals by a slain Lamb "having seven horns and seven eyes, which are the seven Spirits of God sent forth into all the earth" (5:6). The subsequent terrors of Armageddon (see **Tarmon Gai'don**) were carefully delineated in some of Jordan's earliest notes for the books.[24] Accordingly, Jordan originally imagined that in The Wheel of Time there were seven "eyes" of the world, each one a source of power associated with one of the seals preventing the Dark One from destroying the world. Further, he decided that the Dark One had tasked a group of former **Aiel** to destroy these "eyes" and the seals within them. While the concept of these secret Aiel remained in the back of Jordan's mind (see *Samma N'Sei*), it's clear that he early abandoned the notion that there would be multiple "eyes" in the world. Instead, he favored a single source of power—in **Randland** terms, a pool of pure *saidin*. He then combined this with elements of Arthurian mythology by having the pool guarded by the **Green Man** and only able to be found when needed. This second point was fitting twice over. First, the well-known story of *Sir Gawain and the Green Knight* depicts the Green Knight awaiting Sir Gawain in a mysterious "Green

Chapel" that Gawain only locates in a moment of desperation after a long journey from Arthur's court. Second, at the end of the larger myth of King Arthur, the king's sword Excalibur is returned to the Lady of the Lake after he is mortally wounded, and he himself is taken by boat to mystical Avalon, where he is said to be resting until he is once again needed—the "once and future king." The Eye of the World, accordingly, is the place to which **Rand al'Thor**, an analogue to Arthur in The Wheel of Time, is taken to recover from his "sleep" of not knowing that he is himself a reborn figure of power: the Dragon, with its own mythical ties back to the book of Revelation and far more.

F

Faile Bashere. Born Zarine ni Bashere—echoing the English *serene* and the Arabic *bashir*, meaning "bringer of good news"—she was called Faile by her father. This was then the name she took when she joined her future husband, **Perrin Aybara**, in the hunt for the **Horn of Valere**. Jordan probably found the name in the Lia Fáil, a standing stone on the Hill of Tara in Ireland: this was, according to legend, the stone upon which the kings of Ireland were long crowned.

Fal Dara. This heavily fortified city in the Borderlands echoes Dara, the Roman fortress that stood on the border between the Eastern Roman Empire and the Sassanid Empire in the sixth and seventh centuries. See **Tarwin's Gap**.

Far Madding. Described by Jordan as "the only true matriarchy in the lot,"[25] Far Madding is an independent city-state sitting alone on the **Plains of Maredo**. Its name hearkens to Thomas Hardy's 1874 romance, *Far from the Madding Crowd*, though its practice of ensuring that weapons must be "peace-bonded" inside its walls is probably a nod to the laws of Tombstone, then in the Territory of Arizona, that were integral to the famous shoot-out at the O.K. Corral.

Fearil. A Darkfriend Warder who liked to kill; his name combines the English words *feral* and *fear*.

Feast of Lights. A celebration of the winter solstice that occasioned wild parties in Cairhien and a time of charitable gift-giving elsewhere, the Feast of Lights echoes the Roman festival of Saturnalia, with a nod toward the traditions that developed from it and are still celebrated in association with Christmas today.

Field of Merrilor. The first parts of Jordan's Wheel of Time intentionally reference Tolkien in many aspects, so it's only fitting that the series would close with one more reference. The Field of Merrilor, site of the **Last Battle** in The Wheel of Time, is meant to recall the Pelennor Fields, site of the great battle for Minas Tirith in Tolkien's *Lord of the Rings*.

Floran Gelb. A duplicitous and generally cowardly sailor. His name derives from Florianus, who was proclaimed Roman emperor in July 276 after the death of his brother, Emperor Tacitus. His own army, dissatisfied with his ineffective leadership, killed him that September. His surname means "yellow" in German—a subtle comment on his personality.

Fortuona Athaem Devi Paendrag. See **Tuon Athaem Kore Paendrag**.

G

Gaebril. An alias of **Rahvin**, this name derives from the Archangel Gabriel, God's messenger in Christian mythology, showing just how well the **Forsaken** has disguised himself.

Gaidal Cain. One of the **Heroes of the Horn** who is always linked to **Birgitte Silverbow**, Gaidal shares with her a Celtic lineage. In this case, it's Goídel Glas, who, according to the influential eleventh-century text *Lebor Gabála Érenn,* crafted the Gaelic language (and thus founded the Gaels, who are named for him) in the confusion that followed the destruction of the Tower of Babel in the Bible (Genesis 11:1–9). Jordan combined this figure with the biblical figure of Tubal-Cain, a descendant of Cain who was the first to make tools of bronze and iron (Genesis 4:22). According to tradition, Tubal-Cain was also the first maker of weapons of war, and he was responsible for the death of his ancestor, Cain.

Galad Damodred. In his early notes, Jordan imagined Galad Damodraed (as it was then spelled) as a "Galahad/Mordred figure,"[26] a combination from which he created the name. It is possible that a secondary component in the form of his surname is the story of Damocles, as told by Cicero in his *Tusculan Disputations* (5.1): a courtier was enamored of his king's luxurious life, so the king offered to switch places for a time; the courtier hastily did so, but found that he couldn't enjoy the magnificence because an unsheathed sword hung over the throne, held up by single strand of hair. The "sword of Damocles," as it came to be called, represents the dangers and threats inevitably drawn against those in power—and the dangers of ignorant grasping for that power.

At any rate, Jordan's idea of combining the Arthurian figures of Galahad and Mordred into a single man is fascinating: aside from their shared status as bastard sons, they could hardly be more different. Galahad, the son of Lancelot and Elaine of Corbenic, is the perfection of knighthood, so free of flaw that he alone was able to complete the quest for the Holy Grail. Mordred, the son of Arthur and Morgause, is characterized as an agent of chaos and destabilization: he tries to usurp Arthur's throne, tries to marry Arthur's wife, and ultimately he and his father kill each other and end the Arthurian kingdom. Jordan's first intention, it seems, was to use Galad—who would be the secret son of **Lan Mandragoran** and **Morgase Trakand**—to show how even the most pure-minded person, working on the most pure of intentions, can take actions with terrible unintended consequences: "After Rand decides that he is indeed the Dragon his first ally will be Morgase, who becomes his lover for a time. This makes Galad his bitter opponent, and sends Galad over to Sha'tan."[27] Elsewhere in his notes, Jordan indicates that Galad is himself a wielder of the **One Power**—even if he himself does not yet realize it at the end of the series.[28]

Galina Casban. A member of the Black Ajah. Her name reflects the secret danger she holds: since ancient times, the mineral galena has been mined and smelted to extract lead, a toxic element. Her surname appears to be indebted to Caliban, the half-human monster from Shakespeare's *Tempest*.

Garen's Wall. It is, one suspects, the garden wall, just outside Jordan's office window.

Gareth Bryne. The youngest son of Queen Morgause and one of the finest knights of King Arthur's Round Table in Malory, Sir Gareth is accidentally killed by a crazed Lancelot, who was attempting to rescue Guinevere. In The Wheel of Time, Gareth is unrelated to **Morgase Trakand**—though he served under her as one of the great generals of the Westlands until being relieved of that duty when it was discovered he was under the Compulsion of **Graendal**. He was Warder and husband to **Siuan Sanche**, and after her death he went berserk and was killed. In the formation of Gareth's character as a military man, Jordan relied heavily on what he knew of the reputation of Confederate general Robert E. Lee—a parallel made clear in their beloved horses, both named Traveler. His surname derives from a *byrnie*, the name given to a long coat of mail in the Middle Ages.

Gates of Paaran Disen. See **Paaran Disen, Gates of**.

Gawyn Trakand. The son of **Taringail Damodred** and **Morgase Trakand** in The Wheel of Time, Gawyn is based on Sir Gawain—one of King Arthur's knights of the Round Table and a son of Queen Morgause in Malory. In that earlier text, Gawain's dedication to his family causes numerous tragedies, including his own death at the hands of Lancelot. Gawyn is likewise deeply dedicated to family, but he dies at the hands of **Demandred** (who was himself killed by the Lancelot analogue, **Lan Mandragoran**).

Geofram Bornhald. Both his name and his surname are on Jordan's name lists for potential characters as early as 1987, though it's uncertain where he found either.[29]

Gerard Arganda. There are two Gerards in Malory: one a Welsh knight slain by a giant and the other one of two brothers killed by Gareth. Neither seems to have a direct bearing on the character in The Wheel of Time, so it may be that Jordan simply liked the name.

Ghar'ghael. The name of this band of **Trollocs** echoes the word *gargoyle*. See **Trolloc Bands**.

Ghealdan. Several aspects of this small country are based on Lebanon and Israel. Its capital of Jehannah references the valley of Gehenna in the city of Jerusalem, and its flag of three six-pointed stars may allude to the three religions that claim that city as home. Jordan appears to have been inspired to the name by biblical references to the men of Gebal. As he recorded them in his notes (referencing 1 Kings 5:18), they were "men of the 'moutain-heights' [*sic*] who worked stone for Solomon's temple."[30]

Ghenjei, Tower of. See **Tower of Ghenjei**.

Ghob'hlin. The name of this band of **Trollocs** echoes the word *goblin*. See **Trolloc Bands**.

Ghoetam. A sage fed by birds during the forty years he sat beneath *Avendesora*, Ghoetam matches Gautama Buddha, who meditated beneath the bodhi tree for forty-nine days before achieving enlightenment. Jordan has combined this with two biblical figures: the prophet Elijah, who was fed by birds (1 Kings 17:1–17), and the prophet Moses, who wandered in the desert for forty years before he was allowed to see the Promised Land.

Gho'hlem. The name of this band of **Trollocs** echoes the word *golem*. See **Trolloc Bands**.

gholam. In The Wheel of Time, the gholam were six artificial constructs made for no other purpose than to murder **Aes Sedai**. They're based on the golem, an artificial creature of Jewish folklore that in many stories turns against its maker.

Ghraem'lan. The name of this band of **Trollocs** echoes the word *gremlin*. See **Trolloc Bands**.

Gitara Moroso. Few cultures are more stereotypically associated with fortune-telling than the Romani, often called Gypsies in English. In Spanish, they are the *Gitanos,* from which the prophetic Gitara takes her name. Her surname likewise refers to her Talent for Foretelling: in Greek mythology Moros is the son of Nyx, the goddess of night. A brother of the Moirai (the Fates; see **Moiraine Damodred**), it is Moros who drives a person to their fated end. In some stories, Moros is also said to give some people glimpses of their coming death. A more fitting match for Gitara's role in The Wheel of Time could hardly be found.

golliwog. In *Winter's Heart,* Mat thinks to himself that "a man given a loaf should not complain that a few crumbs were missing, but **Aes Sedai** and **Seanchan**, **gholam** stalking him and old men poking their noses in and skinny girls staring at him was enough to give any man the golliwogs" ("News in a Cloth Sack"). The final term is defined as an extreme sense of nervousness in the *Companion* (303). It appears that Jordan thought he was making up a silly-sounding term to replace what would, in American colloquialism, be called the jitters or the heebie-jeebies: he had Taraboners, for instance, call a confused mess a "jolly-bag," which he undoubtedly imagined as derived from the same phonemes that were behind "golliwog." Problematically, however, a *golliwog* in our world happens to be the name of a doll with black skin and a large mane of frizzy hair that was popular in the United Kingdom and elsewhere in the early decades of the twentieth century: these dolls are, today, regularly recognized as offensive racial caricatures. There's no indication that Jordan knew this, but it should be noted nonetheless.

Graendal. Her original name was **Kamarile Maradim Nindar**. Her name as one of the **Forsaken** comes from *Beowulf*—an Old English epic that was standard reading during Jordan's time at The Citadel—in which the hero must defeat both the man-killing creature Grendel and his vengeful mother. Though neither creature is described as beautiful in the original poem, Jordan combines them into a single female entity whose sensual beauty was matched by her incredible skills of compulsion: she fed, figuratively, on those she manipulated. The more beautiful they were, the greater her hunger for them.

Great Hunt of the Horn. The hunt for the **Horn of Valere** parallels the Wild Hunt, a motif that appears in many northern European cultures: a hunt in wild pursuit, its hunters typically otherworldly and led by a figure of legend, passes by. Those who witness it are often caught up in tragedy as a result: their own death or abduction, the coming of war or strife.

Great Serpent. Jordan's decision to symbolize the Wheel of Time as a dragon-like serpent eating its own tail is rooted in the ouroboros (from the Greek for "tail-eating") of ancient mythology, which often represented the never-ending cycle of life and death.

Green Man. The Green Man is a figure with significant antiquity, likely connected to the spring rebirth of the natural world. Often associated with both fertility and the wilderness, the Green Man was particularly popular in the Middle Ages. The most famous of the stories involving him is the Middle English poem *Sir Gawain and the Green Knight*, which describes him as a massive and tall man—his skin, hair, and armor entirely green—with the supernatural ability to survive a beheading. See **Eye of the World**.

Guaire Amalasan. The false Dragon who started the War of the Second Dragon, his name derives from Guaire Aidne mac Colmáin, a seventh-century king of Connacht who features in several stories of early Ireland.

Gyldin. An alias of **Moghedien** while she posed as a servant, it derives from the English word *gilden*, a now-obsolete spelling of the adjective *golden*—this often refers to something that is gilded: a process by which a thin veneer of gold is overlaid on something far less valuable.

H

hadori. This braided cord that holds back the hair of Malkieri men derives from the Japanese surname *Hattori*, meaning "weavers."

Halima Saranov. An alias of **Aran'gar**. The name *Halima* is Arabic, meaning "gentle"—a far cry from the murderous **Forsaken**.

Haral Luhhan. The blacksmith to whom Perrin Aybara is apprenticed in Emond's Field. His first name is derived from Old English *Harold*, meaning "leader of an army," and his surname comes from the Welsh name *Llewyn*, short for *Llewellyn*, meaning both "leader" and "lion." Ironically, Haral is a man who doesn't like the sight of blood.

Hattori Gatano. Her first name comes from Hattori Hanzō (d. 1596), a ninja who in legend was attributed with supernatural abilities. Her surname derives from the weapon most commonly associated with men like Hanzō: the katana (Japanese *uchigatana*).

Hawkwing, Artur. See **Artur Hawkwing**.

Hend the Striker. One of the **Heroes of the Horn**, he is John Henry, an American folk hero. According to legend, he was a former slave who in a competition managed to hammer a steel drill into rock faster than a steam-powered drill could do so, but died in the effort.

Heroes of the Horn. The promise of a great leader returning—from death, from sleep, or from some other means of separation—is found in numerous mythologies. Jordan sets many of these figures within *Tel'aran'rhiod* as a place of waiting, their fates tied to the **Horn of Valere**.

heron-marked sword. In The Wheel of Time, the sword of a blademaster is marked with a heron, a bird that frequents the waters around Jordan's home in Charleston. Herons are symbols of both patient serenity and graceful action across multiple cultures and mythologies. Japanese folklore tells of the Aosaginohi, a black-crowned night heron that can transform into a spirit with blue-illuminated scales.

Herot's Crossing, Battle of. The name of this battle, at which the final stand of the Malkieri took place—a slaughter from which the infant prince, **Lan Mandragoran**, was saved by being sent away—alludes to the Old English epic *Beowulf*. According to the poem, Hrothgar's hall, variously spelled Heorot or Herot, was visited each night by the monstrous Grendel, who killed every living thing he found inside. So, too, did the Shadowspawn kill all that they found at Herot's Crossing.

Hessalam. The name given to **Graendal** when she was resurrected in a less-than-beautiful body. Jordan connected the name with Salem, site of notorious witch trials in 1692.

Hinderstap. This small town, which at the time of the Last Battle has been cursed such that its inhabitants go into a killing frenzy each night only to be reborn whole the next morning, is akin to the

Welsh mythology of the Pair Dadeni (the Cauldron of Rebirth). This legendary object gave its name to Lloyd Alexander's fantasy classic *The Black Cauldron*. The name of the town appears to derive from the Gundestrup Cauldron, a remarkable but mysterious artifact that may or may not present early forms of Celtic mythology upon its ornate silver panels.

Horn of Valere. The blowing of horns was a standard way of sending commands to troops in ancient and medieval warfare. As a result, they frequently appear in legends and myths. Jordan's Horn of Valere is particularly reminiscent of the Horn of Gjall in  Norse mythology. When the time comes for Ragnarok, the **Last Battle**, the god Heimdall will blow this horn to summon the slain warrior-heroes from Valhalla to fight. At the same time, in the instant of its sounding by **Olver**, it echoes the oliphaunt that Olivier begged to be blown in *The Song of Roland*.

"How Goodwife Karil Cured Her Husband of Snoring." A folktale in the **Westlands**, it was originally entitled "How Anteve Cured Her Husband of Snoring" in Jordan's notes.[31] He changed it to its current name when composing the Test Manuscript of *The Eye of the World*.[32]

"How Susa Tamed Jain Farstrider." A folktale in the **Westlands**, it was originally entitled "How Susa the Milkmaid Tamed Haran the Farwalker."[33] Then, in the Test Manuscript of *The Eye of the World*, it became "How Susa Tamed Jarad Far-strider."[34] See **Jain Farstrider**.

Hundred Companions. The 113 male **Aes Sedai**, led by **Lews Therin Telamon**, who sealed the Dark One in his prison, originate in the Hundred-Handed Ones: three giants with fifty heads and a hundred arms who were the offspring of Uranus and Gaia in Greek myth. They helped Zeus overthrow Cronus and the Titans. Jordan had early intentions of incorporating the Hundred-Handed Ones into his story: they first appear as "members of a group who study martial arts that use only hands and feet and staffs" in some of his earliest notes, before evolving into Aes Sedai.[35] Jordan appears to have taken the notion that a group of more than a hundred men was rounded down to an even hundred from the Hundred Years' War, which rather famously lasted 116 years.

Hurin. A man with the ability to smell violence. His name appears to have been lifted from that of Húrin, an important figure in Tolkien's *Silmarillion*.

I

Illian. The name of the kingdom comes from Ilium—that is, Troy—but its culture is far more indebted to that of Troy's enemies in the Trojan War: the Greeks. From the names of its people to its foods, from the laurel crown of its king to his elite fighting force (see the **Companions**), Illian has many echoes of Greece and the Hellenic world of the Mediterranean. At the same time, its namesake capital city, with its canals and mercantilism, parallels the city of Bruges, in Flemish-speaking Belgium, and many of Illian's fashions are likewise Dutch or Flemish in origin.[36]

Illuminators. A secretive guild with chapter houses that controls the production of fireworks, the Illuminators are akin to the many guilds of the Middle Ages, as well as their modern descendants, like the lodges of Freemasons, an organization to which Jordan belonged. The name chosen by Jordan for the guild not only shines a light on their work, it also echoes the supposed secret society of the Illuminati.

Ilyena Moerelle Dalisar. Often called Ilyena Sunhair, she derives from Inanna, the Mesopotamian goddess of fertility and power (Assyrian Ishtar), who is associated with the planet Venus. That Ilyena's husband in The Wheel of Time, **Lews Therin Telamon**, is likewise associated with Venus underscores their connection to each other and a world in balance: her death at his hands is the breaking of that balance, thereby instigating the Breaking of the World.

Isam Mandragoran. Rooted in Arabic, his first name means "bond." As for his surname, mandrake plants (genus *Mandragora*) feature in many stories owing to the fact that they are highly poisonous, but their roots—which can appear quite human-like—are often associated with witchcraft or black magic. The fact that his name can also be read as "man-dragon" indicates his special place in the fight against the **Dragon Reborn**, especially once Isam is fused with **Luc Mantear** into the figure of **Slayer**.

Ishamael. In the Bible, Ishmael was the first son of Abraham, born from Hagar, the handmaiden of Sarah, his wife who was thought to be infertile. After Sarah did conceive a son, Isaac, Ishmael and his mother were cast out of Abraham's house. Islamic belief is that Ishmael was one of the great patriarchs, who became the progenitor of many Arabic peoples and played a key role in the construction of the Kaaba. In The Wheel of Time, the **Forsaken** Ishamael was originally a philosopher named **Elan Morin Tedronai** who declared his allegiance to **Shai'tan** and was cast out by **Lews Therin**. He went on to became one of the Dark One's key lieutenants and, during the main plot of the books, the **Nae'blis**. He eventually began to call himself **Ba'alzamon**.

J

Jaem the Giant-Slayer. "Jack the Giant-Killer" is a Cornish fairy tale, first published in 1711. It is one of a number of tales involving a popular folk hero of the countryside named Jack. The most popular of these tales today is "Jack and the Beanstalk." Jordan playfully hinted at his own given name by changing the name of the hero from Jack to Jaem (i.e., Jim).

Jahar Narishma. Sent early to the Black Tower, Jahar was chosen to accompany Rand after **Dumai's Wells**. His first name derives from Shah Jahan, the powerful Mughal emperor of India who ordered the construction of the Taj Mahal for his beloved wife. His surname associates him with Narasimha, a "man-lion" avatar of the Hindu god Vishnu who represents the heroic resistance against evil.

Jaichim Carridin. Jaichim used the alias Bors among **Darkfriends**, a name that appears in Malory. Jordan's primary source for the first name Jaichim, however, appears to have been the two freestanding pillars that Solomon placed on either side of the First Temple's porch. Called Jachin and Boaz (1 Kings 7:21; meaning "it will establish" and "strength," respectively), these became prominent symbols in

Freemasonry and are found in most Masonic lodges. The Boaz pillar is associated with darkness (Jaichim as a Darkfriend), while the Jachin pillar is associated with light (Jaichim as a **Whitecloak**). His surname may connect to Ceridwen, the enchantress who controls a cauldron of poetic inspiration in Welsh mythology (see **Bowl of the Winds**): he is inspiring by deceit.

Jain Charin. See **Jain Farstrider**.

Jain Farstrider. One of the **Heroes of the Horn**, and a man made famous in **Randland** for what he wrote about his far wanderings, Jain is broadly indebted to many historical figures, including Marco Polo and John Mandeville. His specific name, however, comes from the Frenchman Jean Chardin (1643–1713), who wrote about his extensive travels throughout Persia and beyond. When trying to hide his identity, Jain Farstrider takes the name Noal Charin, and among the stories surrounding Jain in Randland was "**How Susa Tamed Jain Farstrider**." Susa, the ancient capital of the Achaemenid Empire, was one of the most famous stops Jean Chardin made in his travels. As for the name *Noal*, he was indeed someone who seemed to "know all."

Janduin. The biological father of **Rand al'Thor**. In his role leading the **Aiel** across the Spine of the World and to an eventual victory at the **Battle of the Shining Walls**, Janduin takes on the role of the historical Hannibal. His name derives from Joachim, who in Christian mythology is the father of the Virgin Mary: he and his wife, Anne, long childless, were promised a child after Joachim fasted in the desert for forty days. When he returned, he met her at the golden gate of Jerusalem.

Jangai Pass. It appears that Jordan named this pass for *Django,* a 1966 spaghetti Western film that takes place on the desolate border between the United States and Mexico. The film was, in its time, known for its extreme violence.

Jarna Malari. An **Aes Sedai** who seemed saintly but was secretly the head of the Black Ajah until **Ishamael** killed her after discovering that she was seeking to find and kill the **Dragon Reborn** on her own.

Her first name appears to derive from Jara, the hunter who accidentally kills the Hindu god Krishna with a single arrow. Her surname
derives from the infectious disease *malaria* (Latin for "bad air").

Jasin Natael. A gleeman alias of **Asmodean**. The surname is an abbre-
viated version of the Hebrew name *Natanael,* meaning "gift of God."
He indeed falls short of the name.

Jehannah. The capital of Ghealdan. Its name appears to derive from
Gehenna, a valley on the western edge of Jerusalem believed by many
to be a cursed place in which children were once sacrificed by fire.

Jenn Aiel. See **Aiel Tribes**.

Jeordam. The first **Aiel** to fashion a *darei* and an ancestor of **Rand
al'Thor**. His name appears to derive from *Jordan:* his story of fighting
the necessary fight to protect his people was, in one sense, Jordan's
own. In his role as the inventor of the *darei*, however, he parallels
King Shaka of the Zulu Empire (1787–1828).

Jesse Bilal. An **Aes Sedai** of the Brown Ajah. Her name derives from
two men who stand near the roots of their faiths. Her name Jesse is
shared with the father of King David in the Bible. Her surname is
shared with Bilal ibn Rabah, who was chosen by the prophet Muhammad to be the first *mu'azzin*—the one who would give the call to
prayer—in Islamic mythology.

Jezrail. An **Aes Sedai** who joins with the Shadow. Her name is taken
from the biblical figure of Jezebel, who for her violent attempts to in-
stall the worship of Baal across Israel became synonymous with the
worship of false prophets—and with a promiscuity that might follow
from such worship.

ji'e'toh. An **Aiel** term for honor and obligation, it combines the Japanese
concept of *giri* (meaning "obligation") with *bushido,* the code of moral-
ity and honor that defined the Samurai: "giri-bushido" becomes *ji'e'toh*.

Jimar Chubain. A general who thought he deserved more credit than he
got, Chubain is based on Bahrām Chōbīn, who rose to be a general of
the Sassanian Empire in the late sixth century. From this position he
helped to depose his king and then took the throne himself, to rule

as Bahram VI. This lasted only a year before he was himself defeated and assassinated.

Joar Addam Nessosin. The original name of **Asmodean**. His surname derives from the centaur Nessos, who tried to rape Hercules' wife, Deïanira. Shot by Hercules with an arrow, the dying centaur told Deïanira to collect his blood and use it as a love potion. It was instead a poison that killed her husband.

jolly-bag. See **golliwog**.

Jonai. An ancestor of **Rand al'Thor** who during the Breaking of the World led the **Aiel** from **Paaran Disen** along with many objects of power. His reluctance to leave objects behind during his journey, but his ultimate determination to see his oath through to the end, ties him to Jonah, the biblical prophet who reluctantly traveled (partly in the belly of a great fish) to Nineveh to pronounce God's judgment upon it.

Jumara. A jumart is a legendary crossbred animal that is half cow and half horse; the word is French, with a pronunciation akin to "jumar" in English.

Jurah Haret. An innkeeper whose negligence allowed **Faile Bashere** to be trapped in *Tel'aran'rhiod* by the Black Ajah. His surname derives from Harut, one of two angels in Islamic mythology who tempted humans with forbidden knowledge.

K

kaf. This bitter drink from **Seanchan** is coffee.

Kaisin Pass, Battle of. A conflict during the Trolloc Wars in which Rashima Kerenmosa earned a hard victory, it may be an echo of the fierce fighting in the "Bloody Gorge" during the Korean War's Battle of Chosin Reservoir.

Kamarile Maradim Nindar. The original name of **Graendal**. She was a great psychiatrist and an ascetic before turning to the Dark One. Her name, like many others in The Wheel of Time that don't have mythological connections, appears to be an amalgamation of place names.

Kandor. Like other kingdoms of the Borderlands, Kandor is a rich mix of real-world influences, this time stretching from Eastern Europe to the Black Sea.

Karaethon Cycle. This work, which contains the Prophecies of the Dragon in The Wheel of Time, is derived from the Black Book of Carmarthen. A medieval Welsh manuscript, it is one of the so-called Four Ancient Books of Wales. Among the Black Book's contents are a number of mythological and prophetic texts, including some about Merlin and King Arthur.

Kari al'Thor. Though Kári (meaning "wind") is a figure in Norse mythology, Jordan primarily based Rand al'Thor's mother on Kali, the four-armed Hindu goddess of both creation and destruction, time and change, who is sometimes referred to as the Divine Mother. See also **Calian the Chooser**.

Katar. This is undoubtedly a reference to Qatar.

Katerine Alruddin. A member of the Red Ajah (who is secretly of the Black). Her first name likely derives from Catherine de' Medici, the influential and at times ruthless ruler and mother of rulers in sixteenth-century Europe. Her surname takes Jordan's prefix of "al" and combines it with a form of the English word *ruddy*, meaning reddish in color.

Katrine do Catalan a'Coralle. The first queen of Murandy. Her name derives from Catherine of Aragon, the first wife of King Henry VIII of England. During Catherine's time, the Kingdom of Aragon and the Principality of Catalonia were united as the Crown of Aragon.

Keille Shaogi. An alias of **Lanfear**. The name comes from the English word *kill* and the Chinese politician Liu Shaoqi, who was chairman of the People's Republic of China at the outset of the Vietnam War but was purged by Mao Zedong in 1968.

Kerene Nagashi. One of the strongest **Aes Sedai** since **Cadsuane Melaidhrin**. Her surname matches a popular form of traditional music in Japan associated with the working class. It seems more likely, however, that Jordan meant to echo the similar Japanese word for "intermediary"—Kerene was among those chosen by **Tamra Ospenya** to search for the **Dragon Reborn** on her behalf.

Kiruna Nachiman. An **Aes Sedai**; her first name appears to derive from the Sanskrit word *karuṇā*, meaning "compassion," which is one of the most vital concepts in both Buddhism and Hinduism. That she wasn't the perfection of this principle is evident from her surname, which alludes to Hachiman, the god of archery and war in Japanese mythology.

Kno'mon. The name of this band of **Trollocs** echoes the word *gnome*. See **Trolloc Bands**.

Knotai. An Old Tongue name given to Mat by Tuon because he seems to bring destruction everywhere he goes, it is an English pun on the idea that he has "no ties" as a result.

Ko'bal. The name of this band of **Trollocs** echoes the word *kobold,* a creature from German folklore. See **Trolloc Bands**.

L

Laila Dearn. Her name, it seems, was likely modeled on that of actress Laura Dern.

Laman Damodred. According to the Book of Mormon, Laman was the eldest son of the prophet Lehi, but unlike his younger brother Nephi, he was rebellious against God's will. In a vision, Lehi saw that Laman would refuse to eat from the Tree of Life. Many Mormons believe Laman's descendants are Native Americans. In many respects, Jordan uses this story while also subverting it in The Wheel of Time. His Laman cuts down a tree sacred to the **Aiel** in order to make a throne for himself, thereby setting in motion the Aiel Wars and the birth of the **Dragon Reborn**. Laman's sword was taken from him by the Aiel after they killed him for his display of pride and power. On Laman's surname, see **Galad Damodred**.

Land of Madmen. See **Mad Lands**.

Lanfear. Her name derives from French *L'enfer,* meaning "Hell," combined with the English word *fear.* It's a fitting name for this **Forsaken**. Her original name was **Mierin Eronaile**.

Lan Mandragoran. Lan gets his name from Lancelot: the most able of Arthur's knights in Malory. When he was first putting his story together, Jordan planned for Lan to be a temporary antagonist for **Rand al'Thor**, just as Lancelot was for Arthur: "Lan's love for Nynaeve makes him break from Moiraine and brings him into conflict with Rand, into open opposition. (??)He will flee to become a hermit, though he wil [*sic*] return for the final battle.(??)"[37] Elsewhere, Jordan had early on thought Lan would be the secret lover of **Morgase Trakand** and thus the father of **Galad Damodred**. On his surname, see **Isam Mandragoran**.

Last Battle, the. With the forces of the Light reeling from a series of defeats, command of the remaining armies is given to **Matrim Cauthon**, who decides that the Last Battle will be fought upon the **Field of Merrilor**, on the borders of **Arafel** and **Shienar**, near the confluence of the River Mora with the Erinin. This enormous, wide-ranging battle is based on the historical Battle of Austerlitz, fought on December 2, 1805. Also known as the Battle of the Three Emperors, Austerlitz was a remarkable victory for Napoleon Bonaparte: though he was greatly outnumbered, his tactics enabled the Grande Armée of France to beat the combined armies of the Russian and Austrian Empires and effectively end the Third Coalition.

Having trapped and defeated one Austrian army at the Battle of Ulm in mid-October, Napoleon seized Vienna on November 15. He had little time to savor the success, however, as the remaining Austrian forces, under the leadership of Emperor Francis I, were converging with an enormous Russian force under the direct command of Emperor Alexander I. Napoleon, then in possession of the town of Austerlitz (modern-day Slavkov u Brna in the Czech Republic), feigned weakness as the allied coalition approached. He sent word of his willingness to discuss peace, while at the same time he pulled his forces out of Austerlitz and away from the commanding position of the Pratzen (Prace) Heights to its west. His troops dutifully obeyed the order not just to retreat, but to do so in a disorganized fashion in the face of enemy scouts—further suggesting to the allies that the French were weak, demoralized, and frightened. The Grand Armée then took up a position running from Telnitz (Telnice) in the

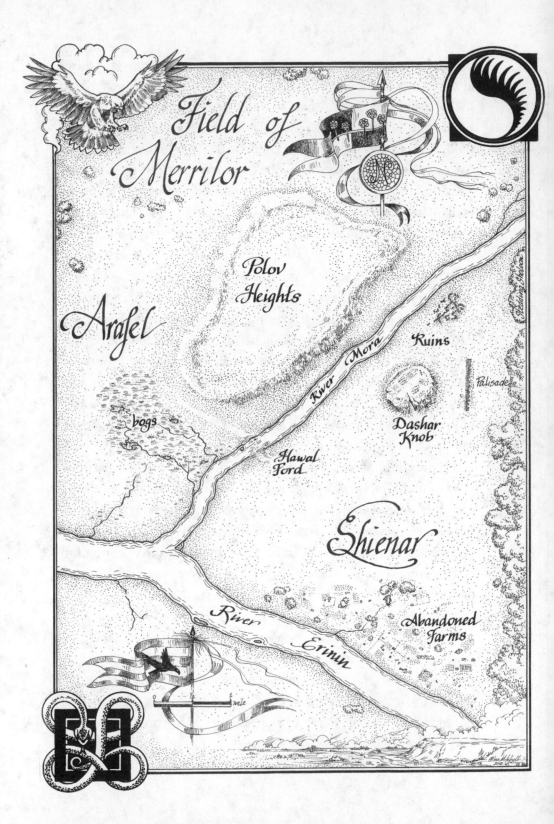

Field of Merrilor

Polov Heights

Arafel

Ruins

River Mora

Palisade

Dashar Knob

bogs

Hawal Ford

Shienar

River Erinin

Abandoned Farms

½   1 mile

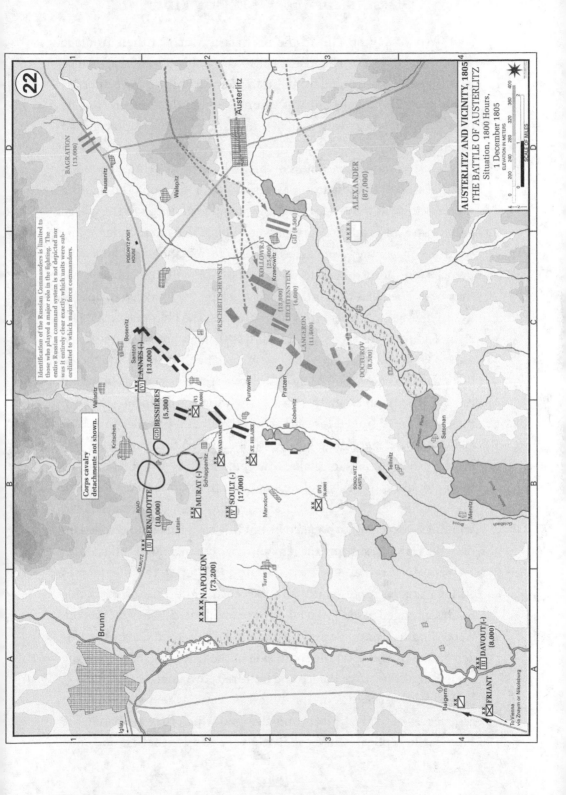

22

Identification of the Russian Commanders is limited to those who played a major role in the fighting. The entire Russian command system is not depicted nor was it entirely clear exactly which units were sub-ordinated to which major force commanders.

Corps cavalry detachments not shown.

Brunn

Iglau

Raigern

To Vienna via Znaym or Nikolsburg

Schwarzawa River

Turas

NAPOLEON (73,200) ×××××

Latein

BERNADOTTE (10,000) ××× I

OLMUTZ ROAD

Welatitz

Kritschen

BESSIÈRES (5,300) GD

MURAT (-) ×××

Schlappanitz

VANDAMME ××

ST. HILAIRE ××

SOULT (-) (17,000) ××× IV

(V) (6,000) ⊠

Marxdorf

(IV) (6,000) ⊠

Kobelnitz

Pratzen

Puntowitz

Santon

Bosenitz

LANNES (-) (13,000) ××× IV

POGORITZ POST HOUSE

Walspitz

Raussnitz

BAGRATION (13,000)

Austerlitz

Littawa River

PRZBRITSCHEWSKI

KOLLOWRAT (25,400)

Krzenowitz

(13,500) LIECHTENSTEIN (4,600)

LANGERON (11,600)

GD (8,500)

DOCTUROV (9,500)

SOKOLNITZ CASTLE

Telnitz

ALEXANDER (87,000) ××××

Satschan

Menitz

Goldbach

Brodt

Satschan Pond

Menitz Pond

DAVOUT (-) (8,000) ×× III

FRIANT ×× ⊠

AUSTERLITZ AND VICINITY, 1805
THE BATTLE OF AUSTERLITZ
Situation, 1800 Hours,
1 December 1805

SCALE OF MILES
0   1   2

ELEVATION IN METERS
200 240 280 320 360 400

N

southwest to Santon Hill in the northeast. Much of their frontage was defended by a small stream, called the Goldbach (Říčka). Napoleon himself commanded from Zuran (Žuráň) Hill, on the center left of his lines. The allied army was stunned to find the Pratzen Heights open, and they hurriedly marched into the position Napoleon had vacated.

Napoleon showed weakness on his right flank at Telnitz, convincing the allies to send their initial attack at that position. The fighting was ferocious, as the armies fought back and forth through the village and the stream beside it. More and more allied lines were brought forward to engage: they were determined to turn Napoleon's flank. The French were pushed back to the castle of Sokolnitz (Sokolnice), but they held. The allies then ordered an attack on the French left, hoping to pin it down to prevent it from reinforcing the beleaguered French right. Fighting had been going on for less than an hour, but it was just as Napoleon had hoped: his flanks staggered but didn't fall, and the allied might was now completely drawn away from its center. He sprang his trap: the main strength of the French lines, still unengaged with the enemy, now surged forward across the stream in order to assault the Pratzen Heights directly. The stunned allied forces were pushed off the position, only to retake it in fierce fighting when its reserves were brought to bear. Napoleon now sent his own reserves forward. The Heights buckled. The right allied flank, seeing the center falter, withdrew. French units peeled off from this engagement and rolled up onto the Heights, sending the remaining forces there into full retreat.

Napoleon's center now turned south to fall upon the allied forces still engaged around Telnitz on the French right. Pinned in by this double-pronged assault, the allies were obliterated. The rout was on. According to stories, fleeing Russians tried to retreat across the frozen Satschan Ponds on the south side of the field, but shots from the French artillery broke the ice and hundreds drowned.

Unlike most battles in The Wheel of Time, which typically take only pieces of the historical conflicts upon which they are based, the Last Battle replicates its base battle very neatly: that is, once one realizes that Merrilor is a mirror image of the Austerlitz battlefield rotated 90 degrees clockwise. The River Mora is the Goldbach stream. The Polov Heights are the Pratzen Heights. Dashar Knob is Zuran Hill. The bogs are the Satschan Ponds. Interestingly, only the ruins on the northwest of the Field of Merrilor are in the wrong position: by the actions of the Last Battle, these would seem to correspond to Sokolnitz Castle, but their corresponding topographical position ought to be at Hawal Ford, to the southwest.

On the mythological underpinnings of the Last Battle, see **Tarmon Gai'don** and **Eye of the World**.

Leane Sharif. In her difficulty to regain the Domani arts of seduction that she left behind to become **Aes Sedai**, Leane has a kind of parallel in actor Omar Sharif, the so-called sultan of seduction who enchanted as a leading man in 1962's *Lawrence of Arabia* before Hollywood moved on to other, younger actors.

Lenn. A decorated Marine pilot, John Glenn (1921–2016) was the third American in space and the first to orbit the Earth when he flew Friendship 7 in 1962. An enormously popular figure, he was ultimately considered both too old and too valuable to NASA's public image to be risked on the Apollo lunar missions. Instead, astronauts Neil Armstrong (1930–2012) and Buzz Aldrin (1930–) were the crew members of the Apollo Lunar Module Eagle that brought the first human beings to the moon. There have been debates that Jordan's "Lenn . . . [who] flew to the moon in the belly of an eagle made of fire" is therefore Armstrong—his name being derived from "Neil" spelled backward—but this isn't so. Jordan wanted his references to be organically developed rather than random puzzles: "Glenn" could easily become "Lenn" under natural linguistic development, but "Neil" could not develop likewise. Jordan, in fact, later sent an autographed copy of *The Eye of the World* to Glenn, noting his appearance. The fact that Glenn's role in the space program has been confused in Randland's cultural memory is also readily explicable, just as it is for Sally Ride (see **Salya**) having never conducted a spacewalk.

Lews Therin Telamon. The word *lucifer,* meaning "light-bearer," originated as a simple reference to the morning star—that is, the planet Venus, which often appears just before the dawn. Isaiah 14:12 condemns a Babylonian king by referring to him as this morning star that falls to earth. Christian writers later associated this passage with Luke 10:18, wherein Satan is described as falling from Heaven. Lucifer thereby came to be thought an alternative name for the Devil in Christian mythology. At the same time, however, the planet Venus became associated with John the Baptist, a forerunner of the "light" of the Christian Messiah (i.e., the Sun). The duality of these two readings of the morning star—one the great evil and the other bringing about the great good—define Lews Therin's role in The Wheel of Time. Telamon, in Greek mythology, is the father of Greater Ajax, one of the Greek heroes in Homer's *Iliad.* Likely due to a story of him hastily constructing an altar of stone to prevent his death at the hands of Hercules, Telamon's name is given to the architectural feature of colossal stone columns in the shape of men; Graves argues that Telamon is, in fact, a misremembered representation of Hercules himself.[38] In The Wheel of Time, Lews Therin is both the strongest of channelers and one who makes of himself a kind of colossal stone altar: **Dragonmount**. See **Ilyena**.

Lian. A legendary hunter of the **Horn of Valere** who may have become one of the **Heroes of the Horn**. The name derives from the English word *lion.*

Liandrin Guirale. A fearsome member of the Red Ajah of the **Aes Sedai**—and secretly a member of the Black. Her first name derives from the English word *lion.* Her surname echoes the word *guerrilla,* as in the secretive violence of guerrilla warfare.

Lillen Moiral. Original name of **Moghedien**. Her surname derives from the Greek *Moirai*: they wove fate; Moghedien weaves traps. See **Forsaken**.

Logain Ablar. A powerful False Dragon; it's often been pointed out that his name echoes Logan Street, just a stone's throw from Jordan's home on Tradd Street in Charleston. There may also have been a mythological source for him, however, in the legendary Irish king Lugaid Riab nDerg. In either case, Logain's surname likely comes from Abel, who was killed by his brother Cain in the Bible.

Loial. This **Ogier** appears early in Jordan's outlines: "Rand befriends a young Ogyr, Jak Vladad, much the same age as himself, and this youngling—who has the urge, strange for an Ogyr, to see other lands and have adventures—joins their party."[39] By the time *The Eye of the World* was being composed, however, he'd been renamed for what he is: *loyal*.

Lothair Mantelar. The founder of the **Whitecloaks**. His name is a garbled echo of Martin Luther (1483–1546), who ignited the Protestant Reformation by rejecting multiple practices of the Roman Catholic Church. The struggle between Protestants and Catholics would result in an enormous amount of bloodshed across the following centuries—just as would the struggle between the Whitecloaks and the **Aes Sedai**.

Luc Mantear. A prince who left home in hope of saving it, and who was taken by the Shadow and along with **Isam Mandragoran** made into **Slayer**, Luc has connections to Lugh, one of the most important figures in Irish mythology. Lugh was born into the Tuatha Dé Danann: a spear-wielding warrior, poet, and craftsman who came to be associated with the idea of rightful kingship.

Lugard. The capital city of Murandy. Its name looks similar to that of Lugarde, a small town in France, but just as plausibly could derive from Logres (itself from Welsh *Lloegyr*), one of the most common names for Arthur's kingdom.

Luthair Paendrag Mondwin. The son of **Artur Hawkwing** who led an army to **Seanchan**. His name combines that of Uther Pendragon, King Arthur's father in Malory, with Lugaid Riab nDerg (often Anglicized as Lothar), one of the triplet sons of Eochaid Feidlech, the legendary high king of Ireland. According to stories, the great hero Cú Chulainn split the Irish coronation stone (the Lia Fáil; see **Faile Bashere**) when it would not acknowledge Lugaid as king himself.

M

Machin Shin. The Black Wind, as the **Ogier** called it, consumed the souls of any it found in the Ways. It was, in its heedless destruction, a *machine of sin*, from which Jordan derived the name.

Maddin Todande. The nobleman whose founding of **Altara** is celebrated on Maddin's Day in late January, he likely echoes John Madden, who was a frequent color commentator of Super Bowls in late January beginning in 1982.

Mad Lands. This landmass in the southern seas of **Randland**, known for its violent and unpredictable male channelers who've turned the land itself into a chaotic, tortured sight, is an echo of Australia—a play on stereotypes of both Australia's original penal settlements and the postapocalyptic landscapes of the Mad Max series of films. For reasons unknown, it was labeled the "Land of the Madmen" on the map of Randland drawn up for *The World of Robert Jordan's Wheel of Time;* Jordan objected to this, writing several notes stating that this was a mistake. As one reads: "Land of Madmen is wrong. Should be The Mad Lands."[40] Why his requested changes (see also **Seanchan**) didn't make their way into the book is unknown. Even the finest of **Aes Sedai** make mistakes! In any event, they are correctly established on the map of Randland included in this book.

Maerion. Jordan's basis for this, one of **Birgitte Silverbow**'s names in a previous incarnation, is *The White Goddess* (362), in which Graves speculated about the possibility of a proto-goddess connecting the Mariandyni of Bithynia, legends of Mariamne, and the Virgin Mary—a goddess furthermore associated with Arianrhod (see *Tel'aran'rhiod*). Beyond this, it seems likely that Jordan was also nodding toward Francis Marion (1732–95), an officer of the American Revolution who became known as the "Swamp Fox" due to his skillful campaign of guerrilla warfare in the Lowcountry around Jordan's hometown of Charleston.

Mah'alleinir. The Power-forged hammer of **Perrin Aybara**. Its name derives from Mjölnir, the hammer of Thor.

Maighande, Battle of. An ancient battle at the time of The Wheel of Time, and the one in which Rashima Kerenmosa died, Maighande was the decisive battle in ending the Trolloc Wars. Jordan took its name from the Battle of Magh Rath, fought in 637. Supposedly the largest battle ever fought in Ireland, it saw Domnall II defeat and kill his foster son, Congal Caech, king of the Ulaid. Jordan probably first found the battle referenced in Graves' *White Goddess* (441–42).

Maighdin Dorlain. An alias of **Morgase Trakand**. She took the first name from her mother: it likely derives from the English word *maiden*. The surname derives from the French *d'Orléans*. Her whole name, then, is a reference to the "maid of Orléans," better known as Joan of Arc.

Malden, Battle of. Fought at the town of Malden in **Altara** between **Shaido Aiel** and a new alliance of **Seanchan** and **Westland** forces, this enormous battle presumably takes its name from the historical Battle of Maldon, which was fought between Viking raiders and English militia on the banks of the River Blackwater near the town of Maldon in 991. Little else connects the engagements, however.[41] At Maldon, the forces were relatively small: the Viking force was encamped on a small island connected to the shore by a low-tide ford, and the English arrayed against them on the shoreline. In a decision that continues to be debated by scholars today, the leader of the English allowed the Vikings free passage across the ford so that the two forces could engage in a melee battle on land. The English subsequently lost the fight, but the Vikings soon withdrew from the area. The Battle of Malden, on the other hand, is massive in scope, taking place in and around a landlocked town: its only connection to water is the aqueduct by which the Seanchan introduced an incapacitating drug into the water supply of the Shaido.

Instead, the tactical situation of Malden appears to match the earlier Battle of Cannae, from the Second Punic War, in 216 BC. One of the most famous battles in history, this fight saw the Carthaginian army of Hannibal meet and completely overwhelm a much larger Roman army on Italian soil. Outnumbered, Hannibal pinned his position to a river to prevent his left flank from being turned. As the lines met, Hannibal's line either fell back in the center or extended on its flanks—there are debates in the scholarship—such that the Carthaginian position formed up into a kind of crescent shape, partially encompassing the Roman position. Meanwhile, the Roman cavalry made a fierce attack intended to turn the Carthaginian flank. It was met with fierce fighting from Hannibal's Numidian cavalry and held off long enough for other units of Carthaginian horsemen to surprise them from the rear. Even as the Roman cavalry was routed off the field, the Carthaginian cavalry rounded back onto it: the main lines of battle were still engaged in a pitched struggle, and the horsemen fell upon the undefended rear of the Romans, who were now disastrously surrounded. The result was close to annihilation in a resounding Carthaginian victory that's still studied today.

Malkier. A nation of the Borderlands swallowed by the Blight just prior to the main story events of The Wheel of Time, Malkier is frequently viewed as an echo of Tibet, a region whose control by the Chinese government was a matter of much concern during Jordan's life. A number of Malkieri customs have parallels in the cultures of Tibet. That said, much about Malkier seems drawn from Japan, as well. (See, for instance, *hadori*.)

Manetheren. The ancient kingdom that once stood where the **Two Rivers** are in The Wheel of Time. Its name was originally *Etheran* in Jordan's notes, presumably a play on the word *ethereal*. Its final form may have been achieved by Jordan connecting it to Manetho (Greek Manéthōn), a historian of the third century BC whose chronology of ancient Egypt is vital to our understanding of the past. Alternatively, it could be that he read aloud his notes about the Fall of Manetheren, which refer to the "men of Etheran" (see **Aemon al Caar al Thorin**).[42]

Maradon, Battle of. A series of engagements in which the army of **Rodel Ituralde** conducted first a brilliant stand in a mountain pass, followed by an organized, fighting retreat that severely damaged and slowed the Trolloc armies advancing into Saldaea. Then, as he was trying to re-form his defenses near Maradon, miscommunication sent his men into a rout that was saved by a small company that rode to his rescue from the city. There, Ituralde organized a sequence of tactical ambushes of Trollocs in street-to-street fighting.

The sequence contains echoes of several ancient Greek battles, from Thermopylae to Marathon—the latter of which being the source of its name.

Marigan. An alias used by **Moghedien**, while she was disguised, it derives from the Morrigan ("phantom queen"), an Irish mythological figure whose appearance is a foretelling of battle.

Marin al'Vere. The mother of **Egwene al'Vere**. Her name derives from that of a Hindu goddess of rain, Māri or Mariamman, who is particularly popular in rural areas.

Masema Dagar. In his turn from an antagonistic view of **Rand al'Thor** to a fervent, fevered adoration of him as **Dragon Reborn**, Masema has strong parallels with the figure of Saul/Paul in the New Testament. The fact that his enthusiasm turns him into a "prophet" for Rand makes sense given that his first name appears to derive from Musaylimah, a seventh-century religious leader considered a "false prophet" by traditional Muslims. His surname comes from the English word *dagger*.

Mashadar. This horrific force within **Shadar Logoth** is *ash* and *shadow*, with the Latinate prefix *mal-*, meaning "bad": "evil ash darkness."

Materese the Healer, Mother of the Wondrous Ind. Through her service to the poor beginning in Calcutta, India, the Roman Catholic nun Mother Teresa (1910–97) became famous worldwide for her charity work. In the summer of 1985, as Jordan was beginning to plan The Wheel of Time, President Ronald Reagan awarded her the Medal of Freedom.

Matrim Cauthon. Like many of the main characters, Mat has influences far beyond a single individual. From Jordan's notes we can see that he began with the Welsh mythological figure of Math fab Mathonwy, the king of Gwynedd. It is Math who, tricked by his nephews, meets Arianrhod, who gives birth to Lleu Llaw Gyffes—a story repeatedly referenced in *The White Goddess*.

Within the larger contexts of the culture, Math becomes a figure of good fortune, which coincides neatly with the idea that Mat in The Wheel of Time would be a clever gambler of incomparable luck. Jordan furthered this with Mat's original surname: Piket, derived from piquet, an early sixteenth-century card game. The change of his surname to Cauthon allowed Jordan to echo the name of Cotton Mather (1663–1728), a Puritan minister from New England. From the witch-hating Mather, Mat got his distrust of **Aes Sedai**, though a great many of Mat's other interests are ones of which the conservative minister would not approve.

An arguably more important influence for Mat's character arc is the Norse mythological figure of Odin. It is from images of this war deity that Mat's wide-brimmed hat is derived, as well as many of his other titles and symbols. Odin carried a magical spear, for instance, and had two ravens, named Hugin ("Thought") and Munin ("Memory"). In addition, to gain knowledge, Odin sacrificed one of his eyes and was hung upon the world tree, Yggdrasil, for nine nights. Mat, who ultimately gains the knowledge of past generals, was similarly hung by a powerful spear suspended between two branches of the tree **Avendesora** in **Rhuidean**. That spear, an *ashandarei*, is adorned with two ravens and an inscription referencing memory and thought. Later, Mat sacrifices one of his eyes to rescue **Moiraine Damodred**. For a time Mat was also associated with the **Horn of Valere**, which will summon legendary warriors to fight at the Last Battle—just as the valorous dead live in Odin's hall, waiting for the horn calling them to Ragnarok. Other obvious mythological influences on Mat's character are the trickster gods that are found in many cultures: Jordan himself cited Loki (from Norse mythology), Coyote (Native American), and the Monkey King (Chinese).[43]

Mat is also one of several individuals in The Wheel of Time to have aspects of the American Revolutionary military leader Francis Marion, whose remarkably successful guerrilla tactics against the British in the Lowcountry around Jordan's hometown of Charleston led to him being called "the Swamp Fox."

Mayene. Jordan once stated that "Mayene is based culturally on the cities of the Hanseatic League, as well as Venice and Genoa when those cities were world commercial powers and city-states in themselves."[44] Its name, however, derives from the small French town (and river) of Mayenne, as well as its lords (among whom was Cardinal Mazarin; see **Mazrim Taim**).

Mazrim Taim. His name alludes to Cardinal Jules Mazarin (1602–61), who succeeded his mentor, Cardinal Richelieu, as France's preeminent clergyman and statesman under King Louis XIII. After that king's death Mazarin served as regent of France until Louis XIV came of age. He had an enormous influence on the course of European politics, not only across the decades of his career, but well beyond his life. When Taim was raised to the rank of **Forsaken**, he took the name **M'Hael**.

Mesaana. The **Forsaken** takes her name from Messalina, the third wife of Roman emperor Claudius and cousin to both Nero and Caligula. Messalina is most commonly remembered for her ruthless conspiracies against other members of the ruling classes in Rome and a scandalous reputation for promiscuity.

M'Hael. The title **Mazrim Taim** gave himself—and the name he took when made one of the **Forsaken**—M'Hael is said to mean "leader" in the Old Tongue. It's a clearly broken version of the name of the leader of God's armies, the Archangel Michael. The corrupted derivation says much about Taim's corrupted nature, especially as it also echoes the German word *Heil,* meaning "hail," which is commonly connected to the phrase "Heil Hitler."

Mierin Eronaile. The original name of **Lanfear**, it echoes the Irish mythological figure of Muireann (or Muirne), a woman with many suitors—her epithet is "beautiful lips"—whose father tried to prevent her marriage. Abducted and impregnated, she gave birth to the hunter-warrior Fionn mac Cumhaill. Mierin's surname might be an allusion to the Erinyes: the Furies of Greek mythology.

Mikel of the Pure Heart. According to Revelation 12:7–12, the Archangel Michael ("He who is like God") leads God's angels in battle against the "old serpent" Satan during the apocalyptic war in heaven. The patron saint of many warriors in arms, in Christian iconography he is often depicted carrying a sword and trampling on the Devil. See **Heroes of the Horn**.

Moghedien. Originally named **Lillen Moiral**; her name as one of the **Forsaken** comes from Mogadon, the brand name for the hypnotic drug nitrazepam, which is used to treat insomnia.[45] This is enormously appropriate given her fondness for working her will upon victims through compulsions and *Tel'aran'rhiod*.

Moiraine Damodred. Moiraine is present as "Emorgaine" in Jordan's earliest handwritten notes from Malory, where she's listed as his parallel for Morgan le Fay, with an additional possible connection to "Amyrlen," the parallel to Merlin.[46] Jordan ultimately abandoned his plans to make Moiraine the **Amyrlin Seat**—this part of her character was split off, it seems, to form **Siuan Sanche**—but the idea of her taking a Merlin-like role in advising his Arthur analogue, **Rand al'Thor**, remained. In Malory, Morgan le Fay is the youngest daughter of Igraine and the duke of Tintagel; since Arthur is Igraine's son by Uther, this makes him Morgan's half-brother. She also, in Malory, attempts to destroy Guinevere, repeatedly attempts to destroy Arthur's kingdom, and arguably is the greatest agent of his mortal wounding, but she is nevertheless the sorceress who takes him to Avalon for his final rest. Little of this ultimately survived in The Wheel of Time. Rand's mother is **Tigraine Mantear** (an analogue of Igraine), but her relation to Moiraine is far more distant: Tigraine's first husband was Moiraine's half-brother, **Taringail Damodred**.

As he often did with his main characters, Jordan combined the character of Moiraine with additional figures. She wasn't just Morgan and Merlin from Arthurian mythology—though that was already a fascinating mix—but she'd also incorporate aspects of the Moirai, the Fates of Greek mythology: for Rand and the other main characters, she was the one who set them on their paths toward destiny. In her position as an early guide, she also fulfilled the role of Gandalf within the Tolkien-inspired beginning of *The Eye of the World*. Thus did she serve as a focus for Jordan's aims to create a more feminist fantasy.

On her traveling name, meant to obscure her identity, see **Alys**. On her surname, see **Galad Damodred**.

Mordeth. The cursed, dark soul that overtook the city of Aridhol and turned it into **Shadar Logoth**, Mordeth comes from (and provides) *more death*.

Morgase Trakand. In the same early handwritten notes from Malory that first theorize **Moiraine Damodred** as a parallel for Morgan le Fay, Jordan listed Morgase as a parallel for Morgan's sister, Morgause—with the further possibility of potentially connecting the same character to Morgan.[47] Jordan clearly let go of any direct overlay of Moiraine and Morgase, but they remain associated: in The Wheel of Time, Morgase is Moiraine's half-sister-in-law. In Malory, Morgause is the half-sister of Arthur, the mother of both Gawain and Mordred, the latter being Arthur's son by incest, and a full sister to Elaine of Garlot. Jordan's Morgase is likewise the mother of his Gawain-analogue, **Gawyn Trakand**, but she's only a stepmother to the (initial) Mordred-analogue, **Galad Damodred**. Furthermore, rather than being a sister to an Elaine, she's the mother of one: **Elayne Trakand**, who ultimately becomes one of **Rand al'Thor**'s three loves.

Moridin. The name, used as an incarnation of **Ishamael**, derives from a mistaken English pronunciation of the Welsh name for Merlin: *Myrddin*. As Jordan summarized his character from Malory, Merlin was "said to be sired by the devil on a nun. Prophet and magician. Arthur's advisor from his birth until his marriage to Gwynevere, at which time Merlin departs with Nyneve, who seals hi[m] up in an enchanted cavern."[48] A disguised Moridin similarly advised **Artur Hawkwing** (and even **Rand al'Thor** at times), and there's no questioning his great powers.

Mosk the Giant. For most Americans growing up in the second half of the twentieth century, nothing defined their worldview more than the competing interests and threatening antagonisms between the United

States and the Soviet Union (after its dissolution, Russia), with its capital in Moscow. The Cold War arguably reached its zenith with the development of intercontinental ballistic missile (ICBM) systems capable of carrying a nuclear weapon around the globe—remembered in The Wheel of Time as a "Lance of Fire that could reach around the world."

Mountains of Dhoom. These are, quite recognizably, meant to recall Mount Doom, where the One Ring must be destroyed in Tolkien's *Lord of the Rings*.

Mountains of Mist. Echoing the Misty Mountains—the central topographical feature in Tolkien's *Lord of the Rings*—their presence as the first geographical location given in the present story of The Wheel of Time is among the many ways Jordan tried to make his world initially familiar to fans of the earlier work.

Murandy. Though it may look like "Burgundy," Murandy more likely owes its name to "Moorish al-Andalus": that is, that part of the Iberian Peninsula under Muslim control in the Middle Ages. From their naming conventions to their historical relationships with the powers around them, the people of Murandy have much in common with the people of Spain. See also **Katrine do Catalan a'Coralle**.

Myrddraal. These twisted Halfmen who command Trollocs want to *murder all,* from which their name derives.

N

Naean Arawn. An Andoran noble who opposed **Morgase Trakand**. Her surname reflects the king of the otherworld Annwn in Welsh mythology.

Nae'blis. The title given to the most favored of **Shai'tan**'s followers on Earth in The Wheel of Time, Nae'blis derives from Iblīs, a name of the Devil walking the world in Islamic tradition.

Nakomi. Among the materials Jordan left behind at his passing was a single line of instruction about a mysterious character who would appear to **Rand al'Thor** as he left **Shayol Ghul**: "An unknown woman says to Rand, 'Yes, that's good, that's what you need to do.' She hurries off."[49] Brandon Sanderson explains:

Well, the team had no idea who this was and—like the infamous pipe—had no idea why Jordan had chosen to write what he had. But I found it an intriguing seed, reminding me of other mysterious events (like the voice Rand hears at the end of *The Eye of the World*). Therefore, as I was working on the Aviendha scenes, I decided to bring in this mysterious woman—whom I named Nakomi. A foreshadowing of the scene Jordan had created at the epilogue.

I decided that this woman was the Creator's version of Shaidar Haran, something Jordan had explained a little in the notes. A vessel, kind of an avatar, but not quite. Shaidar Haran for the Dark One. Nakomi for the creator. But again, not actually the Creator. Something else, something close to the Creator—and inhabited in part by something *of* the Creator. As many have guessed, her birth is Jenn Aiel. Yes, they're still around. A few of them. And providing the vessel who was the counterpart to Shaidar Haran was part of their purpose, lore, and identity. Nakomi (which is her birth name among them) is the latest in this line.[50]

Narasim Bhuran. A leader from the War of the Hundred Years; his name relates to Narasimha, the man-lion avatar of the Hindu god Vishnu.

Narg. This name for a Trolloc who talked to **Rand al'Thor** and was killed by him early in *The Eye of the World*—Rand's first taking of a life in The Wheel of Time—is a word that has literally dark meanings in Tolkien's *Lord of the Rings*.

Neferi. The first *Soe'feia* of **Tuon**; her name alludes to the Ancient Egyptian queen Nefertiti.

Nemene Damendar Boann. The original name of **Semirhage**; her middle name echoes the English word *demander,* while her surname is that of an Irish goddess who personifies the River Boyne.

Nine Rings, The. An inn in Cairhien; its name is a nod toward the nine rings of power given to men in Tolkien's *Lord of the Rings*.

Noal Charin. See **Jain Farstrider**.

Nynaeve al'Meara. The detail given to Nynaeve's character within Jordan's early notes—only Rand gets equal attention so early—

indicates how important she was to the scope of The Wheel of Time.[51] She was, in origin, his parallel to Malory's Nyneve (Nimue in Graves' *White Goddess*), the fairy-like Lady of the Lake who enchants and entraps Merlin but faithfully helps carry a wounded King Arthur back to Avalon. Jordan's initial thoughts had Nynaeve accordingly trapping **Moiraine Damodred** "below ground, apparently slain. She is actually trapped halfway between life and death."[52] In the final scheme of things, of course, Moiraine is instead trapped within the **Tower of Ghenjei**, and by hands other than Nynaeve's.

The first surname Jordan gave her was Bayal.[53] This family name likely derived from Belili, which Graves believed to be the Sumerian White Goddess—the sister or lover of the "corn god" Tammuz—whose name had been warped into the wicked god Belial of the Bible, as well as "the Slavonic word *beli* meaning 'white' and the Latin *bellus* meaning 'beautiful'."[54] Jordan abandoned this complexity, however, in favor of the surname al'Meara, which was derived from the English word *mere,* meaning "lake": his analogue to Nyneve, the Lady of the Lake, would be Nynaeve of the Lake. As for the spelling of her name, which has confused many readers, Jordan's choice enabled him to attach her also to Nana, a Naiad in Greek mythology, probably descended from a Phrygian goddess whom Graves had identified as a counterpart to Arianrhod (*The White Goddess,* 305). Jordan surely nods at this when he has Nynaeve take the name "Nana" to disguise herself.

O

Ogier. Looking for a word that would echo the word *ogre,* Jordan first used the spelling *ogyr* before settling on *Ogier,* which was coincidentally a street name not far from his home in Charleston. As for his depiction of them, Jordan claimed to have been inspired by "a dozen different sources, at least."[55] Something of this variety is clear from his very early notes, which begin with them appearing much like the dwarves in Tolkien's *Lord of the Rings:* "a mountain people. Moderately short and very stocky, with big noses, men and women alike. Men wear full beards and hair very long. Quarreymen [*sic*] and stone-masons, most are. Practice ritual cannibalism in the fashion of the Maori. Other people look on them with a measure of horror for this."[56] By 1987, Jordan had changed his perspective significantly. His ogre analogues were now something of a cross between Tolkien's dwarves and ents: still "a mountain people," but at this point "very tall and very stockily built, men and women alike. Men wear full beards and hair very long. Very flat of face. Considered ugly by most who know of them. Excellent stoneworkers. Major occupations are stoneworking and forresting [*sic*]. Goats tended by children. Men speak of forests and trees as if they were a flock of animals."[57] Among the other changes that the Ogier underwent in drafting is how they came to **Randland**. In the published books, it was via the Book of Translation, but in early notes they instead arrived by means of the Book of Changes—which is the most common English translation of *I Ching*, the influential book of ancient Chinese divination. Ironically, Jordan's notes also inform us that there are no Ogier in the Chinese-akin land of **Shara**: "no Ogier found their way to that part of the world after the Breaking and those who were already there were killed or died of illnesses, accidents etc."[58] See also *stedding*.

Olver. An orphaned boy who idolizes **Matrim Cauthon** and sounds the **Horn of Valere** for the **Last Battle**. Olver has obvious connections with the title character of Charles Dickens' *Oliver Twist*. In his sounding of the horn, however, he ultimately parallels Olivier, a brave warrior and best friend of Roland in the medieval epic *Song of Roland*. Though founded on the historical Battle of Roncevaux Pass between Charlemagne and local Basques in 778, the story of *Roland* is a fantastical account pitting Charlemagne's betrayed rear guard against an enormous force of enemy Muslims. In it, Olivier begs his commander, Roland, to blow the oliphaunt—a horn that would alert Charlemagne to their fight and bring him and the rest of the main army into the fray. Roland stubbornly refuses to blow it until it's too late for their lives to be saved. Thankfully, Olver doesn't wait as long.

One Power. Split into male and female halves that should work in harmony, the One Power is represented in The Wheel of Time by a symbol that mimics the yin-yang. Unlike the actual yin-yang symbol, however, Jordan's is missing the corresponding dots—thus signifying that the two halves of the One Power are seen as entirely distinct from the other.

oosquai. This light brown **Aiel** alcohol, distilled from *zemai* (that is, maize or corn), is a thinly veiled American whiskey. Jordan was a fan.

Osan'gar. After they were killed at the **Eye of the World**, **Balthamel** and **Aginor** were resurrected by the Dark One as **Aran'gar** and Osan'gar, respectively. These are said to be the names of twin daggers in the Old Tongue: the word *gār* means "spear" in Old English. Born **Ishar Morrad Chuain**, Aginor was a biologist during the Age of Legends. His rebirth as Osan'gar reflects this past: Òsanyìn is a manifestation of God in the Yoruba mythology—a one-eyed, one-armed, and one-legged man associated with healing herbs.

Otarin. One of the **Heroes of the Horn**, he derives from Oscar, a popular character in the Fenian Cycle of Irish mythology. Oscar is the son of the warrior-poet Oisín and grandson of the great hero Fionn mac Cumhaill.

Owyn. The nephew of **Thom Merrilin** who was tragically gentled by Red Ajah. Owyn's name derives from the Welsh name Owain, which was shared by several knights in Arthurian legend—most important among them Arthur's nephew, often translated as Yvain—as well as the historical Welsh rebel leader Owain Glyndŵr, who likely influenced the **Dragon Banner** in The Wheel of Time.

P

Paaran Disen, Gates of. The site of a battle between **Lews Therin Telamon** and **Ishamael** in the Age of Legends, it takes its name from Genesis 3:4, in which God places angelic cherubim and a flaming sword before the gates of Paradise, in order to prevent an expelled humanity from returning to Eden. By the time of the battle in The

Wheel of Time, it was clear that the peace and prosperity of what had been a kind of earthly Paradise was irretrievably lost.

Padan Fain. To "feign" something is to fake it—a fitting name for this Darkfriend peddler. Though originally named Eward White, he was renamed Mikal Fain by the time Jordan was writing his Test Manuscript of *The Eye of the World*. It was in the review of this, though, that his first name is crossed out by pencil and changed to the now-familiar Padan.[59] This final name derives from Padan Aram, a land repeatedly mentioned in Genesis. According to the fourth-century Jewish midrashic interpretation of Rabbi Isaac, the region was populated with deceitful wicked-doers. (See also **Aram**.)

Paedrig. One of the **Heroes of the Horn**, he derives from Saint Patrick, who (among other things) supposedly banished the snakes from Ireland.

Paitar Neramovni Nachiman. The king of **Arafel**. His surname derives from Hachiman, the god of archery and war in Japanese mythology.

Pedron Niall. Born in **Murandy**, he rose to become the Lord Captain Commander of the **Whitecloaks** and was murdered by **Abdel Omerna**. Pedron's name is derived from Pedro I, the king of Aragon and Pamplona with a prominent role in the Christian Reconquista. On November 15, 1096, he defeated a Moorish army in the Battle of Alcoraz: according to legend, Saint George had appeared on the battlefield to signal support for the Christian forces. After the battle, the Aragonese adopted as a heraldic coat of arms the Cross of Alcoraz: a Cross of Saint George with a decapitated Moor's head in each quarter. The next year, Pedro joined with Rodrigo Díaz de Vivar to defeat a Muslim army at the Battle of Bairén. Rodrigo is more popularly known as "El Cid"—the same nickname given to Jordan's alma mater, The Citadel. As for Pedron Niall's surname, it matches the name of Niall of the Nine Hostages, a semi-legendary high king of Ireland from whom the Uí Néill dynasties claimed descent. (See also the **Band of the Red Hand**.)

Perival Mantear. The young cousin of **Galad Damodred** and **Rand al'Thor**, Perival is an analogue to Percival, one of the most exceptional of King Arthur's knights, who was originally the knight of the Grail quest before he was replaced, by the time of Malory, with Galahad.

Perrin Aybara. An apprentice blacksmith who grows to be a massive and capable fighter. Perrin's name derives from Perun, a Slavic god of war and sky whose weapon of choice was an axe. As with other main characters, however, he is far more. Unquestionably, Perrin also represents the Norse god of thunder, Thor, even to the point of wielding a similarly named weapon to Thor's hammer, Mjölnir (see ***Mah'al-leinir***). His massive strength ties him to figures like Hercules.

But Perrin is far more than his strength and size. From the beginning of *The Eye of the World*, he is characterized by his gentle ways, by his empathetic consideration of others. Of the two possible origins of his surname known, both reflect this "priestly" side of his personality. One is that Jordan derived it from the Welsh *ab Aaron*, "son of Aaron"—referencing the biblical brother of Moses from whom the high priests of the Israelites claimed descent. The other possibility is that Jordan found the name in that of a somewhat obscure saint, Romanus Aybara, who was martyred by beheading at Nagasaki in 1628—along with his father, Paul, and his brother, Leo.

The other key aspect of Perrin's personality and character arc is that he is resolutely tied to the natural world, most obviously in his status as a **wolfbrother**. In this, he represents the collision of civilization and wilderness: he recognizes that social connections are necessary, but they inevitably corral freedoms. This tension consistently informs his plot, as does his solution to see the problem through the eyes of love.

pipes. An avid collector of pipes who was often smoking one at his writing desk, Jordan made a number of early notes about the use and manufacture of pipes and "tabac" (that is, tobacco) in **Randland**. Here, for instance, is his discussion of the social aspects of pipe-smoking in The Wheel of Time:

> In the villages a pipe of fired clay, or more so, of stone, is expensive, and will only be had by the more relatively well-to-do. All others

smoke pipes carved of wood, some worked quite fancifully. Stone pipes are sometimes carved, as well. Stone pipes and clay pipes usually have long stems, but wooden pipes sometimes are short.

day-pipe: a pipe with a small bowl, holding enough pipeleaf for such a short smoke as a man might take during a break from work.

even-pipe: a pipe with a large bowl, of the sort smoked in the evening when a man can relax for a goodly length of time.

Pipe smoking is considered a male habit, and the women who do it are so few as to occasion comment. Some women consider it a filthy vice, while others enjoy the smell of the pipeleaf.

Pipeleaf is grown in every village, and it is one of the trade items bought by the yearly graintraders and others. There are a number of strains of pipeleaf, just as there are different kinds of tobacco.[60]

Most fascinatingly, he also ensured that one of the final, arguably most mysterious images in The Wheel of Time is Rand lighting his pipe with a mere thought.

Pipkin, the Fall of. A battle from the memories of **Matrim Cauthon**, it presumably alludes to the Gulf of Tonkin incident in 1964, which precipitated the fateful escalation of American involvement in what would soon become the Vietnam War. As it happens, aboard the USS *Maddox* in those fateful days was Commander Herbert L. Ogier.

Plains of Maredo. These wide and wild flatlands take their name from the town of Laredo, Texas, which features in many Western novels, movies, and TV shows.

R

Radhanan Paendrag. The mother of **Tuon Athaem Kore Paendrag**. Her name—but none of her attributes—is taken from Radha, a Hindu goddess associated with love and compassion. She is, essentially, "Radha none."

Rahvin. Though it looks a lot like *Raven* in English, the **Forsaken**'s name comes from Ravana, a Hindu demon. In the *Ramayana*, Ravana abducts the wife of Rama and is ultimately killed for it; in The Wheel of Time, Rahvin abducts **Morgase Trakand**, and **Rand al'Thor** kills him for it.

Rand al'Thor. Unsurprisingly, the character in The Wheel of Time with the most complicated origins is Rand al'Thor, the **Dragon Reborn**. In Jordan's early notes he began as a character named Rhys—an Old Welsh name meaning "fiery warrior" and perhaps related to the character's red hair—before Jordan switched his name to Rand.

Of the many mysteries Jordan left behind, the lack of a clear answer to the question of where this name came from may be the most frustrating. There's no obvious example to draw from in Graves' *White Goddess* or Malory's *Morte d'Arthur*. It may well be that the author simply had a personal affinity for the name: the main character of his unpublished Western, *Morgan*, was named Randall (Ran) Morgan.

Another possibility—we can only speculate—is that Jordan took it from Tolkien's Middle-earth. In the Sindarin language of the Elves, *randir* means "wanderer": thus, in *Lord of the Rings*, the Elves' name for the wizard Gandalf was *Mithrandir*, meaning "grey wanderer" and reflecting his rather nomadic life. From early on in his planning, Jordan envisioned that Rand would "wander as a beggar."[61] In one of his first accounts of this:

> At some point hero is taken prisoner by queen of country he has grown up in. He is charged with treason. Her daughter doesn't want him killed. Thge [sic] sentence is commuted from death, but he is blinded by hot irons and his right hand is cut off. Then he is throuwn [sic] out of the city to become a mendicant. By this time he has the dragon marks on his forearms. Beyond the city he is set on by mounted men, who are ready to slay him when he raises him arms to fend them off and shows the dragon marks. His upraised staff draws a lightning bolt, which kills some of the men and frightens the rest off. He sees glimmerings of light afterwards, but thinks it is after-affect [sic] of lightning bolt. In next book he regains his sight and his hand.[62]

And then there is this: the name Rand in English derives from Old English *Randulf*—meaning "shield-wolf," a metaphor for a good protector. Put it all together and it certainly seems a suitable match for Jordan's hero. Rand is, after all, a magic-wielding protector hurrying to save the world, who would ultimately be left a wanderer within it.

His original surname was "Al'thur,"[63] but Jordan changed this early to al'Thor, an exceedingly clever combination of King Arthur and the Norse god Thor. Using the Arabic prefix *al-*, a definite article meaning "the," and echoing the Welsh patronymic naming convention where *ab* means "son of," Jordan's *al'Thor* can mean the "son of Thor," "*the* Thor," and "Arthur," depending on how one looks at it.

Even more than this, Rand is a nexus of the gods and savior figures across a wide variety of mythologies and traditions. He has multiple aspects of the Norse god Tyr, for instance, and his wounds that won't heal are stigmata akin to the wounds of Christ or the Fisher King from the Arthurian legends. The latter parallel-tracks across the whole of The Wheel of Time: the tainting of *saidin* is called the "Mournful Stroke" in Jordan's notes,[64] a clear reference to the Dolorous Stroke of Arthurian myth. In this respect, Rand is both the Fisher King whose health is tied to the health of the land—something that shows up in particular within the last books of the series—and the seeker of the Holy Grail (see ***sa'angreal***) who can heal the wound.

Randland. Though not used within the books, this is the term used to refer to the fullness of Jordan's world in The Wheel of Time. It is our Earth in a different age: the result of a different shifting of tectonic plates along with the cataclysmic Breaking of the World. Something of our geography is nevertheless written into the rocks of Randland. We conventionally describe Earth as having seven continents—Africa, Antarctica, Asia, Australia, Europe, North America, and South America—but in terms of contiguous lands there are four continental landmasses: Afro-Eurasia (Africa, Asia, and Europe), the Americas (North and South America), Antarctica, and Australia. Jordan's world is based on this concept. Most readily apparent is his "Antarctica" (under the Southern Ice Cap) and his "Australia" (the **Mad Lands**). North

and South America is the continental landmass containing **Seanchan**. The continent from which the Seanchan colonists came—and the one upon which most of the series' action takes place—must thereby contain the broken remnants of our Africa, Asia, and Europe. In Jordan's world, this continent is split in two by the horizontally running Mountains of Dhoom, above which is the Great Blight. Below this line of peaks are three general regions from west to east: the **Westlands**, the **Aiel Waste**, and **Shara**. How these map to the Earth is perhaps predictably imprecise. A direct reading might connect the fertile Westlands to the west coast of sub-Saharan Africa, the desolate Aiel Waste with the Sahara, and Shara with China and Southeast Asia. Everything north of this—Europe and the former Soviet Union—would be within the Great Blight. The Isles of the **Sea Folk** between this continent and the Mad Lands would be an echo of the islands of Indonesia, Malaysia, and other countries. In its historical contexts, however, the Westlands are far more connected to Europe: it is here that **Artur Hawkwing** arises (an analogue to King Arthur), and from here that the colonists were sent to Seanchan (an analogue to the Americas). In this view, the Mediterranean appears to have been erased, with parts of northern Africa having been shoved upward to be east of Europe beyond the mountain range called the Spine of the World. And we have, among Jordan's papers, notes that the Sea Folk were based on Polynesians and the Māori.

The map of Randland presented here differs from that included in *The World of Robert Jordan's Wheel of Time* in two substantial ways, both explained in the corresponding entries in this guide. First it correctly labels the Mad Lands, which were previously and incorrectly given the name "Land of the Madmen." Second, it significantly resizes and reshapes Seanchan.

Raolin Darksbane. One of the most powerful False Dragons ever to have existed. His name comes from China's Shaolin Temple, where a distinct strand of martial arts was developed.

Rhadam Asunawa. The zealous High Inquisitor of the **Whitecloaks**. His name echoes that of Rhadamanthus, one of the three judges of the dead in Greek mythology.

Rhiannon. Needing a name for a haughty past queen humbled by the **Aes Sedai**, Jordan chose Rhiannon, which Graves translated as "Great Queen"—though the stories of Rhiannon in Welsh mythology bear relatively little resemblance to the plot in The Wheel of Time.[65]

Rhodric. There are numerous historical figures with some form of the name Roderick—from a Visigothic king to a martyred saint—in addition to Welsh rulers with the name Rhodri—including the remarkable king of Gwynedd, Rhodri the Great—but none are a perfect fit to the few details we're given about this **Aiel** ancestor of **Rand al'Thor**. Jordan may have simply liked the name.

Rhuidean. A city built by the **Jenn Aiel** to house a great number of powerful objects preserved for the **Aes Sedai**, as well as the sacred tree, **Avendesora**, Rhuidean has a name that echoes Irish *bruidhean*—which refers to the residences of fairies similar to the *aos sí* (see **Aes Sedai**)—while also implying the *ruin* into which the city has fallen. More importantly, just as the **Aiel** have a number of parallels to the ancient Israelites, Rhuidean can be seen as a parallel to Jerusalem: in particular, it holds echoes of the sacred precinct atop the Temple Mount, which was maintained by a specific tribe of the Israelites, the Levites. In this parallel, the glass columns of Rhuidean, which reveal the truth of the Aiel but cause many to go mad and die, is akin to legends—some quite recent in origin—of the Ark of the Covenant, and its place within the Holy of Holies and the Well of Souls. Of note: the glass columns were originally a circle of standing stones akin to Stonehenge.[66]

Rodel Ituralde. A capable military commander, he owes much to Rodrigo Díaz de Vivar, the Spanish hero known as "El Cid"—a nickname shared by Jordan's alma mater, The Citadel. Both men are renowned warriors and leaders of men, considered fair-minded, loyal, and strong.

S

sa'angreal. Looking to find a name for objects that allow channelers to draw more One Power than they otherwise can, Jordan found in Malory the *Sangreal*, another name for the Holy Grail. For a time in the early drafting of The Wheel of Time, Jordan considered changing the name of these objects—or at least some of them—to *cris*.[67] This notion was built from the Javanese kris, an asymmetrical, finely crafted dagger believed to have magical properties. After more consideration, he returned to using the word *sa'angreal* generally, but decided that those which were weapons—in particular, a set of power-imbued swords in what would become the Stone of Tear—would be called *cris*.[68] Eventually, he resorted instead to a tiered grouping of objects using the derived names of *angreal* and *ter'angreal*.

Saldaea. Asked about its origins, Jordan said, "Saldaea is based, in part, on a number of Middle Eastern cultures and several cultures in countries surrounding the Black Sea. In part."[69] The name itself derived from Chaldea, a small country in ancient Mesopotamia, and its cities of Tyr and Sidona echo Tyre and Sidon in Lebanon.

Salya walking among the stars. An astronaut and physicist, Sally Ride (1951–2012) was the first American woman in space. The enormous cultural impact she had for women marks her as John Glenn's "daughter" within the American space program (see **Lenn**). While she didn't take part in a spacewalk herself, she was on the same 1987 mission during which Kathy Sullivan became the first American woman to do so.

Samel Crawe. A man from **Emond's Field**, Samel echoes Samuel Crowley, a young man who died during the Battle of Point Pleasant in 1774. Some consider this engagement the first fight of the American Revolution—making Crowley arguably the first victim of the war.

Sammael. In Jewish literature, Samael is among the most complex of the angels: the angel of death and the accuser of God's enemies. Christian literature can take this even further, branding him a fallen angel—perhaps even a stand-in for Satan himself. Within The Wheel of Time, Sammael may also echo Napoleon. Both are remarkable generals, and both are perceived to be sensitive about their height relative to other men and what it says about their power. Furthermore, when he reenters the world, he does so as Lord **Brend** of **Illian**: Napoleon's imperial emblem was a bee, and Illian's symbol is nine golden bees. Before he became one of the **Forsaken**, Sammael's original name was Tel Janin Aellinsar. His first two names reveal him to be close to (but still short of) the equal of **Lews Therin Telamon**; his surname connects him to the second-century Greek military writer Aelianus Tacticus, showing Sammael's mastery of field command. Among the **Shaido Aiel** his alias was Caddar, which derives from the Welsh name *Caddaric*, meaning "battle leader" (i.e., "general").

Samma N'Sei. Jordan originally imagined that there was not just one **Eye of the World**, but *seven*. Each of these would be associated with a seal of the Bore, and the Dark One had tasked a group of red-veiled former **Aiel** to destroy them. His concept of having multiple "eyes" was abandoned, but the idea of these secret Aiel was not. Among Jordan's directives for the end of The Wheel of Time was the fact that these, in addition to attempting in vain to find and "blind" the Eye, were "being held back as a surprise for the Last Battle," and that they were called "something along the line of 'Sight blinders' or 'Eye blinders'."[70] Elsewhere in his notes he favored "Eyeblinders," who "have been confined to the Blight, and to Thakandar, for reasons of security, so they will come as shocking surprise."[71] Their Old Tongue name, *Samma N'Sei*, derives from Japanese, meaning "honored master."

Sarainya Vostovan. A proud noblewoman of **Arafel** who became an (arguably ill-deserved) Accepted among the **Aes Sedai**. Her name derives from the Hindu goddess Saranyu (alternatively Sanjna), the chief wife of the sun god. She's often considered the mother of the god of death, Yama, in addition to other deities.

sa'sara. A sensual and provocative dance performed in **Saldaea**. Its name is likely taken from the salsa. Whether any moves are likewise echoed is up to the reader's imagination.

Sea Folk. In his early notes, Jordan likens them to Polynesian people and, specifically, to the Māori.[72] See **Atha'an Miere**.

Seanchan. Senchán Torpéist was a legendary bard of seventh-century Ireland. Among the stories of

Senchán is that he became aware that the full text of the great early Irish epic *Táin Bó Cúailnge* had been lost and so went on a journey with his fellow poets to find it. Jordan was captivated by the name Seanchan, as he found it spelled in Graves' *White Goddess,* and he ultimately employed it in conjunction with those people who departed the **Westlands** under **Luthair Paendrag Mondwin**: like Senchán needing to return to Ireland to take his rightful place as the chief bard, so, too, would the Seanchan be driven by their need to return to the Westlands to take what they believed was their rightful place in ruling it. Though meant to recall America in the location of their land (west across the ocean; see **Randland**) and their practice of slavery (see *a'dam*)—to the point that he suggested they had a Southern American accent[73]—Seanchan culture is otherwise largely indebted to Asian nations. As Jordan once noted, it's based on "a good deal of Japan, of the Shogunites, Imperial China, and in general a good many rigid hierarchical stratified societies. Too many to list really, I suppose."[74]

As with the **Mad Lands**, Seanchan was mistakenly presented in *The World of Robert Jordan's Wheel of Time.* Of the map of Randland that was printed in it, Jordan noted a need to "extend Seanchan a little farther south. Make southern portion of Seanchan wider by 75%, all south of equator."[75] Despite the fact that he repeatedly pointed out that the map "needs correction,"[76] his requested changes didn't make their way into the book for reasons unknown. They are, however, correctly established on the new map of Randland included in this book.

This re-dimensioning of the Seanchan continent not only aligns with Jordan's vision, but it also helps to explain what was previously a mystery: Why did the Seanchan cross the wide expanse of the Aryth Ocean to get to the Westlands when the distance to reach them was seemingly less across the Morenal Ocean? Part of the answer, we now know, is that Seanchan was much closer than the published map had shown.

Selene. An alias of **Lanfear**, it comes from the Greek goddess of the moon.

Semirhage. The **Forsaken**'s name derives from Semiramis, a powerful legendary Assyrian queen. In the Middle Ages, she became a figure of sinful lust: so  well known that in his *Divine Comedy,* Dante Alighieri puts her in the Second Circle of Hell. Jordan combines her name with the English word *rage*.

Sevanna. A Wise One of the **Shaido Aiel** who unmistakably thirsts for power. Her name derives from the city of Savannah, Georgia, only a few hours from Jordan's hometown of Charleston. Both cities have a great beauty, while also sharing a dark history as seats of slavery and the old South. Perhaps it is for this reason that Jordan leaves Sevanna, in the end, in the very chains with which she hoped to bind others.

Shadar Logoth. It appears that Jordan constructed this name from the word *shadow* combined with *Morgoth* from Tolkien's *Lord of the Rings*.

Shaidar Haran. Jordan's primary inspirations are once again the word *shadow* and various words associated with evil in Tolkien's *Lord of the Rings*.

Shaido Aiel. They are, of course, the *Shadow* **Aiel**.

Shaiel. The name taken by **Tigraine Damodred** among the **Aiel** is one of Jordan's most interesting constructions. Its origin lies, first and foremost, in Tigraine's relationship to **Shayol Ghul**: her son, born upon a volcano, will ultimately confront the Dark One within a volcano. Her name would be a parallel to this, and to its biblical origins in Sheol. But Jordan managed more: among the names given to God in the Bible is *El Shaddai,* often translated "God of the Mountains." By inversion and truncation, Jordan's Shaiel echoes this, too. Not that she is the Creator, of course, but through her son the Creator's will would be done.

Shai'tan. The word *satan,* from the Hebrew word for "adversary," was in early Old Testament materials an epithet rather than the name for an individual being. Over time, however, it became associated with the Devil alone: a singular entity that was, particularly in Christian mythology, adversarial to the God. It is this near-dualist notion of good and evil that is captured within the conflict in The Wheel of Time between the Creator and Shai'tan, the Dark One. Jordan originally toyed with naming the Dark One Sa'khan—perhaps trying to find a middle ground between Satan and the khans of Central Asia—before abandoning the name in favor of Sha'tan and finally arriving at Shai'tan.

Shara. This large and, for much of the series, rather mysterious part of **Randland** is part Africa (its name comes from *Sahara*) and part China (its location in the "far east," its silks, and its closed ports).

Shayol Ghul. Jordan apparently favored Ghul Shayol early on, before deciding on the reverse order among his notes.[77] The name originates with *Sheol,* another name for the place of the dead in the Hebrew Bible. Though Sheol was often conflated with Christianity's Hell, Graves had described it as "the uninhabitable parts of the world."[78] To this Jordan appended an echo of the word *ghoul,* to better equate it with a frightening place of living death. On the way in which the mountain appears and is balanced in The Wheel of Time, see **Dragonmount**.

Shienar. Though largely modeled on the feudal period of Japan in its culture and linguistics, Shienar actually takes its name from Genesis 14:1, which refers to the biblical kingdom of Shinar, whose king is given as Amrafel, alongside the kingdom of Elasar (see **Arafel** and **Easar Togita**).[79]

Shining Walls, Battle of the. The Aiel War, in which four clans of **Aiel**, after **Laman Damodred** cut down a tree grown from **Avendesora**, crossed over the Spine of the World and descended on the **Westlands** in a bloody, massive invasion lasting over two years, is based on the first phase of the Second Punic War, which began in 218 BC. In that year, the Carthaginian general Hannibal led his troops in an unprecedented march from the Iberian Peninsula across southern Gaul and through the Alps to descend upon Roman lands. At the Battle of the Trebia in late December, Hannibal handed the Romans the first of three massive defeats in three years, culminating in the extraordinary Battle of Cannae. The Aiel, in Jordan's reimagining, represent the Carthaginians, and the Great Coalition of Westland kingdoms are the Romans.

The culminating battle of the Aiel War—a three-day engagement called the Battle of the Shining Walls or the Battle of the Blood Snow, among other names—has much in common with Trebia. In that fight, the sudden appearance of Hannibal's army out of the Alps shocked the unprepared forces of the Romans and the loosely allied tribes settled in the region. Hannibal descended on Turin and seized it. Its numerous supplies replenished his own, and his success brought more and more tribes into his force. The Roman consul Publius Scipio rushed to meet the threat and in late November suffered a hard defeat at the Battle of Ticinus. He himself was badly wounded and would have died, had it not been for a successful rescue led by his sixteen-year-old son. Scipio retreated with what remained of his army, and Hannibal continued to gather strength. Meanwhile, the second Roman consul arrived, Sempronius Longus, who was anxious to succeed where Scipio had failed. Hannibal, recognizing an overeager opponent, took position across the Trebia River from the Romans near modern Piacenza. On a cold and snowy day in late December, Hannibal used fast attacks by his Numidian cavalry to goad Sempronius into an attack. The Romans advanced in loose order, wading through the frigid, chest-high waters of the Trebia and up onto an open floodplain atop which the Carthaginian army was formed up. General battle ensued, but Hannibal had secreted a force of two thousand men south of the field. As the armies struggled, they burst forth into the Roman flank: a hammer to crush the pinned Romans against the anvil of the stout Carthaginian lines. Sempronius fled, but he'd lost perhaps twenty thousand men in the disaster. At the news, the people inside the walls of Rome were sent into a panic.

Much of this matches the Battle of the Shining Walls, especially when one recognizes that the **White Tower** within **Tar Valon** has a strong parallel with the Vatican inside Rome (see also **Amyrlin**

Seat): the unexpected descent from the mountains, the assault across a river, the superior tactics of the invading army, even the blood on the snow. But the Aiel War is not a simple rewriting of the Second Punic War. For one thing, the Aiel, having killed Laman Damodred in the fighting, withdrew across the mountains, their goal achieved. Hannibal's victory at Trebia led to no such withdrawal. Hannibal tried to secure his territorial gains while the Romans tried to gather forces for another attempt to dislodge him. This resulted in a second major Roman defeat, even closer to Rome, at the Battle of Lake Trasimene in June 217. Hannibal then rolled south, past the Eternal City, seeking still more allies on the Italian peninsula. In August of 216 he handed Rome perhaps its greatest military defeat at the Battle of Cannae (see **Malden, Battle of**). But even *this* didn't end the Second Punic War. Hannibal campaigned in Italy for another thirteen years before a Roman counterattack on Carthage forced him to sail home. At the Battle of Zama in October 202, Hannibal was met by the now-grown son of the Scipio he'd wounded at Ticinus. The Romans won, and the victorious commander became known as Scipio Africanus.

As ever, of course, Jordan didn't simply rewrite a single event. Rather, he interlaced it with bits and pieces from elsewhere. The rotation of command among the allied nations in this culminating engagement of the Aiel War, for instance, comes not from Trebia but from stories about the far earlier Battle of Marathon in 490 BC.

Shivan the Hunter. One of the **Heroes of the Horn** along with his sister, **Calian the Chooser**, Shivan echoes Kali, a Hindu god of destruction—and of the creation that follows it.

Shol Arbela. The capital city of **Arafel**. Its name alludes to Arbela, where Alexander the Great destroyed the Persian army of Darius III in the Battle of Arbela in 331 BC.

Siege of the Pillars of the Sky, The. In the 1956 film *Pillars of the Sky*, Native Americans under the leadership of a chief named Kamiakin besiege a company of U.S. cavalry in a trading outpost. Jordan was a dedicated fan of Westerns.

Silvie. An alias of **Lanfear**, the name is French, deriving from the Latin word *silva,* meaning "forest." The name also further implies the word *silver*—a color often associated with the moon and thereby with Lanfear.

Siuan Sanche. When Jordan decided that **Moiraine Damodred** would not be the **Amyrlin Seat**, he split that aspect of her character off into the figure of Siuan. At her core, then, Siuan shares many of Moiraine's original connections, like those to Merlin and the Lady of the Lake in Malory. It is probably from the imagery surrounding the latter that Jordan became fixated on the image of the swan, which along with the crane made frequent appearances in Graves' *White Goddess* in the form, as Jordan noted to himself, of "sacred birds."[80]

Slayer. This combination of **Isam Mandragoran** and **Luc Mantear** into a single being of the Shadow has several origin points. Perhaps most familiar is the story of Hermaphroditus, the beautiful son of Aphrodite and Hermes, in Greek mythology. In the version of his story told in Ovid's *Metamorphoses,* the lustful Naiad Salmacis threw herself upon the boy while he was bathing in a natural pool: her prayer to the gods that she never be parted from him was heard, and the two of them were fused into one entity, half man and half woman. Hermaphroditus' parents subsequently imbued the pool with such power that any man who bathed in the same waters would be weakened in strength. The darker turn taken in Jordan's series appears to be indebted to the Chimera of Greek mythology: a monstrous hybrid of a lion, goat, and serpent that was more menacing and horrific than the three separate species.

Snakes and Foxes. This children's game, in which victory requires the breaking of the rules, reflects the Aelfinn and Eelfinn. Jordan based it on a variety of "Fox games," like Fox and Hounds, in which one player tries to move their piece to evade the pieces of the other player on a checkerboard. See **Eelfinn**.

Soe'feia. A person charged with speaking the truth to the **Seanchan** royalty. The title comes from the Greek word for wisdom: *sophia*.

stedding. These refuges, where channeling is sup-
pressed and so much of the world is set aside, get
their name from their role as being the *homestead*
of the **Ogier**—a word with connotations of fron-
tier settlement, which is similar to the position the
Ogier must take relative to our world. In appearance, the *stedding*
are akin to sacred groves in Greek mythology. Interestingly, most
of the *stedding* in The Wheel of Time have names that appear to be
Chinese in origin—though there were few Ogier in The Wheel of
Time's closest China analogue, **Shara**, and those all vanished after
the Breaking.

Stepin. The Warder of **Kerene Nagashi**, he was known to be an excellent
guitarist: he is John Kay, guitarist and front man for the rock band
Steppenwolf.

Stone of Tear. Originally the Stone of Stair and then the Stone of Aeltar,
at which point Jordan described it as "the great fortress city where
the <u>SWORD</u>, the <u>sa'angreal</u> which it is prophecized that the Dragon
will grasp, is located inside a clear block that is impervious, even to
the Aes Sedai now."[81] In any case, it's based on the historical Rock of
Gibraltar.

stones. Jordan based the game on Go, a Chinese game that may be the
oldest continuously played board game, in which players take turns
placing their chosen color of stones (white or black) on a board in
an effort to control more territory than the other. Though simple to
learn, it is a remarkably complex game with more legal board positions than there are atoms in the observable universe.

Sulamein so Bhagad. A great historian. Her name comes from Sulei-
man the Magnificent, sultan of the Ottoman Empire from 1520
to 1566. Though uncountable deaths resulted from his military
conquests—among them, securing control of the great seat of learning, Baghdad—he ultimately oversaw a period of enormous cultural
prosperity for his empire.

sul'dam. See *a'dam*.

T

tabac. See **pipes**.

Talia. The Wheel of Time story about a sleeping girl named Talia who will be awoken by a kiss from the Sun King is familiar to most readers today as the story of the fairy tale "Sleeping Beauty." Less well known is the source of that famous tale: an Italian story first written down in the seventeenth century by Giambattista Basile, "Sun, Moon, and Talia."

Tamlin al'Thor. Though he originally named him "Tamtrin" in his notes, Jordan settled on the name Tamlin in order to echo the fairy-tale figure Tam Lin, who took something from any young woman who wandered through the enchanted woods in which he himself had been captured by the Queen of the Fairies: either one of her possessions or her virginity. In The Wheel of Time, Tam similarly took something (the child, Rand) from a woman he came upon in an enchanted place (Dragonmount). On Tam's surname, see **Rand al'Thor**.

Tamyrlin. Building on the idea of using the name Merlin as a title—"a Merlin," thus **Amyrlin Seat**—Jordan constructed an originating, first amyrlin—"*the* amyrlin," thus Tamyrlin. It is possible that Jordan less directly intended for the word to serve double duty by echoing the historical figure of Timur, popularly known as "Tamerlane," who founded the Timurid Empire in central Asia in the fourteenth century. Undefeated in battle, by the time of his death in 1405 he'd become one of the most successful and feared military commanders in history. While his leadership brought prosperity and a cultural renaissance to the heart of his empire, it did so at the price of the millions who died as a result of his conquests.

Tamyrlin, Ring of. The titular jewelry of H. Warner Munn's 1974 fantasy novel *Merlin's Ring* bestowed a supernaturally long life on Merlin's godson. Jordan, building **Tamyrlin** from Merlin, nodded at this. If he was also making an indirect reference to Timur, a ring could fit here, too: there is a legend that Timur had a calligrapher named Umar Aqta' who wrote the Qur'an in such tiny letters that the entire text of the book could fit upon a single ring. When this feat failed to impress Timur, the calligrapher created a copy of the Qur'an that was so large it required a cart to hold it. A few seven-foot-tall pages from this copy have survived and are on display in the Metropolitan Museum of Art in New York City.

Tarabon. Tarabon has much in common with the Ottoman Empire after the taking of Constantinople in 1453: that city is the parallel for the beautiful port city of Tanchico, and the country's name is derived from the phrase "the Arab one." Tarabon's fashions, too, are largely of this culture. In its co-ruling diarchy of a king and panarch, however, it is quite unlike the Ottoman sultanate.

Taren Ferry. One of the closest settlements to Emond's Field and the first one to which the protagonists go in their adventure in *The Eye of the World*. Its name is a nod to Taran, the protagonist of Lloyd Alexander's classic fantasy series the Chronicles of Prydain. That the village has a ferry allows it to echo the plot of Tolkien's *Lord of the Rings,* when the hobbits similarly escape the Shire and the pursuit of a Black Rider by using the Bucklebury Ferry.

Taringail Damodred. His name derives from Malory's duke of Tintagel, upon whom he is based.[86] It was this duke's wife, Igraine, whom Uther Pendragon seduced while in disguise as her husband—a trick of Merlin's magic—thus begetting the future King Arthur, who was born after the duke's death. Taringail's wife, **Tigraine Damodred**, was also manipulated by a magic-user (**Gitara Moroso**) into abandoning her husband. On his surname, see **Galad Damodred**.

Tarmon Gai'don. The name of the **Last Battle** is meant to echo *the Armageddon*, the final conflict between good and evil in Christian mythology. That name, in turn, derives from the hilltop settlement of Tel Megiddo. For further discussion, see **Eye of the World**.

Tarna Feir. A member of the Red Ajah who is ultimately turned to the Shadow. Her name appears to derive from the words *tarnish* and *fear*.

Tar Valon. Though in his early brainstorming Jordan had placed the city of the **Aes Sedai** "on the slopes of Dragonmount," he quickly changed it to an island.[82] His intention was to attach his story more firmly to the Arthurian mythology, in which Avalon was among the most fabled places: an island, as Morgan le Fay says in the Vulgate Cycle, *"ou les dames sont qui seiuent tous les enchantemens del monde"* [where the women are who know all the magic of the world].[83] It was here that Excalibur was forged and here where the wounded king was taken—depending on the story—either to die or to recover from his wounds and one day return. It's been identified with many historical places, including Glastonbury Tor—a prominent hill in Somerset, England, topped by the single remaining tower of a fourteenth-century church dedicated to Saint Michael. In Tar Valon, Jordan united the Tor and Avalon, making it the home of his powerful Aes Sedai, and crowning the island with a **White Tower** that could be seen from afar, just like the ruined tower atop the Tor. Simultaneously, he was able to hint at Tara, the legendary seat of the high king of Ireland and of the Tuatha Dé Danann (see **Tuatha'an**). As if this wasn't enough, Jordan built yet one more reference into Tar Valon. In Jordan's Old Tongue, *tar* means "tower" and *valon* means "guard."[84] In Tolkien's Sindarin language, *Minas Tirith* means "Tower of Guard."[85]

Tar Valon, Battle of. See **Shining Walls, Battle of the**.

Tarwin's Gap. The pass of Tarwin's Gap near **Fal Dara** was frequently used by **Trollocs** attempting to raid the **Westlands** from the Blight. There are at least two major engagements depicted here in The Wheel of Time, just as there were multiple engagements at and around the fortress of Dara on the border between the Byzantine and Sassanian Empires. One of the historical battles was the Battle of Dara in 530. A victory for the Byzantine forces, led by Belisarius, it's one of the best-described late Roman battles, thanks to a lengthy contemporary account of it by Procopius. It's likely this battle that Jordan had in mind when describing the horrific battle at Tarwin's Gap into which **Rand al'Thor** first appears as the **Dragon Reborn** in *The Eye of the World*.

ta'veren. When the Pattern of the Wheel of Time is awry, it corrects itself by temporarily weaving new designs around individuals. For the time that these chosen individuals are caught up in this web of destiny, they cause, quite literally, *the veering* of the threads of the lives around them.

Tear. The Stone of Tear is an analogue to the Rock of Gibraltar, and Tear itself has much in common with Spain.

Tel'aran'rhiod. Her name meaning "silver wheel," Ari-anrhod is an important figure in Welsh mythology: she gives birth to the hero Lleu Llaw Gyffes. In *The White Goddess,* Graves suggests that the souls of the dead are taken to her castle (Caer Arianrhod);  Jordan observed this connection early in his notes, where he catego-rized Arianrhod as a "castle where men wait to be reborn. a frigid place."[87] Within The Wheel of Time, *Tel'aran'rhiod* is a parallel world of dreams that can alter the reality of those dreamers who access it. Importantly, it is also a place where the **Heroes of the Horn** wait to be recalled into the world. Jordan's prefix *tel* derives from the archae-ological term for a hill built up beneath a human settlement and is one of a number of prefixes that he listed in his early notes as useful for word making.[88] Adding it to *Arianrhod* allowed Jordan to echo the word *telaraña,* which in Spanish means "spiderweb"; notably, the spider-like Moghedien is known to be able to navigate the dream world well.

Tenobia Kazadi. The queen of Saldaea, she echoes the magnificent Ze-nobia, queen of the Palmyrene Empire in the third century, whose life became legend.

ter'angreal. See *sa'angreal*.

Termool. Smothered by endlessly shifting sands, this desert region is so barren and challenging that the **Aiel** will not go there. The land itself is in *turmoil*.

Thakan'dar. This fog-choked valley at the foot of **Shayol Ghul**—scarred and twisted as if the land itself were being tortured—takes its name from the English word *thunder*.

Thomdril Merrilin. As he did with King Arthur (see **Artur Hawk-wing** and **Rand al'Thor**), Jordan essentially split Malory's Merlin into pieces, and the two most prominent of them are **Moiraine**

Damodred and Thom. Their union at the end of The Wheel of Time is thus a microcosm of what has happened in the course of the series: it brings the male and female halves of Merlin together, just as the two sides of magic once split can now be united. Another important aspect of Thom's character is the first role we see him take: that of a bard. In this, he echoes the greatest of bards in Welsh legend: Taliesin. As for Thom's first name, it's likely a nod toward Jordan's friend and publisher, Tom Doherty, the man who had pushed him to write The Wheel of Time.

Thorin al Toren al Ban. The grandfather of the last king of **Manetheren**. His name is taken from one of Tolkien's most well-known characters in *The Hobbit*: Thorin Oakenshield.

tiganza. A dance of **Tuatha'an** women. Its name comes from "Tzigane," an alternative name for both the nomadic Romani people and their music.

Tigraine Mantear. The biological mother of **Rand al'Thor** in The Wheel of Time, she initially parallels the story of Igraine, mother of King Arthur. Among the **Aiel** she took the name **Shaiel** and fell in love with clan chief **Janduin**.

Tinkers. See **Tuatha'an**.

Tower of Ghenjei. This featureless tower of metal—a gate to the realm of the Aelfinn and **Eelfinn**—might have been inspired by the far smaller iron pillar of Delhi, which has long been the subject of stories to explain the "mystery" of its resistance to rust. An inscription on the column refers to Gupta emperor Chandragupta II (d. 415) moving to another world, though there is much contention on whether this means physically (that is, a retirement of some kind) or spiritually (an afterlife). As for the name of the tower, it's popularly connected to the eleventh-century Japanese novel *The Tale of Genji*, or even to the Genji samurai, but these have little direct connection with the tower in The Wheel of Time. More probably, Jordan coincidentally created a similar spelling to these words as he tried to reverse-engineer a word that would echo *djinn* or *genie*: supernatural creatures in Islamic mythology that are popularly said to be able to grant wishes for an often-unexpected price.

Trolloc Bands. Trollocs are born into one of a number of bands, or chapters; the names of those known likewise recall mythical monsters: Ahf'frait echoes the word *ifrit* (a demon in Islamic mythology), Al'ghol echoes *ghoul*, Bhan'sheen echoes *banshee*, Dha'vol echoes the *devil*, Dhai'mon echoes *demon*, Dhjin'nen echoes *jinn*, Ghar'ghael echoes *gargoyle*, Ghob'hlin echoes *goblin*, Gho'hlem echoes *golem*, Ghraem'lan echoes *gremlin*, Ko'bal echoes *kobold*, and Kno'mon echoes *gnome*.

Trollocs. Though primarily identified with the writings of Tolkien today, trolls and orcs had a long history as mythical monsters prior to *The Lord of the Rings*. Combining these creatures into a disparate breed of beast-men, Jordan created an enemy soldiery that was at once familiar and terrifyingly new.

Tsutama Rath. A seemingly permanently angry **Aes Sedai** of the Red Ajah. Her name comes from the words *tsunami* and *wrath*.

Tuatha'an. The Tuatha Dé Danann are a race of supernatural beings in Irish mythology who dwell in the Otherworld. In Graves' *White Goddess* (45) Jordan found the theory that they were a hazy memory of a people who had been driven out of Greece and into Ireland long ago. Jordan planned on their inclusion from his earliest sketches for The Wheel of Time, where he noted that there would be "Tuathaan: The Traveling Ones, The Traveling People, The Travelers."[89] His presentation of these people within The Wheel of Time is often connected with the Romani (often erroneously called Gypsies in English), and certainly their wagons have this appearance. Just as equally, however, the author likely had in mind a similarly peripatetic people called the Irish Travellers. The largest population of Irish Travellers in the United States lives in Murphy Village, South Carolina, not far from Jordan's hometown of Charleston. Due to their history of itinerant metalworking, the Irish Travellers were often called "tinkers," and their genetics makes "Irish" red hair common among them (which rightly connects them to the **Aiel**).

Tuon Athaem Kore Paendrag. Tuonela is the place of the dead in Finnish mythology, ruled by a king and queen: Tuoni and Tuonetar. Kore is also associated with the underworld, though in Greek mythology: it's an alternative name for Persephone, the daughter of Demeter (goddess of the earth's fertility), who was abducted by Hades (god of the underworld) just as Jordan's Tuon is abducted by **Matrim Cauthon**. The agreement made by which Kore would spent half the year with Hades and half the year free in the world was an ancient explanation for the changing of the seasons—readers will recall that Tuon asked Mat to take her to a hell in Maderin. Her other given name, Athaem, appears to reflect both her intelligent leadership of troops in the field by echoing Athena (the Greek goddess of wisdom and warfare) and her relationship to the **Aes Sedai** by echoing athame (a ritual knife used in certain magic traditions). On her surname, see **Artur Hawkwing**.

Her title, Daughter of the Nine Moons, derives from the nine months of human pregnancy, indicating her association with fertility. In Norse mythology, the goddess most associated with this is Frigg, the wife of Odin (who is paralleled by Tuon's eventual husband, Mat). As empress, she later took the name **Fortuona Athaem Devi Paendrag**, reflecting both Fortuna, the Roman goddess of luck, and Devi, a Sanskrit word meaning "goddess."

Two Rivers. Jordan's hometown of Charleston, South Carolina sits on a peninsula between two rivers: the Ashley and the Cooper. Its residents like to say that the Atlantic Ocean forms where they meet at the peninsula's point—a fifteen-minute walk from Jordan's home.

U

Urien. An Aielman loyal to the Dragon, he shares the name of a Welsh king who by the time of Malory had been made the unhappy husband of Morgan le Fay and father to their child, Ywain.

V

Vasa. A massive sailor, he takes his name from the Swedish warship *Vasa*, which was one of the most magnificent ships of her age when she began her maiden voyage on August 10, 1628—and sank fourteen hundred yards into it.

Verin Mathwin. In 1611, Aix-en-Provence, France, was rocked with a sequence of people claiming to be possessed by demons. One of the supposed victims said that she was possessed by a demon named "Verrine." This would seem fitting enough as a name for a member of the Black Ajah in The Wheel of Time, but Verin's character has redeemable qualities in that she does, in the end, expose many truths— *verities*—about the plans of the Shadow. As with many of Jordan's characters, her secrets were present in her name from the beginning. That said, her surname derives from Math ap Mathonwy, an important king of Gwynedd in Welsh mythology, and in this case it seems only because Jordan liked the name: a reminder that the creative process is in the realm of imagination, not mathematics.

W

Warder. Jordan first called them Wardens, likely due to an initial view of them through the lens of Tolkien's rangers from *Lord of the Rings*.[90] This had changed as early as 1987, however, as they'd become Warders and were attached to the **Aes Sedai**.[91] This relationship between male bodyguards and female power-wielders allowed Jordan to explore using the concept of a "feminist" fantasy while also staying true to what he'd been taught as a boy about the responsibility that men had to protect women.

War of the Hundred Years. This war "when men battled men and the nations of our day were wrought" (*The Eye of the World*, "The Gleeman") is an echo of the Hundred Years' War, fought between England and France from 1337 to 1453, which had an enormous role in defining the shapes of the states of Europe.

Wayland's Forge. An inn near the border between Ghealdan and Murandy. Its name derives from tales of Wayland the Smith, which are present in several Northern European literatures.

Weiramon Saniago. A self-confident nobleman from coastal Tear. His first name probably derives from the English words *weir*—a fish trap—and *a man*: a Darkfriend, he traps other people in service of the Dark One. His surname likely connects to the fisherman San-tiago, the main character in Ernest Hemingway's *Old Man and the Sea,* who might have influenced Saniago's appearance. At the same time, Jordan's spelling of the name brings it closer to Shakespeare's Iago, which is a fitting connection to his character.

Westlands. Though not used in The Wheel of Time itself, this is the name given by fans to the main region of the world in which the action of the book series takes place: the lands west of the Spine of the World.

Whitecloaks. Though around 1987 he was calling them "Whiterid-ers," Jordan eventually settled on Whitecloaks for the group's common name.[92] At a 2001 book signing, Jordan said that the group reflected "any group that believes to know the Truth with a capital T and want you to believe the same. Mostly it's based on groups like the Teutonic Knights, however, since they don't hide behind anything."[93] Elsewhere, he similarly likened them to the KKK or the Taliban. While Freemasons refer to themselves as "Sons of Light," it doesn't seem that Jordan had them in mind—he himself was a Mason, and the Whitecloaks are rarely portrayed in a good light.

White Tower. There are many white towers throughout the world—from the Tower of London to the Taj Mahal—but the initial inspira-tion for the tower of the **Aes Sedai** appears to have been the ruined tower of St. Michael's Church atop Glastonbury Tor (an inspiration for the name and shape of **Tar Valon** itself, the city in which the White Tower is found). Beyond this, the White Tower as home of the **Amyrlin Seat** is reminiscent of the Vatican City, the Pope's center of power in Rome.

In its naming, however, Jordan likely had in mind the iconic white tower of Padgett-Thomas Barracks on the campus of his alma mater, The Citadel. Somewhat famously, thanks to the bestselling novel *The Lords of Discipline,* by fellow Citadel alumnus Pat Conroy, graduates of the school earn a ring by which they identify themselves and each other—just as the Aes Sedai earn their rings.

wolfbrother. According to Jordan, this concept de-
rived from "any number of myths from Europe,
North American Indians, and the Australian ab-
origines."[94] The European myth of the werewolf is
certainly the most well-known of these, but stories
of shape-shifting between humans and canine species are remarkably similar across the globe. Interestingly, most of these myths and
stories depict wolves in a less than kind light. It's possible that the
idea that wolves are misunderstood—indeed, that they are a positive
force in the world—is heavily influenced by Farley Mowat's 1963 au-
tobiography, *Never Cry Wolf,* which was made into a film of the same
name in 1983.

Z

zemai. A staple crop of the **Aiel**, this is maize, from which the Aiel made
oosquai. Since Jordan wanted his echoes to make linguistic sense,
he very likely built his word out of the scientific name for maize:
Zea mays. The fact that he spelled it in such a way that it could be
rearranged into the more familiar form *maize* must have left him
smiling.[95]

zomara. These mindless servants, created by **Aginor**, are zombies—but
beautiful instead of rotting.

ACKNOWLEDGMENTS

The idea for this book was not mine. It was my agent, Paul Stevens—formerly the in-house editor assigned to The Wheel of Time series at Tor—who made the offhand suggestion that something like this could be done. It was a good idea, to say the least, and I'm grateful to him, as well as to my friends and family who helped keep me upright and pushing onward as it advanced.

But no idea becomes a book without the help of a *lot* of people. And that's especially true of a work like this.

First and forever: Harriet. Without the support and encouragement of Harriet and the Rigney Estate, this book simply does not exist. I was humbled and thrilled to have this chance to work so closely with The Wheel of Time. The fact that I was able to do so alongside such a wonderful human being ensured that every moment spent in the endeavor was a joy. Harriet's clear memories, keen editorial hand, and kind heart improved these pages in every regard. I—and Jordan's fans the world over—cannot thank her enough.

Maria Simons and Alan Romanczuk have for many years graced me with their friendship. Like Harriet, they are good people in the truest of senses. The fact that they've allowed me into the smallest of circles continues to leave me astonished, and my debt only increased as I wrote this book: they both helped me to sort through multiple puzzles and inch closer to understanding the mind of the man who gifted us a world.

Speaking of world-makers, Brandon Sanderson sat for an extensive interview and answered my many questions while providing key insights of his own. He generously did so despite his own crushing schedule of the multiple projects and book releases of his own incredible career. He was an inspired choice to finish the main sequence of The Wheel of Time.

The Tor community has been enthusiastic in its support of this book, and I'm particularly grateful to Tom Doherty and Robert Davis, my editor, for helping me sift through reminiscences and materials on their end while they shepherded this book to its conclusion. Copyeditors often save authors from themselves, and I gratefully acknowledge that Terry McGarry did just that for me. My thanks, too, to the rest of the design, production, and marketing folks who have made this complex project a success: Peter Lutjen, Eileen Lawrence, Desirae Friesen, Jessica Katz, Heather Saunders, Greg Collins, Rafal Gibek, and Jim Kapp. Fans around the world will surely join me in also praising Ellisa Mitchell for giving us a wonderful new map of the world we love.

The archive of the Rigney Papers is today held in the Special Collections at the Addlestone Library of the College of Charleston. Despite the difficulties of doing so in a pandemic, the Special Collections staff patiently welcomed my presence for the many, many days I spent sifting through their materials. I'm so grateful to them all, but I must highlight in particular the research services coordinator, Mary Jo Fairchild, for her help facilitating my visits, and archives specialist, Samuel Stewart, for taking the terrific photos of the archival materials printed herein.

Robert Jordan's fandom found an early home on the internet, and the enormity of The Wheel of Time's presence on the web today is astounding. Seemingly every day I've worked on this book I've had a reason to be grateful for resources that were put together simply for the shared love of Jordan's work: from fan theories and observations to searchable databases of Jordan's interviews and chapter contents. Among these, I found myself most often turning to three in particular: Dragonmount, Theoryland, and the Thirteenth Depository. It's been a pleasure to record these sites in my endnotes: those running them and contributing to them ought to be commended for their excellent and helpful work in connecting and enriching fandom.

Though she's specifically noted in several such instances, I need to give a more general shout-out to Linda Taglieri, of Thirteenth Depository fame, who has done more than anyone else I know to recognize the potential influences on The Wheel of Time. I often found myself sighing with relief to see that she and I had gone down the same particular rabbit hole! A shout-out is also owed to Jason Denzel, founder of Dragonmount, who was enormously enthusiastic when he learned of this project, and who also helped me connect with a resource I otherwise wouldn't have had.

Along with the fan sites come the fans. I might be biased—seeing as how I count myself among them—but I believe Robert Jordan's welcoming and generous fans to be the best example of what fandom can and should be. I want to highlight in particular the wonderful folks who run and attend JordanCon, which I've attended on several occasions. The degree to which they open their arms to new folks is a model for the kindness that we could use more of in this world.

I have dedicated this work to Robert Jordan. I don't know what hand of fate moved me to pick up *The Eye of the World* as a boy, but I know that it was Mat's own luck that I had enough allowance in my pocket to buy it. Year by year, book by book, I can look back and measure my life to the turning of The Wheel of Time. For that company alone, I am eternally grateful. I truly hope I have done justice to the world—the gift—that he gave us all.

One day, not long after I penned the letter at the start of this book and began working through this project in earnest, a wind arose around the White Tower of The Citadel, stirring palm trees and easing along the sidewalks where a young Jordan once strode. It carried in through my open window and down upon that same beloved copy of *Eye*, which lay open on the desk that was his. The pages stirred and fluttered before I pressed them back down. A wind. Only a wind.

But a reminder, too: Jordan gave the world the great gift of his imagination, and to open The Wheel of Time is to know him. He lives there still.

Thank you, Jim.

ENDNOTES

Introduction

1. As of this writing, The Wheel of Time has sold an estimated 90 million copies in thirty-three languages.
2. Jordan never named his fantasy world, in part, as we'll see, because it is our own. Coined and populated by fans, the term *Randland* is by some used to refer exclusively to the initial lands in which the story takes place—the Westlands—but I'll be using it to refer to the *whole* of Jordan's fictional world.

1. The Wheelwright: The Life of Robert Jordan

1. "Robert Jordan Bio," Rigney Papers, box 24, folder 1, p. 1.
2. David Aiken, *Fire in the Cradle: Charleston's Literary Heritage* (Charleston Press, 1999), 198.
3. "Eulogy for James Oliver Rigney, Sr., delivered on June 19, 1988," Rigney Papers, box 1, folder 16, p. 2.
4. Ibid. p. 3.
5. Interview with Matt Hatch, April 21, 2012. Archived at https://www.theoryland.com/intvmain.php?i=759.
6. Interview: Writing on the Web, 2002. Archived at https://www.theoryland.com/intvmain.php?i=141.
7. Robert Jordan's Blog: One More Time, October 4, 2005. Archived at https://www.theoryland.com/intvmain.php?i=212.
8. Interview: Writing on the Web, 2002. Archived at https://www.theoryland.com/intvmain.php?i=141.
9. Ibid.
10. Interview with William B. Thompson, *Starlog*, January 1991. Archived at https://www.theoryland.com/intvmain.php?i=9.

11. Aiken, *Fire in the Cradle*, 200. The library was then in the Isaac Jenkins Mikell House on Rutledge Avenue.

12. Ibid. 201.

13. Interview: Writing on the Web, 2002. Archived at https://www.theoryland .com/intvmain.php?i=141.

14. Interview with William B. Thompson, *Starlog*, January 1991. Archived at https://www.theoryland.com/intvmain.php?i=9.

15. Interview: Writing on the Web, 2002. Archived at https://www.theoryland .com/intvmain.php?i=141.

16. Ibid.

17. Aiken, *Fire in the Cradle*, 202.

18. Interview: Writing on the Web, 2002. Archived at https://www.theoryland .com/intvmain.php?i=141.

19. Interview: Bridlington Today, November 22, 2005. Archived at https:// www.theoryland.com/intvmain.php?i=251.

20. *Lord of Chaos*, "Connecting Lines."

21. Interview: Fast Forward, November 1, 1994. Archived at https://www .theoryland.com/intvmain.php?i=52.

22. Interview: Wotmania and Dragonmount Q&A, December 9, 2002. Archived at https://www.theoryland.com/intvmain.php?i=142.

23. Interview: Writing on the Web, 2002. Archived at https://www.theoryland .com/intvmain.php?i=141.

24. Robert Jordan's Blog: Steady as She Goes, April 9, 2007. Archived at https:// www.theoryland.com/intvmain.php?i=301.

25. Robert Jordan's Blog: Hi, There, April 26, 2007. Archived at https://www .theoryland.com/intvmain.php?i=302.

26. Robert Jordan's Blog: Hi, There, April 26, 2007. Archived at https://www .theoryland.com/intvmain.php?i=302. In a quiet tribute to the author, Brandon Sanderson would echo this image with Mat, sitting on a dead Trolloc at the end of the books (*A Memory of Light*, "The Last Battle").

27. Interview with William B. Thompson, *Starlog*, January 1991. Archived at https://www.theoryland.com/intvmain.php?i=9.

28. Interview: Waldenbooks, October 1998. Archived at https://www .theoryland.com/intvmain.php?i=82.

29. Interview: Writing on the Web, 2002. Archived at https://www.theoryland .com/intvmain.php?i=141.

30. Aiken, *Fire in the Cradle*, 204.

31. Interview with Deirdre Donahue, "For Jordan, Fantasy Remains Fertile Field," *USA Today*, January 22, 2003.

32. Interview: Writing on the Web, 2002. Archived at https://www.theoryland .com/intvmain.php?i=141.

33. "Talking with Tom: A Conversation Between Tom Doherty and Harriet Mc-Dougal," March 18, 2013. Archived at https://www.tor.com/2013/03/18/talking -with-tom-a-conversation-between-tom-doherty-and-harriet-mcdougal/.

34. *Warrior of the Altaii*, Foreword.

35. Aiken, *Fire in the Cradle*, 206.

36. *Warrior of the Altaii*, Foreword.

37. Interview: Writing on the Web, 2002. Archived at https://www.theoryland .com/intvmain.php?i=141.

38. Aiken, *Fire in the Cradle*, 207.

39. Frank P. Jarrell, "Author Continues Charleston Saga," *The News and Courier*, May 24, 1981, 3-E.

40. "Talking with Tom: A Conversation Between Tom Doherty and Harriet McDougal," March 18, 2013. Archived at https://www.tor.com/2013/03 /18/talking-with-tom-a-conversation-between-tom-doherty-and-harriet -mcdougal/.

41. Aiken, *Fire in the Cradle*, 209.

42. Interview with William B. Thompson, *Starlog*, January 1991. Archived at https://www.theoryland.com/intvmain.php?i=9.

43. Rigney Papers, box 48, folder 3 (*April the 15th*, under the pseudonym of Peter X. Sanford); box 49, folder 1 (*Jon One-Eye*, under the pseudonym of Jordan Reynolds); and box 49, folder 2 (*Morgan*, under the pseudonym John Ryan). His original typescript of *Warrior of the Altaii* also had the pseudonym of Jordan Reynolds before it was crossed out and Robert Jordan was written in its place; Rigney Papers, box 48, folder 1.

44. And sales have continued to go well: in 2022, the audio version of *The Eye of the World* became Jordan's latest number one on the list.

45. After his death, this writing desk, along with Jordan's corresponding chair, was donated to The Citadel. By a staggering coincidence, these were installed in my office just weeks before the decision was reached for me to write this book—with the result that I am sitting in his chair at his desk as I write these words.

46. Despite a shared family name of Livingston, we are not related in any way known to us.

47. "Advice to New Writers," Rigney Papers, box 24, folder 1.

48. Interview: AOL Chat 1, October 21, 1994. Archived at https://www.theoryland.com/intvmain.php?i=1.

49. Interview: MSN eFriends, November 11, 1998. Archived at https://www.theoryland.com/intvmain.php?i=96.

50. A fine example of these lists is his "Daily Notes" for November 8, 1985, in the Rigney Papers, box 24, folder 1.

51. "Miscellaneous Random Thoughts," Rigney Papers, box 24, folder 1, pp. 4–7.

52. Typescript, Rigney Papers, box 24, folder 1.

53. "Robert Jordan Bio," Rigney Papers, box 24, folder 1, p. 1.

54. Personal interview, November 16, 2021.

55. Aiken, *Fire in the Cradle*, 212.

56. Michael Carlson, "Obituary: Robert Jordan," *The Guardian*, October 17, 2007.

57. Letter to *Locus*, March 23, 2006. Archived at https://www.locusmag.com/2006/Features/03JordanLetter.html.

58. "My Author, My Life," *Forbes*, December 1, 2006. Archived at https://www.forbes.com/2006/11/30/robert-jordan-illness-tech-media_cx_hc_books06_1201jordan.html.

59. Ibid.

60. Personal communication, October 24, 2021.

61. Interview: MSN eFriends, November 11, 1998. Archived at https://www.theoryland.com/intvmain.php?i=96.

62. Robert Jordan's Blog: Rumors and Rumors of Rumors, September 10, 2007, https://dragonmount.com/blogs/entry/380-rumors-and-rumors-of-rumors/.

63. Quoted on Robert Jordan's Blog, September 23, 2007, https://dragonmount.com/blogs/entry/382-from-harriet/.

64. Robert Jordan's Blog: Rumors and Rumors of Rumors, September 10, 2007, https://dragonmount.com/blogs/entry/380-rumors-and-rumors-of-rumors/.

65. Interview with Maria Simons, posted October 4, 2010, https://dragonmount.com/forums/topic/51898-my-interview-with-maria-simons/.

66. Robert Jordan's Blog: Sometimes Even When You've Fought Your Best. . . . , September 17, 2007, https://dragonmount.com/blogs/entry/381-sometimes-even-when-youve-fought-your-best/.

67. Rigney Papers, box 57, folder 7.

68. Robert Jordan's Blog: From Harriet, September 23, 2007, https://dragonmount.com/blogs/entry/382-from-harriet/.

69. "Goodbye, Mr. Jordan," September 19, 2007, https://www.brandons anderson.com/euology-goodbye-mr-jordan/.

70. Ibid.

71. Sanderfaq 5, November 4, 2020, https://www.youtube.com/watch?v= MITTIur3Ytk.

72. Brandon Sanderson, personal blog, October 10, 2013, https://www.brandons anderson.com/the-wheel-of-time-retrospective-the-process/.

73. Brandon Sanderson, personal interview, October 21, 2021.

74. Brandon Sanderson, personal blog, October 15, 2013, https://www.brandons anderson.com/the-wheel-of-time-retrospective-the-gathering-storm -writing-process/.

2. The Axle and the Wheel: Tolkien and Jordan

1. Interview: Writing on the Web, 2002. Archived at https://www.theoryland .com/intvmain.php?i=141.

2. Personal interview, November 16, 2021.

3. John H. Timmerman, "Fantasy Literature's Evocative Power," *Christian Century*, May 17, 1978: 533–37.

4. J. R. R. Tolkien, *The Tolkien Reader* (Ballantine Books, 1966), 75.

5. Edward Rothstein, "An Adored Fantasy Series Now Hints at 1990s Angst," *New York Times*, October 26, 1998. Archived at https://www.nytimes.com /1998/10/26/books/connections-an-adored-fantasy-series-now-hints-at -1990-s-angst.html.

6. Interview: COT "Glimmers" Ebook Q&A, July 2002. Archived at https:// www.theoryland.com/intvmain.php?i=5.

7. Robert Jordan's Blog: One More Time, October 4, 2005. Archived at https:// www.theoryland.com/intvmain.php?i=212.

8. Interview with William B. Thompson, *Starlog*, January 1991. Archived at https://www.theoryland.com/intvmain.php?i=9.

9. Well, this is the story he *told*, anyway. As I've suggested elsewhere, I suspect the professor might not be telling the whole truth about his accidental invention of the word *hobbit*. See my "The Myths of the Author: Tolkien and the Medieval Origins of the Word *Hobbit*," *Mythlore* 30, no. 3 (April 2012): 129–46.

10. Unless cited otherwise, all translations are my own.

11. The Modern Hindustani word for "daughter" is, instead, the word *beti*.

12. J. R. R. Tolkien, *The Letters of J. R. R. Tolkien*, ed. Humphrey Carpenter, with the assistance of Christopher Tolkien (Houghton Mifflin, 1981), 264.

13. Invented, that is, in the sense of discovery. Such words, more often than not, would undoubtedly have been real, only being missing due to the chances of history that have failed to preserve them. For more discussion of this process in relation to Tolkien, see Shippey's *The Road to Middle-earth: How J.R.R. Tolkien Created a New Mythology* (Houghton Mifflin, 2003), 1–54.

14. Michael Livingston, "The Shellshocked Hobbit: The First World War and Tolkien's Trauma of the Ring," *Mythlore* 25, no. 1 (October 2006): 77–92; reprinted in Janet Brennan Croft, ed., *Baptism of Fire: The Birth of Modern British Fantasy in World War I* (Mythopoeic Press, 2015), 9–22.

15. By a peculiar coincidence, Augustine's concerns about time—those reflected by Tolkien but I think rejected in Jordan's work—are the subject of a 1955 essay, "Time and Contingency in St. Augustine," which was published in *The Review of Metaphysics* by one Robert Jordan, then a professor at the University of the South. Reprinted in R. A. Markus, ed., *Augustine: A Collection of Critical Essays* (Anchor Books, 1972).

16. *The Shadow Rising*, "What Lies Hidden."

17. *The Eye of the World*, "The Gleeman."

3. The Wheel Turns: Jordan at Work

1. Interview with Dave Slusher, October 1994. Archived at https://www.theoryland.com/intvmain.php?i=63.

2. Personal interview, November 16, 2021.

3. "Talking with Tom: A Conversation Between Tom Doherty and Harriet McDougal," March 18, 2013. Archived at https://www.tor.com/2013/03/18/talking-with-tom-a-conversation-between-tom-doherty-and-harriet-mcdougal/.

4. Interview: MSN eFriends, November 11, 1998. Archived at https://www.theoryland.com/intvmain.php?i=96. Some silent emendations made to the transcript.

5. Alan Romanczuk, August 22, 2019. Archived at https://www.reddit.com/r/WoT/comments/q82pjo/why_did_robert_jordan_write_wheel_of_time_alan/.

6. Rigney Papers, box 45, folder 2.

7. Rigney Papers, box 24, folder 1, p. 1.

8. The phrase is the title of Graves' first chapter in *The White Goddess: A Historical Grammar of Poetic Myth*, ed. Grevel Lindop (Farrar, Straus and Giroux, 1997).

9.   Interview: Waldenbooks Hailing Frequency, August 1996. Archived at https://www.theoryland.com/intvmain.php?i=842.

10.   "Background Notes No.2," Rigney Papers, box 45, folder 2, p. 11.

11.   Interview: Orbit, December 2000. Archived at https://www.theoryland .com/intvmain.php?i=127.

12.   "*The Wheel of Time*: Outline, Book One," Rigney Papers, box 45, folder 2, p. 4.

13.   Ibid. p. 3. The blank for the Dragon's name was Jordan's.

14.   Untitled handwritten notes, Rigney Papers, box 45, folder 2.

15.   Interestingly, he at one point considered changing them to number nine before discarding the idea: "QUERY: Should the AGES number 7 (as is in so many legends and myths, and the Bible as well) or 9, which would be a number of magical properties." See "Second Notes from *The White Goddess*," Rigney Papers, box 24, folder 1, p. 2.

16.   "Notes from *The White Goddess* for Us [*sic*] in *The Wheel of Time*," Rigney Papers, box 45, folder 2, p. 4.

17.   "*The Wheel of Time*: Outline, Book One," Rigney Papers, box 45, folder 2, p. 4.

18.   Ibid. pp. 15–16.

19.   Though it was still being formed, the series would ultimately acquire multiple figures of "King Arthur": not only would there be a "present-day" King Arthur in the main character about to be discussed, there would also be a "past" King Arthur in Artur Hawkwing.

20.   "Namelist 2," Rigney Papers, box 45, folder 2, p. 1.

21.   "Notes from *The White Goddess* for Us [*sic*] in *The Wheel of Time*," Rigney Papers, box 45, folder 2, p. 1.

22.   Ibid.

23.   Ibid.

24.   Untitled handwritten notes, Rigney Papers, box 45, folder 2.

25.   "*The Wheel of Time*: Outline, Book One," Rigney Papers, box 20, folder 2, pp. 1–2.

26.   "Namelist 2," Rigney Papers, box 45, folder 2, p. 1.

27.   Ibid. pp. 8–9.

28.   Ibid. p. 2.

29.   "Notes on Course of Books (All of This Is Merely Possibility)," Rigney Papers, box 24, folder 1, p. 2.

30.   "Namelist 2," Rigney Papers, box 45, folder 2, p. 1.

31.   "Notes from *The White Goddess* for Us [*sic*] in *The Wheel of Time*," Rigney Papers, box 45, folder 2, p. 7.

32. "Namelist 2," Rigney Papers, box 45, folder 2, p. 3.

33. Ibid. p. 1.

34. Ibid.

35. See, for instance, "Background Notes on *The Wheel of Time*," Rigney Papers, box 45, folder 2, p. 3.

36. Thus both terms appear in his "*Wheel of Time*: Notes 13a" manuscript, Rigney Papers, box 45, folder 2, pp. 2–3.

37. "*Eye of the World* Outline: Part One," Rigney Papers, box 20, folder 2, p. 2.

38. See, e.g., Graves, *White Goddess*, 438.

39. "Miscellaneous Notes and Prophecies from *Le Morte d'Arthur*," Rigney Papers, box 20, folder 2, p. 1.

40. "Random Notes on Course of *The Wheel of Time*," Rigney Papers, box 45, folder 2, pp. 1–2. Similar plot points are found in "Extremely Tentative Notes on the Course of Books," Rigney Papers, box 24, folder 1, p. 1.

41. "*Eye of the World* Outline: Part One," Rigney Papers, box 20, folder 2, p. 1.

42. Graves, *White Goddess*, 53.

43. "*The Wheel of Time*: Outline, Book One," Rigney Papers, box 45, folder 2, p. 7.

44. "*Eye of the World*: Test MS," Rigney Papers, box 17, folder 1.

45. Personal communication. Doherty, in signing Jordan to the six-book contract in 1984, had shrugged off concerns from Jordan about what would happen if he didn't write a series that long: "If it ends up just being a trilogy, we can do the other three books on something else," the publisher replied (personal interview, November 16, 2021).

46. He was introduced later in the series, albeit in a far more limited role. See *The Wheel of Time Companion*, 199.

47. "*Eye of the World*: Test MS," Rigney Papers, box 17, folder 1, p. 46.

48. "*The Eye of the World*, "The Peddler."

49. Rigney Papers, box 18, folder 1.

50. "*Eye of the World* Outline Part 2," Rigney Papers, box 20, folder 2, p. 4.

51. Ibid. p. 12.

52. "Prologue (Revision 3)," Rigney Papers, box 21, folder 3, p. 1.

53. "Second Notes from *The White Goddess*," Rigney Papers, box 24, folder 1, p. 3.

54. Graves, *White Goddess*, 113.

55. Ibid. 463.

56. Personal communication. October 18, 2021.

57. "Notes on Books Two Through Six," Rigney Papers, box 45, folder 2, pp. 4–5.

58. Personal interview, November 16, 2021.

59. "Notes on Books Two Through Six," Rigney Papers, box 20, folder 2, pp. 1–2.

60. *"Eye of the World*: Test MS," Rigney Papers, box 17, folder 1, p. 325.

61. Ibid. pp. 329–32. This sequence would have appeared at the end of chapter 16 of the published version of *The Eye of the World*: "The Wisdom."

62. *A Crown of Swords*, "Diamonds and Stars."

63. "Notes on Books Two Through Six," Rigney Papers, box 20, folder 2.

64. Ibid. pp. 4–5.

65. This observation was first made by an anonymous commenter at https://13depository.blogspot.com/2002/02/character-names-t.html.

66. A lengthy list of character names derived from readers' names is maintained by Linda Taglieri: https://13depository.blogspot.com/2002/02/character-names-derived-from-readers.html.

67. "Ramblings on Form of Story," Rigney Papers, box 24, folder 1, p. 2.

68. "The Forsaken," Rigney Papers, box 45, folder 2, p. 1.

69. *Lord of Chaos*, "The First Message."

70. *Lord of Chaos*, "The Answer."

71. Interviews: DragonCon Report—Isabel, September 3, 2005. Archived at https://www.theoryland.com/intvmain.php?i=197.

72. "Rand," Rigney Papers, box 58, folder 6, p. 34. The first person to make this information publicly known is Theresa "Terez" Gray, though she wrongly cited it as box 55: https://www.theoryland.com/forums/discussion/8767.

73. "People," Rigney Papers, box 58, folder 6, p. 15. The first person to make this information publicly known is Theresa "Terez" Gray, though she wrongly cited it as box 55: https://www.theoryland.com/forums/discussion/8767. It's clear from the subsequent entry on "Messana" [*sic*], which notes "SHE TOOK THE PLACE OF **DANELLE**," that Jordan was suggesting Demandred's appearance as Taim was a permanent disguise rather than a temporary ruse.

74. "Nynaeve," Rigney Papers, box 58, folder 7, p. 19. The first person to make this information publicly known is Theresa "Terez" Gray, though she wrongly cited it as box 55: https://www.theoryland.com/forums/discussion/8767.

75. This, one of the most sought-after bits of information among Wheel of Time fans, was only revealed at last in *The Wheel of Time Companion*, 83.

76. "People/Things to Work Out/Bk12," private files.

77. Personal interview, October 21, 2021.

78. These drafts were heavily rooted in the 1970s barbarian fantasy mode of "slaves who love their masters": two women in the first transcript ("*War-*

riors of the Altaii Typescript," box 48, folder 1, pp. 312–13), but then very specifically revised in the second transcript to *three* who would bear Wulfgar's children: Elspeth, Talva, and Eilinn ("*Warriors of the Altaii* Typescript," box 48, folder 2). The published version abandons all of this in favor of Elspeth alone, newly freed, freely choosing to stay with Wulfgar ("And So, We Ride").

79. "Notes from *The White Goddess*," Rigney Papers, box 45, folder 2, p. 25.

80. Aiken, *Fire in the Cradle*, 214.

4. The Real World in The Wheel of Time

1. "Notes from *The White Goddess* for Us [*sic*] in *The Wheel of Time*," Rigney Papers, box 45, folder 2, p. 25.

2. The possibilities he considered but abandoned can be almost as interesting as those he kept. In those handwritten notes, for instance, he was certain that Malory's King Pellinore would make it into his text as "Pell _____ of Nore"; see Rigney Papers, box 45, folder 2.

Glossary

1. "Book One: *The Eye of the World* Outline, Part 2," Rigney Papers, box 20, folder 2, p. 11.

2. Graves, *White Goddess*, 231–32.

3. "Name List for *The Eye of the World*," Rigney Papers, box 20, folder 2, p. 1.

4. "Notes from *The White Goddess*," Rigney Papers, box 24, folder 1, p. 5.

5. "Aes Sedai-General Notes-Bk10," Private Files, p. 41.

6. "General Notes and Thoughts as They Occur," Rigney Papers, box 20, folder 2, p. 1.

7. "Eye of the World: Fourth Word List," Rigney Papers, box 45, folder 2, p. 4.

8. "Notes from *The White Goddess*," Rigney Papers, box 24, folder 1, p. 5.

9. Graves, *White Goddess*, 45–46.

10. Ibid. 73–74.

11. "Miscellaneous Notes for *The Wheel of Time*," Rigney Papers, box 24, folder 1, p. 2; this name was, for a short time, transferred to Thom before it reached final form in Merrilin.

12. Graves, *White Goddess*, 54.

13. This was first pointed out by Linda Taglieri on her blog: https://13depository .blogspot.com/2002/02/character-names-b.html.

14. Graves, *White Goddess*, 385–86.

15. Ibid. 71–72.

16.   Private files.

17.   "Namelist 2," Rigney Papers, box 45, folder 2, p. 10.

18.   Ibid. p. 15.

19.   "Miscellaneous Notes for *The Wheel of Time*," Rigney Papers, box 24, folder 1, p. 4.

20.   "Notes from *The White Goddess* (Part II)," Rigney Papers, box 24, folder 1, p. 9.

21.   *A Crown of Swords*, "Lightnings." This observation was made by Linda Taglieri on her blog: https://13depository.blogspot.com/2002/02/character -names-e.html.

22.   Graves, *White Goddess*, 398.

23.   Ibid. 283.

24.   Untitled handwritten notes, Rigney Papers, box 45, folder 2.

25.   Robert Jordan's Blog: This and That, December 19, 2005. Archived at https://www.theoryland.com/intvmain.php?i=254.

26.   "Names," Rigney Papers, box 45, folder 2, p. 1.

27.   "Notes on Books Two Through Six," Rigney Papers, box 20, folder 2, p. 3.

28.   This is suggested even as early as Jordan's handwritten notes on Malory, where "Morgase's son" (a parallel for Mordred) will be a "potential power weilder [*sic*]." Rigney Papers, box 45, folder 2.

29.   "Namelist 2," Rigney Papers, box 45, folder 2, pp. 10 and 15, respectively.

30.   "Notes from *The White Goddess* for Us [*sic*] in *The Wheel of Time*," Rigney Papers, box 45, folder 2, p. 17.

31.   "Name List for *The Eye of the World*," Rigney Papers, box 20, folder 2, p. 4.

32.   Rigney Papers, box 17, folder 1, p. 71.

33.   "Name List for *The Eye of the World*," Rigney Papers, box 20, folder 2, p. 4.

34.   Rigney Papers, box 17, folder 1, p. 71.

35.   "Notes from the *White Goddess* for Us [*sic*] in *The Wheel of Time*," Rigney Papers, box 45, folder 2, p. 8.

36.   To this end, it should be noted that in a letter from March 2000, Jordan suggested that the accent of Illian might have sounded Dutch (that is, Flemish). Archived at https://www.theoryland.com/intvmain.php?i=116.

37.   "Extremely Tentative Notes on Course of Books," Rigney Papers, box 24, folder 1, p. 1. In an even earlier set of notes, Jordan was unsure whether Lan would fall in love with Nynaeve or Egwene (which would've been more appropriate to the Arthurian mythology): "Notes on Course of Books," Rigney Papers, box 24, folder 1, p. 2.

38. Graves, *White Goddess*, 131.

39. "*Eye of the World* Outline Part 2," Rigney Papers, box 20, folder 2, p. 4.

40. Rigney Papers, box 51, folder 9, p. 34.

41. For this reason, it may be that the similarity of the names is mere coincidence. As Maria Simons notes: "Jim also used Maldon salt on a daily basis" (personal communication, January 19, 2022).

42. "Book One: *The Eye of the World* Outline, Part 2," Rigney Papers, box 20, folder 2, p. 11.

43. On a back page of his early summarizing of the book of Revelation, Jordan scribbled down the word "Elok," as "the trickster name given to Mat"; handwritten notes, Rigney Papers, box 45, folder 2.

44. Interview: Barnes and Noble Chat, November 11, 1997. Archived at https://www.theoryland.com/intvmain.php?i=80.

45. This reference was first identified by Linda Taglieri on her blog: http://13depository.blogspot.com/2002/03/names-of-shadow.html.

46. Handwritten notes, Rigney Papers, box 45, folder 2.

47. Ibid.

48. "Synopsis of Names and Characters from *Le Morte d'Arthur*," Rigney Papers, box 24, folder 1, p. 3.

49. Private files.

50. Personal communication, March 3, 2022.

51. See, for example, the half page devoted to her background and character in the undated "Ramblings on Form of Story," where Egwene is only described as the daughter of "the tavernkeeper and Mayor" (Rigney Papers, box 20, folder 2, p. 10).

52. "Extremely Tentative Notes on the Course of Books," Rigney Papers, box 24, folder 1, p. 1.

53. "*Eye of the World* Outline: Part One," Rigney Papers, box 20, folder 2, p. 1.

54. Graves, *White Goddess*, 53.

55. Interview: AOL Chat 1, October 21, 1994. Archived at https://www.theoryland.com/intvmain.php?i=1.

56. "Notes from *The White Goddess* for Us [*sic*] in *The Wheel of Time*," Rigney Papers, box 45, folder 2, p. 2.

57. "Namelist 2," Rigney Papers, box 45, folder 2, pp. 8–9.

58. "Ogier-Bk11," private notes, p. 42.

59. Rigney Papers, box 17, folder 1, p. 44.

60. "Miscellaneous Notes for *The Wheel of Time*," Rigney Papers, box 24, folder 1, pp. 6–7.

61. "Notes on Books Two Through Six," Rigney Papers, box 45, folder 2, p. 2.

62. "*The Wheel of Time*: Outline, Book One," Rigney Papers, box 45, folder 2, p. 13.

63. "Namelist 2," Rigney Papers, box 45, folder 2, p. 1.

64. "Name List for *The Eye of the World*," Rigney Papers, box 24, folder 1, p. 6.

65. Graves, *White Goddess*, 411.

66. "Notes on Books Two Through Six," Rigney Papers, box 45, folder 2, p. 3.

67. See, for instance, "Background Notes on *The Wheel of Time*," Rigney Papers, box 45, folder 2, p. 3.

68. Thus both terms appear in his "Wheel of Time: Notes 13a" manuscript, Rigney Papers, box 45, folder 2, pp. 2–3.

69. Interview: DragonCon SciFi Channel Chat, June 28, 1997. Archived at https://www.theoryland.com/intvmain.php?i=79.

70. "Bk12 What Has to Happen," private notes, p. 3.

71. "Eyeblinder Ramble Bk12," private notes, p. 1.

72. "Namelist 2," Rigney Papers, box 45, folder 2, p. 3.

73. Letter to Paul Ward, March 2000. Archived at https://www.theoryland.com/intvmain.php?i=116.

74. Interview: AOL Chat, October 18, 1996. Archived at https://www.theoryland.com/intvmain.php?i=74.

75. Rigney Papers, box 51, folder 9, p. 34.

76. Letter, November 25, 1996, Rigney Papers, box 32, folder 2.

77. "Phrases, Words, Names and Sayings," Rigney Papers, box 45, folder 2.

78. Graves, *White Goddess*, 260.

79. Jordan in fact first records it in his notes as the "Plain of Shinar," matching the description, from Genesis 11:2, of where the Tower of Babel was built. "Notes from *The White Goddess*," Rigney Papers, box 24, folder 1, p. 9.

80. "Notes from *The White Goddess*," Rigney Papers, box 24, folder 1, p. 6.

81. "Miscellaneous Notes for *The Wheel of Time*," Rigney Papers, box 24, folder 1, p. 4.

82. "*The Wheel of Time*: Outline, Book One," Rigney Papers, box 45, folder 2, p. 10.

83. *La Mort le Roi Artus*, in H. Oskar Sommer, ed., *The Vulgate Version of the Arthurian Romances, vol. VI* (Carnegie Institute, 1913), 238.

84. *Companion*, 569–70.

85. Ruth S. Noel, *The Languages of Tolkien's Middle-earth* (Houghton-Mifflin, 1980), 170.

86. For a time, he was named "Maric." See "Notes on Books Two Through Six," Rigney Papers, box 45, folder 2, p. 4.

87. "Notes from *The White Goddess* (Part II)," Rigney Papers, box 24, folder 1, p. 10.

88. "Miscellaneous Notes for *The Wheel of Time*," Rigney Papers, box 24, folder 1, p. 12.

89. Rigney Papers, box 45, folder 2.

90. "Notes From *The White Goddess* for Us [*sic*] in *The Wheel of Time*," Rigney Papers, box 45, folder 2, p. 1.

91. "Namelist 2," Rigney Papers, box 45, folder 2, p. 5.

92. Ibid. p. 3.

93. Interview: Amsterdam Signing Report—Aan'allein, April 5, 2001. Archived at https://www.theoryland.com/intvmain.php?i=133.

94. Interview: AOL Chat 2, October 21, 1994. Archived at https://www.theoryland.com/intvmain.php?i=403.

95. Credit for the realization of how Jordan made this work goes to Maria Simons, who figured it out when the scientific name for maize was the subject of a *Jeopardy!* question posed by Ken Jennings—who for a short time happened to be Brandon Sanderson's roommate in college. The Wheel weaves as the Wheel wills!

INDEX

INDEX

The Wheel of Time®

By Robert Jordan

By Robert Jordan and Brandon Sanderson

By Robert Jordan and Teresa Patterson

By Robert Jordan, Harriet McDougal, Alan Romanczuk, and Maria Simons

ABOUT THE AUTHOR

MICHAEL LIVINGSTON, Ph.D., is the foremost academic interpreter of Robert Jordan's literary accomplishments and legacy. His many other books include the Shards of Heaven trilogy and multiple award-winning studies of military history. At present, he serves as the secretary-general for the United States Commission on Military History and teaches at The Citadel.

michaellivingston.com
Facebook.com/michael.d.livingston
Twitter: @medievalguy
Instagram: @livingstonphd